DASHELL

— AND —

CAROLINE

DASHELL

— AND —

CAROLINE

ELIZABETH CHANTER

ISBN: 978-1-956074-51-2 (Paperback Edition)
ISBN: 978-1-956074-52-9 (Hardcover Edition)
ISBN: 978-1-956074-50-5 (E-book Edition)

Some characters and events in this book are fictitious. Any similarity to the real persons, living or dead, is coincidental and not intended by the author.

Book Ordering Information

Phone Number: 315 288-7939 ext. 1000 or 347-901-4920
Email: info@globalsummithouse.com
Global Summit House
www.globalsummithouse.com

Printed in the United States of America

Contents

DASHELL AND CAROLINE

The missing documents have been found and Caroline now knows her real name, yet much mystery remains. Dashell and his brother, Maxwell, travel to Yorkshire to find out what they can.

On their return, Dashell meets a previously unknown male relative of Caroline, who thought he had no relatives. He, on his part, is astounded at what he is told, and helps to reveal more of the truth.

Amazingly, two other people come forward later, and tell their part of the story.

In the end everything is brought to light, including someone's cruel deception of Isobel, Caroline's mother.

Now Dashell and Caroline can look forward to their wedding.

Acknowledgments

I would like to express my thanks and appreciation to the members of the Cedar Creek Writers' Group, Shawnigan Lake, Vancouver Island, British Columbia, for their interest and helpful comments. In particular I would like to mention one member, Elizabeth Symon, for her continual encouragement, chiefly because she was anxious to read the next episode so she could know "what happened." And for her patient reading of my original rough notes.

My thanks also to Judy Baxter, Library Manager of the South Cowichan Regional Library, in Mill Bay, Vancouver Island, and her staff, for their assistance.

Finally, my thanks to Manuel Erickson, for his considerable encouragement and helpful critiques, and for editing this sequel.

Author's Comments

There is no such place as Becket Lane in Fulham, there is no village of Sutherfield in Sussex, nor is there a village called Skorrcliff in Yorkshire. They will not be found on any map.

Any description of landscape or terrain beyond Pateley Bridge is from the author's imagination.

The Darley Arabian and Eclipse were real horses. All others are named from the author's imagination.

Some references and incidents in this sequel may be puzzling to those who have not read the first book. Reading *The House on Becket Lane* should make things clear.

CHAPTER ONE

Caroline Learns Many Things

It was quite late when Caroline awakened, slowly at first, as though the sleeping potion was reluctant to let go. She lay in a state of confusion of strange dreams and hazy recollections, and it was some minutes before she realized she was not in a familiar room. She stirred anxiously and cried out for Hannah, who came at once.

"Miss Caroline! Oh, thank goodness you are awake. How do you feel?"

"I'm not sure. My arm aches. My face feels stiff one side. And my mouth hurts. I don't know where I am, Hannah, but I am glad you are here. What room is this?" Her speech was slurred and slow because of her injuries.

"We are in the house of Lady Smythe, Lord Lonsdale's aunt, who kindly gave us shelter."

Caroline stared at her, still not comprehending. She tried to speak again but could only cough because her throat was so dry. Hannah fetched some water in a cup from the ewer on the washstand, and began to give her sips to help ease her throat.

"Thank you, Hannah," she managed to say.

Hannah put the things back on the washstand, then came and sat carefully on the bed. "Now, Miss Caroline, I don't really want to push you, but I must ask you this: What is the last thing you remember?"

Caroline leaned back on her pillows and tried to think, passing her right hand over her forehead only to wince when she touched it. "The last thing I remember?" she repeated slowly. Gradually the horror came back. "Papa. Oh, yes, I remember. I was going downstairs and he was coming up. He waved a newspaper about and was very angry about something. He—he taunted me about Lord Lonsdale. Oh, it was horrible. May I have a little more water, please?" After a few more sips, she continued. "I saw him raise his cane and then I felt pain in one arm. Then he seized my other arm and dragged me into my bedroom, at least I think it was, and I remember crying out again and I think I remember falling to the floor." She carefully touched her bandaged arm. "Is that how it got hurt? Papa did it, but why? I don't remember what happened afterwards."

Hannah could have hugged her. "Yes, he did, dear. But oh, thank goodness you can remember even that. It shows you will get better. I know you will. And do not worry any more about your Papa. Lord Lonsdale would never let him hurt you again; he doesn't even know you are here."

Caroline felt relieved about that, and asked, "How long have I been here?"

"Two days."

"Two days!" she echoed. "But how did I get here?"

"It's a very long story, dear, far too much to tell you now. I sent Johnny to find Lord Lonsdale, and he came, and Dr. Meldicott came and bound up your arm and soothed your other hurts. Then we all left the house. Lord Lonsdale carried you downstairs and into the cab and upstairs here when we arrived."

"He carried me?" echoed Caroline in wonder.

"Yes, dear, just like you were a feather. And then when in the cab you regained consciousness for a few moments. Do you remember?"

"No, not a thing."

"Well, you did; and when you lapsed back again he gently kissed your face, your hair. Oh, I'm sure he loves you, Miss Caroline," she concluded, beaming happily at her. "Oh, mercy me, here am I talking away to you when I should be telling Lady Smythe you are awake and almost yourself again." With that she bustled away.

Caroline rested on the pillows again and held the top of the bedsheet to her with her good hand as though holding something precious. What were those dear words Hannah said? *He carried you. He kissed you gently.* She gave a little start when the door opened and Lady Smythe came in, followed by Hannah.

"Caroline, my dear, I am so pleased to hear you have regained your senses and that you can recall things. I know of one person who will be very pleased,"

"Thank you, Lady Smythe. You are very kind to take me in, and Hannah also," replied Caroline slowly and carefully.

"Tush, girl. What else could I do when Dashell asked me to do so? There was nowhere else you could go." Caroline could think of nothing to say to that but still felt she was imposing upon Lady Smythe's goodness. "Now, I can see it pains you to talk so I will not stay. I will have my cook bring you some nourishing soup. You must be feeling quite hungry."

While the two of them waited Hannah smoothed out the sheets and plumped up the pillows, as Caroline carefully asked, "Did Dashell—Lord Lonsdale—come into this room at all? I thought I heard him speaking to me, only a few words I think. I don't know what he said. Or was it just a dream? Perhaps it was. I don't remember."

"Yes, he did," replied Hannah, as she tenderly brushed out Caroline's hair, "but I am not sure how long he stayed. Lady Smythe may know, for they came out together, I believe."

Caroline did not like the idea of asking Lady Smythe so let the matter drop. Instead she asked, "Where is Johnny? Is he all right?"

"Yes, he is. Lord Barrandale kindly allowed him to stay with the stablemen at Barrandale House."

"So that means no one is at Becket Lane at all, except Papa?"

"Yes, that's right, dear. Well, I suppose he's there, though I don't know who will 'do' for him." Nor did she care.

"I seem to have caused a lot of trouble," said Caroline with a sigh.

"It's not you that has caused any trouble," Hannah reminded her grimly.

The soup had been brought up and Caroline had managed to swallow some carefully, which pleased Hannah. Another sign she was going to get better. Hannah gathered up the dishes and took the tray downstairs to the kitchen. On her return she found Caroline sitting up expectantly.

"Hannah, you must tell me more. Please."

"Oh, my. There is so much to tell you but I don't think you are strong enough yet."

"Whatever do you mean?"

"Just that, Miss Caroline. But there is one piece of wonderful news I must tell you, and that is birth certificates have been found for you and Miss Maude."

"Birth certificates found!" Caroline's voice cracked in her excitement. "You mean Mother hid them away, like all those jewels?"

"Well no, not exactly. Your Papa had them, and we think he stole them away from her. So after a lot of searching Johnny found them in a secret cupboard in your Papa's room downstairs.

I must show them to you for they are now here in a drawer for safe keeping."

Caroline looked at the two certificates in wonder and joy as Hannah handed them to her. "How I wish Maude had seen these. What a difference it would have made to us. And Mother was going to tell us in her own good time. I wonder why. Oh, Hannah, will we ever understand what really happened? Look at my name: Caroline Diana Waterton. I like the name Waterton. And my father was Sir Arthur Waterton, just some country gentleman. And look, there's that name which you could never recall—Sutherfield—a village in Sussex; and we were planning to go to Sussex, weren't we?"

"And now you need never use that name Wardlock again," Hannah pointed out.

"No, never again," repeated Caroline slowly. She laid the documents down and thought for a moment. "You know, Hannah, even if Lady Smythe allows us to remain here, we cannot do so indefinitely. What are we going to do? Where can we go, for did you not tell me that Lord Lonsdale said I was not to set foot in that house again?"

"We cannot worry about that just yet, Miss Caroline, for it is more important for you to get better. Anyway, I haven't finished yet. You will never guess what else Johnny found; I'll go and fetch it." So saying she went away, leaving Caroline in a state of wonder. What other surprise could there be?

Hannah came back carrying the portrait with a joyful look on her face. "Johnny found it in a room right at the top of the house. Here you are!" She turned it round for Caroline to see, and Caroline, confused by the youthfulness of the man, thought it was a brother. "No, dear, this was painted years ago by your mother. This is your father."

Caroline gave a little scream. "Another one of Mother's secrets?" she faltered. "My father?" and collapsed back on her pillows.

A conscious-stricken Hannah hastily put the painting down. "Miss Caroline, what have I done! I should never have told you in such a fashion. I only wanted it to be a surprise."

Caroline, her thoughts in a whirl, could only repeat, "I don't understand."

A few minutes later a more composed Caroline sat up in bed again, hardly able to take her eyes off the portrait which Hannah had left propped up on a chair for her to see. She had requested to be left alone to rest and to think.

In truth Caroline was still in shock from being assaulted by her stepfather. She could feel her face was swollen on one side and one eye was closed, and one side of her mouth hurt. She went over again in her mind what Hannah had just told her. Round and round it went like a windmill. It terrified her that but for Hannah's intervention Papa might have killed her and she could not imagine why he would want to do so, anyway. She had been told briefly of Johnny's part and doubtless she would hear his full story later.

Her mind dwelt mostly on her mother, the strong and courageous one, to whom her daughters had always turned. And the question that always worried them, why she never told them who their real father was, when all the time she had those documents in her possession and had hidden that portrait at the top of the house. And the time when they had spoken to their mother and she had run from the room, and when she returned she begged them to say nothing more. Only shame or fear would have driven to her to such silence. And why did she keep all those jewels secretly hidden, preferring instead to struggle along as best she could? A feeling of desolation began to appear and she tried to control the tears that wanted to come.

Caroline looked again at the portrait, and on impulse slipped out of bed, but felt shaky on standing up. Carefully she made her way to the chair and picked up the portrait and sat down. After studying it for a while she held it as close to her as she could, putting her arms round her father in the only way possible. How different their lives would have been with him instead of the strange, cold substitute they had. She read what was written on the back. "*To my darling Arthur*". Yet Hannah had said no death certificate for him was found; and Caroline was sure Mother would never have remarried if he had still been alive.

How she wished Maude had been able to see this portrait! They had both loved being at the Academy and Mother would have been so proud of them. Now she was gone. Maude was gone. Only she was left. All Mother's struggles seemed wasted. What now all that education? She must think of her future and find some means of support, but all that came to mind was opening that tea-shop somewhere in Sussex. But wait! She could write to Miss Osgood at the Academy and ask if she had an opening for a teacher, or did she know of one. But that might mean leaving her dear kind Hannah. Once more the sails of the windmill turned.

She could not possibly marry Dashell even if he still wanted her to. What had she to offer him? She had no dowry. And had he not said his family had suddenly lost their wealth because of the foolish actions of one of his brothers? Brother! That was why Papa was so furious, waving that newspaper at her. There must have been something printed in it and he used it as an excuse to quarrel with her. She was glad she had stood up to him in spite of the consequences. Dashell had helped her so much. The forget-me-nots and pansies he had sent her, and the roses given to her earlier. She hoped Hannah had remembered to pack the sachet of dried petals and flowers; her precious keepsakes. She would never, never forget him. He had to marry some heiress or other to save his family. She wondered who her next-of-kin were, and how could she find them. Would they be kind to her? She would sell some of the jewels and go to her birthplace and make some enquiries. Again the windmill turned.

Those jewels! Her heart almost stopped and she turned cold as yet another thought came to her. Had her father stolen those jewels and died afterwards? Was Mother too terrified to say anything? Perhaps she did not know how to return them, even if she had dared. She looked once more at the painting. That kindly looking man whom her mother had loved and who reminded her of Maude—a felon? There was no stopping the tears now and there was only one eye open to release them.

By now Caroline had a splitting headache, her thoughts unstoppable, making her injuries throb. Suddenly she put the portrait down and hastened blindly and shakily to the basin on the washstand and thankfully reached it just in time. She poured herself a little water and swallowed a little, easing her throat. Then she poured a little onto a washcloth and tried to cool her face, and then to her embarrassment had to use it as a handkerchief, not knowing where her own were packed. Such humiliation. Feeling somewhat more at ease she covered the basin with a towel, and as she turned to go she caught sight of herself in a mirror and gave a cry of horror at her reflection. Her swollen face was now made worse from weeping.

The gentle sounds of sleep that had been coming from Hannah's room suddenly stopped; and there were sounds of movement. "Miss Caroline? Did you call?"

Caroline turned quickly away still horrified at her reflection. She made a little run to her bed, but not being able to see properly she knocked into it and slipped to the floor, and cried out once more.

"Miss Caroline, whatever are you doing out of bed? Here, let me help you get up." Her strong arms soon had Caroline onto her feet and into bed. "Now move your feet over and let me tuck you in."

"I am so sorry, Hannah," Caroline managed to croak. "I had to get to the basin and I saw my reflection in the mirror. I feel so ashamed."

"Hush, now." Hannah put her arms round her young mistress and comforted her and then felt her burning forehead and feared she could be getting feverish. Her sharp eyes had noticed the altered positions of both chair and portrait and guessed what had happened. She chided herself. "I am the one who should be sorry, dear, for telling you things too soon. I should have waited until you were stronger."

"The basin," Caroline croaked again.

"Don't worry, dear. I will put everything right. Just lie back and close your eyes and I'll be back as soon as I can. I'll close the curtains a little to shield you from the sunlight."

On her way downstairs, she had in mind to make them both a nice cup of tea, and realized she would have to ask the cook first. Although they were glad to be away from Becket Lane, living there did have its advantages. The cook was slightly put out when Hannah asked where she might rinse out the basin and the washcloth, and when she begged a little barley water to settle Miss Caroline's stomach.

Once back in the bedroom Hannah deftly wrung out the cloth in some water and moved over to the bed. "How are you, Miss Caroline?" she asked gently in case she was asleep.

"About the same," came the weary reply. "My poor face aches."

"Here is a cold compress for you," said Hannah, as she laid the cloth on Caroline's forehead with a practiced hand, "and I have also requested a little barley water for you."

"It sounds just like when we were children," remarked Caroline, "but that reflection shocked me. I did not know I looked so awful."

"Now, dear, stop fretting. With rest you will get better. I know you will. And I blame myself too for you have had so much to contend with lately."

"Hannah," persisted Caroline, "please promise me you will not let Lord Lonsdale see me like this. I should be quite mortified."

"Of course I will. He will understand. He is a gentleman."

There was a knock on the door from the maid who brought up the barley water, which Hannah answered at once. She did not wish Miss Caroline to be seen by any of the servants.

"Now, Miss Caroline, try some of this; it will help to settle you. And when you have had enough I must inform Lady Smythe."

"Need you? She will think me quite foolish."

"I am sure her ladyship will not. We must remember we are guests in her house, and at very short notice, and I did ask her servants for things without her prior knowledge."

"Yes, of course you are right," sighed Caroline. Drinking slowly by the spoonful was tiring and after a while she put the bowl to one side. "Thank you, Hannah."

"All right, dear. I'll leave it there and you can have some more later." She laid her hand on Caroline's forehead and thought it felt a little less feverish. "I will give you a fresh compress before I go." A minute or two later the door closed behind her.

Caroline looked quickly for the portrait but Hannah had wisely moved it. Of course she had been upset over everything. She must learn to be strong and to have faith. One other thing she resolved to do was to stop calling her stepfather "Papa", for he was not. From now on she would refer to him, if she had to at all, as her "Step-papa".

"It was my fault, Lady Smythe," explained a contrite Hannah, "but I was so wanting Miss Caroline to know the wonderful news."

Lady Smythe was sympathetic. "I believe you did right; Caroline had to know. Please tell her not to worry about being here for she is quite welcome. I will inform my nephew and we will both respect her wish not to see her until she feels ready for us to do so." She felt a trifle doubtful about Dashell's reaction to that but he would have to wait. "As soon as Caroline feels able to travel she must stay in the country somewhere; the peace and quiet would help her considerably. I will enquire amongst my friends and I am sure someone will allow her to stay with them."

"Thank you, Lady Smythe, you are very kind." Her ladyship graciously inclined her head and Hannah left the room.

Lady Smythe promptly wrote a note to Dashell requesting him to call. Her maid came back with the reply that Lord Lonsdale had left earlier that morning to go to Becket Lane, and it was not known when he would return.

CHAPTER TWO

Happenings Continue

S uch was the situation when Chadwick answered the door to Dashell's knocking. "We have been expecting you, Lord Lonsdale. Lady Smythe has been concerned about Miss Waterton."

Dashell's heart missed a beat. "Miss Waterton—Caroline? I will go up at once." Although he was anxious to see Caroline, manners required that he see his aunt first. He knocked briefly on the door of her salon and went straight in.

"Dashell!" cried his aunt, "I am so glad you came. I sent you a note."

"I have not been to the house yet, I came straight here from Becket Lane." But fearing the worst he asked quickly "Is Caroline all right? Chadwick said you were concerned about her."

"It's just that she got out of bed without Hannah's knowledge and had a fall, but let me reassure you"—as she saw his anxious frown—"it is not her actual hurts but her state of mind."

"You mean her head injury is more serious that we thought?" he asked.

"No, no, nothing like that at all. Let me explain." So his aunt repeated almost word for word what Hannah had told her, and what she said in reply.

Dashell sat back with a sigh of relief, thankful that Caroline was all right. "Aunt Letty, you are wonderful. I agree, I think a stay in the country would do her a world of good. Now perhaps I should have a word with Hannah and ask her to reassure the dear girl, for we know what her future is going to be. Before I do, however, I have something important to tell you."

"Oh?" she said, wondering why he looked so intense.

"Thomas Wardlock is dead. We found his body on the floor of his downstairs room. He discovered his black box empty of all papers and it is my belief he intended burning them, for he had lit a fire in the grate, only Johnny had found them first, and he must have had some kind of seizure."

"Oh," said his aunt again, not knowing what else to say, except to think it was rather convenient.

"We informed the authorities, who came and removed the body." He sensed his aunt was not particularly interested about that, so he changed the subject. "Now, if I may, I would like to speak to Hannah."

"Yes, of course. But wait a moment, I will have her come here." With that she left the room and returned with a rather contrite Hannah.

Dashell saw this and tried to put her at her ease. "My aunt has just been telling me of Caroline's unhappiness and discomfort and her unfortunate fall. I only wish I could come and reassure her myself, but I know you will take the greatest care of her. She must not concern herself over her future either, for surely she knows what it is going to be."

Of course, Lord Lonsdale," Hannah said, simply and sincerely. "I will tell Miss Caroline she has nothing to fear."

"And now, Hannah, I have something to tell you, and that is that Thomas Wardlock is dead."

Her eyes widened in surprise. "Well, sir, I suppose I should be sorry, but I am not. Nor will I pretend I am. He was a wicked man."

Dashell looked at her keenly. "I will leave it to your discretion when to tell Caroline of the death of her stepfather."

"Sir, this means we can now fetch that last box from the house in safety."

"Ah, yes. That box. I believe Johnny wishes to speak to you about that and certain other matters concerning the house, now that Caroline inherits everything." He said nothing about the mutilated dresses. "Thank you, Hannah, you may go."

When the door closed behind her, Lady Smythe grimly remarked, "Well, all I can say is—is—well, perhaps it would be better to say nothing."

"I know exactly how you feel, for I feel a great relief, too." Dashell thought for a moment and said, "It must be terrible to die and have nobody mourn your passing. Now," he continued briskly, "I must go. Father will be wondering what is happening, although I told Johnny to inform Matthew where I was." He turned to go, but stopped. "Oh, by the way, I want to speak to Hannah some time, perhaps tomorrow." His aunt looked faintly surprised. "I have in mind to give Johnny some kind of reward for all his wonderful help. Maybe she could suggest something."

"Dashell, you are so good. I truly admire you."

"Now, Aunt Letty, don't—don't—well, whatever the word is—don't," he begged.

"Go away," she laughed at him, as he kissed her on both cheeks.

It took him only a few minutes to return to Barrandale House. "I believe Lord Barrandale is waiting to see you, sir," Matthew informed him.

I bet he is, chuckled Dashell to himself. "When Johnny returned what message did he give you?"

"He said that you were at Grosvenor Square, and that you had instructed him not to say anything to anybody, not even

Lord Barrandale." Dashell, nodded; he always knew Johnny was reliable. "I did pass all this on to his lordship."

"Of course." He turned to go to his father, and with a brief knock on the door, he entered the room.

"Come in, Dashell, come in. I was wondering how much longer you would be." Barrandale had been playing solitaire while waiting, but now left the card table and sat down in his favourite armchair, while Dashell settled himself in a chair opposite.

Barrandale placed the tips of his fingers together. "Tell me, how did you get on with Wardlock when you returned the papers? What did you say to him, or what's more important, what did he say to you?"

Dashell looked at his father levelly. "I never gave him the papers, nor did I speak to him. We found him dead when we arrived at the house, his body was in his downstairs room." Barrandale's eyebrows rose considerably at this item of news. "But I have a great deal to tell you, as you may guess. After discovering Wardlock's body I knew the authorities had to be informed, so I went to Scotland Yard."

Again Barrandale's eyebrows rose. "Indeed?" He could not help showing some aversion to that fact, which Dashell noticed.

"I think, sir, you will understand once I explain."

"Very well; I am listening."

Marshalling his thoughts carefully, Dashell related all that they had discovered in the house; why he had gone to the police; his impressions of Inspector Cockburn and Sergeant Springer; his conversation with the Inspector who was astounded to learn of the real identity of the felon so long sought by them; their return to the house; Johnny's helpfulness; and the Police saying they would be at the house again the next morning; and ending with his own request for anonymity.

When the two policemen had gone, he asked Johnny to show him where the thread had been attached across the top stairs; the attic where the portrait had been hidden; and the room where Isobel died. The incidents of the slashed dresses convinced him of Wardlock's imbalance of mind, or even outright insanity. His death did indeed solve a lot of problems. Caroline would inherit the property and all its contents, such as they were, except all the stolen goods, which by law had been seized by Inspector Cockburn; and he certainly did not inform the Inspector of the violent suspicious deaths of Isobel and Maude. That would have been most unwise; let it be.

How, after stopping at the Bishop's Head Inn, he went straight to Grosvenor Square to advise Aunt Letty and Hannah of Wardlock's death. Caroline was not to be told yet. She had completely distressed herself over what Hannah had revealed about her real name, and the discovery of her father's portrait, and especially why her mother had never told Maude or herself anything. All this had equally upset Hannah for not being more careful; and that Caroline had got out of bed without Hannah's knowledge and on returning had slipped and fallen. She therefore did not wish anyone to see her until she felt ready to receive them. Hannah had told him in confidence that all Caroline's weeping had suffused her face. *What a request,* sighed Dashell to himself, just when he longed to put his arms round her and kiss away all her fears, and say that her future was secure, to have and to hold.

"Aunt Letty said that when Caroline is well enough to travel she must go and stay in the country somewhere. She is going to write to one or two friends to see if they could accept her for a while."

"That is exceedingly kind of her," remarked Barrandale. "I think your aunt is as much intrigued by Caroline and her story as I am."

"Yes," observed Dashell, "I have had that impression. You are both very sympathetic people. And I must also write to the Rector of Sutherfield; it will be interesting to see what his reply will be." He paused for a moment or two. "There is one other matter I must attend to, and I am sure you will agree, and that is to give some suitable reward to Johnny. I really do not know what we all would have done without him."

"I do most certainly agree," said Barrandale. "What had you in mind, may I ask?"

"I'm not sure," replied Dashell slowly. "That is why I wish to speak to Hannah."

Barrandale returned to his playing cards, and Dashell stayed where he was quietly thinking. To be honest he was relieved Thomas Wardlock was dead—although it troubled his conscience to think so—and that he had been too late to speak to him. It would have been an unpleasant interview to say the least. He also wondered how Inspector Cockburn would get on with the cab driver that had come to the house each morning during the week. The man might be co-operative but on the other hand he might refuse to talk. He doubted if Cockburn would let him know; it was no concern of his now, anyway.

His thoughts returned to Caroline and he wondered what he could do to cheer her up. He would send her some flowers. What was it he had said in that second letter? "*I would send you a hundred pansies if I could*". Tomorrow he would return to the flower sellers at St.Paul's Cathedral, and on to Piccadilly Circus and Covent Garden if he had to, and buy all the pansies he could. He could just imagine Caroline's surprise and delight.

Barrandale turned round in his chair to speak to Dashell and saw the smile on his face, and turned back again with a smile of his own, and left his son to his dreams.

"Sir," said Dashell, some minutes later.

"Yes, my son?" enquired Barrandale gravely, looking up from his cards.

"Do you remember that ring you gave Mother for your tenth wedding anniversary, the one with pearls and rubies?"

"Indeed I do." He had carefully chosen it for its meaning: pearls for "*a pearl of great price*" and rubies for a woman "*whose price is far above rubies*".

"Mother left it to me as an engagement ring for any future Lady Lonsdale."

"Yes, I remember that too, except there is one serious drawback."

"Yes, I know," agreed Dashell with a heavy sigh. "Who is Caroline's next-of-kin, meaning her nearest male relative, whom I must ask for permission to marry her, for she is not of age. Well, I am sure we will find out sooner or later." *And I'll find out the truth even if I have to drag it out of them*, Dashell promised himself, remembering at the same time his father's earlier warning.

"What are you planning to do tomorrow?"

"I have a matter to attend to in the morning," replied Dashell, without saying what it was, "and then speak to Hannah about Johnny, and then to Johnny later. Then the next day I shall go to Windsor for the ring—Simmonds will know where it is—and I should be back by dinnertime." He caught sight of his father's look of surprise and laughed. "Forty miles or so is nothing to Sparkle. His endurance is phenomenal."

"Oh, then in that case perhaps I should transfer my concern to you for your endurance. Ah me, such is youth," quipped Barrandale, "although no doubt I would have done the same at your age." He stood up from the table. "I think I have had enough of cards for the time being. Matthew will be announcing dinner soon."

CHAPTER THREE

The Next Day

Ever since returning to the stables Johnny had been unusually quiet. He had to go and see Hannah and tell her about the ruined dresses and that it was his fault for leaving the knife where it could be seen. He still had to go to the livery stable and say that the horse and cart was no longer required as there had been an accident.

His plaintive sigh caught Matthew's attention. "Everything all right?" he asked kindly.

"Well, sort of," he replied carefully. "There are fings I hafta do for Miss Caroline tomorrer."

"Do what you have to," continued Matthew, "but remember, that while you are under the Barrandale roof we are responsible for you and we have to know your whereabouts."

"Oh," said Johnny. That had not occurred to him and he was quite impressed.

He did not spend an entirely happy time that day, although he did do justice to the afternoon tea and evening meal. After the latter, the servants remained at the table talking amongst themselves as they usually did in the evenings, while Johnny stayed in the background quietly listening.

The next morning Johnny slipped out very early to go to the livery stables.

"Just be back in time for breakfast," Stephen reminded him, as he opened the postern gate for him, watched by Reuben.

"Don'tcha worry," Johnny grinned back at him.

"Strikes me that boy has had too much freedom," grumbled Reuben, and as he was in charge of the stables he was not going to let Johnny get away with anything.

Later when Dashell came into the yard for his horse for his morning ride round Hyde Park, Reuben mentioned that Johnny said he had errands to do for Miss Caroline. He was relieved to learn that was correct or else he would have given Johnny a flea in his ear.

At Grosvenor Square Caroline awoke feeling much better after a good night's sleep, and her movements brought the ever-ready Hannah to her side. She began feeling her face and eye carefully with her good hand, because Hannah would not allow her to have a mirror. "I think the swelling has gone down. My face does not feel so hot. Do you think so, Hannah? Do you think I look better?"

"Yes, dear, I do. And now you are awake I will see about some breakfast."

Caroline felt her face again and tried opening her left eye, but still could not do so. She was determined not to let tears suffuse her face again; the sooner she was better the sooner she could see Dashell again. She must ask Hannah more about her rescue and wished she had been more aware of his arms around her. She smiled to herself as she thought of asking him to do the same thing again so she would know what it felt like. She was sure he would oblige.

Hannah came in with the tray. "It does me good to see you more cheerful, Miss Caroline," she said, as she put the tray on Caroline's lap.

Caroline ate a good breakfast but slowly, while Hannah had tidied up the room and straightened the bedclothes. With nothing much to do she hoped the passage of time was not going to be too tedious. Her thoughts, of course, turned to Dashell, not knowing that at the same time his thoughts were of her.

Dashell had set off in his carriage straight to St. Paul's Cathedral and began to search among the flower sellers there. He found the one from whom he had purchased those earlier pansies and bought all she had.

"Your lady-love must be very special," she laughed at him.

"Or need a lot of convincing," joked another, causing laughter all round.

An embarrassed Dashell returned to his carriage. Of course his lady-love was special, why else would he be doing this?

At Grosvenor Square he ordered Stephen not to wait. Chadwick could not help showing a flicker of surprise when he answered the door to admit Lord Lonsdale, with his armful of sweet-smelling flowers.

"For the lady upstairs," he said simply, as he handed them over, trying not to look too sheepish.

"Very good, your lordship. I shall have her ladyship's maid see to them."

"Would you inform Hannah as well, she will be pleased to help. I know Miss Waterton will love them," he said slightly tartly, in case Chadwick thought they were meant for his aunt, heaven forbid. "Is her ladyship up?"

"I believe she is, sir."

"Then I will announce myself." He left his hat and gloves on the hall table to indicate he would not be staying long, also leaving behind a rather perplexed Chadwick.

A few minutes later there was a knock on the door of Caroline's room. It was the housemaid, smiling broadly, saying Hannah was required downstairs and would she be pleased to come. Mystified, and after glancing at Caroline who was equally puzzled, Hannah went down as requested.

On entering the kitchen she stopped short at the sight of numerous little pansies laid out on the table. "Oh! They must be from Lord Lonsdale."

"Indeed they are," said an interested Chadwick. "There is a dish put out for them."

"Why would Lord Lonsdale want to give the lady so many pansies?" asked Cook.

"Well," explained Hannah, "in flower language it means, *"My thoughts are always of you"* or something like that."

"Does that mean Miss Waterton could become the new Lady Lonsdale?"

"I am sure of it," replied Hannah.

Chadwick cleared his throat. "It's time he settled down," he stated, as though reinstating his authority.

"I think it's ever so romantic," sniffed Cook, her eyes filling with tears. "I really do." Chadwick stared at her; he had no idea she was like this, although Chadwick himself was heard blowing his nose a few minutes later.

Caroline could hardly believe it when Hannah came in with the dish." I don't need to tell you who sent them," she smiled.

"I can certainly guess," said Caroline. "I must get up and look at them. How lovely they are," as she bent to smell their delicate scent. "Is Dashell still here?" she asked. "Hannah, would you go along to Lady Smythe's salon and see if he is, and thank him most sincerely for me for his kindness."

"Come in," called Lady Smythe, in response to Hannah's knock on the door. "I know exactly why you have come. I have heard all about them from my nephew himself. In fact I have heard nothing but."

"Begging your pardon, your ladyship, Miss Caroline wishes me to thank Lord Lonsdale most sincerely for his kindness. She says they are lovely."

"How is she?" asked Dashell.

"She is much better, sir. I am sure a few days rest will help her considerably."

"Before you go, Hannah," continued Dashell, "I will come back this afternoon as I wish to speak to you about something."

"I trust that will be convenient, Aunt Letty? I wish to talk to her about a reward for Johnny for all his helpfulness."

"Yes, you told me that yesterday. And if you talk to me any more about Caroline, I shall scream."

"I promise," laughed Dashell, "at least for today."

After Dashell left, Lady Smythe went along to Caroline's room to satisfy her own curiosity, and when Hannah answered the door she said, "Oh, how charming: I can smell the flowers from here. By the way, Caroline, can you see well enough to read? I have two books here you may like to have. There is no haste for their return." She looked once more at the pretty blooms. *"Completely besotted,"* she muttered, shaking her head.

CHAPTER FOUR

To Return to Johnny

Johnny finished his breakfast, and Matthew saw him glance at the kitchen clock. "You said last night that you had to go to Becket Lane this morning."

"Yes, that's right," replied Johnny. "I might not be back for tea but I will be back for supper."

"That's all right. As long as you tell us so we don't have to worry where you are."

Johnny smiled, thinking once more that Matthew was nicer and kinder than he looked.

So many memories came back to him as he walked along exactly the same road he had taken some four years or so ago, when he first went to Becket Lane; all the incidents that had happened at that house, almost as if he was meant to be there, except being a boy, he brushed aside such foolish imaginings.

He had to think about his future now that he would be on his own, for he knew things would never be the same again. Miss Caroline would become Lady Lonsdale and therefore Hannah would go with her, for Miss Caroline would never leave her behind. And what would happen to the house now that nobody would be living in it? Probably it would be sold.

He looked at the Bishop's Head Inn as he passed it. He had liked being there, he had made friends with Sammy Cullen, the under-ostler; Perkins, the head-ostler, was all right if he was in a good mood.

A few minutes later he was at the house, which now had a grey and forlorn look about it. He looked inside the old tree stump but no letters were there. The front door was locked, and thank goodness Lord Lonsdale had given him back the key. Inside the hall he saw the tell-tale scuff marks on the floor which led to the cupboard under the stairs. He looked at the door to Wardlock's room but did not go in.

Upstairs the bedrooms looked bare and desolate. The door to the linen cupboard was open although the key was in the lock. He locked it again, grinning to himself, how mad 'is Nibs must have been when he discovered he had been tricked! The rooms at the top of the house looked better in daylight, and in moving around he felt sure the floors were uneven and there was still that odd smell, which he later learned it indicated dry rot in the floor boards. He returned downstairs carrying the easel with him as there was no point leaving it there.

Down in the kitchen he noticed the door to his own small room was open. He never left it open, so 'is Nibs must have been in there as well, not knowing which door led where. He had forgotten all about his bedding which he had just dumped inside Saturday morning, and now folded it up carefully. And there was still that tell-tale little pile of ashes in the fire grate.

He went into the pantry and was greeted by the smell of mouldy food and sour milk. The ham was all right and there were still plenty of pickles.

There were two errands he had to do. The first was to call round at the postman's cottage and explain that the house was empty because old Mr. Wardlock had died, and Miss Waterton and Hannah had gone to live with a friend in London, and could any letters still be left in the tree stump, as he would take care of them.

The next errand was to call at the vicarage to say that Mr. Wardlock had died on Saturday and that funeral arrangements had already been made, in case the vicar felt he had to do something about it. Johnny thought it was clever of him to word it that way. He said Miss Waterton had gone to live with a friend in London, and Hannah was with her. He did not say where Miss Waterton was staying in case the Guv didn't want anyone to know. It was none of their business anyway.

Back at the house he went into the pantry again and made a meal from whatever he could find that was still edible, then washed all the things he had left on the draining board. When he had finished he went outside and dug a deep hole and buried all the mouldy food and sour milk.

Now he must see what needed to be done in both the front and back gardens. It was more important to tidy up the front one to make it look as though someone was still about. He dead-headed some of the rose bushes and wondered what would become of them now. The mistress had so loved them and it would be a pity to neglect them. The vegetable garden needing weeding and he set to with a hoe. Strange how the weeds grew so quickly; it was almost as though they waited until you were not looking and then sprang up. That had always been the missus' little joke. When that was done he swept along the paths.

It was time to leave. He locked the front door from the inside and put the key back in his pocket and went out by the side door, locked it, and hung up that key in its own hiding place. If he really hurried he might be back for afternoon tea at four o'clock after all.

From listening to the servants' previous talk, Johnny had learned that Barrandale House was up for sale and why, and the next house was going to be smaller. He had heard from Matthew that many pieces of furniture were going to be sold, and that there was bound to be other items in the country house at Windsor being sold as well, and that carters would have to be hired.

This quickened Johnny's interest. If only he could do something like this! There was still that forty pounds Uncle Joe had left to him which he would not get until he was twenty-one, and he was not yet eighteen. But that was why he wanted to talk things over with Hannah, what to do with all the things that were still in the old house. It would have to be discussed with Miss Caroline first and that would take time, yet he could not just sit around getting under people's feet because he had nothing to do. Oh, what a worry and bloomin' mess it was, an' all. Tea was now over, and Matthew had just returned with the silver tea tray when the front door bell rang and he went immediately to answer it.

It was Dashell, who had been all afternoon at his aunt's house.

"Would you send Johnny to me, Matthew? Show him into the small front salon in fifteen minutes, for I wish first to speak to my father." Dashell went to join his father and sat down, smiling at him. Barrandale saw he had something interesting to say and left him to speak first.

"I have had an interesting talk with Hannah," he began. "It seems this Uncle Joe Barlow left Johnny the sum of forty pounds which he will receive when he is twenty-one. Apparently the man never married, worked hard, saved hard, and then he died in some unfortunate accident. Also Johnny's parents were lost in a house fire three years or so before that, so apart from his half-sister he has no relatives at all."

"Indeed?" responded Barrandale gravely, "so young, too."

"I wish to reward him in some way for all his help, but we cannot offer him a position on our estate or household here, for it would not be fair to those servants whom we have had to let go."

"That is true," replied Barrandale, with a slight frown at being reminded of the "difficult situation". "But go on, I see you have something more to say."

"It is just this, sir. The inventories have shown there are a considerable number of items no longer required which will need to be carted away. I intend to ask Johnny to do this, for he could at least take the smaller ones."

"Most admirable," agreed Barrandale, "but would it not require him to have a horse and cart?"

"I intend to reward him by giving him enough money to purchase his own. Once he has done all he can for us he is free to do what he will."

Barrandale placed his fingers together and looked at Dashell. "I think that is most magnanimous of you, just the sort of thing you would think of doing."

"I cannot do anything less. He saved Caroline's life and he has done a great deal for us also." Both men fell silent as they heard footsteps pass the door.

Matthew returned and knocked on the door, "I have ushered Johnny into the salon, Lord Lonsdale," he said.

When Matthew told Johnny that Lord Lonsdale wished to speak to him, he promptly got up to go, but Matthew stopped him. "Oh no, you don't. Not like that. Not so fast. We'll have to tidy you up first." A brush and comb for his hair was produced from somewhere. His hands and fingernails were inspected and he was told to scrub them, and he was told to give his boots a quick clean. Johnny meekly submitted to these ministrations but inwardly he was quite indignant. When Matthew was satisfied he was ready he led him to the front room. Johnny was left feeling rather like a lamb led to the slaughter and wondered why the Guv wanted to see him anyway, and hoped all was well with Miss

Caroline. He braced himself when he heard footsteps coming and Lord Lonsdale entered the room.

"You wanted to me abaht somefink, Guv," he ventured, not sure if this was the correct way to proceed.

"Yes, Johnny, I do," replied Dashell, "but to begin with I was at Grosvenor Square this afternoon and learned Caroline is much better."

"Oh," said Johnny, looking pleased.

Dashell smiled at him again. "Caroline will be staying now at Grosvenor Square and Hannah, of course, will be with her."

"Yes, Guv," put in Johnny quickly, 'I wuz at the 'ouse today lookin' over everyfink and seein' wot I could do. All the fings left be'ind 'ave all gotta be sorted out now that the 'ouse is empty."

"That brings me to something else," continued Dashell. "There will be a considerable number of unwanted items here in this house and in the one at Windsor. They need to be taken away and sold for whatever price they will fetch. Would you be willing and able to do this?" He paused to assess Johnny's reaction.

"Would—I—be—willin'," Johnny echoed slowly, hardly daring to believe his ears. This was his dream! He knew the Guv would mean what he said. "But—how could I?"

Again Dashell smiled. He went over to a small bureau and took out a leather purse tied at the neck with a drawstring, and held it out to Johnny. "Here are twenty pounds for you, with my sincere thanks for all you have done for Caroline, for your resourcefulness and bravery, because but for you I think Caroline would have died; and also for all your help to my own family. I am sure there will be enough for you to purchase your own horse and cart."

Johnny stammered his thanks, quite at a loss for words. "I—I just don't know what to say, Guv. I never expected this." Twenty pounds! It was certainly more than enough to make his dream become reality; and already his agile brain was thinking he would have to find stabling premises somewhere. He hesitated, wanting to say more but not sure if he should.

Dashell saw this. "Yes, Johnny?" he encouraged.

'Y'know, Guv, I would've done anyfink for Miss Caroline," he confessed. "I remember when I first went to that 'ouse an' Miss Caroline opened the door to me, I felt there was somefink speshell 'bout 'er then. P'raps it was becos she wuz the first of the three I met, I dunno, and now"—with a rueful sigh—"she's the last of the three. They were all good to me, the Missus, Miss Maude and Miss Caroline. They made 'annah an' me feel like family." Then the irrepressible Johnny began to grin. "Y'know, Guv, I'm glad it wuz you 'oo found Miss Caroline."

Dashell smiled his quirky smile. "You know something, Johnny, so am I. And now I believe my father would like to see you."

Lord Barrandale was the only person who ever held Johnny in complete awe. What with that and the fact he had been given a reward, he found it hard to listen. He did, however, remember being told that overnight accommodation would be provided for him and his horse at Windsor, if required. "Simmonds will be informed of this. I think my son would agree."

Again Johnny could only stammer his thanks. "Thank you, Lord Barrandale. Thank you, sir," he said, turning to Dashell. He never personally addressed him as "Guv" again.

Dashell rang the bell for Matthew. "Matthew, I am sure you have learned of the ways in which Johnny has been of great assistance to Miss Caroline and me. He has been engaged to cart away the smaller unwanted items for sale from this house and the one in Windsor. I am sure you and he will come to some arrangement about the matter."

"Very good, sir," replied Mathew, looking at Johnny's glowing face.

Johnny followed Matthew back to the kitchen, still clutching that precious leather bag. He really had to go and see Hannah and tell her the wonderful news, although she might know something already. He glanced hopefully at Matthew. "I hafta go an' see me sister," he said.

"All right, lad. Off you go. Just be back in time for supper."

Johnny did not need to be told twice.

Johnny sped round to Grosvenor Square as though his feet hardly touched the ground. Just wait until he told Hannah the news! The servants' side door was opened by a rather surprised Chadwick, for nobody was expected. "Please could I see 'annah," he panted. I'm Johnny Faulkner, her bruvver. I'm staying wiv the servants at Barrandale 'ouse."

Chadwick's manner changed at once. So this was the young hero. "Come in," he said. "I will have Hannah informed you are here."

A few minutes later Hannah came down. "I hoped you would come, Johnny, there is so much to talk about," she said, looking curiously at his beaming face.

"Where can we talk, 'annah? It's gotta be where no one can 'ear us."

"Oh? Well, I suppose outside in the yard," she replied, wondering what the secrecy was about.

Johnny brought out the leather bag from his coat pocket and shook it. "You'll never guess," he said gleefully, "Lord Lonsdale gave me this as a reward for everyfink I've done fer Miss Caroline. An wot's more, 'e sed there's a lot of fings to be taken away from the 'ouse 'ere an' the one at Windsor, which all have to be sold. An' he wants me to do it."

"How can you? You don't have a horse and cart." Hannah could be quite logical too.

"That's just it." In his excitement Johnny shook the bag again. "The Guv gave me twenty pounds. I can buy me own 'orse'n cart an' set meself up in business. An' I've got the money I've bin able to save, and there is still that forty pounds to come from Uncle Joe."

Hannah gasped out loud. "Oh, Johnny, that's wonderful," and in her delight gave him a hug. "But how will you go about it?"

"Oh, I've thought it all out," he grinned, as indeed he had. "I'll go to Paxton's Yard where Uncle Joe useta be an' see if they can 'elp."

"Johnny, I am so pleased for you. I should tell you Lord Lonsdale spoke to me this afternoon as he wanted to reward you in some way, but I had no idea he would be that generous. I had been wondering, too, what you would do now that that house is empty."

"That reminds me. I was there this mornin' lookin' around." He came to a stop and gulped. "I gotta tell you this, 'annah," looking anxiously at her, "It's all my fault an' you will be so cross, and so will Miss Caroline."

"Tell me what?" said Hannah, as Johnny hesitated.

"Well, y'know that box we couldn't take wiv us last Friday night which Stephen an' me 'ad to put it into the cupboard under the stairs. Well, "e found it, 'e musta seen the marks left on the floor when we pushed it in. An' that's not all. I left a sharp knife on the drainin' board in the kitchen just to annoy 'im an' 'e found that as well." Johnny floundered to a stop and Hannah waited for him to continue. "Well, 'e took Miss Caroline's dresses outa the box, and cut 'em."

"What!" shrieked Hannah.

"Well, 'e cut one dahn the middle an' the sleeves of anuvver, well, all four of 'em."

"Oh, that horrible, horrible man!" exclaimed Hannah. "I'm glad he's dead. There. I've said it, and I'm not sorry."

"But I've gotta tell Miss Caroline it was my fault," wailed Johnny.

"Look, don't worry. He would have found a knife anyway. I'm sure he did this out of sheer spite and I'm not letting him get the better of us. There's enough remnants and pieces packed away somewhere for the dresses to be repaired and altered and made almost new again. I'll tell Miss Caroline myself."

"Please tell 'er I'm so sorry," begged Johnny.

"Of course I will. And by the way, I told her that you and Lord Lonsdale found him dead when you went to the house on Sunday."

"So she knows. What did she say?"

"Nothing much; what was there to say?"

They stared at each other. "Blimey," muttered Johnny, "it must be 'orrible to die and nobody cares," unknowingly echoing Dashell's words. Hannah opened her mouth to say something but decided against it. No, there was nothing to say, not any more. "I'll get that box over 'ere somehow," persisted Johnny, "an' you an' me will hafta go through that 'ouse an' sort fings out."

"Yes, all right. But there is plenty of time. Besides, you must attend to both the Barrandale houses first."

"Oh, mm, yes," he said, "you're right, as always," but before Hannah could think of a suitable answer, Johnny continued. "I still 'ave two uvver fings to tell yer. I 'ad a word wiv the vicar an' told 'im wot 'ad 'appened and that Miss Caroline 'ad gone to live wiv a friend in London and you were wiv 'er. I didn't say where. An' I asked the postman if 'e could still leave letters in the old stump, and that I would look after em."

They parted company with Hannah reminding Johnny to "remember Uncle Joe". They had often used that phrase with the underlying meaning that anything private they said to each other was to be kept between them.

Johnny returned to the Barrandale stableyard smiling, for more than one reason. After their evening meal he was quite content to sit once more in the background listening to their talk until it was time to go to bed. He slept with the money bag held to his chest, still hardly able to believe it was there.

Hannah had gone back upstairs, eager to tell her young mistress what Johnny had been given by Lord Lonsdale; and what Johnny had been doing at that house during the day. She would not mention the ruined dresses until last. Coming quickly into the room she paused for breath, declaring she hardly knew where to begin.

Caroline looked up in wonder, catching Hannah's excitement. "Hannah, what is it?"

"Lord Lonsdale," she puffed. "You will never guess, Miss Caroline. He has given Johnny twenty pounds to buy his own horse and cart as a reward for everything he had done to help you and their own Barrandale family." She then went on to tell about the removal of all the unwanted items from both the Barrandale houses which he was to do. "Oh, he will be so busy, I'm sure, and how fortunate for him. But begging your pardon, I said he should attend to all that first before we look over things at that other house."

"Of course you were right in saying that, Hannah. And I am so pleased for him. That was a very generous gesture from Dashell."

Hannah then mentioned the four dresses that had been cut. "He was so upset about those dresses, and that it was his fault for leaving the knife out," then added with a sniff, "Even if he had not, that man could easily have found one in a kitchen drawer somewhere. Anyway, Miss Caroline, he asked me to say for him that he is so sorry."

"Poor Johnny," sympathized Caroline, "of course I would not have him upset for anything. There must be enough remnants or other pieces left over from their making. I know nothing was thrown away. Between the two of us I am sure we can repair or alter them like new."

"We certainly will," said Hannah rather grimly. "We will not let that man get the better of us." There followed a rather awkward silence after that remark, so Hannah went on to say what else Johnny had been doing.

After listening carefully, Caroline said she would write to the vicar and say that now her stepfather had died she would prefer to be known by her real name of Waterton.

"And what a stir what will cause," remarked Hannah.

"It probably will," said Caroline, with a chuckle.

CHAPTER FIVE

The Two Ladies Leave for St. Albans

The next morning Dashell decided he could wait to go to Windsor after all. It was more important to write to the parish priest of Sutherfield and ask him what he knew of a family by the name of Waterton who had once lived in that vicinity; and in particular a Sir Arthur Waterton, who, it was believed, had died about eighteen years ago. And he, Lonsdale, would be most obliged if he made the most discreet enquiries.

That same morning, Caroline wrote to Dashell thanking him for all the flowers, and for his generosity towards Johnny. Her letter now gave him a wonderful excuse to go to Grosvenor Square and tell her he had just written to the parish priest of Sutherfield, and that should raise her spirits even more.

Ignoring convention, he called in the morning. "I'll announce myself, Chadwick."

An astonished Lady Smythe exclaimed, "You are early," when Dashell entered the salon. "Is everything all right?"

"My father and I are in good health, thank you, Aunt Letty. And I see you are blooming, too. But more to the point, how is Caroline? I have just received her letter. I trust she is better?"

"Thank you, Dashell, for putting me in second place," laughed his aunt. "Yes. I am glad to say she is, and do please sit down.

Hannah says the discolouration and swelling have gone down, and her arm is less painful. She has been out of bed but remains in her room."

"I am so glad, for her sake, when I think of how she looked a few days ago,"

"Caroline is not at death's door," his aunt reminded him rather tersely.

Dashell laughed, and then became serious. "By the way, I have written to the parish priest of Sutherfield in Sussex, asking him what he knows about a family by the name of Waterton that once resided in that area. It may take him some days to reply, particularly if he has to obtain information first."

"I find it rather exciting," admitted Lady Smythe, "except goodness knows who will turn out to be her relatives. Poor girl; she may not even like them. I know many people who thoroughly detest their relatives."

Dashell laughed again, grimly this time. "We will just have to take that chance, for I am determined to find out everything. I would like to know about that shameful treatment to her mother, Isobel, for one thing."

Lady Smythe sighed to herself. She knew her nephew too well. Tactfully she changed the subject. "Will you be staying for lunch?"

"No thank you. But if you will tell your cook to make some of her shortbreads, I shall be here for tea."

The next two days passed in much the same manner. Dashell came round every day to enquire after Caroline, which nearly drove his aunt to distraction. She was almost at the point of begging the girl to hasten her own wellness.

There was one instance when that could have been said to happen. Lady Smythe, learning from Hannah that Caroline was so much better, had gone to see her. Caroline was seated at the table looking at the dish containing the pansies, which were still quite fresh. She had the elbow of her right arm on the table and her right hand supporting her chin, regarding the flowers with a tender, dreamy look on her face. *Oh, for goodness' sake,* thought Lady Smythe, *now they are both at it. If they don't get together soon, I really will scream'.*

"Oh!" Caroline gave a little start. "Your pardon, ma'am, I didn't hear you come," she said, beginning to get up.

"No matter, child, but I seem to have disturbed you. Pray be seated again."

Caroline did so, and glanced up at the older woman. "You must be wondering what I am doing, just looking at these pansies. I know Dashell told you all about them."

Lady Smythe flung her hands in the air. "He has, several times over."

Caroline gave a little choking sound, trying not to laugh. "Indeed, ma'am, he could not have given me anything more delightful than these; for I now understand why the wild ones are called "heart's ease." Their very charm, fragrance and fragility truly do ease the pain in one's heart," laying her hand over her own as she said it.

That had never really occurred to Lady Smythe before and she was quite touched by it. "I think that is a lovely thought," smiling at her. "And now, my dear," she continued, "if I may coax you away from your meditation, I have received a letter from a very dear friend of mine, Mrs. Farling, who resides near St. Albans in Hertfordshire. I have touched very discreetly upon your misfortunes, and she says she will be delighted to have you stay with her for as long as you wish."

Caroline flushed, not sure if she wanted a stranger to know of her "misfortunes" but she did not wish to offend Lady Smythe. "How very kind of her," she said pleasantly, "and you also, ma'am, for going to all that trouble on my behalf."

"No trouble at all, child; you will enjoy being there. The house is charming, and the gardens are lovely although not extensive, and there are many country walks to take. Today is Tuesday, so do you think you would be ready to travel by Friday? We could leave early and take our time."

"I am sure I will be by then, ma'am. But you spoke of "we." Does that mean you will be journeying too?"

"Oh, yes. But I will not stay for long. I have not seen my friend for some time, although we correspond regularly."

"That will be pleasant for you. But why is everyone so kind to me?"

"Because, my dear, your story is the most astonishing and intriguing one we have ever heard. Both Lord Barrandale and I wish to help you all we can."

"You mean Lord Barrandale himself is sympathetic to my situation?" queried Caroline with some surprise.

Before Lady Smythe could answer they both heard a knocking at the front door. "I am sure you know who that is," she remarked. "I shall leave you for now."

A rather pink-faced Caroline had returned to her "meditation." She felt a glow spread over her face for she knew who it was at the front door. She knew now she loved him. She always had, only she never really allowed herself to do so at first, because she had thought he was just a-man-about-town, amusing himself. Yet from the time they met so dramatically when Dashell had lifted her to her feet and they had looked into each other's eyes, she knew. She knew too, what her answer would be when—oh, no, that was being too forward—if Dashell asked her to marry him. He had not done so yet. Then she smiled at her next thought: she would have to say "yes" because it would be expected of her by others who had gone to so much trouble on her behalf, so she could not possibly say "no." She was still smiling to herself when Hannah came in with their tea tray.

"I've said it before, Miss Caroline, and I'll say it again, but it does me good to see you so much better," she said as she set down the tray.

"You will never guess, Hannah," began Caroline eagerly. "Lady Smythe has just been to see me. She has now heard from her friend who lives near St. Albans, who says we may stay with her for as long as we wish. Of course, I would not presume upon her generosity, but isn't it wonderful!"

Hannah's face lit up at the news. "It will do you good, Miss Caroline. You will be yourself again in no time at all."

"Lady Smythe asked if we would be ready to travel by Friday. We can look through the boxes that were brought here. We do not need to take everything. By the way, did you pack my sketching and painting materials? I would love to paint some of these pansies before they all fade."

"I did indeed, Miss Caroline. I knew you would want to have them with you."

"Hannah, you are wonderful. You think of everything."

"Now, now, don't go buttering me up like that, Miss Caroline."

After they finished their tea, Caroline remarked thoughtfully, "It was amazing we had those boxes packed ready to leave on Monday, which was yesterday, and we would have been well on our way to Sussex by now. It was four days ago that Step-papa spoke to me on the stairs, and it seems much longer than that, for look how much has happened since then."

Hannah agreed, and then went on to say, "If you want to think what he did to you, just be thankful it was his cane he used and not that knife, like he did on those dresses."

As far as Lady Smythe was concerned, Friday could not come soon enough, not only for Caroline's own health and well-being of course, but also for her own sanity, as she put it, because every time Dashell called he could only talk about Caroline. When he was told they would be leaving on Friday for St. Albans he asked if he could see Caroline when he came on Thursday afternoon.

He duly turned up at that time, expecting to see Caroline in the salon with his aunt; however, he was disappointed. "Where is she?" he wanted to know, remembering just in time to greet his aunt first.

"Caroline will be joining us later on, or rather we will be joining her. You will doubtless understand she is still a little slow in eating and drinking and does not wish to embarrass herself in front of us. Her mouth still hurts and she still cannot open it too far, although she is talking a little better. Nor can she open her left eye properly."

Dashell was contrite at once. "Of course," he said. "I do understand," reminding himself that it was six days ago that Caroline had been injured, and of course that dear face would still be discoloured. "Caroline will be all right, won't she?" he asked with an anxious frown.

"I am sure she will be. A long rest in the country will do her a world of good."

"And her broken arm," he persisted.

"Dashell," replied his aunt patiently, "the doctor agreed to allow Caroline to leave on Friday as long as we travel in easy stages, and it is not such a long journey anyway."

At last Hannah came to say that Caroline was ready to receive them, much to the relief of Lady Smythe. Dashell would have gone at once but his aunt firmly declared she would lead the way.

Caroline was standing up holding onto a chair to welcome them when they came in, Lady Smythe doing so with a rustle of skirts. "My dear," she said, "Dashell has never stopped plying me with questions about your health and welfare. I have told him you are much better, but he wanted to see for himself."

"Thank you, Lady Smythe, and you too, Dashell, for your concern," replied Caroline, speaking carefully. "I must also thank you, Dashell, for your generosity towards Johnny. Hannah tells me he is overjoyed."

"It was the least I could do for him," said Dashell gravely. "He has that rare quality of being at the right place at the right time." He looked towards the dish of pansies. "My aunt tells me you greatly enjoyed them. I am so glad."

By now Lady Smythe and Caroline were sitting down, and the former broke in with a laugh. "Caroline, you must ask Dashell some time the story behind their purchase. It really is quite amusing."

Dashell was mortified. "Aunt Letty!" he cried. That made Caroline smile, rather too much in fact, for it pulled at her mouth causing her to put up her hand with a little wince. "There now," he said reproachfully, "you made Caroline hurt herself."

"Not really. I'm all right."

They talked together for a little while until Lady Smythe decided it was time for them to leave, or rather for Dashell to leave. "But I have only just got here," he protested. However his aunt was adamant, so reluctantly he stood up. "I hope you have a safe journey tomorrow," he said, addressing Caroline and taking hold of her right hand, "Just remember I love you, and come back safe and sound."

She mouthed the words carefully, "I love you too, Dashell," in a quiet voice so that only he heard. His eyes widened in joyful wonderment and he stood there almost transfixed.

Lady Smythe had moved towards the door. "How much longer are you going to stand there holding her hand?" she wanted to know.

"For ever, if I could," replied Dashell.

"Oh, no, you're not," his aunt stated flatly. "We must not make Caroline tired and we still have a lot to do before we leave," disregarding the possibility that what still had to be done could also make Caroline tired.

"I was only going to kiss her hand—" he was going to say.

"That's enough of that. There will be plenty of opportunities later for that nonsense."

"I have a whole litany of missed opportunities." Dashell pointed out.

"Go away," said Lady Smythe, beginning to laugh herself.

"But I only—"

"Dashell—will you SHOO!"

He looked appealingly at Caroline, whose own shoulders were beginning to shake, as he was pushed backwards towards the door. It only made matters worse when she blew him a kiss, but the door was firmly shut in his face.

As Lady Smythe turned back from the door she said, "You mark my words, my girl," wagging a finger at Caroline, "Dashell can be very persistent."

"But he is such a tease."

"Humph," she snorted, but smiled at the same time.

Dashell went slowly downstairs smiling, almost rejoicing in those three precious words: "I love you." He paused thoughtfully at the bottom for a minute or so, and then rang the bell for Chadwick to enquire of him the arrangements for the next day.

"The ladies are leaving after an early luncheon, sir, and the carriage has been ordered for one o'clock. Hannah will be travelling behind in a hired carriage with the boxes."

Ah, so one o'clock was the intended time. Knowing his aunt he knew they would keep to that time and it would not take him long to catch up, especially as Lady Smythe's horses never went faster than a trot. Nor was St. Albans really that far. He knew the road they would take: straight along the Edgware Road through Edgware itself and on to St. Albans.

"Chadwick, would you inform Lady Smythe's coachman and the hired carriage that I shall be following, so they will not be alarmed. But do not inform the ladies as I wish to surprise them."

"Very good, sir."

Dashell left the house still smiling. So was Chadwick, when he closed the door behind him, fairly certain there was a romance brewing.

Dashell could not help telling his father that he was planning to catch up with his aunt's carriage tomorrow as a surprise.

"To see Caroline, no doubt," observed Barrandale.

"Of course. Who else?"

"Well, I did not think it was really to see your aunt," drawled Barrandale, who was fast coming to the same conclusion as his sister.

Dashell did not elaborate on the real reason why he was doing this. It was the impulse to hear Caroline say those three precious words again.

"And how long will Caroline be staying at St. Albans?"

"About a month or so, I am told," Dashell sighed, thinking it was going to seem a long while and yet she needed that time for a complete rest. Well, perhaps he could go and visit her there. That cheered him up.

The next day after luncheon he called for his horse and set off.

It was shortly before they reached Edgware that Lady Smythe became aware of a horseman beginning to overtake her carriage on its near side, but instead of completely passing the horseman kept level. Alarmed and a little annoyed she had in mind to stop the carriage to give the impudent fellow a dressing-down and send him on his way. She looked angrily at the rider, who swept her a bow from the saddle, while his well-trained horse paced sideways. She closed her eyes and leaned back against the upholstery with a little groan. "I might have known. Oh, I might have known."

Caroline, who had been looking out of the right-hand window, turned her head. "I beg your pardon, ma'am, but did you say something?"

"I did. It's him," complained Lady Smythe, rather ungrammatically. "He must have followed us. I told you he was persistent. Dashell," she explained to a rather puzzled-looking Caroline.

"Oh!" she cried, leaning forward and looking to the left. "Where is he? I can't see him." Nor could she, for Dashell had reined Sparkle behind the carriage to appear on the other side, which Caroline did not realize at first. She turned to the right at the sound of hoofbeats alongside. "Dashell!" she cried again.

With a sigh Lady Smythe knocked on the roof of her carriage, thus ordering it to stop, and requested Caroline to lower the window in the door. "Dashell, what foolishness is this?" she demanded as he dismounted, yet ascertaining from his expression that nothing untoward had happened. "Why, you might have frightened the horses or driven my poor coachman into thinking you were a highwayman."

"Oh, no," said Dashell easily, "not at all. I told Chadwick yesterday to warn him I would be doing this."

"Oh, did you. And why, may I ask?"

"Just to see Caroline again," he replied, placing his hand on the window sill.

"What on earth for? We are not going to the other side of the world, you know."

"I just wanted to hear Caroline say those three words again," he said, smiling at her tenderly.

Lady Smythe looked at Caroline helplessly.

"Which three words?" Caroline asked innocently, pretending not know. "Oh, I know the ones: 'You are impossible.'"

"Caroline!" cried Dashell. "Those are not the words I came all this way to hear," flushing as his aunt burst out laughing.

"But you are, Dashell, in a delightful way. Another reason for me to say I love you," placing her hand on his.

Still laughing, Lady Smythe did not hear those last words. "Oh, really. I could not have thought of better words myself. Oh, dear. Caroline, you are fast becoming a girl after my own heart. And now, Dashell, instead of keeping my carriage standing on the road perhaps you would go ahead to Edgware and order a private room at the inn."

"Certainly, Aunt Letty." He kissed Caroline's fingertips before riding away.

"Really," said Lady Smythe, shaking her head. I have never known him like this," while Caroline just smiled demurely.

They did not stay long at the inn, just enough for some light refreshments. Dashell offered to escort them to their destination, but was firmly turned down by his aunt. "I would rather you did not, thank you. I would feel much safer without you. Besides, your frivolous behaviour would terrify the whole household and I will not be held responsible."

Dashell laughed as he handed the two ladies into the carriage and watched it go, followed by the second one. He waited until they were out of sight before returning to London.

He arrived back at Park Lane tired but happy, to find his father greatly cheered by the arrival of Maxwell.

CHAPTER SIX

The Rector of Sutherfield Receives a Letter

I n Sutherfield a certain letter had been delivered to the Rector on quality paper with the Barrandale crest on the back of the envelope and at the top of the sheet inside, and it awed and impressed him that such a letter should be sent to him. It must have been quite important for this gentleman by the name of Lord Lonsdale to have done so.

A simple man of letters, a kindly man, yet shrewd and observant, the Reverend David Swanson had been offered this incumbency about a year ago. He was well liked amongst his parishioners, as were his wife and children, as they found him easy to approach. He, in his turn, learned all he could about his flock. Soon after their arrival he, his wife and children, had explored the graveyard and read all the tablets and memorials inside the church itself.

There was indeed a family by the name of Waterton in the parish since the early 1700s. The original Waterton had died in battle and another drowned at sea. The third Waterton, old Sir Godfrey, had the foresight to be buried in the family vault. He had left everything to his son, Arthur, who had married the daughter from another family in the neighbourhood, and they had two daughters. Sir Arthur died young and everything passed to the nearest male relative, a distant cousin. This cousin, Sir Richard Irving, could hardly believe his good fortune and took up residence as soon as he legally could, together with his wife and children. Swanson knew the family well for his own children often played with the younger ones.

Now here was the difficulty: the writer of the said letter had requested him to be particularly discreet. He could not go to Sir Richard himself and ask questions outright for he would then have to explain what he was doing and why, and then it would become common knowledge. Nor could he ask his parishioners one Sunday morning for the same reason. No, that would not do at all.

When the Swanson family had first gone round the church yard his son had observed that there was a memorial tablet to Sir Arthur Waterton inside the church, but no corresponding headstone outside. What with settling in and meeting so many new people and becoming integrated into the life of his new parish, he had paid scant attention—until now. He went into the church and studied the Waterton memorial more carefully and also noted the date. The letters and numbers had been beautifully carved by an obviously master hand, no expense spared. He then went into the vestry where all the parish records were kept and looked for a volume marked "Burials."

Beginning two years before the actual date, just to be sure, he checked very carefully all the names of the deceased but could find no mention of the name Waterton, apart from Sir Godfrey. Even with a family vault something would have been noted, some burial service or other, which was puzzling. It could only mean that Sir Arthur Waterton had been buried elsewhere. Surprising, for he was a local person, and why, and what's more, where? Swanson closed the volume thoughtfully and placed it back on the shelf, and pondered his next move, as even he was becoming intrigued.

The vestry door opened suddenly. "Ah, there you are, Reverend," said the gravedigger, with the inappropriate name of Merriman. "I've been looking all over for you," sounding peeved about it. "I'd like to ask you summat about this new grave to be dug and where exactly it should be." He stood with his hand on the latch of the open door. "Me roomatticks are getting to me and I don't want to waste time digging in the wrong place."

"Yes, of course I will come," replied Swanson and followed Merriman out, who was grumbling about the hard work it involved and maybe it was time to find a younger man. "How long have you been gravedigger here?" he enquired casually, seizing his chance.

"Long enough, I'd say, Reverend. Nigh on thirty years. And don't ask me how many graves I've dug for I've lost count. If you want to know," he added, with a dry chuckle, "you can look in the parish records."

Swanson smiled gently, without saying he had already done so. A few minutes later the two of them had decided exactly where Merriman was to start work.

Nigh on thirty years, thought Swanson, that should be plenty of time. He sensed it might be difficult to get this taciturn man to talk but he would have to try. Taking a deep breath he said, "Could you tell me something, Merriman, if you would."

"Oh, ar, what?" he replied, without turning his head as he thrust his spade into the earth.

"When we first came here my boy looked at the names on the various memorials and tablets inside the church and went looking for the matching headstones, but could not find one for Sir Arthur Waterton."

Merriman paused in his digging to stare at Swanson. "Why do a daft thing like that? Don't seem natural for a boy to do that. Anyway, he won't find one. One was never dug, at least not here. But I can tell you where one was dug."

"Oh, where?" Swanson's words slipped out, too quickly perhaps. Was he showing too much interest?

"Somewhere up in Yorkshire, of all places. My uncle's neighbour had a brother who drove a stage coach on the road between Grantham and York, or somewhere like that, and he heard talk about some terrible accident from the other drivers. He said it was known all over the west side of Yorkshire. Reckon that saved me a lot of work, being buried elsewhere. Some other poor fool had to do that."

"You said there was some kind of accident?"

"Supposed to have been, so I heard," said Merriman. "Some carriage overturned, Or was it a drowning? Don't remember which. Must be nigh on twenty years ago so it don't mean much now, so why bother to remember. Don't believe in cluttering up one's mind with stuff you don't need to think about." All these remarks were said between pushing in his spade and lifting out mounds of earth. Swanson murmured something in agreement, but did not point out that it was precisely those minor details that could be so important. The spade grated against some stones. "Anyway," continued Merriman, "I've got my work to do, so if you don't mind I'll get on with it, instead of gossiping and wasting time." So saying, he turned his back on the Rector.

"Yes, of course, Merriman. I quite understand. Thank you." Swanson walked away smiling to himself, feeling he had accomplished what he had set out to do and more, with Merriman's further comments sounding in his ears: *Fancy a boy wanting to know summat like that. Daft.*

There was one more thing Swanson had to do but he would require some help.

That evening after their meal, when the younger children were in bed, he spoke to his wife and son about the letter he had received and what he had done that day. It caught their interest at once, especially the boy, but they were reminded that the writer of the letter had particularly asked them to be discreet, which meant they were to be quiet about it and to remember it was none of their business. Those last few words were Swanson's own.

Early the next morning when nobody was likely to be around, they entered the church bringing with them certain items. Mrs. Swanson and the son stretched a large sheet of parchment over the said tablet and held it in place while Swanson made a charcoal rubbing of the lettering. It was dusty work and he tried not to get the parchment too smudged, but on the whole the result was credible and easy to read, and he felt pleased with his efforts.

Now all he had to do was to reply to this gentleman by the name of Lord Lonsdale and inform him of what he had been able to discover about the Waterton family, and trust it would provide the answer to his enquiries.

CHAPTER SEVEN

Maxwell

The morning Lord Barrandale had left for London, Maxwell came out with him to the front steps to see him off. "You are quite sure you wish to stay here?" asked Barrandale. "There is still time to change your mind."

"Thank you, sir," he replied. "I would prefer to do so just to thinks things over," and his father nodded at him approvingly as the footman closed the carriage door. Maxwell waved him goodbye and stayed a few minutes watching the carriage roll away.

He turned round wondering what to do at first, and decided to walk through the grounds for a while and get some fresh air. He had not done this kind of thing for some time; boys of his age usually did not and, as Dashell had done, marveled how much everything had grown, what landscape alterations had taken place, and all without him really noticing because he thought it would always be there. Now he realized it might not.

He made his way slowly along the path towards the river and sat on the same bench where Dashell had told him he could not now go to Oxford, and why. Oh, how angry he had been! The months he had spent looking forward to it; seeing some of his friends there who were also going; his bitterness and disappointment which he found difficult to handle; and how he wished his mother had still been alive to encourage him along other ways. He knew the onus was on him to decide and he was resentful about that too. Damn Walden. How could he have been so thoughtless? He looked towards the boathouse but was not really in the mood for rowing. He could order a horse to be saddled but he was not in the mood for riding, either. He got up and walked back to the house. Inside everything seemed so quiet and empty. The servants were about their business and needed no orders from him. For want of something to do he went into the library where he had helped his father sort out the books, some to keep and some to be sold. Barrandale had given him permission to keep a few if he wished, which he had done. Maxwell had tried hard to keep his feelings from his father, but he must have known if only from the fact that Maxwell has been so quiet.

He occupied himself until it was lunch time when he found himself sitting alone in the large dining room. He had been used to the company of his father and brothers and all the bustle and activity at Eton, and it all made the situation even more desolate.

Now Maxwell had to decide how to occupy himself for the next few days for he had promised to think things over. He was annoyed on the one hand that he had been left alone to do so, but on the other hand he had been trusted to come to his own decision. He remembered when he was little he had gone to Windsor on his own to see what the new building alterations at the castle looked like and he had ended up in the St. George's Chapel. He was amazed at the intricate carvings of the vaulted roof and that was when his dreams of being an architect had started. When he had arrived late for the evening meal he had not received the scolding he had expected, but his father wanted to know exactly why he was late. He was only about ten years old at the time and his father was impressed at his answer, and that he intended to go round the countryside sketching anything he liked.

With a sigh he hoisted himself out of the chair in which he had been slouching and decided to make a tour of the house, or what was left of it, for so many rooms had been closed off and dust sheets put over everything.

Eventually he came to the family portrait gallery, a long corridor on the north side of the house. Here again memories came to mind. One cloudy afternoon when he and Walden were small, even before the Windsor Castle adventure, they had dared each other to walk along the gallery alone and back again. They looked up at the people in the portraits, who appeared to look down at them and their impudence. When it was Maxwell's turn the sun suddenly went in and the ensuing gloom frightened him, and he ran to go downstairs. In his anxiety and haste he tripped and fell, and by the time he got up and rubbed his bruises Walden was out of sight, leaving him to find his own way down. It was quite a long time before Maxwell ventured into the gallery again.

Now with his tuition and trained eye he could study the paintings with more appreciation. Moving along slowly he came to his parents' portraits painted in their younger days. How like Dashell was to Father and he to Mother! Lady Barrandale appeared to stare ahead of her and he could glean nothing from her expression. It was as though she was saying he must think for himself, for she could not help him.

As he turned away he remembered that one Christmas a visiting guest had sketched the head and shoulders of the three brothers, and they had been framed and hung in a row. They were considered to be very good likenesses, and as Maxwell looked for them he stopped short with an audible gasp. Walden's likeness had been removed, just leaving a space in the middle. Simmonds would not have removed it without an order, and only Lord Barrandale himself would have given it.

There was a heavy feeling in Maxwell's stomach as he laid the palm of his hand over the space, in some kind of wordless gesture. He realized more than ever what a terrible blow all this must been to their father: the stooped shoulders, the whitened hair, yet being so proud and stoical, just the sort of thing he would do. There was still the threat of financial ruin and the possibility of losing the estate. No wonder there had been so many stringent economic measures, no wonder rooms had been closed off and servants let go. He had been too preoccupied with his own anger and resentment to realize fully what all this meant. Feeling ashamed he turned to go downstairs, then looked back at the empty space. It was as though Walden was no longer a son of the house and, what was more, he had lost a brother. Dashell had never mentioned this and he wondered if he even knew about it.

The next morning he looked carefully at all his sketches and paintings; those he had done at school and those done in his own time, and there were a considerable number of them. Besides having a genuine talent he also had the good fortune to have had an excellent art master. Good old Mr.Creppan. A bit dotty and excitable at times, but he knew the art world inside out. He lived with his unmarried sister somewhere not too far away. He should go and call on him and ask his advice. It would mean going back to Eton to find out exactly where he lived, but the school caretakers or someone should be able to tell him. His decision made, after luncheon he ordered a horse to be saddled for him.

It was strange for Maxwell to be back at Eton again, now that all the boys had gone. The caretaker stared in surprise at the sight of Maxwell, who prided himself on remembering the names of all the young gentlemen, and he was seldom wrong. "Mr. Maxwell Romford? This is indeed a surprise. Did you forget something? There was nothing left behind in your old room." Boys could be quiet forgetful sometimes.

"Oh, nothing like that at all, Mr.Barnes. I was wondering if you could give me Mr. Creppan's address, as I wish to call on him. I believe he lives somewhere locally."

"Mr. Creppan, eh?" replied Barnes. "Well, I suppose it would be all right for me to tell you, although I don't think he is too well at the moment."

"Oh," said Maxwell. "Then perhaps I should not go."

"You could send a letter first that you wish to call," suggested Barnes. "Let me just make sure of the address. Ah, yes, here we are, Laurel Cottage, in the village on the road to Reading."

"Thank you very much, Mr.Barnes." Maxwell went away feeling he was beginning to make progress. Stopping at the Post Office he sent a letter to Mr. Creppan that he wished to call upon him and hoped it would be convenient, but would understand if it was not. That was the best he could do and he would now have to wait for a reply.

A reply did come from Mr. Creppan, that he would be welcome to call as long as he made his visit brief.

The cottage door was opened by Mr.Creppan himself, who told Maxwell to make him comfortable in a chair, then sat down as his sister brought in the tea things.

"Now, young Romford, this is most unusual. I am interested to know why you wanted to call upon me." Creppan sat regarding Maxwell, who had been one of his best students.

Taking a deep breath Maxwell said, "I came to ask your advice, sir," pausing as Creppan's eyebrows rose in surprise. "You see, it is not now possible for me to go to Oxford to study architecture."

Creppan's expressive face fell. "I am truly sorry to hear that, Romford, for I thought your future was firmly fixed for you. But how I can help you?"

Maxwell hesitated. "I now have to consider the possibility of painting for a living."

"Ah," said Creppan. He helped himself to more tea and cakes and gestured to his guest to do the same. "I will be frank with you, Romford. You certainly have talent, quite remarkable in one so young. Your work shows your love of nature and the countryside. However, you are not so good with portraits or still life, so stay with what you do best." Mr. Creppan looked again at Maxwell with his wise eyes. "Did you never consider that your aptitude lay just with painting and not architecture?"

Maxwell stared at him in amazement, for that had never really occurred to him. He always believed that the one led to the other, mainly because he always knew he would have to seek his own remuneration, son of an earl or not. That wonderful vaulted ceiling in St. George's Chapel in Windsor which had held him spellbound, and the interior of the Henry VII Chapel in Westminster Abbey, had stirred the artist in him. Now he understood. But the art master was speaking again.

"To fully answer your question, many people have tried to earn a living from their art work and many have failed. Many aspiring artists have literally starved in garrets; and even some Old Masters were never recognised in their own lifetimes."

Maxwell's heart sank. "Do you suggest, sir, I should not even try?"

"No, I am not suggesting that at all. But I would strongly urge you to find some visible means of support and carry on painting as you can. Has this been of help to you?"

"Yes, indeed it has," replied Maxwell eagerly. "I am most grateful to you."

"Before you leave, I must give you the name of a man in Windsor who does framing for me. He may display your work and you will find his prices quite reasonable. Of course, you will not receive anything unless there is a sale. And I will also give you the name of a place in London."

"I will not keep you any longer, sir, and thank you again for your advice."

Maxwell was now in a much better frame of mind than when he had set out, yet the words *"find some visible means of support"* kept running through his head. He had been so centred on architecture that he had never considered anything else, but Oxford was now out of the question altogether. He must seriously think of something else, but what?

He remembered when his father once took him into his bank on Lombard Street he had been quite impressed, except everyone looked so stern all dressed in black, and no unnecessary word said. The older clerks looked as though they had been there for years and had forgotten how to smile. No, Banking was not for him. That just left the Law. Well, he would see.

The next day he went to the picture framer in Windsor and left two of his paintings which the man promised to display for him when he had framed them. Then he went to the coaching station to book a seat on a coach to London and learned there were no seats until the 2 o'clock stage tomorrow. He had never travelled on a stage coach before and remembered tales he had heard of outside passengers being frozen or soaked, or having to hold onto their hats, and he just hoped the weather would hold.

Early the next morning he was out for a brisk ride, which he knew he was going to miss when in London. He had seen Lively and Daisy Chain out on a training session and back at the stables asked how they were progressing, for he was sure his father and Dashell would want to know.

"Well enough, sir," replied James carefully, "but begging his lordship's pardon, training racehorses does not come easily to me, I do not know enough about it. Now give me a young horse on a lungeing rain then I know what I am doing."

"I will mention this to my father," promised Maxwell. "Now I would like to order the trap for this afternoon. I am catching the 2 o'clock stage to London."

There was still one more thing he wanted to do before he left: to go to the portrait gallery again as it could be a long time before he had another opportunity. Once more he surveyed his mother's portrait long and carefully. If he could not build houses he could still paint them; and yes, he would study Law. Was it his imagination or was it a trick of light and shadow, or did her eyes look at him and she seemed to smile? Whatever it was, it was enough; he knew he had made the right decision.

The trap was at the front door and Maxwell's leather bags were placed into it, one of which contained some more paintings. Simmonds came out to see him leave and to wish him well for the future. He watched the trap drive away, and he too felt that things were never going to be the same again.

Maxwell did not enjoy the journey. He was on an outside seat right over a rear wheel, giving him the odd sensation he might fall off; squeezed next to a stout gentleman who never stopped talking and voicing his opinion on every subject. He thought the journey would never end.

Arrival at one of the London coaching stations was even worse. With so many coaches coming and going he wondered how they all knew in which direction to go. It took several minutes to obtain a cab, but he eventually arrived on the doorstep of Barrandale House, thankful to be there, resolving it would be a long time before he travelled by stage coach again.

CHAPTER EIGHT

More About Maxwell

Matthew answered the door not knowing whom to expect. "Why, Mr.Maxwell," he said, beaming a welcome. "Come in."

"Hello, Matthew. I travelled by stagecoach, if you can believe it. What a journey." He was still young enough to talk like this. "Is my father in?"

"He is in the sitting-room, sir," replied Matthew and ushered him in.

Barrandale looked up sharply. "Maxwell, come in!" he cried, and stood up to greet him. He put his hand on his son's shoulder and looked at him critically. "Maxwell," he observed, "you look different somehow."

"I feel it too. Oh, Father, I have so much to tell you."

"And I am anxious to hear you. How did you get here, by the way?"

"By stagecoach," replied Maxwell, "and never again. I sat over a rear wheel and got jolted all the way. Where's Dashell? Is he here?"

"Dashell has gone to St. Albans. Your Aunt Letty travelled with a Miss Waterton and he went with them."

Maxwell was faintly surprised, thinking this Miss Waterton was a friend of his aunt and imagined them as two elderly ladies.

Poor Aunt Letty must be getting on if she required a companion and an escort.

Matthew entered with a tray of refreshments and an extra cup and saucer for Lord Barrandale in case he fancied another cup of tea.

"Now Maxwell, I am very interested to hear what you have to say."

"Well, sir, after you left last week…" began Maxwell, and so he related his thoughts, his visit to his old art master, and then his final decision. The only fact he did not mention was the missing sketch of Walden, and if his father thought of it he gave no sign.

Barrandale regarded him all the time with increasing admiration for his enterprise and the courage of his final decision. "Maxwell, you amaze me. Actually, I was not sure what you were going to do, and if I may say, I think you came to a wiser, better decision on your own than if you had taken someone else's advice."

At once Maxwell saw the wisdom of being left on his own, and it had been a hard lesson to learn. He realized too, that during these last few days he had grown up. His father then asked to see the paintings Maxwell had brought with him and Maxwell went up to his room to fetch them.

Barrandale looked them over carefully. "I am no connoisseur of art but I like what I see. I congratulate you. What will you do with them?"

"Well," replied Maxwell thoughtfully, "I will have some framed and will show them to the galleries Mr. Creppan mentioned, and hope they will display them for me."

His father nodded approvingly, and then asked, "Had you considered entering the Diplomatic Service or the Foreign Office at all? I could put in a good word for you."

"No, sir, that had never really occurred to me. But I will give the thought careful consideration if all other options failed."

Barrandale laughed at his response. "Well said, Maxwell."

It was just after this Dashell joined them, entering the room looking pleased and happy about something, and caught sight of his brother. "Maxwell! I had no idea you would be here."

"Maxwell has been telling me what he was doing last week in Windsor," explained Barrandale. "You should hear what he has to say. I am quite proud of him."

Maxwell flushed as Dashell turned his interested gaze upon him. "Come on, Maxwell," said Dashell, encouraging him. "Don't be your usual diffident self."

Maxwell glared at him as only a younger brother can. "Well, as I was saying to Father…" and so he carefully related everything again, but still did not mention the missing sketch, while Dashell listened with increasing interest, and laughed at the account of travelling on the stage coach. Maxwell did have a way of saying things.

"I take my hat off to you," declared Dashell.

Maxwell turned red. "Oh, shut up," he muttered.

"And some fellows I know," Dashell went on, "would not have the foggiest notion how to think about their future anyway, let alone how to get on a stage coach."

"Oh, really?" laughed Maxwell, "and how do you know such nincompoops in the first place?"

They stopped at a deliberate cough from their father, who tactfully changed the subject. "Tell me, Dashell, how was your journey to St.Albans?"

'Dashell sat up in his chair. "It went very well I caught them up a mile or two south of Edgware. Poor Aunt Letty, I gave her quite a surprise"

"And how is Miss Waterton?"

"She was surprised too," replied Dashell, smiling tenderly as he recollected their conversation.

His expression caused Maxwell to stare wide-eyed at him, and he glanced quizzically at his father, who gave him the briefest of nods and a ghost of a wink, so Maxwell deliberately asked, "Who is Miss Waterton? Was she some elderly companion travelling with Aunt Letty?"

Dashell was caught off guard. "Elderly companion!" he cried indignantly. "She—she—" and stopped short at his brother's expression.

"Ah," asked Maxwell, "is she beautiful, this lady-love of yours?" delighted to see Dashell's face colouring up. "Well, I reckon she must be beautiful. Trust you to pick a winner. But who is she?"

"Miss Caroline Waterton is the younger daughter of the late Sir Arthur Waterton and the late Lady Isobel Waterton," answered Dashell with dignity. Oh, how thankful he was to say that with confidence; no more concern about her background and lineage.

"Oh. So why was she with Aunt Letty?"

"She sustained a recent injury when her arm was broken and she has been staying with Aunt Letty, and she will now be staying for some days with a Mrs.Farling, who is a friend of Aunt Letty."

Maxwell sensed from the dark frown on Dashell's face not to ask any more questions, which surprised him. However, he did ask; "How is Aunt Letty?"

"She is keeping very well," replied Barrandale instead. "I am sure she would appreciate a visit from you when she returns."

"Oh, yes, I would love to go," said Maxwell. Then he sat bolt upright, "Oh, I almost forgot. Yesterday morning when I was out riding I saw Daisy Chain and Lively being exercised, and I asked James back at the stables how they were coming along as I thought you both would like to know."

"And…?" So Maxwell repeated word for word what James had told him.

"It sounds he was respectfully asking if a more experienced trainer could be found," remarked Dashell.

Barrandale looked at him. "How would we go about finding one?"

"I have no idea," he answered, and sighed to himself. Here were two good horses not able to show their full potential until the right man was found.

Later that evening Maxwell drew Dashell aside when they were alone. "I say, Dashell," he whispered urgently," do you remember those sketches of us hanging in the portrait gallery, which were done years ago? Did you know the one of Walden had been removed?"

Dashell stared at him. "No, I did not. And only Father would have given that order." They regarded each other in dismay. "Poor Father," muttered Dashell.

"I wonder what Walden is doing now?" Maxwell could not help remarking, which caused Dashell to scowl angrily.

CHAPTER NINE

Walden

Walden had spent a miserable time after his dismissal from Barrandale House. When he left he had pulled his hat down as far as he could, enduring the looks and titters of passers-by, and walked back to his rooms feeling shaken and mortified by all the words and actions that had transpired between himself and his brother; and so sudden and unexpected too. His horrified and disgusted manservant, not knowing what had happened, began to say that Lord Lonsdale had called several times, asking for him. Walden curtly cut him short and sent him out for a beefsteak for his black eye. Butcher's shops were not easy to find in that area and the servant was away for quite a while.

On his return the servant refused to hand over the package until he had been given the wages owing to him. Walden swore at him for his damned impudence, but pulled out some gold sovereigns from his pocket and slammed them on the table. The man scooped them up and only then handed the package to Walden.

Walden lay down on his bed holding the raw meat to his eye. He heard his servant moving about and was just about to shout at him to be quieter when the man appeared in the doorway.

"I am leaving. I cannot stay here. I have my reputation as a gentleman's gentleman to think of." With that, he turned away and slammed the front door behind him.

Infuriated, Walden sat up sharply. The noise made his head spin causing him to curse and swear again, and he sank back with a groan and lay there for several minutes. He began to feel hungry and would be forced to go out to some eating-place and return before dark. When he left he made sure he had his cane with him; it was wise to be careful.

He went to a place he knew and was thankful to find a corner seat. The soup he ordered was hot, but by the time he finished spooning it into his bruised mouth it was getting cold. He ordered some slices of buttered bread and put them into his pocket to eat the next day. When he got up to leave a party of four men came in, one of whom stared hard at Walden, who turned his face away and kept to the shadows. On the way back to his rooms he bought two meat pies from a vendor near a cab stand, again for the next day.

He used the beefsteak the second day, and by the third day he threw it into the gutter in disgust when he went out. He was beginning to need a shave but had to wait for the cuts and bruises on his face to heal first.

All this staying in during the day time forced him to think in a way he had never done before; there was really not much else he could do. It had been a great shock to him to learn of the amount of his debt and, as Dashell had asked him, how in the name of wonder had it amounted to so much.

He began with his time at Oxford. Gentlemen's sons often went to university even if nothing spectacular transpired or was expected. True, it had started off well enough until he became mixed up with the wrong crowd. Wine, women and song were a much better option. He left Oxford before he was sent down and went to London, and was soon attracted to the gaming dens.

In one of these places was a man by the name of Augustus Lassiter. Lassiter remarked to Walden that someone he knew had got hopelessly into debt and had shot himself, and Walden heard later this man's property had to be sold to pay off his debts.

Shortly after this Lassiter had invited Walden to join a party of his which was going to Newmarket racecourse. The men in the party were all young and wealthy, and were flattered by the attention of this older man of the world, who had suggested they went to one racecourse after another, never noticing the direction in which they were being taken.

Then someone remarked that Ridgeway had not been seen for a while. "Gone to the North of England, so I've heard," said Lassiter. But that was not the case, as discovered when the body was pulled out of the Thames. Ridgeway had borrowed money to pay his debts and the moneylenders were demanding their repayment. They had forced the sale of his house, and his widowed mother was now living in genteel poverty somewhere.

A while later Walden had come across an acquaintance walking, or rather lurching, along some street. He looked wild-eyed, almost as if in shock. Walden stopped to speak to him as they had known each other in the old days. "Greythorpe, what the devil are you doing here?" he asked. "You look terrible. Are you ill?"

Greythorpe stopped on hearing his name and peered about, his eyes glazed. When he focused enough, he recognised Walden. "Oh, it's you, Romford, is it?" Then he rambled on. "That devil. That devil. Don't let him near you. Keep away from him," swaying slightly as he spoke.

"Who?" Walden demanded. "What are you talking about?"

"That devil," repeated Greythorpe. "First he gets you into debt, damn him, then tells you about those accursed men." He swayed so much he clutched Walden for support, and then muttered, "He was there. I saw him. He was there when I went to see them. Oh, dear God, what am I going to do. Dear Flora, you must forgive me. You must." He staggered away leaving Walden staring after him, then he turned round and said, "It happened to Ridgeway, you know. And to Brennan. And to Hunterton. They were all in debt and they all shot themselves." Then he was gone, and with a sudden chill Walden watched him leave.

Walden recalled reading in the London Times a few days later:

"Unfortunate death of Sir Edmund Greythorpe, who appeared to have shot himself. His house and estate will have to be sold to pay off mounting debts, and it is believed that was why the gentleman took his own life. His widow, Lady Flora, who is shortly expecting to be confined, is naturally greatly distressed."Walden was not too surprised to read that after his strange meeting with his friend. Odd that he should have met him just as he himself was getting into debt.

So it was along those lines his thoughts ran as he lay on his bed with his hands laced behind his head. The names kept on repeating themselves. Ridgeway. Brennan. Hunterton. And now Greythorpe. They had all been in debt and they had all been unable to repay, and they had all gone to the same moneylenders and all that was too much of a coincidence. What was the common factor between them, what connecting link? Then suddenly his eyes flew open and in one movement he sat up straight and swung his feet to the floor. *There was a connection: Lassiter. Augustus Lassiter.*

Walden recalled that about two years ago he had a run of losses on cards and he had a number of IOUs. Then Lassiter took him to one side and asked if he was in any kind of trouble as he had noticed Walden was beginning to look worried, and if so perhaps he could help. He knew of some discreet moneylenders who could amalgamate the debts so Walden was responsible only to them. It seemed a good idea at the time as his creditors were becoming restless.

Now a terrible truth was rearing its head. It was impossible, unthinkable. But no, it *was* possible. There were too many coincidences. And how did Lassiter know about his debts because he had never spoken of them. And why had the four other men been recommended to the same moneylenders? Could it be that Lassiter had deliberately lured them into debt? Walden sat appalled as the truth began to take hold.

So that was what Greythorpe had meant! He had been talking sense after all. And when Walden met him, Greythorpe had been coming away from the moneylenders and by chance had seen Lassiter on their premises. So that was it. Lassiter was in league with them. Walden drew in his breath with a sharp cry. *Now it was his turn!* He, the son of a wealthy man. No wonder his debt had been allowed to accumulate.

Now he could see what a complete blind fool he had been. It was all so clear. What fools they were, trusting that man, and he had betrayed each one of them. Now it was too late; he had involved his whole family because of his own folly. He could never go back and explain; he could never go back at all.

Too late, he recalled his father's admonitions, the tears in his mother's eyes. And too late, he remembered his often insolent attitude. Dashell was right about that, damn him. He had forfeited the love of his father and brothers, for what? He had lost everything and ended up being disinherited. And now he gave way to shame and remorse. The only way for Walden to redeem himself would be to accept that commission, in case Dashell made enquiries to see if he actually had.

His face had almost healed, but before going to the Barracks in Hyde Park Walden had two letters to write. The first was to Simmonds at Barrandale Park asking him to send certain items from his old room, to be addressed to him at Hyde Park Barracks. That should be enough to satisfy Dashell, Walden thought grimly.

The other letter required more care and thought. Walden paused, pen in hand, wondering who to send it to. Frensham was a good possibility, and so was Ogilvy. He decided on the latter, and began carefully outlining the whole history of events with Lassiter, his strange meeting with Greythorpe, his suspicions about the deaths of the other men whom he named, and his own situation. He sat back with a sigh of relief when he had finished.

The next morning Walden hailed a cab and was soon outside the Barracks, and stood looking up at the façade. Then bracing his shoulders he stepped forward to face his unknown and unwanted future. By evening he had been kitted out with a uniform and introduced to the other officers in the mess hall, and had met Colonel Stratton, the tall grizzled Commander-in-Chief of the Regiment.

Walden soon sensed an air of urgency and learned that the regiment was due to leave for India and that there was to be more intensive training. All the officers were good horsemen and most were good marksmen, but swordsmanship was also required. Wielding a rifle or sabre on foot was well enough but doing so on horseback required more skill. Colonel Stratton watched all this with interest and commended Captain Romford on his progress. Only Walden knew how he had done this. Every time he wielded his sabre or fired his rifle—he was aiming at Lassiter.

For all that, Walden was not a popular officer, for the others found him cold and distant, with an air of suppressed anger. Pleasant enough if you knew how to approach him but definitely not a man to cross.

A few weeks before the regiment was due to sail the family of one of the officers came to bid him farewell and left behind a copy of the *Times*. By the time it reached Walden it was several days old. "Better read it, Romford," joked someone, "it could be your last chance for weeks." Walden laughed good-naturedly and began quickly scanning the pages, pausing to read anything that took his interest. Then something did; and he snatched the paper closer to him for a better look.

The skipper of a Thames barge noticed a body floating in the river and hauled it on board and at once alerted the river authorities. It was later ascertained that the body was that of a Mr. Augustus Lassiter, a well known financier in certain circles. It appeared the unfortunate gentleman had been struck on the head heavily from behind and thrown into the river and left to drown. The police were helped in their enquiries by certain information given to them.

Slowly Walden put the newspaper down. Well, well, well. So that devil did get his just desserts. Perhaps there was justice after all, and wondered who it was who struck him.

Two days later an orderly approached him. "Captain Romford, sir, there is a gentleman to see you." Surprised and intrigued, he followed the orderly to a small room, wondering briefly if it was Dashell, but it was not.

"Ogilvy!" exclaimed Walden as he shook hands with his friend, "I trust you received my letter?" He was genuinely pleased to see his friend.

"Indeed I did. And I showed it to Frensham, as you asked. But I must tell you that Lassiter is dead."

"Yes," replied Walden briefly, "I read it in the *Times*."

Walden listened intently as Ogilvy explained how he and Frensham were amazed and shocked at his letter, but the more they read it the more sense it made. They spoke to others who had known Lassiter, and they expressed disgust and loathing as they saw the pattern repeating itself. As far as they knew Lassiter was alive at the time. It might have seemed pointless to approach the Police after Lassiter's death but the other two villains had to be apprehended; by the time they arrived at their premises the birds had flown, taking their ill-gotten gains with them.

Enquiries at the coaching stations produced nothing, but at private hire places it was learned two men answering their description had hired a carriage, travelling post all the way to Dover. By the time the Police arrived it was too late.

"That must have been them," said Walden when Ogilvy finished speaking. "Cursed luck they got away."

"The Police asked some questions," continued Ogilvy, "but we merely said we had our suspicions because there were too many coincidences."

"Have you any idea who killed Lassiter?"

Ogilvy shook his head. "None at all. It could have been anybody. And even if we had known we would not have said anything. By the way, did you know Flora Greythorpe was Frensham's cousin? The shock and manner of Greythorpe's death was too much for her; she died in childbirth and the little one with her."

Walden's eyes widened in surprise as he thought of that little family destroyed. "I hope Lassiter rots in hell."

They continued talking quietly together until Ogilvy ventured to remark: "You have changed a great deal, Romford."

Walden gave him a bleak look. "Yes. I know I have, but at least I'm still alive. Not like some other poor devils."

Ogilvy nodded in understanding, then stood up saying it was time he left.

Walden got to his feet too. "I must thank you for coming, Ogilvy. It was very good of you. And now, I would like to ask a favour of you."

"Of course, if I am able."

"If your path should ever cross Dashell's in the future, perhaps you would explain to him Lassiter's dealings with others and me.

Do not seek him out, and on no account approach my father, Lord Barrandale. It is possible you might meet him one day and I would like him to know the truth."

"I understand. I promise."

"Thank you for that," said Walden, as they shook hands.

Ogilvy left and Walden remained where he was to think by himself.

Within a few days the regiment, led by Colonel Stratton, embarked from Greenwich in a transport ship, accompanied by a supply ship, for the long voyage to India.

When the ships entered the English Channel all the soldiers were out on deck to watch the white cliffs of Dover and the green coastline of England receding in the distance; some wondering out loud if they would be lucky enough to see that scene again.

Walden had no such doubts. He had a premonition he would never see England again.

Well, if that meant an early death, then so be it.

CHAPTER TEN

More About Johnny

That same morning Johnny was still thinking about his future. He could not expect to stay at Barrandale House much longer; he wondered where was he going to keep any horse and cart when he got them, and what premises could he afford. As far as he could see his work would be between Barrandale House on Park Lane and Barrandale Hall in Windsor, and anything in the house on Becket Lane would have to come last, as he and Hannah had agreed.

That house was now empty and he must keep an eye on it somehow. Then a wide grin spread over his face as a wonderful thought came to him. The old stable behind the house! It had not been used for years but was still in reasonably good repair; he knew that for he had been inside often enough. Miss Caroline now owned the property and he knew she would not mind if he used it.

There was another reason why he wanted to go to Becket Lane, or rather the Bishop's Head Inn, and that was to speak to his friend Sammy Cullen about something.

Johnny left Barrandale House after breakfast, making sure to tell Matthew where he was going and that he would be back in time for the evening meal. Now that Matthew knew he was carrying out orders he did not mind Johnny's absence so much.

As before Johnny walked along the road to Fulham whistling to himself, and eventually turned into the inn courtyard, keeping a wary eye out for old Perkins.

Sammy turned round at the sound of footsteps. "Johnny!" he exclaimed in surprise. "What brings you here? Looking for your old job again?"

"Not likely. But I want to tell you about one. Y'know I've bin staying at Barrandale 'ouse and I've bin listening to the two coachmen talking in the evenings."

"Oh?" said Sammy, wondering what Johnny was getting at.

"Well, Lord Lonsdale and 'is farver 'ave these two 'orses they want to race."

"Look, Johnny, you know I can't ride any more, not with this bad leg of mine. Besides, I'm too heavy now."

"They're looking for a trainer, not a jockey," said Johnny patiently.

Sammy stopped what he was doing. "A trainer, did you say?" he repeated slowly. "Do you really mean that? Cross yer 'eart and hope to die?" He regarded Johnny suspiciously. "You're not having me on, are you?"

"No. Honest. Cross me' eart an' 'ope to die," replied Johnny, going through the motions. "They really are looking for a trainer, an' I thought of you at once. I 'aven't sed anyfink to anyone yet cos' I wanted to mention it to yer first."

Sammy scratched his head. "Well, I dunno, Johnny. It's nice of you to think of me but I'll have to think it over."

"I wish yer would. I'm going to the old house now to see wot needs doing, and I'll come' ere again when I leave."

After Johnny had gone, Sammy gave serious thought to what he had been told. He hardly dared believe such a wonderful piece of luck was true, yet he knew Johnny would not make it up, but what an opportunity to get back into racing once more! The excitement, the roar of the crowd when approaching the winning post! He had been away from it for so long after his accident. About that same time the gentleman he rode for died, and his string of racehorses was broken up and sold, leaving him without any work, for nobody wanted a jockey who could not ride however good he had once been. Horses were his life and they were all he knew. He had managed to find work in coaching inns and such like, gradually drifting his way to London, but working in such places was noisy and tiring, what with his limp, and he eventually found his way to the Bishop's Head Inn, which was much quieter.

Deep down he had missed it all a great deal, and he should surely know something about training and wondered what these two horses were like. Well, he would wait and see. Better not build up too many hopes just yet.

At the house Johnny checked the old tree stump. He next went to the old stable and looked around with a more critical eye. Two stalls, one for the horse and one for himself, for he had decided not to sleep in the house. Plenty of storage for hay and straw and a bin for oats, and there was water available, and a cart would fit inside the carriage house. Yes, the stable would do very well, after he swept it out and made everything ready.

Nothing had changed inside the house, except that it felt cold. The pantry was still much the same. If Johnny was planning to live here for a while, he would have to purchase some food for himself.

Now he must work in the gardens again. He began with the front one to give the impression that someone was about, in case people came round looking for what they could see. The back one took much longer because it was larger and he was also careful to weed the kitchen garden and water any vegetables he could find. It was getting late and he was anxious to know what Sammy had decided.

This time Perkins saw Johnny and sourly asked why he came back when he was supposed to have left, and Johnny meekly replied he wanted to speak to Sammy. Perkins glared at the two of them and walked away.

"'ave you thought it over?" Johnny asked Sammy.

"Yes, I have," he replied, "I would like you to speak to those two coachmen for me."

"Right you are," said Johnny, "I will."

When Johnny arrived later at Barrandale House, Reuben and Stephen were talking together in the yard. Here was his chance. "Please, Reuben," he began, "could I speak to you about somefink?"

"What is it?" said Reuben, wondering what Johnny had to say. He still felt the boy needed firm handling.

Johnny hesitated at first, not sure how to word it, but he had better be polite in any case. "I 'ave 'eard you an' Stephen talking about the two racehorses Lord Barrandale an' Lord Lonsdale 'ave and that they need to find a trainer." The two men still stared at Johnny, causing him to wilt. "Well, I know someone 'oo might be 'oo you are lookin' for."

"Oh, yes?" said Reuben. The cheek of him! What did Johnny or this man know about training racehorses?

"'e's the under-ostler at the Bishop's Head Inn in Fulham Village," continued Johnny doggedly, "and useta to be a jockey until 'e 'ad an accident and couldn't ride any more."

"Oh, yes?" said Reuben, sounding bored. "What's his name?"

"Samuel Cullen."

Both men almost snapped to attention. "Did you say Samuel Cullen?" asked Reuben, astonished. "Samuel Cullen, who rode three Derby winners in seven seasons, and goodness knows how many other winners as well. I can't believe it. He just seemed to disappear after his accident and nobody knew where."

"You know," put in Stephen, "I have seen a small man with a limp when I have driven passed that inn, but I never knew he was Cullen."

"What did you tell Cullen?" asked Reuben.

"Just that I had 'eard you talking' about a trainer, and that I would only say anyfink if 'e wanted me to."

"Thank you, Johnny, you did well," said Reuben, "I will go and tell Matthew I would like to mention this to Lord Barrandale."

"Your lordship," began Matthew, "Reuben requested me to inform you that a possible trainer has been found for the two racehorses, and may he speak to you about it."

Father and son looked at each other. Already? When as yet Dashell had not said anything? They were intrigued. "Show him in, Matthew."

Several minutes later after explaining the whole incident, Reuben was given orders to speak to Samuel Cullen first, and if he was considered suitable he would be interviewed by Lord Barrandale and Lord Lonsdale.

"That Johnny really is remarkable," laughed Dashell when Reuben left the room.

The next morning Johnny sped eagerly to the inn to tell Sammy everything and that Reuben, Lord Barrandale's coachman, wished to see him for an interview.

Sammy was surprised. "Really? I didn't think it would happen that fast. I will have to get time off if I can."

"Get time off?" echoed Johnny. "Of course you should 'ave it. An' treat yerself to a cab. Ask for Barrandale House, Park Lane."

Johnny did not go to the house again. Instead he called at Paxton's Yard on his way back.

Mrs. Paxton hardly recognised him at first. "Johnny!" she cried. "How you have grown. Quite the young man, in fact. Wait till Mr. Paxton sees you."

"I want to see him about somefink," explained Johnny, without saying what. "I'll just have to call again," trying not to sound too disappointed.

"You're not in any kind of trouble, are you?" asked Mrs. Paxton, knowing Johnny of old.

"Oh no," said Johnny, "I have enough money to buy me own 'orse an' cart, and I thought he might be able to 'elp me find one."

She blinked at him in surprise. "You must be having me on. Where did you get the money, anyway? I hope you didn't steal it."

"Certainly not. I earned it," replied Johnny indignantly.

Mrs. Paxton gave her head a perplexed shake. "Try going to the stand. You could find him there." Mr. Paxton was not at the stand when Johnny got there. No driver knew when he would be back once he was out on the road.

Johnny spoke to the drivers who were there. "I'm looking to buy me own 'orse an' cart. Does anyone know where I could get one?"

"Do you really mean it?" said one man, incredulously, thinking Johnny looked rather young to buy anything. "A neighbour's older brother has a good horse for sale. He does hauling and carting but is having to give it up because his sight is getting bad. Come to think of it, he may be willing to sell his cart too." He looked hard at Johnny again. "You're not having me on, are you?"

"Of course not. Me uncle died an' left me some money."

"If this is for real I'll drive you to the man's premises," said the man, not wanting to lose a fare.

"Done," said Johnny, not wanting to lose an opportunity, and hardly daring to believe his luck.

Another driver scratched his head as the cab drove away. He knew Johnny was not getting his uncle's money until he was twenty-one, yet he was claiming he already had it. Like Mrs.

Paxton, he wondered how Johnny had obtained it and hoped it wasn't stolen.

This was definitely something to tell Paxton.

The cab drove along narrow streets until it stopped outside a small yard. "This is it," said the driver, "and I'll wait to take you back if you want."

At the sound of someone calling out a man appeared and asked Johnny what he thought he was doing.

"The cab driver 'oo brought me 'ere sed you 'ad an 'orse an' cart for sale," Johnny explained. "Says 'is neighbour knows yer bruvver."

"Oh," said the man. "Well, he's right. I'm having to give up carting because of my eyesight. Come over here and I'll show you what I've got."

A short while later Johnny was the proud owner of a Suffolk Punch mare in need of a good grooming, a set of harness in poor condition, a four-wheeled cart with rusty hoops, and a canvas covering for the same that would best be discarded and replaced.

When the old man, who said his name was Bill Tibbs, learned Johnny would be dealing in secondhand goods he told him of two places where he used to take such items, and also a third which only dealt in quality goods, if he ever got hold of any. Johnny kept a straight face about that. He also told Johnny he did deliveries for a furniture maker once a week. They settled on a fair price for the horse and cart and Johnny paid five pounds down and said he could come the next day and pay off the remainder. They shook hands on the deal.

Back at the stand Johnny paid off the driver, with a tip, and thanked him. "What I bought was exactly what I wuz lookin' for." He looked about him, but there was still no sign of Mr. Paxton.

When he returned to Barrandale House he told Reuben he had given the message to Sammy Cullen about an interview and, with a wide grin, what else he had done.

Early the next morning Johnny was at Paxton's Yard well before six o'clock as it was the only time he knew he could find Mr.Paxton. The man was getting his horse fed and ready before he had his breakfast, when Johnny appeared at his side.

"Hello Johnny," said Paxton pleasantly, then his manner changed. "What's this yarn you've been telling my missus about your uncle's money and buying a horse and cart? You haven't stolen it, have you?"

"No, I have not," said Johnny, still indignant that people thought that. "Lord Lonsdale gave me some money for saving Miss Waterton's life and for finding some very important papers that 'elped clear up a mystery. I say it's me uncle's money 'cos I don't want people to know where it really came from. It's none of their ruddy business."

Paxton looked long and hard at Johnny, noting that indeed he had changed for the good. Those years at Becket Lane had served him well. "All right, I believe you. Come and have a bite to eat before you go."

"Ta," said Johnny, hoping he would say that, "but before I do I'd like to arsk you somefink."

Paxton laughed. "I might have known there would be a catch to it. What is it?"

"I'm going to use the old stable at the 'ouse, but would it be all right for me to come 'ere overnight once or twice just to begin with? I would pay for it of course."

"Well, there would be room for the cart but it might be a tight fit for your horse, but I am sure we can come to some arrangement, as long as it's not too often."

"Oh, thanks," said Johnny.

"Right," said Paxton. "Now let's go and get some breakfast."

During the meal Johnny told the other two only what he cared to divulge, but did say he would be busy carting small items from the two Barrandale houses and take them to secondhand places for sale. He did not stay long and slipped a few coins in the box to pay for his breakfast.

Paxton saw this and said, "Come on, Johnny, I'll give you a free ride to the stand."

A very cheerful Johnny arrived back at Barrandale House to be told he was just in time for breakfast. "I've already 'ad some," he had to admit, although the smell of frying bacon was very tempting.

"Well, you can still come and join us."

Afterwards it did not take him long to return to the warehouse to pay over the rest of the money he owed to the man. Then he proudly led out the mare and proceeded to give her a good grooming, who eyed him warily only because she did not know him.

The old man stood and watched while he told Johnny two other helpful hints. "First of all, when you arrange a time to call at a place, keep to it. Nothing makes folks more crotchety as when someone is late or never shows up at all. Do it once or twice and they won't bother with you again, and word does get round. And don't forget to wipe your feet going inside somewhere or else you'll get an earful from some housemaid or other."

Johnny finished grooming the horse and she was put back in her stall and given a good feed. He asked if he could leave her for one more night, and Tibbs, ever mindful of earning a penny or two, agreed.

By the time Johnny got back to Barrandale House he was beginning to realize the enormity of what he was doing. It was all very well having a dream but it was very different putting it into reality; besides buying a horse and cart, he also had work handed to him with no effort on his part. He was used to looking after horses but had no experience in driving them, so later that evening he asked Stephen to give him a few tips.

CHAPTER ELEVEN

Happenings Continue

S amuel Cullen duly came for his interview with Reuben about his racing experience and what he had been doing since his enforced retirement, and how he thought he could turn what knowledge he had into training racehorses. Reuben admitted that neither he nor James at Windsor knew too much about training which was why they were looking for someone else. Satisfied that Cullen knew what he was talking about, Reuben asked Matthew to inform their lordships that he had interviewed Samuel Cullen and respectfully requested them to speak to Cullen. Cullen must have made a good impression for he was offered the position of trainer which he was very pleased to accept, even though there were only two horses at his disposal.

Lord Barrandale and Dashell were still discussing the interview together when Matthew announced the estate agent.

"Thank you, gentlemen, I will not take up too much of your time. I have here the plans of the new house in South Kensington for you to look at in case there are any alterations you may like to make. A gentleman has made an offer on this house, and a very good one, if I may say so. He understands the other house has to be finished and has agreed to wait." So saying, he bowed himself out.

"Well," remarked Dashell, "that did not take very long. Any regrets, sir?"

Barrandale turned to him with a half-smile. "Yes, I suppose I have. So many memories are coming back. Yet, is it not said there a time and place for everything? Those words, 'To everything there is a season and a time for every purpose under heaven'." Dashell knew where those words came from and did not press him to say anything further. "Shall we say tomorrow morning we look at the new house and see what has been going on?"

Johnny had duly gone to the furniture maker and made his first delivery. Two men from the premises had gone with him for he was not expected to handle anything for heaven forbid there should be any dent or scratch on any new surface. He returned to Barrandale House so proud of his first payment, and loaded the cart with some unwanted items with the help of Stephen and George, and set off to one of the secondhand places. He had to be satisfied with the payment given, but Tibbs said they always gave a fair price. He gave the money and receipt to Matthew and was given his ten per cent.

The cart was loaded again but this time he drove to Paxton's Yard and left it in the carriage house ready for the morning. After seeing to his horse's needs he told Mrs. Paxton he would be back again early in the morning, and walked back to Barrandale House thinking what a wonderful day it had been for him.

When he arrived Matthew told him, "There is someone in the kitchen who would like to see you." Johnny knew at once who it was and went in with a wide grin on his face.

Since his interviews Samuel, Reuben and Stephen had been talking 'horse' and were now in the kitchen celebrating his new position with a cup of tea.

"Johnny!" cried Samuel when he entered, "I was offered the position of trainer, which I accepted. You did me a good turn there and I must thank you for it."

"Aw," said Johnny, "I knoo you might be interested, and good fer you."

"Their lordships would like to see you," Matthew also told him. "I had to tell them you were out so don't keep them waiting, but clean yourself up first," and when Johnny was considered presentable Matthew ushered him into the salon. "Johnny Faulkner, your lordship," he announced.

"It seems that we must thank you once more," began Lord Barrandale, and a few minutes later Johnny returned to the others smiling broadly, and feeling almost two inches taller.

Sammy now felt it was time to go. "Well, Johnny, I've heard of your doings of the last few days or so; and I told Lord Barrandale I will have to work out my week's notice, so it makes a new beginning for both of us. I'll have to make my way to Windsor somehow, probably by stage coach, because I won't be able to walk it."

"Y'know," said Johnny thoughtfully, "I may be able to help yer. I hafta go to Windsor meself to pick up stuff there. so perhaps I could give yer a ride in me cart. Let me know when yer're ready to go," then added with a grin, "old Perkins won't like this, first me leaving and now you."

"That he won't," agreed Sammy. "Well, thanks again, and see you in a week's time."

That morning Maxwell was determined to put aside any thoughts of his useless attempts to obtain some position in a bank. He now prepared himself to face the last of his options—the Law.

He called at a framer with two more of his canvasses and was horrified at the cost involved. "Our prices are considered quite reasonable," he was told. He almost wished he had left more canvases with the man at Windsor although it would have been difficult to get them back, now that he was to be living in

London. When his two paintings were framed he took them to a gallery recommended by Mr. Creppan, where the curator agreed to display them for sale.

Lady Smythe had now returned to Grosvenor Square, knowing she had left Caroline in the good care of Mrs. Farling; at the same time wondering, with an inward smile, how Dashell was going to cope with her absence. At lease he would not now be coming round every day, so she should be thankful for small mercies.

She had sent an answer to Maxwell's note saying she would be delighted to see him. "Come for tea, and dinner too if you wish, as long as you promise not to stay too long."

One afternoon at half past three Maxwell went round to Grosvenor Square. Perhaps Aunt Letty could offer some suggestions, for she knew a multitude of people and surely there could be a barrister or solicitor among them. Whatever else he and his aunt were going to talk about he did not expect to have an incredible story poured into his ears. He knew Walden had disgraced himself and had brought ruin on his family but did not know all the details because his father and Dashell did not wish to talk about it.

CHAPTER TWELVE

Dashell Receives a Reply to His Letter

Matthew went to answer a knock on the front door and a messenger handed him a package addressed to Lord Lonsdale.

Dashell took it eagerly from him and turned to his father. "Sir, this must be the answer to my letter to the Rev. Swanson. It's surprisingly thick." He quickly opened the package and began to read the letter aloud.

"In reply to your letter I have ascertained that there has been a family by the name of Waterton in the county of Sussex since the early 1700s. The first baronet, Sir Edward Waterton, died in battle and his son. also Edward, drowned when the ship he was in sank in a storm while crossing the English Channel. The next baronet, Sir Godfrey, was buried in the Sutherfield churchyard. His son, Sir Arthur, died in what was believed to have been a carriage accident. His wife, Lady Isobel, and their two infant daughters also perished. They were all buried somewhere in Yorkshire where the accident took place. I regret to say I do not know exactly where. Dashell gasped out loud. "What the devil is the man talking about?" forgetting for the moment he was referring to a clergyman. Shakily he went on reading:

"There is a memorial tablet in our church here from which I have taken a charcoal rubbing. The lettering is quite clear and I am sure your lordship will be able to read it exactly." The letter slipped from Dashell's fingers to the floor as he snatched up the folded sheet of parchment and laid it flat on the table which Barrandale had cleared for him. The words seemed to rise up and strike him like a physical blow and almost rocked him off his feet, as he read:

"In Loving Memory of Sir Arthur Waterton and Lady Isobel, and their two infant daughters, Maude and Caroline, who all perished in the same accident. May Their Souls Rest in Peace." Stunned and ashen-faced Dashell stared at his father who, equally astonished, stared back at him. Dashell slumped into a chair and wiped his forehead. "I don't understand," he said at last. "It's impossible. If they are all dead then who are the living, the people using their names? Does that mean they are imposters? It cannot be possible, unless—unless that awful man Wardlock forged the documents we have."

He got up and stood leaning over the table with his hands laid flat on it, staring at the parchment still not able to comprehend what he read. "What am I to tell Caroline?" he said at last, "that she is still not who she thinks she is? This could break her heart, and mine too. How *can* they all be dead." Bewilderment, grief and frustration came to a point and with a cry of, "Damnation! Are we never to get to the bottom of this!" he raised his right arm and with his considerable strength brought his fist down on the table.

"Dashell!" cried his father. "What are you doing! Control yourself!"

Dashell could only stammer an apology. "I beg your pardon, sir. I-I am deeply sorry. But this is beyond comprehension."

"Very well. I accept your apology, considering the mitigating circumstances. Now have the goodness to sit down and we will talk this over together." A still visibly shaken Dashell silently obeyed. "Let us consider the facts as we know them. Under no circumstances can this Reverend Swanson have been mistaken, and I take him to be an intelligent man. This memorial tablet has been in existence for eighteen or nineteen years, placed, I presume, on a church wall for all to see; and a rubbing cannot be falsified for it takes an absolute copy.

"Nor do I believe Wardlock forged all those documents even though Inspector Cockburn knows he had been a forger. If he had, then why did Isobel hide them from him only for him to find them later and steal them back from her; and in that case why did he not forge a death certificate for Waterton himself. He would not have left that undone if he and those three women were cheating. I, for one, believe those documents we have are absolutely genuine. There is also the fact of the hidden portrait, as Isobel obviously wanted to keep it safe, probably from Wardlock himself.

"Another fact to consider is the witness of Hannah. You will remember she came into Isobel's employment when the children were still infants, and that for about two years Isobel was anxious for their safety as though she thought they might be taken away from her. Also, she married a man whom she barely knew for, I believe, obscurity. I am convinced something terrified her into silence."

Dashell, still pale, shaken, and horrified at his outburst, had listened to every word. He let his breath out slowly, "But what, I wonder."

"I cannot answer that."

"And, what's more, why?"

"I cannot answer that either." Barrandale placed his fingertips together and watched his son carefully while Dashell thought things over.

Slowly Dashell's face expressed horror as a particular thought came to mind. "It seems," he began, and hesitated, "It seems that someone wished them dead."

"That is what I think too, but I did not want to be the one to say so."

"But why?" persisted Dashell, "A gentle lady like Isobel. What could she possibly have done to warrant such cruel treatment?" He shook his head slowly. "I have long had a suspicion that she married against her family's wishes, but this? So that could mean that only Sir Arthur is buried in Yorkshire somewhere, and the memorial tablet is a lie, for Isobel and her daughters never died with him; and it is quite possible they never even travelled with him in the first place. So that means someone went to the expense of having that lying memorial tablet cut." He ruffled his hand though his hair. "I wonder what Sir Arthur was doing in Yorkshire anyway. It's a long way from Sussex."

"We may never know," observed Barrandale, "but what better place than the wide empty moors of Yorkshire to hide a guilty secret."

Dashell got up suddenly and stood looking through a window for a few minutes. "Those letters for Caroline that Johnny brought over, I was going to St. Albans tomorrow to give them to her, but now I will not. After what we have learned I would not know what to say to her; and it would be cruel to say anything until we have found out more. Nor can I leave them with Aunt Letty for she might wonder why I could not take them myself."

He turned round to find his father watching him with a half-smile on his face. Barrandale coughed gently, "And—er—when will you be setting out for Yorkshire?" he enquired, studying his fingernails.

Dashell laughed grimly as he sat down again. "You know me very well, sir."

"I should do so by now."

"When I get to York I can make enquiries at the county newspaper office about this accident that took place some years ago, for there is bound to be such a place. I will still accompany you to see the new house tomorrow as I promised, and then set off in the afternoon." He added thoughtfully, "I suppose I should send a note to Caroline for she might wonder what I am doing, being away for a while. That reminds me, all those jewels still in Aunt Letty's safe keeping, probably the truth about them will come to light eventually, like everything else. But what a damnable revelation of something that is practically a heinous crime."

"And that is?"

"Well, to declare a whole family dead when they were not; and that is why I intend to go and see what I can find out."

"Admirable," said Barrandale. "I knew you would."

"One would almost think you were as keen as I am to get to the truth of it all," remarked Dashell.

"Of course I am, if I am ever to welcome Caroline as my daughter-in-law." The look on Dashell's face was enough for Barrandale.

"Oh," exclaimed Dashell, "I never finished reading Swanson's letter. Where is it? Ah, there it is," and picked it up off the floor.

"After the death of Sir Arthur the baronetcy and property was inherited by a distant cousin, Sir Richard Irving. He and his family still reside at Waterton Grange. I trust I have answered your enquiry to the best of my knowledge and ability, and, I assure you, with the utmost discretion. I am, etc.etc." Father and son had the same query in mind. Could this Sir Richard be behind it all just to get the inheritance? Such incidences were known to happen; so an unscrupulous person could gain the inheritance. Dashell's heart ached for Caroline; the "last of the three" as Johnny had so graphically described it, and the innocent victim in all of this.

"I must write some letters," said Dashell. "I will write to Caroline and say I will be out of town for a while as there is more information I am trying to find out, and I will write to the Reverend Swanson to thank him for his help. I will also write to Aunt Letty. Even what little we know about the Watertons may help in discovering any close relatives."

"Why your Aunt Letty?" asked Barrandale, mystified.

"She once told me she knew someone who makes very discreet enquiries about relations and next-of-kin, as a marriage broker or something like that."

"Oh, I see."

Dashell left to go upstairs to his room, while Lord Barrandale summoned Matthew.

"Matthew, when Mr. Maxwell returns from dining with Lady Smythe would you send him to see me. I particularly wish to speak to him."

Not long afterwards Barrandale heard the front doorbell ring and Maxwell entered the room.

"Sir?" he said. "Matthew tells me you wish to speak to me about something."

"Ah, yes, Maxwell, I do. Come and sit down, will you."

Maxwell did so, wondering if he had done anything amiss. Perhaps the expression on his face relayed his thoughts, for his father said, "There is something I want you to do, but first of all how was your time with your Aunt Letty?"

Maxwell's face brightened up at once. "I had a wonderful time and Aunt Letty is such a dear and she asked me how I was getting on, and I told her what I had been doing, which wasn't always very successful, so she gave me the names of some people I could contact. And then—" he paused as he hitched himself up in his chair—"and then she told me this fantastic tale about Dashell finding this lady in Oxford Street one afternoon., and everything else that followed later. Honestly, by the time she finished she made Dashell sound like a knight in shining armour. What a story! I think it's incredible. It sounds all so romantic and medieval."

Barrandale laughed at that, while Maxwell rattled on, until he stopped short, "Oh, I beg your pardon, sir, I believe you want me to do something for you."

"Yes, I do, Maxwell, and it will take up some considerable amount of your time. Now listen carefully."

After several minutes of Barrandale talking and Maxwell listening, they said good night to each other. "Ring the bell for Matthew would you, Maxwell, as you go? I believe Dashell retired early so you should find him in his room."

Maxwell slowly went upstairs, his head full of everything Aunt Letty had told him, but even so he felt that not all had been mentioned. He would have to try and get the old lad to talk somehow. And if that was not enough, there was everything his father had just told him. He stopped outside Dashell's bedroom door and knocked.

"Come in," called Dashell, sounding surprised. "Oh, it's you. Come in."

Maxwell, trying not to grin, remarked he had had a wonderful time with Aunt Letty. "She told me a long tale about you and your lady. She sounds like a real corker."

"Let me tell you, my lad," began Dashell, glaring at Maxwell as only an older brother can, "the word 'corker' does not apply in Caroline's case. She is a very charming and delightful lady."

"She certainly sounds like it. And the way Aunt Letty spoke of you, you sounded like a cross between St. George and Sir Galahad, besides being more besotted than she cared to think about. I had to ask what that meant." Maxwell took great delight in saying that.

Dashell laughed in spite of himself. "Now get out before I throw you out."

"Not yet, old lad."

"Look, Maxwell," said Dashell, beginning to get annoyed. "I'm not in the mood for frivolity. There is a very serious matter on hand and I am worried about it."

Maxwell, contrite now, said, "Yes, I know. You are going up to Yorkshire."

"Yes, I am."

"And I am coming with you as squire."

Dashell stared at him. "Are you indeed? And who says?"

"Father does. He spoke to me when I returned just now."

"Oh. Well, if Father says so then you must."

"And he says I may ride Lively; and I have promised not to damage him."

"Believe you me, if you do damage Lively you can answer to me too; and if you start setting him at five-barred gates, or anything else to jump over," Dashell added grimly. Maxwell was rather taken aback at Dashell's sharpness. "Well, he is one of our two hopefuls, you know."

"Er—yes, I know." Then anxious to change the subject Maxwell asked, "If you are going back to Windsor in your gig could I come with you?"

"Sorry, Maxwell, I always leave the gig here in town so you will have to make your own way there. Father and I are going to look at the new house in the morning and I will leave for

Windsor after luncheon. I will leave again the following morning with you or without you."

Maxwell sighed to himself. He had a feeling this would happen. "All right, I'll be up extra early tomorrow morning and get a seat on the eight o'clock stage." Just when he had promised himself it would be a long time before he travelled on one again. Oh,well.

"You had better tell Matthew you require an early breakfast."

"I already have," Maxwell told him.

"The devil you have. Now go away, I want to be alone. Good night."

Maxwell, thinking that Dashell could sound very like Father at times answered, "Good night," and went away to his own room.

Dashell's door opened suddenly as he called his brother back. "Maxwell! I was rather short with you. Sorry. Yes, I will be glad of your company because it will be a long journey. As my squire, you could begin by asking at the coaching station the best way to the Great North Road for Yorkshire."

Maxwell was up early next morning and was at the coaching station by quarter past seven. Even at that time it was busy, for at eight o'clock many stages would be leaving in various directions. It was here that his problems started. First, the stage to Windsor was fully booked; and amidst great noise and clatter the coach moved off at eight o'clock sharp, leaving Maxwell staring glumly after it as it thundered away. The two o'clock was also fully booked. Perhaps, suggested the clerk in the booking office, the young gentleman could come back in case of a cancellation. Maxwell shook his head. It was too risky to wait and see and then still not get on.

Now what was he to do? He felt he was on some kind of quest to accompany Dashell, and to let Father down was unthinkable.

There was only one thing he could do: with a philosophical shrug he set off to walk the nearly twenty miles to Windsor.

Barrandale and Dashell met at the breakfast table and learned from Matthew that Maxwell had already left.

At eleven o'clock Barrandale's carriage was waiting at the front door and shortly afterwards the two men were outside the new house. It stood three storeys high, built in the still popular, graceful Georgian style. They went over the whole building and when they returned to the hall, Barrandale asked Dashell, "What do you think?"

"I like it very much," he replied. "The interior is larger than one would think when looking from the outside. I am sure we will be very comfortable here."

"Doubtless you are right," demurred Barrandale, "but do you not think it somewhat modern?" He was more used to wooden panelling and heavy ornate fireplaces.

"Modern? No, I think it is splendid; and I like how the skylight in the roof lets so much light into the hall."

After more discussion about any possible alterations they returned to the old house.

"I do not think anything needs to be added or altered," remarked Barrandale. "The design has obviously been very well thought out in the first place. Do you agree?"

"Yes, I do," agreed Dashell, "but I regret leaving you to speak to the estate agent."

"Thank you, Dashell, I consider myself to be quite capable," said Barrandale, drily.

After luncheon Barrandale spoke again to Dashell. "I know you want to leave as soon as possible, Dashell, but there is the question of funds," he said, smiling faintly. "I would willingly offer you the use of my carriage and then you could travel post;

it would be much quicker but also more expensive; and hiring a hackney carriage would be even more so."

"I understand what you are saying, sir," replied Dashell, "but I would much prefer to ride, and there is no extreme pressing need for haste."

"Exactly; and I know that Maxwell will be travelling with you. It will be a long journey and I would rather you were together as it would be safer. I trust to your discretion not to take any unnecessary risks."

"Thank you, sir. I appreciate your concern on our behalf."

"I am glad you are going to Windsor first after all, for you would have had to go there anyway."

"Sir?" queried Dashell.

"I have here a note for Simmonds instructing him to provide you with a certain amount of money which you will keep on your person at all times. I hope it will be enough for your needs."

"That is most generous of you, sir, but with regard to funds I can provide my own."

"Of course, but remember Maxwell will be with you. One more thing, I have also instructed Simmonds to let you have that pair of silver-mounted pistols. I know you are a good shot. Take them with you just to be on the safe side."

"Very well, sir. If I may say, those letters for Caroline should go to Grosvenor Square after all. Aunt Letty can write and tell her she has them. It is not for us to keep them here."

"Yes, that is a good point. Now I will not delay you any more except to say Godspeed, and my thoughts and prayers go with you both."

Less than half an hour later Dashell was on his way.

Meanwhile, a very tired, footsore and hungry Maxwell had arrived at Barrandale Park during the late afternoon, to the great surprise of Simmonds that he had travelled all that way on foot. The first thing Maxwell asked was, "Has my brother, Mr. Dashell, arrived yet?" and was told he had not. "Ah, he should be on his way. Would you bring me some refreshments, Simmonds. I will have them here." 'Here' meant the entrance hall where he had flopped into a comfortable armchair to stretch himself out and relax.

A footman came and left a tray on a low table and Maxwell ate everything there was. He felt much better, and wondered how long it would be before Dashell came. Surely he would be here for the evening meal. He had said nothing to Simmonds about what they would be doing, he would leave that for Dashell to do. A few minutes later he stood up, still feeling somewhat stiff, and went upstairs to his bedroom. He had better decide what to take with him.

When he eventually arrived at Barrandale Park, Dashell did not waste any time. He went straight to his father's study and summoned both Simmonds and James.

"James," he began, "a trainer has been engaged. He is an ex-jockey by the name of Samuel Cullen. He has already been interviewed both by my father and myself, and found suitable. He will be coming within the next week or ten days, so would you see that accommodation is made ready for him. Mr.Maxwell and I are travelling to Yorkshire tomorrow, and would you have my horse and Lively ready at eight o'clock. By the way, how are the two hopefuls coming along?"

"Quite well at the moment, sir," replied James carefully, "but they will benefit from a more knowledgeable trainer."

"Well said," smiled Dashell. "Thank you, James. That is all."

He now turned to Simmonds. "Simmonds, here is a note to you from Lord Barrandale. Would you bring the items here after my brother and I have dined. Is he here yet?"

"Yes, sir. He came an hour or so ago. I believe he is waiting in the hall to see you."

"Thank you, Simmonds. That is all."

Maxwell had just sat down again in the hall when Dashell came looking for him. "So you made it here after all. How was your journey on the stage this time?" he asked.

"Every seat on the eight o'clock was taken. I could not get on; and I was not going to risk waiting for the two o'clock."

"So how did you get here?"

"I walked."

"What!" laughed Dashell. "All the way? Well, I take my hat off to you. I really do."

"Thanks," grinned Maxwell. "I was not going to let you or Father down. By the way, did you go and look at the new house this morning? I made a point of passing by and had a good look at the outside. I must say I was quite impressed."

"That's just what Father said," explained Dashell. "We both went inside," and he described the rooms in some detail.

"Poor Father. I wonder how he is taking it?"

"Over something like this he keeps his thoughts to himself, although he did say he liked it. By the way, did you make those enquiries at the coaching station?"

"Yes, I did. The man said to go through Watford to St. Albans and on to Luton, and then follow any signposts to Huntingdon."

St. Albans! thought Dashell. *What if Mrs. Farling and Caroline were out and about and they recognised him? How was he to explain why he was there? He would just have to take that risk.* "Thank you, Maxwell. I suppose that is what we will have to do."

Later that evening they went into their father's study, and Dashell rang the bell for Simmonds.

"I have here the sum of money I am instructed to give you, Lord Lonsdale. And here are the two silver-mounted pistols." That latter remark caused Maxwell some surprise.

"Thank you, Simmonds, just leave them on the desk. Now, I am taking you into my confidence by informing you that we are travelling up to Yorkshire. It is something of my own undertaking and my brother is accompanying me. This means we shall be away a considerable number of days. Barrandale House has been sold and the new owner has agreed to wait until the new house in South Kensington is finished. A carter by the name of Johnny Faulkner has been hired to take away all items for sale from here. He has a great deal to do first around the old house. When he does come, and if he requires overnight accommodation, he is to have it. He is young but he can be trusted."

"Very good, sir. What time shall I order breakfast?"

"Seven o'clock will suit us," replied Dashell, glancing at Maxwell. "That will be all, Simmonds, thank you."

After Simmonds left, Dashell took the pair of pistols out of their padded case and looked them over, then gave one to Maxwell. "It's not loaded." Maxwell handled it gingerly, prompting Dashell to ask him, "Have you ever fired a pistol?"

"No," Maxwell replied, still eyeing it carefully.

"Do you want to learn? We could go outside."

Maxwell stared at him aghast. "You mean now? Are you serious?"

With a sigh, Dashell took the pistol away from him. "If there is any shooting to be done you had better leave it to me," and carefully loaded both pistols. He then turned to the money in its linen bag on the desk, and Maxwell watched him as he emptied out the coins and counted them. "Fifty sovereigns," he said at last. "Father said to keep it on our persons at all times, Does your riding coat have inside pockets? Good," as Maxwell nodded. "Also, we take nothing else of value with us."

"How long will we be away?" asked Maxwell. "I am beginning to think it is quite an undertaking."

Dashell paused a moment. "Yes, I know," he replied thoughtfully. "I would say three to four weeks, even longer."

Maxwell whistled. "As long as that?"

"Well, if we were riding post with fresh horses it would take less time, but as we are riding the same two horses we must be careful not to over-use them. It's almost two hundred miles to York alone. And after enquiring at the newspaper office about this accident that happened some eighteen years or so ago, that will mean even more riding; and Yorkshire is a very large county."

CHAPTER THIRTEEN

The Brothers Set Off On Their Journey

The next morning Dashell was in the hall waiting for the horses to be brought round to the front of the house just as Maxwell came downstairs. He seemed to be adjusting something in a pocket of his riding-coat.

"What have you got there?" he asked curiously.

"Some sketch pads, pencils and a penknife," replied Maxwell.

Dashell sighed. "I might have known."

The horses were brought round, and without wasting any time the two brothers were on their way. An epic journey neither would ever forget.

Simmonds and James, who had known each other for years, were left alone at the bottom of the steps. "What do you make of this going up to Yorkshire, of all places?" remarked Simmonds. "Seems strange. Doesn't appear to be any call for it, and just when the old house in London has been sold, and leaving his lordship alone."

"Aye," replied James. "Taking Lively away just before the new man comes. I wonder what he is like. Should be good, being an ex-jockey. And what do you make of this young carter who has been hired? 'To have accommodation if required'. Sounds rum to me."

"Probably Reuben could tell us a lot when his lordship returns."

The brothers rode side by side, Dashell being particularly quiet, being preoccupied with his own thoughts. *Was he doing the right thing,* he wondered, *or would it all turn out to be a fool's errand?* Yet he would do anything for Caroline, although she had no real idea what he was doing. His brief note to her gave no indication what he was doing, except making further enquiries. About what, she might wonder.

Although Maxwell sensed Dashell was preoccupied he was beginning to feel piqued at his silence. "I say, Dashell, you might include me in the conversation," he said at last.

Dashell looked at him in surprise. "What?"

"You haven't said a word since we left."

"Sorry, Maxwell, I'm too preoccupied with everything, especially that package from Swanson, which is why we are doing this ride."

"Yes; and that incredible story Aunt Letty told me. I still can't believe it. And there are still some facts I am not clear about."

"Knowing Aunt Letty, I am surprised she left anything out. What else did you want to know?"

So Maxwell asked and Dashell answered.

It was a long ride to Watford through Rickmansworth, and once there they stopped for refreshments before continuing their journey. Dashell had already decided not to call to see Caroline; for one thing, the whole house would be put into a flutter to have two gentlemen arrive unexpectedly, which would be considered ill-mannered on their part, and Mrs. Farling would feel obliged to invite them to stay a while, nor could they hasten away again without some long explanation about why they called in the first place. And that would give Aunt Letty further reason to doubt his sanity. It would be wiser to call on their way back when he had some facts to impart. So some time and some miles later they walked their horses up Holywell Hill as they entered St.Albans and stopped at the White Hart Inn.

"By the way, Maxwell," said Dashell, "I shall not use my title wherever we stay. We will just be what we are, two gentlemen brothers out riding together."

Maxwell took that remark to heart, hoping it meant there would be time to do some sketching. "I could spend all day in St. Albans," he said as they took their seats in the dining area. "Sketching," he explained in answer to his brother's puzzled look. "Just think of it. The Abbey, the Roman ruins, the Fighting Cocks Inn, and goodness knows what else." He caught the look in Dashell's eye. "Well, perhaps on the way back there would be more time," he finished lamely.

All too soon they came to Hitchin and found somewhere to stay for the night. "How far do you think we have come?" queried Maxwell.

"Well, judging by the miles on signposts," answered Dashell, "I should think about thirty-five miles. That's about as far as I thought we would."

They left early next morning for another long ride, hoping to reach Huntingdon by evening. At St. Neots they halted to rest the horses and themselves and Maxwell seized the opportunity to sketch the 15th century church.

"Dammit, I hope you are not planning to stop and sketch every wretched church," complained Dashell rather testily.

Maxwell turned round in genuine surprise. "I thought we stopped to rest the horses," he said innocently.

Dashell muttered something unintelligible and went to sit under a tree in the shade and closed his eyes, and let his mind drift to his favourite subject.

When Maxwell felt he had done enough he went to sit under the same tree, and caught sight of the dreamy smile on his brother's face. The temptation was too great. Quickly finding a fresh page in his book he made a sketch of Dashell's face. He then sat down next to him and nudged him with his elbow. "Are you awake?"

"More or less," murmured Dashell.

"What's it like being in love?"

"Why do you ask?"

"I drew a sketch of you grinning to yourself," showing him the drawing.

Dashell opened one eye and turned his head to look, and laughed. "Hmm. Not bad."

"What's it like?" persisted Maxwell.

Dashell's smile broadened. "Wonderful. You should try it yourself some time."

"Don't be so idiotic," said Maxwell. "How can I? I'm far too young."

"Well, you will just have to wait until you grow up."

Maxwell fell silent, rather appalled at the prospect. "I've heard tell a pair of eyes come into it somehow," he added darkly, thinking it sounded like a whole lot of rot.

"Oh, yes, that too," agreed Dashell happily.

"Hah," scoffed Maxwell, thinking of the poems he had read at school. "Do you mean to tell me that of all the eyes out— out there"—waving a hand vaguely—"one pair is supposed to be meant for me? How awful. And it sounds damn stupid anyway. How does a fellow know which are the right ones?"

"You will know when the time comes."

Maxwell gave such a derisive snort that Dashell laughed out loud. He stood up. "Come on, Maxwell. We had better get going."

Eventually they reached Huntingdon and put up at the George Inn. As they approached it Maxwell decided it was also worth sketching.

That evening, to put their father's mind at rest, Dashell wrote to say they had reached Huntingdon in good time and nothing untoward had happened on the journey, and left the letter to be picked up by the next mail coach going south.

The next morning they planned to ride to Stilton and then on to Stamford. They were in no great hurry to leave as Stilton was only about twelve or thirteen miles away. Once there Maxwell was ecstatic over the Bell Inn and just had to sketch it. After dining they journeyed on to Stamford, roughly fifteen miles, where they stayed the night at another inn called The George, which Maxwell also sketched.

They had now been on the road for three days, long enough to have made some impressions, particularly their surprise at the amount of traffic travelling north and south. There was one aspect that had not occurred to either of them. They were both healthy and young and good horsemen yet they were becoming tired, not because of the distance they had ridden but because of lack of sleep. The London to Edinburgh road, which ran through York, was used by stage coaches, Royal Mail coaches, private vehicles, hackney carriages, waggons, and anything else with wheels, and horsemen like themselves, and even people walking. The rumble of wheels and clatter of hooves arriving or leaving the various inns at all times of day and night, the cries of the coachmen and ostlers kept them awake. It seemed that an inn had barely quietened down for the night before it all started up again at dawn.

On the other hand, there was the cheerfulness of the landlords welcoming weary travellers, the roaring fires where they could warm themselves, the excellent food in most cases and the genial company during the evenings.

If Dashell and Maxwell put aside the real reason why they were there, they would have to admit they were enjoying it. Yet many a time Dashell had wondered why Sir Arthur Waterton had been up here at all, and perhaps they might never know. He and Maxwell could even have stayed in the same inns as Waterton had

They travelled by setting off early in the morning, resting midday at whatever inn or tavern became available, and made enquiries about a night's lodging farther ahead. Even Maxwell was feeling he had done enough sketching, that he could never keep up with all possible subjects, except of course, York itself. Besides, that was not why they had come this way and he did not wish to irritate his brother.

They reached York the next day where the magnificent pile of the Minster was in view the whole time. "No need to ask what you will be doing here," remarked Dashell.

"Oh, yes," replied Maxwell, "That, and catching up on some sleep."

"I'll second that," said Dashell, "and then find the office of the local paper and make some enquiries without attracting too much attention, if possible."

"As your squire, I could go for you," suggested Maxwell. "I could pretend to be doing research on local tragedies, or something like that, then your name would not be associated with it. Better still, I could give a false name, then neither of us would be associated with it. What do you think of that idea?"

"I think it sounds excellent."

So that was what Maxwell did. He found a discarded newspaper where they were staying and made a note of their office address. He had to ask the inn-keeper where the street was and set off on his mission, wondering how he was going to word his enquiries when he got there.

He tried to explain to a disinterested clerk what he was doing and was promptly asked how far back he wanted to look in their archives, because the paper only began printing about fourteen years ago anyway. The clerk deliberately looked at the clock on the wall, and said, "We will be closing in fifteen minutes or so, so you will have to come back tomorrow." He turned to another clerk who had just come to join him. "What was that tragic accident that happened about twenty years ago? You know something about it, don't you?"

The second clerk, with a face that looked as if his whole life was a tragedy, sniffed and said, "So I should. My father dinned it into me enough times that he helped to clean up the mess. Out at Skorrcliff, wasn't it?" he said, looking at the first clerk.

"I thought you said you knew," he replied, with another glance at the clock.

Maxwell thanked both of them for their trouble and left. Skorrcliff! Now he would have to find out where it was, and the most likely place to ask would be the Post Office. He learned it was the other side of Pateley Bridge, and that town was some thirty-five miles or so west of York. Feeling he had made a great deal of headway in a short time he now returned to the inn. Dashell would be delighted.

Dashell certainly was. "I don't know how you do it," he said after Maxwell related everything. "And now for your reward you may sketch all you want tomorrow."

"I was going to anyway," Maxwell grinned back at him, "and while I'm out I'll look for a signpost to Pateley Bridge."

That evening Dashell wrote to his father to say they had reached York safely and had enjoyed the ride, if one may be forgiven for saying so, considering why the two of them were here, and that they would stay a day in York. When Maxwell returned from his meanderings around that city he told Dashell he had seen a signpost to Pateley Bridge.

"Thirty-five miles," repeated Dashell. "That will mean a very early start tomorrow if we are to get there before dark. We will have to ask directions to Skorrcliff when we get there, or rather look for more signposts."

The Yorkshire countryside could be quite varied, with hills and dales, rivers, rocky areas, woodlands, and even great craggy cliffs. Pateley Bridge lay at the edge of the moors which would become more and more desolate and wild, with lonely farms and villages—and sheep. Signposts had indicated that Skorrcliff was another fifteen miles beyond Pateley Bridge.

"So we are here at last," said Dashell, as they settled themselves into a room at an inn in Pateley Bridge. His thoughts had been of Caroline all the time, on falling asleep and on waking. Now, perhaps, this damnable mystery of Sir Arthur's death might be cleared up. "I wonder what we shall find out. We must consider how we are to present ourselves, for we do not want people to think we are here for a specific purpose. I have heard Yorkshire people are very shrewd."

"We could always say we are here because I would like to do some sketching," said Maxwell hopefully, "that we understand there are some interesting views around here."

Dashell laughed. "So your sketching has come in useful after all. I do agree it sounds a plausible idea."

Their departure the next morning was delayed while their horses had to be re-shod and they had to wait their turn. "We might as well stay for a meal before we leave," said Dashell, "because there is no other place until Skorrecliff, so the landlord told me."

CHAPTER FOURTEEN

What They Learn Astounds Them

The lonely road led past the side of a hill which looked somewhat misshapen, set back a little way yet casting a great shadow over them. They were glad to be away from it and into the full sunlight once more. In the distance they could see the Crossroads Inn and the village church in Skorrcliff.

As they rode into the courtyard the clatter of hooves brought out a man from the stables to lead the horses away. The landlord also heard them and came forward to greet them, looking faintly surprised at seeing two lone horsemen.

"Welcome, gentlemen. My name is Prunty," he said, his round genial face beaming at them. "Come in, come indoors and I'll soon get a cheerful fire going and you can warm yourselves."

"Thank you, Prunty, it is rather cold," replied Dashell agreeably.

"And what may I get for you gentlemen? There is some very good ale."

"That will do us very well," said Dashell, as they followed the landlord in.

The two of them sat down and made themselves comfortable, stretching their legs out and enjoying the warmth of the fire the landlord had lit for them. Dashell shook his head, "I can't believe we are actually here," he muttered, keeping his voice down. Footsteps approached and Prunty came in with the ale for them.

"Would you gentlemen be ready to dine? We have some cold mutton."

"It is a little early yet," said Dashell, "perhaps later. I think we will go outside first to stretch our legs after we have tasted your ale."

"Prunty," began Maxwell, "my brother and I have been exploring the countryside and I have been doing some sketching, and I believe there are some splendid views here, or so we have been told. Perhaps you could tell us where we may go?"

The landlord chuckled. "Why, sir, I reckon wherever you look you will see something to suite your fancy; though it's a mite surprising to some folks to know others want to draw pictures on paper."

"That's easy to explain," said Maxwell swiftly. "It is to keep the view for all time. Memories can fade but pictures do not; and we may never be in this part again."

Dashell stared at him in amazement while Prunty scratched his head and then began to name some places. "Now, sirs," he said when he could think of no more, "just call me if you need any more ale."

"Maxwell, my lad," said Dashell, still staring at him, "I am discovering more and more about you all the time."

Maxwell grinned back at him. "I have been surprising myself sometimes."

They finished their ale. "Let's go outside while we can," said Dashell, "the sky is getting darker and it looks like rain," and they went out into the damp, fresh air.

They walked casually towards the church which was a little distance away, and what folks were about turned and stared at them. Maxwell looked around to get the best angle from which to draw but realized he was too close but was not able to stand away for a longer view, so he began to draw the old Norman entrance archway instead.

Dashell watched him for a few minutes then moved away and started looking carefully at the old headstones. It was only a small churchyard and it did not take him long to walk round, and he eventually came to the darker, north side of the church, out of view of the village. It was here that the sight of two headstones brought him to an abrupt halt. He felt his face turn pale. Here was the reason why the two of them had come all this way, so their journey had not been in vain. He looked at them in silence and then went back to Maxwell, who promptly stopped what he was doing and followed his brother over to them. "Look at these," said Dashell, his voice expressionless.

They both stood in silence and regarded the two headstones, each with the barest of lettering. The first was inscribed, "Arthur Waterton, bart," and the date of death underneath, and the other inscription was just "Edwards," with the same date underneath.

"So," said Dashell, "now we are getting closer to the truth. It shows that the charcoal rubbing of the memorial tablet the rector of Sutherfield sent to me was a deliberate lie. I am sure of it. The question is—why?"

A sudden chill in the air caused by the sun going behind a cloud left them in the shadows. "Give me a few minutes while I sketch them," said Maxwell, "while there is still enough light.

"All right," said Dashell, "and when you have finished we will go back to the inn and see how much our friend the landlord knows about this."

By the time they returned the sky had darkened even more and it was beginning to rain. Glad to be indoors again in the cheery room, Dashell ordered some more ale.

When Prunty brought it to them he asked, "Will you two gentlemen be requiring rooms for the night? There is another storm brewing and the next inn is some miles away."

Dashell sensed the man was being honest rather then just trying to detain them. He also felt Prunty was almost hoping for their company. Now here was his chance, he must encourage Prunty to talk willingly, for if he suspected his guests were here for this purpose he might not be so ready to say anything. He took a mouthful of ale, and then a deep breath, "Prunty, I am intrigued about something. In the churchyard we saw two headstones with the barest of inscriptions. They looked bare and stark as though nothing else was known about them."

"Strange you should say that, sir," replied the landlord carefully, "for that is absolutely true. There was an accident round about here some eighteen years or so ago, almost to the day in fact"—which remark sent a chill through his two listeners—"but it is a long story."

"Then join us in some ale," said Dashell lightly but with beating heart. "There is plenty of time, for we will take your advice and stay the night."

"Why, thank you, sir." He went away and came back with a tankard and settled himself down. A sudden gust of wind lashed the rain against the windows. "There won't be many folks about tonight, I can tell you that," he remarked.

"It was a time like this," he began, "only much worse, eighteen years ago, and it seems to me it has rained every year about this time ever since, and laugh at me if you wish. It's a lonely place on this road and folk don't travel much in one direction or another. A stagecoach comes through twice a week and back again. There are sometimes post and private vehicles but not enough to rely on for steady trade. In fact there's nowt much about except sheep. That particular day this gentleman by the name of Waterton stopped here for a meal for himself and his coachman. A very pleasant young gentleman, well-spoken, rather like yourselves, sirs, if I may be so bold to say so. It had rained every day for a week, as it can in these parts, and longer at times, and a strong east wind with it. I told the gentleman it was not going to let up and it would be a bad night, and he very reluctantly agreed to stay. By late morning the clouds did clear away, but only for a while, and he insisted on continuing his journey."

"Did he say what he was doing here?" queried Dashell, as Prunty paused to take a drink.

"Oh, no, sir. If a traveller does not wish to say what he is doing, that's his business, and it's not for me to ask. So the carriage drove off, with a very smart pair of red roans, by the way. About an hour later the storm returned with even more force, with such amounts of rain that one wondered where all the water came from, and I knew the coachman would have trouble keeping the horses' heads into that wind. As the carriage did not return I assumed they had made their way to the next place; and that's what I said at the inquest. By evening time the sky had cleared and some folks turned up at the inn and all we could talk about was the weather. It was getting late when a young lad panting hard from running, burst in among us with the news that part of the hill, which you passed on the way here, had collapsed and was blocking the road."

"You mean a landslide," said Dashell. "Yes, we did see the wide gap as we passed."

"Aye, that's right," continued Prunty, "and because the road was blocked we had to do something about it. There is another way round to get here but it adds fifteen miles more. I remember we all stared at the lad at first, then those who had brought lanterns with them ran outside to see for themselves. Even the vicar, who sometimes came in for a pint, came with us. I seized my own lantern and hastened down the road with the others for a mile or so, and there it was. The earth must have become so sodden with water it could not hold any more, and it collapsed, like the young lad said."

The landlord paused to take another drink but he had already emptied his tankard.

"Here, fills yours again and ours too, landlord," invited Dashell.

"Thank you, sir, very generous of you." He returned with the three tankards on a small tray and sat down to continue his story.

"The next part I shall never forget. Never. There we were, swinging our lanterns, trying to see as best we could in the dark, when someone saw something glinting in the light of his lantern. Curious, he took a closer look and found it to be a piece of metal and pushed away the mud to see what it could be, then stepped back with a terrible cry."

Prunty paused for effect and looked at the other two who had been listening to every word. "It was a horseshoe."

"A horseshoe?"

Prunty nodded. "Yes, a horseshoe. We were all shaken. Then the vicar strode forward and pushed away the mud from the hoof up to the knee. With the light from lanterns we could make out a white fetlock and the roan colouring. Then we all looked at the rear and yes, there was part of the rim of a wheel showing. We found later the axle had been broken, causing the wheel to slant outwards. Nobody moved at first. We were all struck dumb as though we had lost our wits. Then we all slowly backed away in fear as we realized what lay buried under the silent tons of mud, for we heard neither cry nor movement. From the position of the carriage it was obvious it was returning here, and by what terrible misfortune it passed the hill just when it could no longer hold."

Neither Dashell nor Maxwell could speak at first. "Dear heavens," said Dashell at last, "what a terrible tragic story. I can hardly believe it."

"How awful for the people in the carriage," murmured Maxwell, "to die like that."

"There was only the gentleman, and his coachman. There was never anyone else with them." Prunty took another mouthful of ale and did not see the significant glance that flashed between the other two.

"What happened next?"

"Well," said Prunty, wiping his mouth with the back of his hand, "I don't mind telling you we were all afraid, myself included, as the full horror dawned upon us, but there was absolutely nothing we could do right there and then. I believe the vicar said a prayer for their souls, but maybe some wondered what good that might do. So folks returned to their homes with many a fearful backward glance, and we just had to wait for daylight.

"It was truly amazing how word got around. Men came from all directions to help clear the road with buckets and shovels and carts to take away the mud, and some even came with wheelbarrows. It was hard work moving tons of mud like that and it took several days to really clear the road. The womenfolk helped too, with hot soup and pies for the workers. We had to notify the local authorities what had happened, and word was sent out for anyone travelling to take the longer road round. That caused some grumbling from some unkind folks, but there you are.

"Well, eventually the two dead horses were removed and the carriage pulled away, it had been crushed by the sheer weight of mud and rocks on top of it. Then the two bodies were removed. First the coachman, still holding the reins, and then the other one, and were taken into my barn. With the vicar, the coroner from York, the local doctor and myself present, we looked through their pockets for papers and actually found very few, and what we did find was so sodden they were too difficult to read properly. I gave evidence by showing the book all guests have to sign if staying overnight. The entries were 'Arthur Waterton, bart., and coachman.' There was no name given for him, but my man gave sworn evidence he had twice heard the gentleman address his coachman as "Edwards." The carriage was private, no name painted on it that a hired one might have. So that was all we knew."

Prunty paused as though all this talking had made him thirsty. "Everything was removed from their pockets, together with any valuables, and put under lock and key in the church vestry, and the two bodies were given decent burial at the expense of the parish. It was all we could do; and then we wondered how long we would have to wait."

"Wait?" echoed Dashell, surprised

"Aye, to wait and see if anyone came enquiring about an overdue carriage. More than a month later two men did come, agents they said they were, enquiring about a private carriage owned by a certain gentleman, but they never said who they were acting for. They had made enquiries all the way up to York and beyond, going north and east, and then tried the west road. Well, we told them what had happened, that the carriage appeared to have come from Ripon and had started towards York on that particular day. We showed them the scar on the hillside, and where we had buried them, and gave them everything we had kept under lock and key, including the death certificates for each of them which the local doctor had written. They were told of the expenses the parish had paid, and they repaid every single penny. Apart from all that, they never said a word." Prunty sat back as he finished speaking, while the other two looked at him.

"That is an incredible story," said Dashell finally, which was all he could think of saying at the moment. "And is that the end?"

"Aye, except for one thing I thought rather strange, but maybe not. No order was ever given for better headstones and there was plenty of room for more lettering, which I am sure you saw for yourself. Neither at the time nor later. It was as though they were forgotten."

"I must congratulate you, Prunty," said Dashell, "for such a detailed account after so long a time. How well you remembered it all."

"Aye, and it still haunts me. Eighteen years ago almost to the day, as I said. Not many people will be about tonight, not with all this rain. There are still some superstitious folk who will not go near that part of the road in the dark and others swear they have heard the sound of a carriage and pair passing by."

All three men fell silent feeling anything more said would be inappropriate, Dashell and Maxwell in particular. What a coincidence they should be in the very inn where Sir Arthur had stayed and at this very time. It was uncanny.

Prunty slapped his hands on his knees as he got to his feet. "Well, gentlemen, I have taken up too much of your time, but somehow I feel better for having spoken about it. If you are staying the night would you like to be shown to your rooms?"

"Not yet," smiled Dashell. "In fact we are too comfortable to move, we will stay here a while longer."

"Very well. We have chess and cribbage to help you while away the time. I will fetch them for you." He went away and returned with the game boards and boxes, and they watched as he stirred up the fire and put more wood on it before leaving the room.

Neither of the two men moved at first, still thinking of all they had heard. Dashell stayed in his chair but pulled up another one to rest his feet on, leaned back and laced his hands behind his head. "Poor devil," he said at last.

"You mean Waterton?"

"Yes. And how am I to tell Caroline? First her mother, then her sister, and now this; as if she has not suffered enough already; and they all died unnatural deaths." He fell to musing that he was about the same age as Waterton when he had died, and somehow that made it worse.

Maxwell tried to think of something sympathetic to say but could only wonder about the missing death certificates, at least the one for Sir Arthur. "Someone has it, for sure," he finished rather lamely. A few minutes later he pulled out his sketch pad and began to go through each page touching up here and there, just for something to do. "What do we do now?" he asked. "We have done what we came to do."

"Keep you voice down," urged Dashell. "I hope the weather clears up and we can leave in the morning. If not, we may have to stay another day." His eye caught sight of the cribbage box. "Care for a game of cribbage?"

So they whiled away their time until Prunty came and asked whether they would like cold mutton for supper or hot beef pie just out of the oven. They both chose the beef pie. After they had eaten they returned to the cribbage but in a half-hearted manner. Dashell could not concentrate and finally said he had had enough. "Let's go outside and get some fresh air before we turn in for the night." They sauntered along breathing in the cool air, thankful it had stopped raining. Unconsciously their steps took them towards the church.

"I never finished sketching that archway," said Maxwell suddenly, "and somehow I don't really want to. Not now."

They turned and retraced their steps, passing the inn for a short distance and stood looking west along the lonely road that led over the moors. "You know," remarked Dashell, "we may never know why Waterton was up here in Yorkshire."

"Well, it must have been something important," replied Maxwell sensibly. "Come on, I'm going back."

The next morning the weather promised fair. "What do you think, Prunty?" they asked when they ordered their breakfast.

The landlord had already cast a practiced look outside. "I think it will hold for the day, gentlemen."

"We will leave in an hour's time then. Would you have our horses ready for us."

When they had paid their way and were ready to leave, Prunty came out to bid them farewell and was thanked for his hospitality, and Dashell led the way out of the courtyard.

Unbeknown to them Prunty had stood and watched the riders until they were out of sight with a somewhat puzzled frown, and fingered his chin thoughtfully. No other travellers had ever gone to the churchyard and then asked about the headstones, even if they knew they were there. Time passes and memories can fade, except his had not. It was quite true what he had said: that the event still haunted him, it would not go away but remained clear in his mind every time this year. But this time it was different; relating the events in great detail to listeners who really wanted to hear had taken a load off his mind. Or was it he had to retain it all in mind until such a time as this? With a shake of his head he went back indoors; he had plenty to do.

The next day the two of them reached York during the afternoon. Once settled at an inn Dashell began to write a long letter to Lord Barrandale telling him what they had learned about the death of Sir Arthur, and that no one else was with him, except the coachman of course, and therefore someone had gone to the expense of having the damnable lying memorial tablet made.

"I say, Dashell," asked Maxwell, "do you think if I made up a package of my sketch pads they could go with your letter to Father? The pages are getting smudged from being carried around all the time."

Dashell did not know too much of such matters but Maxwell had been a real help. "All right, I suppose they could."

"Oh, thanks a lot. I'll go and get a new pad from the art shop I saw the other day."

"You are not planning on more sketching, are you?" demanded Dashell.

"Oh, no. I just like to have the feel of one with me."

Dashell shook his head with a sigh. "Don't be too long." He had finished his letter by the time Maxwell returned, who quickly wrote his own brief letter to enclose with his package.

During their evening meal Dashell asked, "What are you going to do with all your sketches anyway? You must have quite a number of them by now."

"I'll keep them. I can touch them up here and there before painting some of them or I can leave them as sketches. But I have dozens of ideas for country scenes. Some I can do from memory and others I can make up."

"Do you plan to make a living from all of this?" Dashell sounded quite interested.

"I did have that in mind," replied Maxwell slowly, "but do you remember the art master at Eton?"

"You mean old Creppan?" said Dashell

"Yes," replied Maxwell. "I went to call on him soon after I left Eton. He was very helpful but strongly suggested I found 'some visible means of support' as he put it. I tried doing what he said but did not get very far. I've discovered it's not easy, not for a fellow like me. For any profession it's Oxford, Oxford, all the time." He made that last remark without any trace of bitterness, which Dashell was quick to note. "I had the idea of trying banking," and related his experiences of applying for a position. "Thank goodness I did not accept, I would have hated it."

"So what will you do?"

"There is one option left as far as I can see, and that is the Law. If I could find a place as a clerk somewhere I could study law in my spare time."

"I think that sounds like an excellent idea."

"Ah yes, but the trouble is finding such a place."

"Have you thought of speaking to Father's solicitor in Windsor?" suggested Dashell. "He may be able to help you. He must have colleagues and associates in London."

Maxwell stared at him. "No, I had not. But I will."

"Well, you are a damn fine fellow," said Dashell with conviction, "and you have got a brain, if some of the astute remarks you have come out with lately are anything to go by, so I think you should do well."

"Aw," muttered Maxwell awkwardly. "What are the plans for returning?" he asked, anxious to change the subject.

"With all speed, yet with care," said Dashell. "Leave early, stop at midday, and stay somewhere for the night. Probably the same places we stayed at on the journey up. The last thing I want to do is over-extend the horses, especially Lively, because a lame horse can take a while to recover. They have both been bearing up remarkably well and I could almost say they have enjoyed it." His face darkened as he said, "Then when we return we will see what Aunt Letty has been able to find out about Caroline's next-of-kin. And then, once we know—" He left the sentence unfinished, while Maxwell shifted in his seat.

CHAPTER FIFTEEN

Caroline at Farling House

Caroline had been looking forward to staying in the countryside, and the knowledge that there would be pleasant walks appealed to her a great deal, and Mrs. Farling was kindness itself and made her feel quite welcome; but the situation did not quite turn out as she had hoped or thought.

Lady Smythe stayed the night they arrived and all the next day, and left the following afternoon. The two ladies had known each other for years and naturally had plenty to talk about, and it amused Caroline to hear peals of laughter from them.

Left to themselves she and Hannah would walk around the garden or sit by the ornamental pond and watch the fish. It was quiet and peaceful and Caroline could indulge herself freely with thoughts of Dashell. Confident now he really did love her she allowed herself to love him in return. It did a great deal for her well-being and hastened the recovery of her spirits.

When the time came for Lady Smythe to leave she declared she could see an improvement in Caroline already. "We will soon see the roses in your cheeks again, my dear," and Caroline smiled as she and Mrs. Farling waved her goodbye.

Both Caroline and Hannah had planned to repair at least one of the torn dresses but soon realized it would not be possible. Perhaps it was foolish to have brought even one with them.

Both of them liked to have some kind of sewing on hand which was all right for Hannah, being a maidservant, but Mrs.Farling considered Caroline should be above that kind of thing, so Hannah was left to unpick and re-stitch by herself.

Caroline soon learned that Mrs.Farling was a talker, and kept up a flow of chatter while the other person sat and listened. She was one of those rare people whose chatter was both interesting and amusing, especially when recounting her times abroad and the places she had been to with her dear husband. Any other person could keep up a flow of talk and never say anything worthwhile at all.

"Caroline," Mrs.Farling would say, "You must rest or we will never see those roses in your cheeks, and what would Lady Smythe think about that? Now, as I was saying..." and so she would rattle on. Caroline sighed to herself, feeling it was going to be a long month, yet she also felt Mrs.Farling was rather lonely; and to be quite honest, she found her to be quite likeable.

Hannah came to her rescue by suggesting they go out for daily walks. "At least it will take you away from her," she whispered.

"I was thinking the same myself," chuckled Caroline in return.

In the evening they would play cards or read or Caroline would play the piano, to her hostess' delight. Mrs. Farling would occasionally ask Caroline about herself, but she was a talker and not a listener, and Caroline hardly had time to say a few words before she was off again. And so the days passed.

Then by chance Caroline remarked she loved to do embroidery and Mrs. Farling promptly said she had some unfinished pieces, ones she had put away after her dear husband died and not touched since. Then perhaps you would prefer they were left? asked Caroline. Oh, no, was the reply, choose whichever one you fancy to finish stitching.

So Caroline went to look for them. There was an unfinished pair of men's slippers in petit point which must have been meant for Mr. Farling, and of course her mind flew immediately to Dashell and she smiled at the thought of stitching a pair for him one day. However, she put them aside as Mrs.,Farling might be surprised to see her bring them out. There was a cushion cover with an almost completed floral scene, also in petit point; and a flamboyant Jacobean panel of flowers and leaves designed more to show off intricate stitches and the skill of the needlewoman than any accuracy of foliage. The last was a set of six table napkins, with one still to be hemmed. Caroline was a little surprised at so much unfinished work put away but it went with Mrs. Farling's personality. She decided to hem the last napkin.

In time it was finished, and likewise the petit point floral cushion cover. This alone brought forth a torrent of words of wonder that Caroline was such an accomplished needlewoman. She smiled her thanks and made a start on the Jacobean crewel work.

She had to sort out the wools and more needles than seemed necessary. Mrs. Farling was not exactly tidy when it came to threads and needles. Caroline was doing this after luncheon one rainy day when Mrs. Farling had retired to her room for her usual nap. She too felt a little drowsy and her eyes closed for a few minutes, until Mrs. Farling suddenly burst into the room declaring she had forgotten this was the day her brother said he would call and have afternoon tea with her. He was several years older than his sister, and called once in a while when his health permitted.

Caroline, startled out of her reverie, hastily gathered up her needlework and put it aside. "Do you wish me to stay, ma'am?" she asked.

"Of course you may stay, child," cried a flustered Mrs. Farling. "Why should you need to leave?"

Mr. Talbot duly arrived, a tall thin-faced, but kindly man, and his sister gave him a warm welcome with a flow of words. "I am keeping as well as I can, Ellie, my dear," he managed to say eventually.

His sister barely heard him as she wished to introduce Caroline. "This is Miss Caroline Waterton, Harold. I believe I did tell you I had a young lady staying with me."

"Ah, Miss Waterton. Charmed, I'm sure." He smiled as they shook hands.

"I am pleased to meet you too, sir," replied Caroline gravely.

"Harold, do come and sit down instead of standing about."

Mr. Talbot obediently did so and promptly gave a startled cry as he sat on a needle.

Caroline knew at once what had happened. "Mr. Talbot! I am so sorry! I must have left a needle on the chair. Please forgive me."

"My dear Miss Waterton," he said gallantly, as he picked it up and handed it to her, "think no more of it."

However, Mrs. Farling cried out, "Caroline! How could you be so careless?"

Caroline, mortified, put the needle with the rest of her work and took the workbag upstairs and did not join the others until tea time, as she knew Mr. Talbot wished to discuss something with Mrs. Farling. She was impressed at Mr. Talbot's ability to handle his sister's chatter, and at the same time tactfully drawing her into the conversation.

The time came for him to leave. "Goodbye, Miss Waterton. I am delighted to have made your acquaintance," he said with a gentle smile.

"And I too, Mr. Talbot," Caroline replied, thinking him a very kind old man.

Two women stood at the front door to wave him off, and Mrs. Farling had a worried frown on her face. "I am a little concerned about him," she confided to Caroline, "his health is not too good."

So the days continued. Mrs.Farling chatted away, "I do so enjoy your company, Caroline, my dear," while Caroline listened patiently, as she was beginning to realise Mrs. Farling was lonely.

One morning a letter arrived from Dashell to Caroline's delight. She read it through quickly but the contents were not what she expected; in fact they gave her quite a shock. In his previous letter Dashell had told her he was making further enquiries but did not say exactly what or where, and now he said he had found out how her father had died, in Yorkshire. Dashell had gone all that way on her behalf? And how did he know to go there anyway? More mystery. Would there never be an end to it all? Caroline handed the letter to Hannah for her to read.

"Oh, Miss Caroline, whatever does all this mean?" she wondered, as she finished.

"I don't know, Hannah," replied Caroline with a shake of her head. "I just don't know what to think. I find it all so unsettling."

They set out on one of their walks, Caroline still feeling astonished at the contents of that letter. Eventually she said, "Hannah, we have been here a month and I am beginning to think it is time for us to leave."

"You mean go back to Lady Smythe?"

"Yes, if that is possible. But we have no means of conveyance, nor could we afford to hire a carriage even if one was available. It would mean hoping Mrs. Farling would send us in her own carriage, and I cannot expect that."

They turned and retraced their steps with Caroline still deep in thought. Wishing to return to Grosvenor Square was one thing but she could not expect to stay there indefinitely either, and the only other place she could go to was the house on Becket Lane.

That house, so empty now; what could she do with her time there, because she had to do something. Then a flash of inspiration came to her. She stopped short, her face alight. "Hannah! I have just had a most wonderful idea! We will go back to Becket Lane!"

Hannah, startled out of her own thoughts, almost screeched, "Go back there!"

"Yes, Hannah. Now listen. We originally planned to leave because of Step-papa but now he is no longer there we need not be afraid to go back. We could live there again quite well. I could teach singing and piano playing just like Mother used to do and perhaps some of her old pupils might return. And another thing, it was given out that I went to stay with friends when Step-papa died but nobody knew where or for how long. Now people would think nothing of our return."

Hannah listened in joyful surprise. "Ooh, Miss Caroline, do you think we could?"

"I don't see why not," declared Caroline. "We could sell some of the furniture to get a little money; and if that house now belongs to me it could also be sold and we find a smaller, more convenient one."

They stopped walking and faced each other, for by now Hannah had caught Caroline's enthusiasm. "Oh, Miss Caroline, I think it is wonderful. The only thing is: how do we get to Becket Lane?"

That broke the dream at once. Caroline wondered what she was going to say to Mrs. Farling about wishing to leave, while at the same time Hannah wondered what Lord Lonsdale might have to say about Miss Caroline's plans for her future, after declaring she was not to set foot in that house again.

Mrs. Farling had been anxiously waiting for her return. "Caroline, my dear," she cried as soon as Caroline entered the room, "Do come and sit down. I must speak to you. Oh, dear,

I hardly know where to begin, and it is such a shame, and—oh, dear," she said again, becoming more flustered.

Caroline was surprised that Mrs. Farling had something say and yet could not say it. Usually the words just flowed. "Is everything all right, ma'am?" she asked anxiously.

"Oh, yes, I think so. It's just that it's happened so quickly and yet I had been half expecting it. Mr. Talbot and I did discuss it when he was here the other day, so I must speak to you." She took a deep breath and began. "Shortly after you left this morning Mr. Talbot's groom brought me a letter from him. I believe I told you Mr. Talbot has not been in good health for some time and he has now decided to come and live with me. He did ask me to live with him but I said no because his house is rather draughty and I don't really like it and his garden is not so nice either, so he has agreed to come here. He sold his house sooner than he thought he would, with a great deal of furniture with it, because he did have a very good offer. He will be coming within a few days and will be bringing his manservant with him as he needs a lot of attention. Caroline, my dear, I hate to say this because I have so enjoyed your company, but I will have to ask you to leave. I am so very sorry, and I hope you will understand. I will of course write to Lady Smythe and explain to her why you are leaving so soon."

When at last Mrs. Farling paused for breath, Caroline was able to express her sympathy towards Mr. Talbot, and to say of course she understood, and that she had enjoyed her stay here very much.

"Thank you, my dear, I knew you would understand. It is such a relief to know."

After luncheon Mrs. Farling had her usual nap, and for Caroline this was an answer to prayer almost before she had even asked, although she felt a pang of guilt for thinking that way. But Dashell might come and wonder why she had gone so soon; and she could not possibly ask to stay a few days longer in case he did come.

"Hannah! You will never guess!" she began, when she went upstairs to her room and told her the news, and ended by saying that the carriage had been ordered for them at two o'clock tomorrow. "We had better start packing. It won't take us long anyway"

The last evening was a little difficult as Mrs. Farling talked almost non-stop and Caroline tried to be patient; yet she was touched when Mrs.Farling asked if she would like to keep the crewel panel she had been working on. "Please do. It will remind you of your stay here and I know I shall never finish it," so it too was packed away in a box.

The next day the carriage was ready at two o'clock with boxes strapped on and smaller things put inside. Mrs.Farling gave Caroline a letter for Lady Smythe as she said she would, and said goodbye, kissing Caroline most warmly. "I did so enjoy your company" she said again. "It was wonderful to have someone to talk to."

Caroline just smiled sweetly and said she has enjoyed her stay too, and hoped Mr. Talbot's health would improve, "Please give him my regards."

"Don't forget to write to me!" Mrs.Farling called out as the carriage moved away.

"I will. I promise," Caroline called back as she leaned out of the window, thankful the goodbyes had not been too prolonged.

CHAPTER SIXTEEN

Dashell Calls
at Farling House

E ven though Dashell was anxious to return, they travelled carefully, sometimes walking the horses. They stayed at some of the same inns again, feeling gratified when various jovial, yet shrewd, innkeepers said they were good at remembering faces. Dashell wrote again to his father saying all was well and that he would call on Caroline when they reached St. Albans, and then ride on to Windsor.

He hesitated before beginning another letter to Caroline herself, yet it was time he did so. He explained again that Sir Arthur Waterton had died in Yorkshire and had been buried in the churchyard of a little village called Skorrcliff, and that he and his brother Maxwell had travelled up there to find out the facts for themselves. "I will explain more when next I see you."

They reached the White Hart Inn at St. Albans one day in time for luncheon; and Maxwell was delighted to be told he could spend all next day "scribbling away to his heart's content," as Dashell put it. "You have been a real help, besides being a staunch companion."

Maxwell felt embarrassed at these words, yet admitted he had enjoyed the ride. "And as we are at St. Albans I can guess you will call on Miss Waterton."

That was exactly what Dashell had in mind to do, except he would make himself wait until after luncheon as it would be more the proper time, and then he would be asked to stay for tea. The question was how to occupy his time until then; there was not much a gentleman could do except to wander round the Abbey and the Roman ruins.

At last it was time for him to ride to Farling House, after enquiring where it might be. He was on a hired horse, leaving his own to enjoy another day's rest with his stable companion. Upon arrival at the house he was informed by the maidservant that Miss Waterton had returned to Grosvenor Square. He was greatly surprised at this for he had been so looking forward to seeing Caroline again for her own sake, yet saddened at the news he would have to tell her. Then he realized it was a month or more since he had escorted his aunt's carriage on the way to this house, but Caroline had been assured she could stay as long as she wished.

"Perhaps I may speak to Mrs. Farling," he said at last to the maidservant.

"What name shall I say, sir?" A few moments later he was ushered into the pleasant sunny parlour. "Lord Lonsdale, ma'am," said the maid.

"Oh, oh," began a flustered Mrs. Farling. "Do please sit down, Lord Lonsdale. Would you care for some tea?"

"Thank you," said Dashell as he sat down. "I am sorry to call upon you unexpectedly, Mrs. Farling. I had hoped to see Miss Waterton but I understand she is not here."

"No, Lord Lonsdale. She left at my request. She's such a dear girl. I allowed her the use of my carriage. Oh, dear, it was all so embarrassing. I wonder if I shall ever live it down. I do hope Lady Smythe will not be too angry. Why, we have been friends for years."

All these somewhat contradictory statements came out so fast it caused confusion to Dashell himself. "Mrs. Farling, do you know if Caroline received a letter from me the other day?"

"A letter? Oh, yes she did. And that was part of the problem." Mrs. Farling was compelled to stop talking when the maid brought in the tea things, giving Dashell time to wonder how his letter was a problem. When the maid left Mrs. Farling made an attempt to pull herself together. "I can understand why she was so mortified. I know I was."

By now Dashell was getting more confused, and he wanted to know how his letter had upset Caroline. "Mrs. Farling," he stated firmly, "would you please let me know what has been going on? When did all this happen anyway?"

"Yesterday. Oh no, it was the day before. It was yesterday she left." She looked at the rather formidable young man seated opposite her, albeit rather tired looking and travel worn, and with a frown on his face. "My brother came to tea the other day to discuss something with me."

"And that is why she wanted to leave?" Dashell asked incredulously.

"Oh, no, I asked her to do so. And she is such a dear girl. I felt rather bad about it."

Once more Dashell felt himself getting confused, but Mrs. Farling did go on to explain. "My brother came to visit me because he is not in good health and he has agreed to come and live with me here. He wanted to come within the next few days, with his manservant, so, you understand, I had to ask her to leave. She quite understood as I knew she would, and I also thought she might be embarrassed to meet my dear Harold again—or should it be the other way round?—anyway he was very good about the whole thing."

"Good about what," Dashell asked, as he felt that familiar confused feeling coming over him again.

"Oh, didn't I tell you? She was doing some needlework—and she is so accomplished—but somehow a needle was left on a chair—and Harold sat on it—and that's why she was embarrassed at her carelessness. I know Harold was—although he treated it so lightly, but he is such a gentleman—and that was why she was so mortified."

Dashell stood up and placed his cup and saucer on the tray, trying not to laugh, feeling the only way to pacify Mrs. Farling was to leave. "You have been very kind, Mrs. Farling. I am sure Caroline did enjoy her stay here with you."

"Yes, she did. She told me so."

Dashell made his way back to the White Hart Inn to find Maxwell was already there.

"How was your day?" he asked.

"Quite good," answered Maxwell. "I got a lot done, but it was tiring standing much of the time and then going to the next place. How was yours? How was Miss Waterton?"

"I did not see her. She left for London yesterday. Poor Caroline, staying a whole month with Mrs. Farling. She got me quite confused, yet I rather liked her," then began to laugh at the humour of it as he explained it all to Maxwell. "Well," he continued. "One more night and then we will be at Windsor. I shall never forget our ride, and apart from the reason for it, it has all been a wonderful experience."

"Nor will I," agreed Maxwell. "We saw places we would never have seen otherwise, and spoke to people we would never have met, either. I will always remember that wonderful old stage driver we met at some inn we stayed at, who could quote whole passages from Shakespeare. Richard II, for instance, and Henry

V. He said he often did that when on the road, as he put it. He was a man after my own heart."

"Maxwell," said Dashell, "he was almost old enough to be your grandfather."

"I know," said Maxwell doggedly.

The next morning, their journey's last, was grey and overcast and threatened rain but they were too close to home to worry about it. It was an easy ride of just over twenty miles, and even the horses sensed where they were.

Dashell seemed particularly preoccupied, especially as he was disappointed not to have seen Caroline. There was indeed something on his mind which had to be put right. Twice he had declared he and Caroline were betrothed when in actual fact they were not, at least not yet. He had once asked her to marry him but she had slept all through his proposal—and how he would tease her about that!—so the next time he would make sure she was wide awake. That made him smile and he sighed out of pure joy.

That caught Maxwell's attention and he saw the smile on Dashell's face, and thought *the old lad must be at it again*.

It was not long before they were walking their horses along the poplar-lined avenue leading to Barrandale Park and eventually into the stableyard. James came out to greet them, as Sparkle and Lively were led to their familiar stalls., "We have had a wonderful ride, but I think they are glad to be home, too," said Dashell. "I know you will look after them, James."

"Aye, I will, your lordship," he replied as he ran a practiced eye over them.

Inside the house Simmonds also welcomed their homecoming. "Anything happened during our absence?" enquired Dashell.

"The new trainer, Samuel Cullen, came some days ago, sir," replied Simmonds. "He was brought here by the young carter,

Faulkner, who has also been here quite a few times taking items away."

"Has there been anything from his lordship?"

"No, sir, nothing at all."

An hour later after Dashell and Maxwell had refreshed themselves and changed into clean clothing and had something to eat, they were sitting relaxing in the entrance hall. Even after a footman had taken the trays away they stayed where they were, savouring the fact they were home.

"What are your plans for tomorrow?" asked Maxwell.

"I shall go to London and tell Father everything, and then call on Aunt Letty to see what she has been able to find out about Caroline's next-of-kin; and Caroline is bound to be there. What will you do?"

"Well, I would like to come with you but I'm not sure I can. I want to follow up this idea of calling on Father's solicitors in Windsor, and there's no point in going to London just to come back again, because once I get to London it could be a long while before I come back, even after finding some 'visible means of support'. It's all right for you," he added, grinning at Dashell, "you don't have to worry about your future. Oh, by the way," he went on quickly before Dashell could say anything, "if a package is made up of all my art materials, can they be taken to London?"

"I am sure they can," replied Dashell, "Simmonds will arrange it for you. I suppose everything will eventually go to the new house in South Kensington. It will seem strange going there after going to Park Lane for so long. Nor will it be so convenient to visit Aunt Letty."

Maxwell stood up, declaring he was going to his room to sort out everything.

Dashell took the opportunity to summon Simmonds, and after a brief discussion they went together to where the remaining family jewels were locked away. Dashell watched while Simmonds unlocked a wall cabinet and lifted down the jewel box and records book and put them on a table, unlocked and opened the box and then stood to one side.

"I am looking for the late Lady Barrandale's ring, the one with the pearls and rubies," stated Dashell.

"Indeed, sir?" Simmonds knew the story behind that particular ring and why Lord Lonsdale requested it.

Dashell picked out the ring and waited while Simmonds entered its removal in the record book and the date. Simmonds then placed the book on top of the locked jewel box and returned both to the cabinet.

"May I enquire if congratulations are in order, sir?"

"Not yet, Simmonds, but I have every confidence they will be; but in the meantime do not say anything."

"Very good, your lordship," replied Simmonds with a slight bow.

CHAPTER SEVENTEEN

The Next Day

The next morning Dashell left for London riding one of the mares, for Sparkle and Lively had been put out to grass for a rest. Lively, for one, needed it before resuming serious training.

Maxwell had gone into Windsor and his first call was to the picture framer who had taken two of his paintings and agreed to display them for him. Great was his delight to learn that both of them had been sold.

"Yes, indeed, Mr. Romford," the framer had beamed at him, "I was quite surprised myself. The gentleman who bought the local scene was quite taken with it; and the other painting was purchased as a wedding present for a niece. I must congratulate you on such as auspicious beginning. It must be quite encouraging for you."

Maxwell was thrilled as payment was handed over to him. "It certainly is," he agreed warmly. It was many years before he learned that both paintings had been bought by Mr. Creppan; the framer also being part of the conspiracy.

He now stepped with confidence into the premises of his father's solicitors. A clerk a few years older than himself asked him his business and Maxwell carefully explained what he was about and asked to speak to one of the gentleman.

"What name shall I say, sir?" and Maxwell told him. "One moment, if you please." There was a murmured conversation in one of the rooms, then the clerk came out. "Would you please come in, Mr. Romford."

An elderly gentleman seated behind a desk smiled pleasantly at Maxwell. "Do sit down, young sir. Am I correct in thinking you are one of Lord Barrandale's sons?"

"Yes, sir," replied Maxwell as they shook hands. "I am."

"Ah, I have known your father for many years. And how may I help you? My clerk informs me you are making enquiries about studying for the Law."

"Yes, sir, that is my intention. Perhaps you could give me some advice on how to go about it." So the two of them talked together for a while, only this time Maxwell made no mention of painting in his spare time.

He must have made a favourable impression for he emerged from the premises with a letter of introduction entitled: 'To Whom It May Concern.' "There are no vacancies here, Mr. Romford," the solicitor had said, "but establishments in London are always looking out for bright young men like you. I am sure my letter will help you."

"Thank you, sir, very much." Maxwell went outside feeling that at last events were turning in his favour. He even managed to get a seat on the stage leaving later that day.

Dashell made good time to Park Lane, anxious to impart all the news to his father, whom he knew would be just as keen to hear it. When he clattered into the stableyard it was Reuben who took the mare's reins, surprised to see it was not Sparkle.

"Where is Stephen?" Dashell asked, surprised in his turn not to see him.

"He is helping to move items to the new house, sir," Reuben informed him.

Once inside the house Dashell went quickly to see his father, thinking that he always seemed to be there when needed, a fact he had observed many a time in the past. Matthew also welcomed him back and was ready to announce him, but Dashell said he would announce himself.

Barrandale looked up as the door opened. "Dashell!" he cried warmly and got to his feet to greet him. "Welcome! When did you get back?"

"Yesterday," he replied as they greeted each other.

"And Maxwell? Where is he?"

"He stayed at Windsor, complaining of being saddle-sore," replied Dashell, then explained what his brother was really doing.

Barrandale laughed. "He certainly does not let the grass grow under his feet. But I am anxious to hear all your news. By the way, thank you for your letters. I found them most interesting, besides putting my mind at rest."

Each one settled down in his favourite chair and Dashell began relating their adventures. "To begin with, sir, our journey was not in vain as we did find out what had happened to Sir Arthur Waterton. He and his coachman are indeed buried in the churchyard of Skorrcliff village church, and they died tragically. Here are the sketches Maxwell did of the two headstones."

Barrandale studied them long and carefully as though trying to glean what he could from them. "How empty and bare they look, as though nothing else was known about them," and listened while Dashell explained that was precisely the case.

Dashell went on to say, "So now we know for sure that the memorial in Sutherfield church was a deliberate and damnable lie. But I have so much more to tell you," and for an hour or so he spoke of their adventures, concluding with, "I would not have missed that ride for anything, apart for the reason, and nor would Maxwell. By the way, I am glad he came as my companion, it would have been lonely without him; and he asked me to tell you that he returned Lively to the Windsor stables 'undamaged.' He would also like to know if his sketches arrived safely."

"Yes, they did. Matthew put them in his room."

"Goodness knows how many others he has got."

Barrandale smiled at that. "Now, if you have finished, at least for the time being, I have a great deal to tell you for your aunt was able to find out about Caroline's next-of-kin. I dined with her one evening recently at her request and she told me in precise detail who they are."

Dashell sat up with sharp interest at Barrandale's words. "And who are they?"

"To begin with," began Barrandale, "there seem to be few relatives on either side of the family, which I find remarkable when other people have so many they are almost tripping over each other. However, there were these two sisters, Catherine and Harriet. Harriet, the younger of the two, married Edward, youngest grandson of the then Duke of Fennshire, while Catherine married Lord Bretherton, a distant cousin of the Fennshires. Edward and Harriet both died, I'm not sure how or why, while their only child, Isobel, was still small, leaving her to be brought up by her Aunt Catherine, a scheming and very ambitious woman who used her relationship-by-marriage to the Fennshires to her own advantage."

"Ah," said Dashell slowly, "so that's why I thought I saw a faint likeness between Caroline and some 'family'; and it would have been the Fennshires. The present Duke's two sons had been at Oxford."

He reflected on that situation with extreme dismay. If Lord Runcorn, the elder of the two, and worse still, Lord Carley, learned of a related marriageable beauty in the offing, Caroline would not stand a chance. Lord Runcorn was reasonably all right, but the other—just to be seen with him would finish her. No woman was safe from Carley, nor some men, either. There had always been contention between Runcorn and his brother, the latter being extremely jealous of the other because he, Carley, was not the heir. Suspicious 'happenings' had occurred at intervals during their boyhood, although Carley always protested he had nothing to do with anything. He was quite a plausible liar. As Carley grew up he collected other unsavoury characters around him, and he began to be known as "Devil Carley" and became feared and loathed. He emphasized the fact by driving a coach with a team like the Four Horses of the Apocalypse—one white, one black, one grey, and one red chestnut. Surly animals, as though they knew why they were named Satan, Devil, Lucifer and Hellfire.

Dashell changed the subject by wondering about any other relatives.

"No more on that side apparently," continued Barrandale. "Isobel was an only child and her aunt Catherine never had any children of her own. Now, the Reverend Swanson in Sutherfield described the Waterton lineage in detail, ending with Sir Richard, a distant cousin of Sir Arthur. I do not think we will gain much more from him so there is no point in approaching him. However, there is one other person who may be of help. He is the brother of the late Lady Margaret Waterton, wife of Sir Godfrey, who were Sir Arthur's parents. So if Margaret was Arthur's mother, that means she is Caroline's paternal grandmother. Therefore this man is an uncle-by-marriage to Isobel, therefore a paternal great uncle to Caroline. His name is Sir Ryder Wyecross."

"Who?" cried Dashell. "That peppery old man! Are you sure?"

"Yes, Aunt Letty's informant was quite sure, and I grant he is not known to be an even-tempered person. But here is the great advantage: apparently he spent some considerable time with the

Watertons in his younger days so he would have known Isobel as a child. I should also explain that Arthur and Isobel lived near each other and grew up together, and they played with other local children. If I may so, approach this man first."

"I certainly will," said Dashell, "anything to avoid contacting the Fennshires. I would lose Caroline on the spot."

That very evening Dashell wrote a long but clear and detailed latter to Sir Ryder, and the next morning it was delivered to his house in Hampstead.

CHAPTER EIGHTEEN

Enter the Admiral

R ear Admiral Sir Ryder Wyecross, retired, was having luncheon with some of his former shipmates and officers, all of them weather-beaten old sea dogs. They did this two or three times a year, reminiscing and yarning about old times, and perhaps regret the passing of some fellow officer who had "slipped anchor" and silently drifted away. They were all good men, and if they heard that some widows or orphans needed a little financial assistance, they were perfectly ready to help them.

Sir Ryder was a shrewd judge of men; he should know, he had had enough of them under him over the years. He had his own way of doing it. In his mind he would picture them on the bridge of a warship in the midst of action and try to imagine them under fire and how they would react. He called this his "bridge test". He had joined the Royal Navy as a midshipman when aged fifteen and had made a brilliant career for himself. He had never married. Promotion could be fast in wartime for obvious reasons but he also earned it on his own merit and had served well under Lord Nelson at Trafalgar, and ended up with a knighthood.

He was a stocky well-built man, with heavy features tanned leathery by all kinds of weather. He did not suffer fools gladly and was known to be peppery-tempered, but the men who knew him would have sailed anywhere with him.

During luncheon there was time to talk of many things, and gradually the talk turned to world affairs and up-to-date news, and to any gossip gleaned from the newspapers.

"What's this rumour going around about Lord Barrandale?" said someone, who seemed to know of him. "I heard one of his sons, the second one I believe, had practically ruined the old fellow."

"Yes, that's right," said another. "The moneylenders gave him two weeks to repay all the debts and all kinds of things had to be sold. Property and goodness knows what else. Even the town house on Park Lane had to go, although another much smaller one was bought in South Kensington."

"South Kensington? That's a bit of a comedown, isn't it?"

"Anyway, that son was packed into the Army and sent off to India."

"Army?" snorted Sir Ryder, who had been listening to all this. "Army? Pah! The Army's useless. He should have been packed into the Navy and no mistake. I've seen any number of young 'uns straightened out. Did them the world of good, too,"

But the conversation persisted.

"And now I've heard that young Lonsdale, the heir, has got himself embroiled with some woman or other, but nobody can find out much about it. Nobody knows who or where she is."

Sir Ryder thought that if she was that sort of woman why would anyone want to know, unless they were that sort themselves.

"I believe there is a third son somewhere," said someone, still keeping the talk going.

"How many sons has this Lord Barrandale got?" demanded Sir Ryder. "Three! And he can't control any of them! The man's a fool."

"That's not so. My grandson knew the youngest one at Eton. He said he was a likeable fellow, and clever too."

Sir Ryder was not convinced and muttered something into his glass of port wine. He had had enough of Barrandale and his unruly brood anyway.

Consequently, when he returned to his house in Hampstead later and found Dashell's letter waiting for him, he let out a roar of complete bewilderment, incomprehension and sheer rage in a tone of voice that could have been heard above the sound of any storm or cannon; and promptly rang the bell for Tidmarsh, his long-suffering butler.

"This letter," he spluttered. "When did it come?"

"Shortly before noon, Sir Ryder," replied the man carefully. "A groom brought it."

Sir Ryder glared at the letter in his hand, still fuming. "My carriage immediately!" he bellowed.

Tidmarsh hastened to inform the coachman, warning him to be careful for the Admiral was in right royal rage about something.

Sir Ryder arrived at Barrandale House still enraged, clutching the open letter in his fist, the contents of which were beyond his comprehension. By George, he swore to himself, if this is some kind of cruel hoax I'll expose this Lord Lonsdale as a scoundrel, and this Lord Barrandale; and knocked loudly and angrily on the door.

The door was opened by a passive Matthew who had been earlier instructed that if a certain gentleman called he was to be shown in at once. He barely had time to announce, "Sir Ryder Wyecross," before the said gentleman strode in behind him, as father and son rose to their feet.

Sir Ryder was far too angry to consider manners. He glared from one to the other with a brief blink of surprise, for he had not expected two such well set-up men.

"I take it, sir, that you are Lord Barrandale," addressing the older one, "and that you, sir, are Lord Lonsdale," turning to the younger one. "How dare you write such a letter to me? What is the meaning of it? And how do you know so much about these people? I demand to know," shaking the fist which held the letter while he spoke. Then his eye caught sight of the portrait of Sir Arthur Waterton propped up on a chair. He almost blanched as he gave an audible gasp. "Where the devil did you get that portrait? I last saw it years ago in the Waterton household. How did you get hold if it?"

"Perhaps you should see this as well, Sir Ryder," began Dashell, showing him the charcoal rubbing the Reverend Swanson had sent.

"I recognize that too," snapped Sir Ryder. "It's a memorial tablet in the Sutherfield Parish Church."

"And these are the two sketches of the headstones of Sir Arthur and his coachman. They are buried in the churchyard of the village of Skorrcliff in Yorkshire."

"*What? In Yorkshire?* How do you know that?" snapped Sir Ryder again.

"My brother and I have just returned from Yorkshire. It was he who did the two sketches. We went to find out the truth."

"And what is that?" snapped the admiral for the third time.

"That the tablet is a lie, for Lady Isobel and her two daughters never travelled with Sir Arthur."

"What!" roared Sir Ryder, who was fast beginning to think that either he or the other two were taking leave of their senses.

"Sir Ryder," intervened Barrandale in his calm way of speaking, "we have obviously given you a great deal to think about. My son has a long, intriguing and rather strange story to tell you. May I suggest therefore that you stay and dine with us this evening. If you send your carriage away we will see you are driven to your door."

Sir Ryder, somewhat mollified, agreed, although he was still not fully convinced. "Just do not trifle with me nor waste my time," he growled as he sat down.

The bell was rung for Matthew who was given the necessary order and informed there would be one extra for dinner.

So once more Dashell related his story. "One afternoon when I was walking along Oxford Street…" while Sir Ryder listened carefully to every word.

By the time Dashell had finished Sir Ryder's attitude had changed. Shocked and aghast, he cried out, "Do you mean to tell me that Isobel and her girls have been *alive* all these years? It's impossible. Why should anyone declare them dead? What was the point?"

Dashell hesitated before answering. He glanced at his father, who gave a brief nod.

"My father and I have given this a great deal of thought and this is how it appears to us."

"Go on."

"We know that Isobel was brought up by her aunt, Lady Catherine Bretherton after her parents died, and this aunt was known to be a scheming, vindictive and ambitious woman, who would allow nothing and no one to stand in her way. If anyone did so or refused to agree to what she wanted she formed an implacable hatred for them. We know of her from other sources that she regarded herself as a marriage broker of some kind and moved people about like pawns, often with disastrous results. Many people's lives were ruined because they should never have married in the first place."

"Go on," said Sir Ryder again when Dashell paused for breath.

"Lady Bretherton saw to it that Isobel had the best education possible and watched her grow up into a beauty, and would have had something better in mind for her than the son of some obscure country squire. I have always felt that Isobel married against her family's wishes, for she married her childhood sweetheart. Then Lady Bretherton would have seized her opportunity to punish Isobel with Sir Arthur's tragic death by calling her from Sussex to London on some pretext, and then cruelly abandoning her and her infant daughters. There does not seem to be any other explanation.

"From the later witness of Hannah, the maid-servant, Isobel always seemed terrified for her children, that they could be taken away from her. And another matter, Sir Ryder: Hannah said that for almost two years, her mistress anxiously awaited the arrival of a letter, which never came."

Sir Ryder looked at Dashell sharply. "Let me think. I was probably the only person Isobel could have written to for help, which she could easily have done without her aunt knowing. I was in the West Indies, Jamaica in fact, as Acting Governor at about that time. I remember we were expecting two ships from England, but the supply ship went down with all hands in a violent storm not far from Jamaica itself. It was known that personal items and many letters were lost. If Isobel wrote to me it was quite possible that her letter was among them, which is why I never received it. Oh, dear heavens, I can hardly believe that Isobel and her daughters were alive all these years; and they could have been under my care and protection. What she must have suffered. And you think she married this man, Thomas Wardlock, for a roof over her head?"

"Yes," replied Dashell, "and obscurity. It would have meant a change of name for her."

The admiral sat slumped in his chair. "Forgive me, gentlemen, but you have given me a great deal to think about. I never expected to be told all this. You have completely taken the wind out of my sails." He got to his feet and walked slowly up and down with his hands behind his back, finally addressing Dashell again. "These deaths of Isobel and Maude, you seem to think they are suspicious?"

"Yes, we do. But we have said nothing about them to any authority, nor even to Dr. Meldicott because he would feel obligated to speak up."

"I agree. But the evidence of these two servants, Hannah Faulkner and the boy, would you say they are reliable?"

"Absolutely. And when Wardlock almost killed Caroline herself, it was only the devotion of Hannah, and Johnny running to find me that saved her."

"What a damnable scoundrel that Wardlock must have been," declared Sir Ryder. "I would have had him keel-hauled or strung up on some yard-arm. Pity he's already dead." He sounded disappointed. He stood thinking for a few moments longer, then remarked, "There was something I thought rather odd at the time and still do, when on one of my furloughs I decided to call on the Watertons to see how they were, and found Arthur and Isobel were no longer in residence. I was told by Sir Richard that they had died and he had come into the inheritance some eighteen months ago. You can imagine my astonishment. He was not able to tell me much for not much had been told to him. Nor was I able to enquire anything of the servants for there was not one I recognized. I did learn, however, that Isobel's old nursemaid-companion, Joan Cooper, had gone to the Bretherton household to take care of the Dowager Lady Bretherton. On leaving, Sir Richard mentioned the memorial in the parish church and recommended I take a look."

He picked up the parchment rubbing to view it more carefully and put it down again. "I could not understand why Sir Arthur had been in Yorkshire and why on earth his wife and family were with him. It struck me as odd. But now in view of what you both have told me, they never were with him. However, to continue, as the Brethertons were not all that far away I called upon them. Again I was told very little. I found that the house had been shut up except for the older servants who were left as caretakers, all the others had been given notice. Apparently after the deaths of the Watertons the old Dowager Lady had died not too long after, and Lady Catherine went abroad for a long stay as she found it all too much."

"What you have told us is very interesting, Admiral," observed Barrandale, who had been following everything keenly. "More and more is being revealed about the whole situation."

"By the way," said Dashell, "was anything said about the jewels, the family heirlooms? A whole lot were found hidden away after Isobel's death. And Caroline said some were sold to pay for the fees at Miss Osgood's Academy."

"Jewels? Yes, at the Bretherton House. There had been a robbery and a thief had found his way into the old lady's apartment and frightened her to death—literally—and stole all the jewels he could find. He must have climbed the wall and it would have been easy for a strong man to do. That is what caused Lady Bretherton to close the house eventually and leave for the continent. All the servants were questioned but nothing was found out. I enquired about Joan Cooper and was told she had married John Webster, one of the footmen, and they had gone to London."

"Wait a moment," said Dashell slowly, as a thought came to him. "If there was this robbery, how did the jewels end up with Isobel?"

The three men looked at each other in blank dismay. How indeed?

"I'll tell you what I will do," said Sir Ryder decisively. "I will advertise in *The Times* for the whereabouts of John Webster and his wife, formerly known as Joan Cooper, one time servants of Lady Catherine Bretherton in Sussex. It may bring an answer, even though it was years ago, and anything could have happened. We must try everything possible," as the other two looked rather doubtful.

"That is very good of you, Sir Ryder, said Barrandale gravely.

"By now, after what you have told me, I am as keen as you both are to get to the bottom of this. Where are the jewels now?"

"They are in the safe keeping of my sister, Lady Smythe, of Grosvenor Square," replied Barrandale.

"Where Caroline herself is," added Dashell with a faint smile.

"I should point out, Sir Ryder," continued Barrandale, "that the jewels really belong to the late Lord Bretherton and any family he had, even possibly the Fennshires themselves. They are not ours to keep so they must be returned."

"Before you say anything further, Sir Ryder," said Dashell, "may I speak to you about a subject that affects me greatly?"

"Of course, Lonsdale," said the Admiral, sounding surprised.

"I need hardly say to you, sir, that I love Caroline dearly and wish to marry her, but I have no prospects and can offer her very little, and she on the other hand has no dowry as she herself will tell you, and also she is not of age. By rights I should ask her nearest male relative for her hand in marriage, but the Duke of Fennshire is the last person I wish to approach, not because of him but because of his two sons, Lord Runcorn and Lord Carley, who would be Caroline's second cousins. Once they know of her existence, being blood relatives, they could claim her as their own." Dashell could not finish what he was going to say, leaving it to Sir Ryder to understand. Surely the man would know what he meant?

As it happened, the old sailor did understand; it was just that his thoughts and opinions towards Barrandale and his son had undergone an extremely rapid change. He had been wrong about them because he had been given negative facts, but now with positive ones he saw them differently, and he had warmed towards them both. He saw Barrandale glance anxiously at his son. The Admiral cleared is throat. "There is something I can do, Lonsdale."

"Yes?" said Dashell quickly.

"I have yet to meet Caroline, whom you say is the sole survivor of the Watertons, and if I am satisfied that she is indeed who she claims to be, then I shall take legal steps to make her my ward. Then anyone asking for her hand in marriage will have to approach me."

Their eyes met. "Thank you, Sir Ryder," replied Dashell.

"By the way, when may I see her?"

"Tomorrow evening, if you care to dine with us again," suggested Barrandale at once. "I shall request that both Lady Smythe and Caroline come. I have not yet met her myself, and my son says she is very beautiful."

Sir Ryder's rough face softened somewhat. "Beautiful? Aye, she will be if she is anything like her mother."

They had been talking for a long time now, and it was beginning to get late. Matthew came in to ask if the gentlemen required anything.

"I should be taking my leave," said Sir Ryder.

"Very well. The carriage, Matthew, for the Admiral."

He was a very different man from the angry one that had knocked so vehemently on the front door earlier that afternoon, and Sir Ryder would be the first to admit it.

"I must thank you for your hospitality, Lord Barrandale, and you, Lord Lonsdale, for such an incredible story. The way it all unfolded. My thanks also for all that you have done for my niece. That letter from you, Lonsdale, was beyond my comprehension, but now everything has been explained to me, at least as far as you can, I shall for ever be in your debt. And as I have said, I will advertise for those two servants in the London newspaper and pray there will be an answer. So gentlemen, until tomorrow evening."

After their guest had left Barrandale asked Dashell, "Well, what do you think? I think the evening went very well."

"Yes, so do I," replied Dashell, "once he cooled his temper. I have never seen anyone as angry as he was, but he did have the grace to listen once we caught his interest."

"Yes, and I rather liked him," said his father "And now it is late," stifling a yawn, "I shall go upstairs. Goodnight, Dashell."

"Good night, sir," replied Dashell, rising to his feet, and then sitting down again to savour the evening's conversation, and to think. Of course Caroline would be acknowledged as a Waterton. How could it be otherwise? Sir Ryder, who had once known her mother, must surely see the likeness; and Caroline had known it herself, she had said so often enough. Then once she became Sir Ryder's ward not even the Fennshires could steal her away. He smiled to himself as he fingered the ring in his pocket. He would go to see Caroline tomorrow; there was so much to tell her and Aunt Letty.

CHAPTER NINETEEN

The Next Day

In the morning Lord Barrandale wrote a note to his sister:
"Sir Ryder Wyecross called yesterday in answer to Dashell's
letter, and once we had gained his confidence it became a most
illuminating time, and there is now so much to tell you. He is
most anxious to meet Caroline, and would the two of you be
pleased to dine here tonight for that reason?" "There," he said.
"Your aunt does not like sudden invitations and having to leave
the house, but I am sure she will come for this."

Dashell also wrote a note to his aunt saying he would call after
luncheon and stay for tea, and he would like to see Caroline alone
during some of that time.

George was sent to Grosvenor Square with both notes and
returned with Lady Smythe's reply, *"Of course we will come.
Nothing would keep us away!"*

As he said he would, Dashell called round to Grosvenor Square
after luncheon, and spent the next hour or more describing how
last evening went. "Sir Ryder was astonished beyond measure at
everything we told him, especially that the three of you were still
alive," he told Caroline.

She was overjoyed. "Does that mean I have a family?" Perhaps
that feeling of loneliness would be dispelled for ever.

Lady Smythe was delighted too. "I am so happy for your sake, Caroline. Fancy someone that famous being your great uncle."

"Wait, there's more," said Dashell. "Sir Richard Irving, who inherited from Sir Arthur, has five children I believe, at least that was the total at the last count,"—and paused as Caroline laughed again—"they are not full cousins, only second cousins, but even so, they are still family."

Lady Smythe had told Caroline about her relatives on her mother's side, that she was related to the Duke of Fennshire. How could Lady Bretherton have been so hateful, just because her mother, Isobel, had married the man she loved and then had been so cruelly punished for it. Nor did she like the sound of the Duke himself; and as for his two sons, she did not like the sound of them either.

But Dashell was speaking again. "Sir Ryder said he will make you his ward."

"His ward?" queried Caroline.

"Yes. He will be your guardian until you reach the age of twenty-one. No one can marry you without his consent, so you will be safe."

Safe? thought Caroline. *Safe from whom or what? There is only man I wish to marry.* She wanted to ask more about the letter Dashell had written to her while she was at Mrs. Farling's house, mentioning how he had learned more about her father's death, but somehow it did not feel to be the right moment. Nor was it the right moment to mention her hopes of returning to the house on Becket Lane and of teaching music and singing as her mother had done. She was a little surprised when Lady Smythe stood up saying she ought to reply to Mrs. Farling's letter and would they please excuse her and she would join them later for tea.

Dashell closed the door behind his aunt and then sat down beside Caroline on the sofa. He took her hands in his, which caused her to look at him with some degree of surprise.

"I want to make sure you stay awake. Well, at least for the next few minutes."

"Stay awake! Of course I shall. Whatever do you mean?"

"Well, the last time I tried to talk seriously to you, you fell asleep."

"I did? I don't remember. Oh, wait a minute. You came into my room and began to say something. I remember that; and then your voice drifted away and I must have gone back to sleep."

"And you don't remember anything I said?"

"No, not at all."

"Ah, me," sighed Dashell, "and I made such a long speech."

Caroline was now entering into the spirit of it all. "Can you remember what you said? Was it important?"

"No, I can't remember everything I said, not word for word. Yes, of course it was important."

"Then tell me that."

"I'm not sure I can remember that either." He still had hold of her hands and he regarded her so intently that she felt her heart miss a beat. "Oh, yes, it's all coming back to me, what I was going to say. Caroline, will you marry me?"

She gave a little gasp, even though she had hoped for some time to hear those words, and had she not had her answer ready? She had expected a romantic, even dignified proposal, not this gentle, teasing approach, yet somehow it made her love him all the more. She smiled at him as she stood up. "Stand up, Dashell, and give me your hands," and he, mystified, obeyed. She placed his hands either side of her face and held them there. "Some time ago you tried to kiss me."

"I did? How ungallant of me."

"You also complained of missing so many opportunities, but now you have one."

"An opportunity for what? Do I understand you want me to kiss you?" He sounded incredulous.

"Dashell," said Caroline, "I think we have been teasing each other long enough. You asked me to marry you and I am trying to say 'yes'."

"Then why didn't you say so."

"Dashell, you really are impossible!" She was not able to say anything more before he bent his head down and she slipped her arms around his neck.

He held her closely to him. "I fell in love with you the first moment I saw you," he said.

Caroline had fallen in love too, but had refused to acknowledge to herself that she had, until she was sure of him. "I love you too," she murmured. How wonderful it felt to be able to say that, but Dashell was speaking again.

"Caroline, you know my circumstances, don't you? I have so very little to offer you, so much of my inheritance has gone. In fact, we Barrandales are almost penniless. Half the house at Windsor has had to be closed and a whole number of servants let go. Yet the grounds and gardens are untouched. You will love them. You will not believe the number of times I have pictured you there walking about, especially in the rose garden."

"Dashell, I cannot complain of your circumstances when I have no dowry to give you either. Lord Barrandale might oppose our marriage for that very reason."

"Oh, no, he won't," said Dashell quickly. "He has been following your story closely; and he is looking forward to meeting you."

"He is?" said Caroline in amazement, "how very kind of him."

"And so is Sir Ryder Wyecross, your mother's uncle, which makes him your great-uncle."

Caroline savoured those thoughts before saying, "You don't know how wonderful it is to discover you have a family, to actually feel one belongs; and I should like to meet Sir Richard Irving one day, and all my cousins."

"Of course you will. Now come and sit down, I want to show you something." When they were seated he brought from his pocket the pearl and ruby ring. "Father gave this to Mother on their tenth wedding anniversary, and she willed it to me to give to whosoever would be the next Lady Lonsdale." He placed it in the palm of her hand.

Caroline picked it up and moved it about to catch the light on the stones. "It's beautiful," she said. "They must have loved each other very much."

"Yes, they did," said Dashell, as she handed it back to him. "I will ask Sir Ryder formally tonight for your hand in marriage."

"Suppose he refuses?" said Caroline with a chuckle.

"Well, in that case we will just have to elope," and they both laughed out of sheer delight.

"I can't believe this is happening to me, Dashell," Caroline sighed. "Perhaps I am not awake after all, that this is all a dream."

Before he could say anything they heard footsteps approaching as though someone was being deliberately noisy, then scuffles and an exclamation from the other side of the door. With a wink at Caroline, Dashell got up to open the door. "We heard you coming, Aunt Letty. Do come in. We were not doing anything compromising, you know."

"Don't be impertinent," she retorted, although she smiled as she said it.

"And now, my dearest aunt, may I present to you the new Lady Lonsdale, with or without Sir Ryder's blessing."

Caroline had stood up when Lady Smythe entered the room and was now standing beside Dashell, hand in hand. "Oh, my dear, dear girl," exclaimed her ladyship. "Congratulations! I am so pleased for you. I know you will both be very happy." She kissed her on both cheeks. "You too, Dashell," and he bent his head down. "Of course, this is no surprise to me at all, I knew it was going to happen sooner or later. And now that you are to be my niece-by-marriage Caroline, you must start calling me Aunt Letty."

"That is so kind of you—Aunt Letty."

"Not at all my dear, I have become quite fond of you."

While they had their tea, Lady Smythe remarked to Caroline, "Dashell was considered to be one of the most eligible bachelors in the whole of London."

"Not any more," he corrected.

"Don't interrupt. I was going to say that any number of women were ready to throw themselves at his feet."

"And then when one of them actually did," said Dashell, with a sidelong look at Caroline, "what was a poor fellow to do but to pick her up and fall in love with her?"

"Dashell," laughed Caroline, "you really are a terrible tease, and you know perfectly well I tripped and fell."

"It's pretty well the same thing. The end result was the same anyway."

"But I am glad it was you and not anybody else."

"So am I, that I can make claim to you before any other rogue does."

"Other rogue? By that remark you infer that you yourself are one."

"Caroline!"

Lady Smythe put down her cup and saucer in alarm. "Children! Children! Behave yourselves at once!" But it was all too much for them as they laughed out of sheer happiness. "Oh me, oh my," she cried as she dabbed at her eyes. "I haven't laughed like this for a long time." A few moments later when she had caught her breath she said, "Well, my dears, time is passing and Caroline and I must get ready for this evening."

Dashell stood up. "I will take my leave, my two darlings, and will look forward to seeing you both tonight."

As soon as she could, Caroline ran to her room to tell Hannah the wonderful news that Dashell had asked her to marry him.

"Oh, Miss Caroline, that is wonderful! I am so pleased for you. Just fancy, I shall have to start calling you Lady Lonsdale."

"Not yet, Hannah, not yet. No arrangements have been made. Besides, we still need Sir Ryder's consent, and I shall be meeting him and Lord Barrandale tonight. I must decide what to wear; and that is a strange thing to say when usually I had so little choice," she added wistfully.

Hannah had gone somewhat quiet before asking, "Please, Miss Caroline, what will become of me? I can't help asking, because I'm not grand enough to be a lady's maid, I won't be good enough for you."

"Hannah, dear," cried Caroline, as she put her arms round her faithful companion. "Whatever made you think you would not be coming with me? Of course you will. We have been friends for too long for me to leave you behind. I would never do that." She eventually managed to coax Hannah to dry her tears.

"I'm so sorry, Miss Caroline," she said, swallowing hard. "I suppose I was just being a little foolish."

"We all are sometimes," said Caroline, kissing her again. "Now put those foolish thoughts away." She then became a trifle pensive and said, "I am just beginning to realize what a great step this will be for me. It's like chapters in a book: as one ends another begins. Do you remember that talk we had when we were still at Mrs. Farling's house? All my grand ideas of teaching music and singing? All that will have to be put aside now."

"Do you mind that very much?"

"No, not really. Well, I suppose I do have some regrets, but not when there is a much brighter future for me." Dear Dashell. She had always known he would propose, but just in case he did not, she had felt compelled to think of some other means for herself and Hannah. That made her think of the house on Becket Lane "You and I, Hannah, will have to go over to that house sometime because there will be much to go through and sort out."

A while later Lady Smythe, a stickler for punctuality like all the Barrandales, knocked on Caroline's door. "Ah, there you are. Nearly ready? Perhaps you would like to borrow these earrings. Put them on. Oh, you look lovely."

Indeed she did, wearing one of the dresses Hannah had diligently repaired by inserting a full length panel down the front, making it appear as though it had always been there. "Thank you so much, Aunt Letty. I hardly know what to say."

"There is no need to say anything. Now we must be going."

Two sedan chairs had been ordered, each one carried by two strong burly men, and it would not take them long to reach Barrandale House; for it was too short a distance to call out the carriage.

At Barrandale House Lord Barrandale and Dashell were in the sitting-room with Sir Ryder Wyecross, who had purposely arrived well ahead of the ladies.

"You will understand, Barrandale, I am sure," the latter was saying, "that I have thought of nothing else since I left last evening. I must have been awake half the night going over this incredible story again and again. This question of the jewels does concern me, but by whatever means Isobel obtained them I can see what she had in mind. She herself had the best education a girl in her position could have, which was why she was able to teach her own daughters so much. She had spirit, and I believe she fought back in the only way she knew how, and that was to educate her daughters as much as she could, and then eventually send them to this Academy for Young Ladies.

"From what you have both told me, these young ladies are well-sought after by prospective husbands. Do you see what I mean? Isobel had hoped to obtain help from influential people so she could declare who she and her daughters really were. And that is why I believe she kept silent all these years as she tried to protect her daughters from she knew not what. I think, like you both do, that the fear of that Bretherton woman, if you will pardon me, terrified her into silence, for to speak too soon would have revealed that all three of them were still alive. She would have revealed the truth later on when it was time for her to do so."

Father and son had listened intently to the Admiral's words. "I think that is a very sound theory," remarked Barrandale upon reflection, "and surely that explains why Isobel hid that portrait in the attic, and also the jewels. What a mercy Wardlock never found them."

Dashell also voiced his agreement but with a sinking heart. What if Caroline was now considered too grand for him? He silently cursed Walden for the loss of the family fortune.

"Ah, yes, the jewels," continued Sir Ryder. "That reminds me. I went to the office of *The Times* this morning and placed that advertisement enquiring the whereabouts of John Webster and his wife. We can only hope we do get an answer but it is a very slim hope. I still have to call on my solicitor to make Caroline my legal ward and no doubt I shall require her full name and date of birth before I can do so."

The three men talked together until they heard a knocking on the front door and the sound of Matthew's footsteps crossing the hall.

"Gentlemen," said Barrandale as he rose to his feet, "I believe the ladies are here."

Each man turned expectantly as Matthew announced, "Lady Smythe and Miss Caroline Waterton," and not one of them could take his eyes off the latter. Dashell thought she looked even lovelier than ever.

Barrandale stepped forward to greet Lady Smythe and kissed her on the cheek. "As blooming as always, my dear." He then turned to Sir Ryder, "May I present to you my sister, Lady Smythe."

"Charmed, I'm sure, marm," said the old sailor a trifle awkwardly; he was not too used to female company.

Lady Smythe graciously inclined her head, "Sir Ryder."

Dashell had taken Caroline's hand in his firm grasp and approached his father. "Sir, may I present to you Miss Caroline Waterton."

"My dear, dear child," he said, taking hold of her other hand, "I have long wanted to meet you. Dashell has told me so much about you; and you are indeed as beautiful as he said you are." He said that without any sense of patronizing.

Then Dashell turned to Sir Ryder. "May I present to you Miss Caroline Waterton."

The old admiral had been dumbfounded ever since Caroline had entered the room and had felt his spine tingle. It was almost as though Isobel herself had walked in. He took her hands in his, "My dear Caroline, let me look at you. My dear, you are so like your mother it takes my breath away," and kissed her gently on her forehead. "You will forgive me if I should forget at times and call you Isobel by mistake."

Dashell rejoiced at those words. His Caroline had been acknowledged as a Waterton! No one could dispute Sir Ryder's words about that.

"I am so glad to meet you, Sir Ryder, for you were my mother's uncle."

"Your grandmother, Margaret, was my sister, and was your father Arthur's mother, and Isobel called me uncle too, although there was no blood tie. And now it seems I shall have to get used to being called Uncle Ryder again, but please do not call me Great Uncle, for that would make me feel too ancient." This remark was followed by a little ripple of laughter.

"I should like that," replied Caroline with a smile.

Matthew came and announced, "Dinner is served," which put an end to the conversation.

There was general talk during the meal, but once the gentlemen joined the ladies in the sitting-room they were eager to talk again about that one subject.

Sir Ryder was in a jovial mood. "My mind is fair addled from everything I have been told," he laughed, "I feel quite all at sea and all within the space of two days. Yet I could go listening, and I am sure there is more."

"There is indeed something more, Sir Ryder," said Dashell, beckoning to Caroline, and they stood before him hand in hand. "This afternoon I asked Caroline to marry me and I must now ask you formally for your consent. I have already made known to you my circumstances, but I can offer Caroline a home with love and security, and gardens and grounds to walk in and call her own." Caroline gave his hand a gentle squeeze at the word "home" and he turned and smiled at her. "I love her very much."

"And you, Caroline?"

"I have no dowry to bring with me, and yet I love him, too. Dashell has done so much for me."

"Two penniless people? Aye, I'll not stand in your way, and long life and happiness to you both. So of course I give you my consent."

"Oh, Uncle Ryder, you are a dear!" cried Caroline, and impulsively put her arms round him and kissed him on the cheek.

"Goodness gracious! I have been called many names in my life, but I can't remember ever being called a 'dear'."

"Thank you, sir, thank you," said Dashell, and slipped that precious ring on Caroline's finger and kissed her.

That delighted the others. "My blessings also," said Barrandale. "Welcome to our family."

"And I must welcome you too," stated Lady Smythe. "Mind you, I had known all along this was going to happen." That brought more laughter, and for the first time in a long time Caroline felt tears of happiness.

After a while Caroline went to sit next to Sir Ryder. "Uncle Ryder, I would so love to talk to you about my parents, or rather you talk to me about them. I could ask endless questions."

"Ask away, my dear."

"But I could ask all day," protested Caroline with a laugh.

Lady Smythe overheard this. "Perhaps, Sir Ryder, you would care to join us for luncheon soon. Then you will have all the time in the world."

Caroline looked up in surprise. "Why is everyone being so kind and helpful?"

"Because," she was told, "we are all involved with your story one way or another. We all find it so intriguing."

The remainder of the evening passed pleasantly and eventually the ladies said it was time for them to leave.

Amongst all the goodbyes Lady Smythe reminded Sir Ryder, "We shall expect you for luncheon tomorrow, if that is convenient for you."

"Delighted, marm. I shall look forward to it."

The Admiral had enjoyed his visit to Grosvenor Square. He felt quite at ease with Lady Smythe and Caroline, and in time lost a lot of his awkwardness when in female company. The sea and ships and sailormen had always been his life in which there had certainly been no need or necessity for ladies and their gentle influence.

After their luncheon Lady Smythe had tactfully withdrawn and left the other two to ply each other with questions. Hannah had been sent for as there were many things Sir Ryder himself wanted to know about her early days with Isobel.

"Mother never told us very much about her childhood and growing up and playing with my father and other local children," explained Caroline. "Perhaps it was because she thought we might let something slip and thus reveal her secret. She struggled so hard and yet she was always cheerful, and she never lost faith. She taught Maude and me so much; far more than she knew."

She sat silently for a moment or two while Sir Ryder regarded her with sympathy. "Uncle Ryder, there is something troubling me and I would like to talk to you about it."

"I would not have you troubled about anything, Caroline, my dear. Is there any way I can help you?"

"You mentioned just now that Sir Richard Irving knew both my parents well."

"Yes, that's right. He did."

"Well, I remarked to Dashell the other day that I would love to meet him and his family, but I realise it could cause them some concern. Here am I, a long-lost daughter of Sir Arthur and Lady Isobel Waterton, and they might think I want to claim the house they are in as I have more right to it than they do. Do you see what I mean, Uncle? There is no need for me to have that house when I shall be living with the Barrandales in Windsor, and it would be very cruel of me to send them away. There has been enough unhappiness as it is and enough tears already shed, without more distress being caused. Yet on the other hand I would dearly love to see the house where Father grew up and where Mother lived after they married. What should I do? What do you suggest?"

Sir Ryder was quite touched at Caroline's words. "I think that is very kind and generous of you to release your claim to Waterton Grange. Sir Richard is a quiet, unassuming man and he will be most grateful to you once he knows. I am sure they would find it very hard to leave as they must be quite attached to the place. You leave everything to me and I will get in touch with him. In fact, I would rather like to renew my acquaintance with him as it is."

"Oh, Uncle Ryder, thank you so much!"

That was how the matter was left and Lady Smythe heard all about it when she joined them for tea.

Shortly after their guest left, Caroline excused herself and returned to her room. Hannah had returned a while ago, and when Caroline entered she delightedly showed Hannah the ruby and pearl engagement ring Dashell had given her, and the story behind it.

"Ooh, Miss Caroline. It is beautiful! It really is." And then she showed Caroline the letters Johnny had brought over and given to Chadwick.

"He must have come this afternoon while we were all talking," said Caroline, as she glanced through them. "That means he must have been at the house because he said he would keep an eye on it. I am sorry we missed him. Did he leave any message at all?"

"No, Miss Caroline, Chadwick did not say he had."

"That reminds me, Hannah, we must make arrangements to go over to the house; it is time we did for I am sure the place needs airing out by now. There will be a lot of things to go through and decide what to do with them. Some furniture and other items will have to be sold just to get a little money. We will need Johnny's help but how do we find him? And also how do we get to the house? I suppose we could go by cab."

"How many days would we be there?" asked Hannah.

Caroline thought for a moment. "I should think about a week, or perhaps more."

When Caroline mentioned this to Lady Smythe she was quite agreeable, but was horrified at the idea of a cab. "Certainly not, child. You may go in my carriage. Anyway, there is something I must mention to you first and that is the question of curtains at the new house. I have already mentioned this to Barrandale and he said he had no knowledge at all of such matters and was quite content to leave this to me and you.

"I know of an excellent shop in London, and while you are away I will have their representative go over the house and take measurements of the windows. Matthew can make arrangements with them. They can leave samples of their fabrics here for you to see and decide on before you leave to go to your old house."

"For me to decide?" queried Caroline. "But surely you should?"

"No, my dear. Barrandale said he would leave the choice to you."

Caroline felt overwhelmed at this responsibility and hardly knew what to say.

CHAPTER TWENTY

At Becket Lane Again

Caroline and Hannah left the next morning taking what necessities they required with them. They stood looking up at the house in silence thinking it had a sad, unlived-in look about it, and when they approached the front door they found it locked. "Oh my, suppose we can't get in," cried Hannah in alarm, for the carriage had gone.

"Let's try the side door," suggested Caroline. "The key must still be in its usual place." The side door was also locked but they found the key and were soon inside. Leaving their bags in the kitchen they went from room to room opening windows to air out the house, for it had been closed for some weeks.

"I'll soon get a fire going in the bedroom upstairs for there's the bedding to air out as well," said Hannah. Nothing had changed, it was exactly as they had left it.

Upstairs, they looked at the door leading up to the attic and at the splinters of wood and broken lock as Johnny had left them. "Come on," said Caroline daringly, "let's go up. We will see where Mother hid Father's portrait. Johnny said it had been behind a door. Poor Johnny; in the darkness it must have given him quite a shock. Poor Mother, too," she sighed, "knowing it was up here but never able to come and look."

Hannah went over to a window to look out but felt the floor uneven under her feet and hastily came back. "Ooh! This floor does not feel safe. And it gives me the creeps, and there's a funny smell up here."

"Yes, there is," agreed Caroline. "Well, as these rooms are all empty we need not bother coming up here again so we will not open any windows."

Downstairs again they went into Wardlock's room. Hannah showed Caroline the tiny hidden keyhole in the wooden panel and they both marveled how cleverly concealed it was. Then they discovered the gouge marks on the hall floor leading to the cupboard under the stairs. Caroline gave a little shiver, "I am glad those terrible days are over. Come, let's take a look at the back garden."

When outside, for some reason Caroline glanced through the gap in the hedge by the side door and stopped short in surprise, and went to take a closer look. "Hannah, come here a minute. What do you make of this?" There on the ground were distinct marks of wheels and hoofprints coming and going.

Hannah was mystified. "It looks as though someone has been using the old stable," she said in awed tones. "But who?" They looked at each other in wonder, then with one accord cried, "Johnny!" They went to investigate and sure enough, there were signs of occupation.

"We should have known," laughed Caroline. "Of course he has been here. Did you see how tidy the front garden looked? He must have been taking care of it." They went round the back garden for a look, and found evidence of vegetables being dug up.

"Well, Miss Caroline," said Hannah eventually, "I shall take a look at the pantry. Goodness knows what state it will be in after all this time." When they got there they were surprised nothing was mouldy. The bread, butter and cheese were all quite fresh.

Hannah sniffed the contents of the milk jug and said that was fresh. "Johnny must have been here many times," she remarked, "and he has nearly finished that ham that was left hanging."

"Don't scold him," said Caroline, "it had to be eaten up. Come, we ought to go out and do our own shopping and get something for supper."

An hour or so later she and Hannah returned from purchasing necessary items and they were thankful to be indoors again; and Caroline was also rather annoyed. It was inevitable she would meet people she knew, and it would have to be the ones who asked questions or liked giving advice. Remarks like "Caroline, how lovely to see you again!" were all right, but others like, "You can't live in that horrid old house by yourself," or "It's time you got married, my girl," and having a finger wagged at her, or "You don't want to end up an old maid," would make her seethe.

Although it was a warm day she had resolutely kept her gloves on for she did not wish to expose that precious ring to the curious, particularly as no announcement of the betrothal had yet been made. She could just imagine the hubbub that would cause when it was. She decided she would not wear it for now but put it away for safe keeping.

She took a pinafore apron out of a drawer and gave it a good shake and tied it on. Lady Lonsdale-to-be or not, there was work to be done.

Hannah had got a fire going in the oven range and was now upstairs to light one in the bedroom, so Caroline went to see how she getting on. "Almost done," said Hannah as Caroline entered the room. "I'll soon get a good blaze going."

"Thank you, Hannah. And I'll go and close some windows before they get forgotten as it is becoming grey and overcast." As she went from room to room Caroline looked into drawers and cupboards. "There is much more than I thought," she remarked to Hannah when she joined her. "It is just as well we decided to say a week."

"Tomorrow I shall see about getting a fire going under the copper and getting some things washed," said the practical Hannah. "It is too late now to start."

Later when they were getting supper ready, they heard heavy sounds outside the kitchen and went to investigate and saw a horse and cart going along the lane to the old stable. "Johnny!" they cried together.

He spun round in his seat on hearing his name called and promptly halted the horse. There was a joyful welcome between the three of them. "I didn't expect to see you, Miss Caroline, but it's a lovely surprise. And you, 'annah."

"Oh, so this is the horse and cart you bought," remarked Caroline.

Johnny swelled with pride. "Isn't she beautiful?" turning to admire his horse's strong stockiness. "She's a good girl, and I've named her Goldie." Goldie, however, was more interested in her stall and some feed, so with a shake of her head she moved forward on her own accord, leaving Johnny standing and talking. That caused some amusement; then Hannah said she must return to the supper before anything boiled over, while Johnny ran after his horse.

"Come and join us for supper," Caroline called out after him.

When Johnny had finished attending to Goldie and her needs and entered the kitchen, his immediate question to Caroline was, "Please, Miss Caroline, you don't mind me using the old stable, do you?"

"Of course not, Johnny. It was a good idea of yours."

"I haven't got me own place yet and Mr. Paxton does let me keep Goldie at his place sometimes, but he did say it could not be for forever. Goldie and the cart do take up a lot of room."

Hannah was also anxious to say something. "Begging your pardon, Miss Caroline, but I think Johnny would like to hear your news, if I may tell him." He looked with surprise at Hannah and then at Miss Caroline's smiling face. "Lord Lonsdale and Miss Caroline are betrothed. They are going to be married."

Johnny's answer was to dance round the kitchen, whooping with delight. "I allus knoo he's arsk you sooner or later," giving another whoop. "Just fancy, Miss Caroline, you are going to be a lady." Then he saw that well-known glint in Hannah's eye and added hastily, "I mean you always were, but this is different," and became embarrassed when the other two laughed, until he joined in the laughter himself. "What I mean to say, Miss Caroline, is congratulations," he said with dignity.

"Thank you, Johnny," said Caroline sweetly.

Long after supper they stayed sitting round the table talking, for there was so much news to tell each other, to catch up on.

Caroline told Johnny why she and Hannah were back in the house. "We will go through everything and we will need your help to dispose of anything no longer wanted."

"I'll 'elp yer, Miss Caroline," he said, "I know exactly where to take fings and get a good price."

"I am sure you do," answered Caroline. "Lord Barrandale has kindly allowed me to send anything I wish to keep to their house at Windsor. Will you be able to take them?"

Johnny grinned happily. "'Course I will. I'm taking a cart load of stuff tomorrer from the old 'ouse to the new one in South Kensington. I could come 'ere afterwards."

"Oh, that is a little too soon. We need to go through everything first."

A few minutes later they tidied up the kitchen and said goodnight to each other. Johnny was so happy when he returned to the stable he put his arms round Goldie's neck and kissed her.

CHAPTER TWENTY-ONE

The Irvings Are Greatly Astonished

A day or two after Caroline and Hannah had gone to Becket Lane, Sir Ryder Wyecross left for Sutherfield in Sussex, and passing through the county and the approach to the village and Waterton Grange revived countless memories for him.

The carriage swept up to the house and the sound of its arrival caused some surprise to Sir Richard Irving and Lady Lucy, for they were not expecting anyone to call. They were even more surprised when the housemaid announced, "Sir Ryder Wyecross." In fact Sir Richard Irving was astounded.

"Wyecross, my dear fellow, come in, come in. This is indeed a most welcome surprise. It has been years since we last saw each other."

"Too many," he agreed with a laugh.

"And here is my wife, Lucy. I do not think you have met her before."

"Charmed, marm, I'm sure," said the admiral.

"But how delightful of you to call. I suppose you just happened to be in the neighbourhood and decided to come," joked Sir Richard, "and you will stay and dine with us tonight?"

"Thank you most kindly, but I will put up at the inn."

"Indeed you will not; we will have a room here prepared for you. I insist, my dear fellow. I am sure we will have much to talk about. Lucy, my dear?"

Lady Irving looked to the housemaid who had been waiting by the door, and who gave a bob of understanding.

The three of them settled in their chairs and talked of many things.

It was not until after they had dined and were once again in the pleasant sitting room that Sir Ryder spoke up. "I must not mislead you, Richard, but this is not entirely a social visit. There is a very grave matter I have to speak to you about."

"Oh," said Lady Irving, rising from her seat, "then I will leave you two gentlemen to talk."

"Please do not, Lucy. I would prefer you stayed to hear."

Husband and wife looked at each other in surprise and then at their guest. What could it be that was so serious?

"To begin with," continued their guest, "do you ever see anything of your neighbour, Lady Catherine Bretherton?"

Sir Richard was puzzled. "Nobody sees much of Lady Bretherton. She has shut herself away for years. Why? Has she anything to do with what you have to say?"

"Yes, she has, but be patient and you will learn why," smiled Sir Ryder. "What was her attitude when Sir Arthur died? What was the situation with you?"

Irving was still puzzled, yet he knew his old friend would not have made this journey to ask these questions for nothing. "It was all some years ago now, but I will do my best to remember what little I knew in the first place, because you obviously have your reasons for asking. I was, as you may appreciate, very surprised that Arthur had died so young, and his family with him. I knew I was next in line to inherit but never fully expected to do so. After having two daughters, Arthur and Isobel could easily have had a son. All I was told was that they had all perished in a tragic carriage accident; and that fact truly surprised me."

"And you never thought to question Lady Bretherton?"

"No one ever thought to question Lady Bretherton."

"Were you told where this accident occurred?" continued the admiral, with a faint smile.

"No, not at all; and I was not told immediately that it had happened. Lady Bretherton told me eventually, saying she had been too distraught to have done so earlier. It seemed Arthur had been attending to some matter to do with the late Lord Bretherton's estate, at her request. I believe he was in London staying at the Bretherton town house, and for some reason his family was with him, and she felt she was to blame in some way. Then later she had that memorial put in the parish church."

"Which you have seen, of course."

"Oh, yes, indeed, many times," said Irving. "She had asked the parish priest to see to it for her and had written down the exact words she wanted, and apparently paid very well for it."

"Was that the Reverend Swanson?" asked Wyecross.

"No, his predecessor, the Reverend Latimer. Then some while after that tragedy the old Dowager Lady Anne Bretherton died; she was Bretherton's old mother. There was some talk of a thief getting into her suite of rooms which were at one end of the house and stealing a quantity of jewels, and frightening her to death. I think that was all too much for Lady Catherine for she closed up the house and let go a number of servants, only keeping the older ones to look after the place, and let her town house in London, and went abroad for some years. The next thing I heard was that she had come back, sold the town house and retired to her country house here, completely shunning Society, although I doubt Society missed her very much."

Lady Lucy spoke up. "That's right, Richard. We all tried to draw her into our country ways but she would have nothing to do with us, so we soon gave up. Indeed, there some something about her that I, for one, found repelling, and I believe others did too, if I may be forgiven for saying so. We often wondered what she did in that great house all on her own, with only a few old servants. She just walks around the gardens which have all become so overgrown anyway, and she hardly ever goes out."

Sir Ryder regarded them thoughtfully. "Thank you both for what you have told me. Now, to go back a few more years. When Arthur and Isobel married, was it an elopement?"

"Oh no," said Irving. "It was a quiet private ceremony in the parish church. I was there."

"And Lady Catherine was not?" queried Sir Ryder.

"No. She was in London attending to all her social functions and doubtless matching up even more unfortunate people together."

"And she was not pleased when she heard about it?" queried Sir Ryder again.

Irving gave a short, dry laugh. "No, she was not," he said emphatically. "In fact, she was extremely displeased. She had been making a very good match for Isobel while in London with a young French aristocrat whose family had escaped to England from the revolution in Paris, and who were still residing here. Then when she found out there had been this marriage in her absence, well—you can imagine. She then had to tell this French family what had happened and they just shrugged it off with a laugh. "Ah, les Anglais," and the young Frenchman turned his attention elsewhere, so I heard. That humiliation must have made her seethe with anger, and it could have been the first time she was ever thwarted. She tried to make out the marriage was not legal and wanted the bishop to dismiss the Reverend Latimer. This, the bishop refused to do and declared the marriage was legal, so she could do nothing about it. In time she accepted the situation with good grace, which was surprising for someone with her vindictive temper."

"Ah," was all Sir Ryder said.

"What is all this leading up to?" asked Irving shrewdly, narrowing his eyes. "There is something behind it all, isn't there?"

"Yes, there is," admitted Sir Ryder, "and it will all be revealed to you in good time. Just bear with me."

"As you wish."

"To continue, have you ever heard of Lord Barrandale? He is a member of the House of Lords."

Irving shook his head, but Lady Lucy said she had heard of him in a round about way through a friend. "I have heard he is a good man," she stated.

"That he is," agreed Sir Ryder with a smile. "Now, a few days ago I received a letter from his eldest son, Lord Dashell Lonsdale, the contents of which gave me the greatest shock I have ever had in my life. I promptly went round to Barrandale House in Park Lane to demand an explanation, in no uncertain terms. To say the least, I was extremely angry.

"I was invited to stay for dinner that evening as Lord Lonsdale's explanation would take some time. So I stayed. I was determined to find out what was going on as I suspected a cruel hoax—at first. Lonsdale began by saying he had come to the aid of a young lady who had had a slight accident in Oxford Street in London, whose name he learned later was Caroline Wardlock. He called on her the next day, for he discovered where she lived, and from then on the story unfolded.

"The young lady had been living with her father, mother and sister; and by the time Lonsdale met the lady the mother and sister had already died. So she lived alone with her father, who was a very unpleasant man and whom she began to suspect was not her father, but her stepfather. She therefore did not believe her name to be Wardlock but had no way of discovering her real name. Nor could she understand why her mother had never told her sister and herself who they really were. The mother, by her own efforts, was able to send them to a very good young ladies' academy when they were older. I believe it was her intention to tell them the truth eventually, but tragically and unfortunately she died before she was able to do so; and then when the sister died, also tragically, Caroline was left alone."

Sir Ryder looked at his listeners carefully, who had been following with little murmurs of surprise. "I trust I have your interest and that you begin to understand what I am saying?"

Lady Lucy had been holding her husband's hand and her other hand went up to her mouth, and she said almost in a whisper, "If this girl is called Caroline, would the mother and sister have been called Isobel and Maude? Is that what you have been telling us?"

"You are very astute, Lucy."

"Lucy, my dear!" cried Sir Richard, "how can you say that when they died long ago with Arthur."

"As a matter of fact," stated Sir Ryder bluntly, "they did not."

Sir Richard was dumbfounded. "But—but," he said at last, "Lady Catherine said they had. And what about that memorial she ordered?"

"That was a lie, and placed inside the church where more people would see it there than if it was outside in the graveyard. It was well known that she had a very spiteful and vindictive temper and we, that is Barrandale, Lonsdale, and now myself, believe she seized upon the fact of Arthur's death and deliberately and cruelly abandoned Isobel and her children as punishment for marrying her childhood sweetheart; and for all the humiliation she had been caused. I, for one, can believe her quite capable of doing it."

The other two cried out in genuine horror as the truth sank in. "That's impossible! How did they survive? Did she not care?"

"Isobel must have been desperate because what little money she had been given was running out, for she married this man Thomas Wardlock for security and obscurity. With a change of name she could not easily be traced, for we know she was threatened and told that if she ever tried to declare who she really was, her children would be taken away and she would never see them again." Again there gasps of horror from the other two.

"The saving factor was that she hired a country girl, Hannah Faulkner, as nursemaid and general help, who also came from Sussex, and this girl became devoted to her mistress and who later became an important witness in the whole story. She told us that for about two years her mistress was fearful for her children and could hardly let them out of her sight, which I think proves our theory. Likewise, Hannah's half-brother, Johnny Faulkner, who was later hired by Isobel, also became a witness, and he it was who discovered Arthur's portrait hidden in the locked attic in the house. And he also found certain documents which Wardlock took from Isobel and refused to give them back, among which were the birth certificates for Maude and Caroline."

"Arthur's portrait, "cried Irving. "I remember seeing it hanging in one of the rooms here and then it somehow disappeared; and those certificates must have proved who the girls were. But go on, Ryder. This is becoming more and more absorbing."

"Before I do, do the names Joan Cooper or John Webster mean anything to you?"

"Yes, I remember them both," said Irving quickly. "Joan Cooper was Isobel's maid, and John Webster was a footman. They were both here at Waterton Grange."

"Do you know what happened to them?"

"Now let me think. After Arthur's death Joan Cooper went as maidservant to the Dowager Lady Anne Bretherton and John Webster became her footman. As they were now the old lady's servants Lady Catherine could not do much about it. The old lady thoroughly detested her daughter-in-law and some said she just did it to annoy her."

Sir Ryder smiled at that. "What became of them after the old lady died?"

"As far as I know they married and went to some position together in London. That's all I can tell you."

"You have told me a great deal, Richard, and you too, Lucy."

"Let us go back to Arthur," said Sir Richard. "He was doing something for the late Lord Bretherton's estate I believe, but I have no idea where."

"He was up in Yorkshire," Sir Ryder told him. "That's where the accident occurred."

"Where?" they both cried in unison, thunderstruck. "In Yorkshire?" Sir Richard shook his head as though it was all getting too much for him. "I imagined it was somewhere near London. I had no idea it was that far away. What happened anyway?"

So Sir Ryder carefully described the incident as related to him by Dashell. Again there were exclamations of horror. "Oh, poor, poor Arthur," cried Lady Lucy. "It must have been terrifying for him, and for his coachman."

"How did this Lord Lonsdale know to go all that way up there?" asked Irving.

"Ah," said Sir Ryder. "The village of Sutherfield was mentioned in the birth certificates of the two sisters. He wrote to the incumbent of the church, the Reverend Swanson, and asked him to make discreet enquiries about the Waterton family, and apparently the gravedigger was able to help Swanson; and Swanson also made a charcoal rubbing of that memorial."

"Good man," murmured Irving.

"Determined to find out the truth, Lonsdale, accompanied by his youngest brother, travelled all the way there on horseback. When they got to York they made enquiries and learned of this terrible tragedy in the village of Skorrcliff that occurred eighteen or so years ago. They discovered that only Arthur and the coachman were buried there." Sir Ryder paused, and then said quietly but emphatically, "The landlord of the inn where they stayed, and where Arthur had stayed all those years ago, said there had never been anyone else. So I think that proves that woman did what she did."

Husband and wife sat in stunned silence thinking over all they had been told, and Sir Ryder could tell from their expressions that they were appalled and even shocked. "That memorial," began Lady Lucy, sounding aghast, "which Lady Catherine ordered cut with the very words she wanted. It states that all four members of the Waterton family had died when only one of them actually had. How could she dare to think of being so—so—evil. It is almost beyond comprehension."

Then Sir Richard suddenly spoke up. "Swanson never approached me about the Watertons," sounding somewhat indignant.

"Perhaps he did not wish to distress you at all," said Sir Ryder tactfully. *Good marks for you, Swanson,* he thought. Irving might have spoken too much about it outwardly and he did not want that just yet. "But there is one more thing I have to mention."

"You mean there is more?" echoed Irving, raising his eyebrows, "I find that incredible."

"For the time being Caroline is staying with Lady Smythe, who is Lord Barrandale's sister," continued Sir Ryder. "I called on them the day before yesterday and Caroline herself mentioned this to me. She said she would dearly love to visit the house where her father grew up and where her mother came when she married him."

"Of course she may. We would be delighted to have her come."

"One moment. She went on to say that as she is the long-lost daughter and heiress of Sir Arthur and is the last of the Watertons, she could lay claim to this house as hers."

"You mean we will have to leave!" the other two cried out, "she wants us to go? But we love it here! And yet she is right." They looked at each other in dismay.

"No, no, no. She does not want that at all. She is willing to relinquish her claim to the house and property, although it would have been her home under different circumstances. To use her own words: 'There has been too much unhappiness as it is and too many tears have been shed.' She only wishes to visit."

"That is wonderfully generous of her; we will thank her most warmly when we meet," said Sir Richard.

"So where will she live then?" asked Lady Lucy.

Sir Ryder gave a chuckle. "Caroline will be well cared for. She and Lord Lonsdale are bethrothed, and the Barrandales have a country house and estate near Windsor." He tactfully said nothing of their circumstances. "I should tell you that Caroline plied me with questions about her parents until I felt quite dizzy, and she will probably do the same to you two."

"In that case," they both said, "we had better start recollecting memories now. Is there anything more you have to tell us, although we hardly dare ask."

"Just one or two things more. I have made Caroline my ward as she is still under age. I also intend to make it public that Caroline Waterton is—well, Caroline Waterton, long-lost daughter of Sir Arthur and Lady Isobel Waterton, and why exactly she is long-lost. By doing this I shall achieve for Isobel what she struggled for so long to do herself. I feel it is only right to do so."

Irving pursed his lips. "That, my dear fellow, is going to create quite a stir. The Duke of Fennshire is not going to like that."

"I dare say," remarked the old admiral drily, with determined face and set jaw, "but all this was none of his making anyway. By the way, I am not approaching the Reverend Swanson yet about a new memorial, and I would appreciate it if you both would say nothing at all to anybody until all this is made public."

"Of course," they said together. "We understand."

For the next while they continued talking, the Irvings asking most questions which Sir Ryder did his best to answer.

"I am beginning to recollect so many things," began Sir Richard. "Godfrey, Arthur's father, and I were good friends and I visited here many times. I was some years older than Arthur and I remember the day the two of us tried to teach him to play cricket; it was one of those hot hazy, lazy summer days that always seem to stay in one's memory. Then when I married my Lucy"—turning to her with a smile—"and moved to our old house we somehow drifted apart and went our separate ways. Then out of the blue I was told I was the new baronet and that Waterton Grange was vacant and we could move in."

The clock in the room, with its pleasant chimes, reminded them time was passing. Sir Richard bestirred himself. "Ryder, you must stay here tomorrow, there is so much more I would like ask you, and I am sure Lucy would, too. It has been so long since we last saw each other, as it is. You will be most welcome to do so; and there is still that very good trout stream," he added.

"Yes, please do," urged Lady Lucy.

Sir Ryder laughed. "In that case I shall be pleased to do so. How can I refuse?"

CHAPTER TWENTY-TWO

To Return to Caroline

When Caroline had been injured all those weeks ago and she and Hannah had left the house in such haste, it had always been their intention to return and take away whatever else was needed and dispose of what was not. If Caroline's plan to teach singing, music and needlework had come to fruition, then of course they would have stayed. Also, the earlier plan of opening a tea-shop in a coastal town in Sussex, like Eastbourne or perhaps Brighton, had completely faded away. Dashell's proposal had made her future assured. The two of them had gone through all the rooms upstairs starting with Hannah's old one, taking down curtains and folding bedding and coverlets. Three piles of things were made on the landing at the top of the stairs: those to be kept, those to be sold, and those to be given to charity.

Caroline had gone through the clothing and personal belongings of Maude slowly and with gentle care, keeping any clothing she thought would fit her or could be altered. Too much work had gone into their making for them to be discarded lightly. She would also hold back a few items as keepsakes. It was the same going through her mother's room. She looked at the writing desk with all its neat little drawers at eye level, and the larger ones where Isobel kept her housekeeping and teaching records. "This is one piece of furniture I intend to keep, and the chair with it.

One of my earliest memories as a child is of seeing Mother sitting here, always busy about something."

"In that case," said Hannah, "I will give them a good polishing." She was not about to let anything go to Miss Caroline's new home looking shabby. "Come to think of it I will do the rest of the furniture too. That will make them look better for when Johnny takes them away."

Caroline then turned to the chest of drawers. When she reached the bottom drawer she came across a bundle wrapped carefully in a length of linen, obviously once very precious to her mother. "Whatever is all this?" she wondered as she opened the bundle.

Hannah glanced over in curiosity. "Goodness me!" she cried. "They are the little baby clothes Miss Maude and you once wore. I recognize them. Fancy them being kept all these years."

Caroline held up the tiny garments and examined the fine fabric and stitching. Beautiful little quilted bonnets and baby jackets, little dresses, tiny slippers for the feet and equally tiny mittens for the hands, and one beautiful christening robe. "They are so lovely; Mother must have made them herself. I can hardly believe Maude and I were once tiny enough to wear them. What shall I do with them?"

"Well, as you are going to be married soon, I would keep them if I were you. You will be wanting them yourself one day," said the ever practical Hannah.

"Hannah!" Caroline felt her cheeks flame up, knowing full well what she meant, and yet—if there ever was a little girl would she not be glad she had kept them? She wrapped them up again and put them back in the drawer for the time being; and no, she would not forget they were there. Mother must have kept them for Maude and herself. She got up from kneeling on the floor and shook out her dress and looked about to see what else had to be done, and caught sight of the daffodil-embroidered cushion on the chair, stitched by her mother. "Oh, that cushion. I must not forget it. I can still remember Mother showing Maude and me how to do cross-stitch." She picked it up and Hannah could hardly stop herself from crying out in horror as her mistress examined the cushion more closely. Obviously Lord Lonsdale had not yet told Miss Caroline how her mother had really died, by being suffocated by it. She would never have picked it up the way she did if she had known.

"I'll take it for you, Miss Caroline," said Hannah, perhaps too quickly, but Caroline suspected nothing as Hannah took it from her and placed it on one of the piles on the landing. She would have to find a way to get rid of it somehow. Johnny could deal with it; he would be bound to think of some way or other.

When she came back Caroline said, "There is one more room to do, and then the linen cupboard. I think the room should be done next."

"Aye, let's get it over with," agreed Hannah with a scowl. That room was Thomas Wardlock's bedroom, large and sparsely furnished, a room that Caroline had rarely been in, not that she or her sister had ever wanted to be. Hannah gave a shudder of disgust. "Horrible old man," she muttered to herself, as the two of them took down the curtains, folded the bedding, and looked through the wardrobe and the chest of drawers, the latter with a few personal items and a small hoard of coins.

"Everything can go," said Caroline decisively. "In fact, Johnny may keep the money from anything he sells."

"Does that include the furniture from both rooms?" asked Hannah.

"Yes. I want none of it," said Caroline again, "and I think we have done enough for today. I'll help you carry some things down and we can leave them in the hall." It took quite a few trips downstairs and back again, and Hannah made sure she carried the items containing that particular cushion in it.

"Well, that's that," said Hannah as she came down with the last bundle. "Now you go and sit down, Miss Caroline, while I see to our supper. It won't take long because it's the same as we had last night."

"All right," said Caroline. "I think I will go out into the garden for some fresh air. I'll go out the front door." She sat down at the bottom of the steps as she and Maude had so often done with their mother. It always seemed a special time on sunny days, the late afternoon just before it turned to early evening; they had always loved it. Now she sat alone with her elbows on her knees and her chin on her hands, watching the sunlight as it filtered through the trees.

Daydreaming, she wondered about her forthcoming marriage to Dashell, the heir to an earldom, such as it was, and what would be expected of her. What was a "Lady Someone" supposed to do? She and Maude had always been taught to be occupied and diligent in a genteel way, and considering her background Mother must have known what to do. Dashell would one day take his seat in the House of Lords and she would have to take her place beside him, because she did not have the temperament or even the inclination just to sit around and be "grand." And she was about to do what her mother had worked so hard to achieve for her daughters, and that was to marry into an aristocratic family. Why else had they been sent to that school?

She looked towards the beds of roses, her mother's delight, and got to her feet and began walking slowly round them. Many a time she had pondered that warm feeling that came to her soon after meeting Dashell; and the message it was supposed to convey. Or perhaps it was not supposed to convey anything, it was just there. Now she felt it again, the awareness that her mother could be near. Why? Just when she would be leaving the house for ever. In an instant she thought she knew why. Smiling to herself she returned indoors in a happier frame of mind and went to see how Hannah was getting on and if she needed any help.

"Oh, no thank you, Miss Caroline, it is almost ready. We won't wait for Johnny because he did say to me he never knew when he would be back, and then he has to see to his horse first."

"Did you notice any change in Johnny?" asked Caroline when they were sitting down. "I was surprised, not having seen him for a while. I think Mother would have been proud of him."

"Aye, he's a young man now. He's no longer a boy."

It was not long before they heard the cart pass the house, and within half an hour Johnny joined them looking pleased about something. He was even more pleased when he was told he could keep any money from the sales of anything from Wardlock's old room upstairs, and the small hoard of coins they had found.

"We have not yet been through his downstairs room, we will do that tomorrow," said Caroline. "By the way, how can you manage moving heavy furniture by yourself?"

"Don'tcha worry, Miss Caroline. I know someone 'oo can 'elp. I've already told 'im I might be needin' 'im."

After their meal was finished they fell to talking again and the time passed as pleasantly as the evening before.

All three were up early the next morning to catch as much daylight as possible. Johnny left to do whatever work he had to do, and the two women started on that downstairs room. Again there was little furniture: one leather chair, a table, and the desk which Johnny had searched at one time. Inspector Cockburn had also gone through it and removed a few items of interest. What was left Hannah regarded as rubbish.

"Even so, we can still leave it all for Johnny," said Caroline, as they took down the curtains and folded them. She looked round the room, "Well, I think we have finished here," and left Hannah to do the dusting and polishing.

Meanwhile Caroline busied herself by emptying the linen cupboard and taking the contents downstairs to the front sitting room and putting them on the table and chairs ready to sort them out. It took several trips.

When Hannah had finished and came into the sitting room, she found her mistress sitting on the piano stool looking very pensive. "I am probably being very foolish," she said, "but I cannot bear the thought of parting with this old piano. It has been so much a part of our lives. Do you remember all the singing and playing of an evening? all the pupils Mother taught? It used to be so lovely." She stopped short with a sigh. "We had better stop for lunch and then we can go through all this linen."

When they returned to the sitting room later, Caroline was still in a reminiscent mood. "Oh, look at this," she would say, holding up some article. "I can remember Mother teaching me these stitches. And here is something Maude did. And here are our old samplers. Just look at them all." Finely stitched pillowcases, tablecloths, and tray cloths of various sizes, and little place mats. Then there were the petit point chair backs and chair seats and the cushion covers on the furniture in the room. "It was amazing how much Mother was able to do."

"That's because she had two loving daughters to help her."

"Oh, Hannah," smiled Caroline as she folded a tablecloth. "It seems that most things will be kept and I am rather glad about that." She turned away to pick up something and did not notice a person coming up the front path, but Hannah did.

"We have a visitor coming," she said.

"Oh, no!" cried Caroline. "Just look at the room. We are in no position to entertain anyone. Oh, how tiresome. Did you see who it was?"

"Yes. Someone very special."

"Oh?" Then Caroline saw the smile on Hannah's face. "Oh!" and ran to the door just as there was a knock.

"Dashell! Do come in!"

"What a lovely welcome!" he exclaimed as he stepped inside. "I must come here more often," and Caroline laughed delightedly. "But what is this?" he said, taking a closer look at her. "How does that song go? 'She looked so neat and nimble-o a-wearing of her apron-o—she stole my hea-art a-way.' and kissed her. "I had to come and see you after receiving your note. The beginning and ending were delightful: 'My darling Dashell,' and then 'With love always'. It was the rest of it that puzzled me; all the busy-ness you were planning to do. I felt quite let down. That was not my idea of a love-letter."

"Dashell. Really."

"But you were quite right," he continued on a more serious note, "There is nothing to fear now."

"Thank you, Dashell. I knew you would understand. But please come into the sitting room and you can see how busy we are. I will make some room for you to sit down," and she removed some items off the sofa and put them on a chair already piled high." Please forgive all this confusion; there was more in the linen cupboard than I remembered. But I must not bore you with all this; I am sure gentlemen do not like it."

"I quite understand your confusion, as you put it, for we are in much the same situation ourselves. Father is returning to Windsor soon and I shall go with him, as Aunt Letty told me quite firmly that I could not possibly stay with her if you were to be there as well. Then when everything is over and done with we will go straight to the new house. By the way, we have been amazed at what Johnny has been able to do. He has been so helpful."

"Oh yes, we have seen him," said Caroline. "He has been using the old stables here, and he is so proud of the horse and cart he purchased with the money you gave him." She had been sitting on the sofa next to Dashell because there really was nowhere else to sit, and she impulsively placed her hand on his. "I think he will do well."

"Knowing Johnny, I am sure he will," agreed Dashell with a chuckle. He looked down at her hand, then asked more sharply than he really meant to, "Where is your ring? Where is it?" fearing it might be lost.

It startled Caroline and made her a trifle flustered. "I do have it. I did not wish to spoil it while working around the house so I put it away for safe keeping."

"Oh, I'm sorry," said Dashell, now a little contrite. "That's my clever girl."

Caroline looked at Dashell, wanted to say something, but hesitated then finally said, "There is something I would like to mention it to you."

"I thought there was. Do please tell me."

"As you know, Lord Barrandale has kindly said I may send whatever I wish to keep from this house to your house at Windsor, but I find it rather embarrassing."

"Why?" asked Dashell in surprise.

"Because I am sending furniture and belongings there when at the same time such things are being sent away from that house. It seems a such a contradiction."

"Not entirely. It has been an excuse for us to sell off some things. There was a perfectly hideous Jacobean armoire given to my parents as a wedding present, which Mother hated and she never knew what to do with it. She always suspected the people who gave it wanted to get rid of it themselves." Caroline could not help laughing at that. "Anyway, my father says what he means and means what he says," observed Dashell drily, "and there is plenty of room to store things."

"You do so quickly understand things," said Caroline, pausing as Dashell smiled at her, "and now I would like to ask you something more, if I may."

"Of course you may. What is it?"

"I do not wish to upset you or Lord Barrandale, but is there a piano at Windsor?"

Dashell hesitated a moment before replying. "Yes, there is, but it was never used much after my mother died, except by an occasional guest. We will be selling the one at Park Lane. Why? Are you hoping to take this one of yours?"

"Yes, I would love to. It was Mother's really, and it means so much to me. We used to have such happy times round it."

"Is there anything more?" Dashell wondered.

"Yes. One more special request." She got up, and beckoned him to a window overlooking the front garden. "You remember you said there were gardens and grounds at Windsor I could walk in and call my own?"

"Yes, I did."

Caroline turned to look outside again and pointed to the rose beds. "Do you think that if those rose bushes were carefully dug up there would be room for them at Windsor?"

Dashell smiled and shook his head. "You really are a darling. You love them because your mother did. I will inform our head gardener to expect their arrival some time or other; and any other plants you may wish to send."

Caroline laid her hand gently on his arm. "I think my mother would have loved you."

He looked down at her. "I think my mother would have loved you, too."

They turned away from the window as the door opened and Hannah came in with the tea things.

"I made you some shortbread, sir," she said, beaming at him.

"Shortbread?"

"Yes," said Caroline. "Aunt Letty told me how much you enjoyed it."

"She did? Mmm. I really must come here more often."

"But Dashell," protested Caroline with a laugh, "we will be leaving at the beginning of next week. Monday to be exact. Aunt Letty is sending her carriage for us."

"I know," he grinned. "I was just teasing you."

"Not again!"

During their tea Dashell said, "I must tell you that Sir Ryder left me a note saying he was going to Sutherfield in Sussex to renew his acquaintance with Sir Richard Irving, and to see what more he can find out, if anything. In fact, he should be there already. He said they knew each other well in days gone by. He did not say how long he would be away."

"He is so kind," remarked Caroline. "I told him I would love to visit Waterton Grange to see where my parents lived, but did not wish to cause them any anxiety as that is still their home as I will not be living there."

"And why is that?"

"You know perfectly well why."

"Because you are coming to live with me?"

"Yes. But if you are going to be impossible all the time I may decide to stay here. Would you care for the last shortbread?"

"Yes, thank you, I would, but I did not know I had eaten so many."

When Hannah came in for the tea tray Dashell said he had greatly enjoyed her shortbread. "Thank you, sir," she replied, looking at the empty plate.

Dashell did not stay much longer as he could see Caroline was busy. The two of them walked slowly along the front path to the wrought iron gate. He sighed to himself. He had wanted to speak about his ride to Yorkshire but it was neither the time nor the place, and certainly not to mention the manner of her father's death. "I will tell you all about it some other time," he said.

"I am so sorry, Dashell. I feel so contrite after all your trouble on my behalf. You have done so much for me as it is."

"When Sir Ryder returns from Sussex," continued Dashell, "we will wait to hear what he has to say and see what he plans to do next. I think deep down he is very shocked and angry at the facts that have been revealed to him, and is determined to expose the truth on your behalf. Don't be alarmed, dearest," as Caroline looked apprehensive, "it must be done for the sake of your mother to have this terrible wrong put right."

"Yes, you are right of course. It would be too cruel to sacrifice what she did for herself and for both Maude and me. I have often thought it must have taken a great deal of courage. Then when all that is done and everything put behind me, I can turn and make a new beginning."

"And that means we can start making plans for our wedding."

"That sounds much nicer," said Caroline with a contented sigh. "That is something we can both look forward to." She hesitated again. "Dashell, there is one thing more I would like to ask you, as if I have not already asked enough this afternoon."

"And what is that? Do not be afraid to ask."

"Is it all right for me and Hannah to continue staying with Lady Smythe? If she is finding it too much we could still stay here. It would not be too late to change plans."

"You will do nothing of the sort," replied Dashell decisively. "I know she enjoys having you. She told me so."

"Thank you, Dashell. You have put my mind at rest."

He looked back at the house that to him had always looked so gloomy. "I don't suppose you will be sorry to leave. Monday, you said?"

"Yes. And no, I will not be sorry." She also looked back at the house, thinking of all that had occurred there. There had certainly been happy times when the three of them had been together and yes, there had also been unhappy times, and she was not sure which one outweighed the other. "I will ask Uncle Ryder how to go about selling it. At least I can thank Step-papa for that, I suppose."

A few minutes later, Caroline returned indoors where she found Hannah still sorting the household linen. Hannah, in turn, was pleased to see Miss Caroline so happy.

"Hannah! It's so wonderful! Dashell said I may send the piano to Windsor. And what's more, he said there would be room in the gardens for Mother's rose bushes and anything other plants I wish to take. It is so kind of him and his father."

"Aye, he is a good man. I am sure your mother would have been pleased."

Caroline remembered the warm feeling she had experienced earlier that day. "Yes, I think so too," she said, smiling to herself. It was almost as though Mother had asked for her roses to be moved, if that was not being too fanciful.

After more sorting Caroline said, "I suppose the next thing is to bring down what boxes and trunks there are from upstairs." Between them they managed to bring down two, but the heavier ones would need Johnny's stronger help. "Now it is really time we stopped," she said. "I hope we remember which pile is which."

"Don't worry about that, Miss Caroline. I do. You leave all that to me."

Johnny had worked hard that day, chiefly because he wanted to be back at the house for supper with the others. He had decided he did not really like being on his own and in many ways still hankered after the busy-ness of London. Later, with Goldie safely "tucked up for the night," which expression he had learned from Stephen, Johnny was once more in the kitchen, only too ready to eat. "I always did like yer 'ome cookin', 'annah," he said, grinning at her.

"Well, make the most of it, my lad," she said, "for we will be leaving on Monday."

"Leavin'? Does that mean for good?" he asked, his heart sinking a little.

"Yes, for good. That's why Miss Caroline and I have been clearing out everything. She will tell you what things are to go to Windsor."

Caroline came in just then and heard Hannah's words. "Yes, indeed Johnny, there are quite a number of pieces of furniture to go. Lord Lonsdale was here this afternoon and said I would be able to send the piano and anything else I wished to Windsor. He said there would be room for the rose bushes from here. Do you think you could dig them up if you are careful? I can't bear the thought of leaving them behind."

"That's easy, Miss Caroline," he replied cheerfully. "As long as the roots are wrapped in wet sacking they will be orl right."

"And now that other room downstairs has been done there is that furniture to go; and as I told you, the money from the sale of it is yours too, Johnny. Then there are all the different piles of things in the hall."

"I can explain all that to Johnny," said Hannah quickly.

"I hope you can," Caroline said with a tired little sigh, "for I have almost forgotten."

Johnny listened quietly while the two women talked together about what had been done that day and what needed to be done tomorrow. "We will work in the kitchen, Hannah. It should not take us long, and we can have a quiet day on Sunday before we leave on Monday." Caroline sighed as she said that although she had no real regrets. "It will be a parting of the ways, a new beginning for all of us. Will you be all right, Johnny? Will you find enough work once you have finished what you are doing?"

"I expect so," he replied with his usual optimistic smile, rather touched that Miss Caroline should ask, but he did have a little stab of doubt.

"I suppose it will be all right for you to use the stables until the house is sold, but I do not know when that will be. I shall have to ask my uncle for his advice." Caroline then asked, "How long ago was it when you first came here, Johnny?"

"Just over four years ago, Miss Caroline," he replied promptly.

"And now look at you. You are quite the young man now."

He could not help glowing with pride at that remark. Then plucking up courage and being as polite and diffident as he knew how he asked, "Please, Miss Caroline, could you—I mean—would you," then gulped and became hesitant.

"Yes, Johnny?" encouraged Caroline.

"Could we just 'ave one more sing-song rahnd the pianner just like we useta do, before I take it to Windsor?" as Hannah cried out in agreement.

"That's a lovely idea," cried Caroline herself, "of course we will. Let's make it Sunday, our last night."

Before they went to bed Hannah waited for a chance to speak privately to Johnny, but it was not easy. There was something very much on her mind but she did not want Miss Caroline to hear. It was not until Caroline was actually going upstairs that Hannah made some excuse that she had forgotten to say something to Johnny, and would do so now in case she missed him in the morning. "I'll have to run after him and I'll be as quick as I can," she explained.

Seizing her chance she hurried into the hall to where that particular cushion was hidden in one of the piles, removed it, and ran out of the kitchen towards the stables.

When Johnny heard her calling for him he came out in surprise. "Wot's 'appened?"

"Nothing's happened," she said panting, "but listen. Here is the cushion that man used when—well, you know. I could tell by the way Miss Caroline picked it up that Lord Lonsdale had not yet told her how her mother really died, and it was all I could do not to snatch it away from her."

"Of course!" cried Johnny. "The one with the daffodils. I remember now."

"Now, Johnny. I want you to get rid of it. You will think of something, I'm sure, but just get rid of it," emphasizing the last few words. "If Miss Caroline asks later where it is I shall just say it must have got lost in the move or sold by mistake. Now, I must go before she wonders what's taking me so long." So saying she turned and ran back to the house.

Johnny, open-mouthed, was left holding the cushion, and stared at it in horror. What was he supposed to do with it? How would he get rid of it? He walked slowly back to the stable; he would have to think it over. In the meantime, he put it inside the carriage-house for the night and tried to forget it was there.

CHAPTER TWENTY-THREE

The Last Two Days At The House

Neither Caroline nor Hannah, nor Johnny for that matter, would forget their last two days at the house. The weather for the first day did not promise well as there was a strong wind blowing up. Though the two women would be leaving, there were still some necessary groceries to purchase, and as soon as they could they left to do their shopping.

By now the wind had increased, causing heavy grey clouds to gather. Caroline glanced up at them, remarking, "It looks so stormy, Hannah. We had better hurry back." However, it was not easy hurrying and carrying parcels with the wind pulling at their bonnets and skirts, and they were glad to get indoors.

Johnny went to Park Lane early that morning for a load to take to the new house in South Kensington and then back to Park Lane for more. By the time he completed his second unloading and was returning to Becket Lane, Goldie started a loose shoe in one foreleg, so Johnny had to walk her all the way back. When he arrived at the smithy his face fell when he saw one horse already in the smithy with two others waiting to be shod. "Sorry, Goldie. We'll just hafta wait until Monday."

Hannah heard the cart go by in the lane. "Ah, there's Johnny," she said. "He must be glad to be back." Even as she said that more wind buffeted the house and rattled the window panes. "I hope this wind is not going to last all night," she added.

The evening darkened earlier than usual and they were compelled to light extra candles. The wind increased and seemed to come from all directions, causing draughts everywhere inside the house and making the candle flames flutter.

"I think we should all have an early night," Caroline announced later. "There is no point starting anything now, and we have been busy the last few days."

As it turned out it was a storm to remember, just as Hannah had feared. The two of them had hardly settled into their beds when the wind returned with even more ferocity. It seemed to shake the very house and shrieked round it, and shook the windows again as though some creature was trying to gain entrance. It made the house feel quite eerie.

Caroline was sure she heard footsteps on the stairs. Impossible, she told herself. It was just the woodwork creaking. She lay back again, and then sat up once more with a start. "Did you hear that creak, Hannah?"

"Y-yes," said Hannah. "It came from downstairs. It sounded like a door. There must be a draught but I'm sure no window was left open." As if to add weight to her words a tremendous roar of wind howled down a chimney somewhere causing such a draught that the said door slammed shut, accompanied by startled gasps from the two women.

"Oh my goodness, I'll be glad when daylight comes," declared Hannah.

Caroline lay back once more and pulled the bedclothes up to her chin, listening to the rain now pounding down. One more night in this house after this one, only one more night and she would leave it for ever. Nor was she sorry. Not now. There were too many ghostly noises, or so it seemed, or perhaps she had too much imagination. Old houses were known to creak and crack. What was that noise? It sounded like a sigh. Just the wind, her common sense told her, and was glad to have the solid form of Hannah in the next bed. Her thoughts ran on. Just the two of them living here, it would have been too much. She knew it would have depressed and pulled them down eventually.

Downstairs in the hall the clock ignored the forces of nature and continued ticking and chiming as it was supposed to do, while both Caroline and Hannah listened for the quarter-hour chimes and counted the hours. "I wonder how Johnny is," Caroline said. "I hope he is all right."

Johnny had the same thoughts himself, wondering if the other two were all right. Twice he had to get up to talk quietly to Goldie, who had been moving about in her stall, snorting and pulling at her rope. He lay down again, remembering that cushion in its hiding place and tried not to think how it had been used.

It seemed to him he had hardly closed his eyes before cock-crows from neighbouring farms awakened him and he groaned to himself, but it was no use, Goldie had to be attended to. Besides, he was curious to find out what damage had occurred during the night.

Caroline and Hannah had been up early too, rubbing their eyes from lack of sleep, and went round the house to see all was well, no leaks or bowed-in window panes.

Downstairs they discovered the door into Wardlock's room was the one that had slammed shut. "Might have known it would be that one," muttered Hannah.

Caroline went into the other sitting-room to look out of the window and stared in dismay. "Oh, those poor roses," she exclaimed to Hannah, who had come to join her. "See how the rain has beaten them down, and just look at the rest of the garden."

There were leaves, twigs and broken branches scattered everywhere; the laurel bushes were bent over; earth had been washed away from the flowerbeds, forming muddy puddles where the rainwater had collected. The only thing that had come through the storm reasonably well was the old tree stump.

"This storm would happen," sighed Caroline, "just when I was planning to sell the house and have everything look tidy. But the gardens will have to wait a while."

Johnny and Hannah began carrying downstairs small items of furniture to be left in the hall, ready to be loaded onto the cart on Monday morning.

The drawers from Isobel's desk were removed to make it a little lighter to carry and in taking it through the doorway the desk slipped in Hannah's hand, tilting to one side, and something metallic slid out and fell to the floor. The two of them stared in amazement at it, and then with one word they each cried, "The key!" Johnny snatched it up, while Hannah ran downstairs to find her mistress.

"Miss Caroline!" she called out excitedly, "we have found that missing key!" and breathlessly explained how it happened. "And we always thought it had been lost, but instead it was carefully hidden behind one of the drawers all these years."

All three of them ran up to the attic rooms and Johnny managed to insert it into the rusty keyhole, but even with his strong hands it still would not turn. Yet there was no doubt in their minds that this was the correct key, or else why had it been hidden away?

"Leave the key in the lock, Johnny, there is no need to keep it," said Caroline. "It has served its purpose."

They slowly returned downstairs and finished removing what they could, leaving the heavier things until Johnny's helper came the next morning.

After lunch, when the weather had improved, Caroline and Hannah went outside for a walk along Becket Lane. "This will be our last walk here," said Caroline.

"Oh dear," Hannah ventured to say, "that does sound so final."

They kept to the lane itself as any grassy areas were still wet, each one thinking her own thoughts. Then Caroline remarked, "You know, Hannah, we did have many happy times together, just the four of us. Mother, Maude, you and I."

"Indeed we did, Miss Caroline. I remember when we used to pick blackberries and rose hips to make jams and jellies. And sometimes Johnny helped us." She thought of her wooden spoon and smiled to herself. Yes, she certainly would keep it.

"And that time I tore my pinafore. And when Maude got stung by a bee. And when you nearly fell into that ditch," laughed Caroline.

"Now, now, Miss Caroline," laughed Hannah in return. "Don't go remembering things like that!"

Hannah hesitated a moment before speaking. "Excuse me for saying this, Miss Caroline, but Johnny is feeling rather downhearted about our parting. He has not said anything to me but I know he is."

"Yes, I know he is," she replied slowly. "I shall be sorry to say goodbye to him."

They had reached the front gate by now and were surprised to see how much tidying up had been done. "Although I say it myself," remarked Hannah, "he is a good lad."

"Yes, he is," agreed Caroline again, then said, "I must look for my music and song sheets. Apart from playing for Mrs. Farling, I have hardly played for some time."

They did not stay as long at the supper table because they wanted to enjoy themselves round the piano. Hannah cleared away the dishes quickly with Johnny's help. Caroline went to the sitting-room and lit extra candles as dusk was coming. It was a little strange not to pull any curtains across the windows and it made the room look so bare. She played gently to herself until the other two came in, all smiles and anticipation.

It was a happy evening, one to be remembered by all three. Caroline asked Hannah and Johnny what they would like to hear or sing, and she was only too delighted to play pieces for them, sometimes more than once. Nor did she feel the least awkward about it; a young mistress playing for two servants. The evening passed all too quickly, or so it seemed, as they had been playing and singing for more than two hours.

"That was lovely, Miss Caroline," sighed Hannah, "I enjoyed every minute, but my throat is a little dry from all that singing."

"So is mine," said Caroline. "Did you enjoy it, Johnny? It was a wonderful idea of yours."

"Oh yes, I did, Miss Caroline. It was just like old times," he said. It did not occur to him that he was still too young to have any 'old times,' but Caroline knew what he meant.

She put away the music sheets into the piano stool. "I am sure we are all still tired from last night, and there is still much to do tomorrow. What about you, Johnny?"

"Well, I hafta be very early tomorrer for me to take Goldie to the smiffy. Me 'elper is coming' at nine o'clock, an'—an'—I'd like to be on 'and to see you an' 'annah go orf in the carriage."

"Perhaps we should say our goodbyes now," suggested Caroline, "as I think we shall all be rather busy in the morning."

Johnny was a little taken aback at that and he could feel his face flushing.

Caroline did not embarrass him with a lengthy speech but simply said, "Thank you for all your wonderful help and resourcefulness. We could not have managed without you, as

Mother often said. We will miss you," and then lightly kissed him on the cheek.

Hannah, who had tactfully withdrawn a little way, now stepped forward to say her goodbye. "Goodbye and good luck, Johnny. You will do well for yourself, I know," and lightly kissed him on the other cheek.

He was rather overwhelmed by all this and said hastily, "Thank you, Miss Caroline, and you, 'annah. Good night, both of you," and left the room. Lifting his lantern off its hook and not bothering to light it he stepped outside, glad no one could see him wipe his sleeves across his eyes or hear his sniffs, for he loved them both very much.

As they were going upstairs Caroline remarked to Hannah, "I do wish I had been able to give something to Johnny. Something that he would like. Is there anything you can think of, Hannah?"

"Not right now, Miss Caroline," she said, frowning a little, "but I shall certainly try."

The blacksmith always started to heat his forge at five o'clock in the morning, and Johnny made sure he was first in line, and Goldie came back with two new front shoes. Better to do that now and not have to take her again. He harnessed her and moved the cart ready in position to be loaded and then put her back in her stable.

Hannah was bustling about getting breakfast ready and talking to Johnny at the same time. "Now, Miss Caroline said that any food left in the pantry is yours, and I baked an extra fruit pie for you, and also hard-boiled some eggs. And as you are going to be on your own, you may take whatever pots and pans you want from the pile to go out, and any thing else you want. We have left you all the candles, together with some matches. Oh, and dig up any vegetables you can use after that storm."

Johnny knew Hannah was just being her usual brisk self, but it did give him a sinking feeling.

Andy, his helper came just after nine o'clock, a "bit slow up top" but as strong as a young ox. He lived with his widowed mother and was only too willing to earn some pennies here and there.

Between the two of them Johnny and Andy carried things out and onto the cart, Johnny having to be patient in giving Andy instructions. When the cart was loaded they took any boxes to the front gate, ready for the carriage when it came. Then Johnny paid off Andy, reminding him to be back tomorrow at the same time.

Johnny went to the front gate to keep watch along the road, while Hannah waited by a window for his signal. Caroline sat at the piano quietly playing, more for want of something to do than anything else, at the same time wondering if Dashell was coming as escort. It was a lovely thought.

It was nearly fifteen minutes before Johnny could give his signal. "The carriage is coming," cried Hannah.

Caroline immediately closed the piano and went to the window. There was no sign of Dashell, but the coachman handed a letter for her to Johnny.

My darling Caroline, Forgive me for not being with you on your return to Grosvenor Square. As I told you, my father decided to go to Windsor and I have gone with him and I will return some time next week. Sir Ryder has not yet returned from his visit to the Irvings to learn what more he could, but I know he is determined to go ahead with his plan concerning your mother. Till we meet again, my love always, Dashell.

She smiled a little at the same beginning and ending of the letter that she had used, and was disappointed she would not be seeing him for several days.

They were now ready to leave. They looked about to make sure all the packages were picked up and nothing left before shutting the front door behind them. Johnny had strapped the boxes onto the rack behind the carriage and was now holding the carriage door open for them. All the proper goodbyes had been said the evening before so there was no need to say them again.

As soon as the carriage moved off Caroline took the letter from her purse to read it again. So intent was she on doing this that she never looked back at the house. Neither did Hannah, for her own reasons.

Johnny watched the carriage until it was out of sight. With a sigh and a heavy heart he turned back to the house. After making sure both the front and side doors were locked, he went to the stable. "Come along, Goldie, we have work to do."

CHAPTER TWENTY-FOUR

Maxwell's Progress

Barrandale and Dashell were talking about leaving Barrandale House for Windsor in a day or so and were in the sitting-room, when the door opened suddenly and Maxwell came in.

"Maxwell!" cried his father. "Come in. This is a surprise. Dashell and I will be going to Windsor soon to make it easier for the servants to make the move to South Kensington. We were just talking about it." Barrandale made it sound so matter of fact. "You have just come in time."

"Oh? What shall I do now?" asked Maxwell in surprise, as he sat down. "I suppose I could stay with Aunt Letty."

"I don't think so," said Dashell. "I wanted to do that, but Caroline will be returning there on Monday from her stay at Becket Lane, and Aunt Letty banished me from Grosvenor Square, and told me to think of the proprieties. Doubtless she will say the same to you."

"Oh," said Maxwell again, sounding disappointed. "Perhaps I could stay there until Monday morning, and then go to the new house by the evening."

Barrandale sensed his disappointment and changed the subject. "Those sketches you sent back of your journey to Yorkshire, I thought they were excellent, and such detail."

"Yes, I saw so many delightful country scenes it could take me months to paint or even just sketch them. Oh, yes, I must tell you, some days I have been watching Lively and Daisy Chain at their training gallops. You should see the filly, she is real go-er."

That caught Dashell's interest at once. "We must go and watch her, sir, when we get to Windsor. I shall look forward to that."

"Just one more thing," Maxwell continued, "I called at the office of your solicitor in Windsor, and explained who I was and why I was there, and after speaking to him he gave me a letter of introduction to their office in London. I hope you did not mind me doing that."

"Not at all. I am pleased they could help. So I understand this will be the beginning of your new life. I admire you for keeping to this decision."

"Thank you, sir. So tomorrow I will go to the London office, and then call on Aunt Letty and hope she lets me stay there, at least for a few days."

"By the way, Maxwell," Dashell could not help asking. "How did you get here? Did you walk?"

"Oh no. I got a seat on the stage leaving Windsor, and I must say it was quite a pleasant ride this time," giving him a look that only a younger brother can.

"I think we should tell you, Maxwell," said Barrandale, "that Sir Ryder has gone to Sussex to call on some old friends who knew Arthur Waterton as a boy, to see what else he can learn. I am not sure how long he will be away."

The next morning, after saying goodbye to his father and brother, Maxwell called round to see his aunt. She was a little surprised at seeing him so early until Maxwell explained what he was doing.

"Of course you may stay, but not for too long. Caroline will return here Monday afternoon."

"I know," grinned Maxwell, "Dashell told me I had to think of the proprieties, too."

"Oh, did he? Well, now that you are here would you like to stay for lunch? Then you can tell me your news."

Afterwards, when Maxwell called at the solicitor's office, he really felt his luck was beginning to turn for the good. That letter of introduction had opened a door for him, but not at that particular office.

An elderly man with shrewd eyes read it through carefully as though it was a brief. He then sat back and surveyed Maxwell critically. "Well, Mr. Romford, our associates appear to be quite impressed with you. However, there is nothing here we can offer you, so I suggest you approach some other associates of ours. I will write a note to indicate you were here today, and why." He took a few minutes to do so and then rang a bell on his desk, and a clerk silently appeared. "Would you give this young man directions to the premises of Messrs. Wagstaff & Bickerstaff. And here are your letters, Mr. Romford."

"Thank you very much, sir. I am most grateful to you." Maxwell received a brief nod and a wave of a hand in return.

At the premises of Messrs. Wagstaff & Bickerstaff he was asked to state his business. He was shown into a room containing Mr. Wagstaff, the senior of the two partners, also an elderly gentleman. Maxwell sighed to himself, wondering if all solicitors and their clerks were elderly and bent-looking, and hoped he would not become like them when he was their age.

"It is fortunate you have come at this time, Mr. Romford," said Mr. Wagstaff after reading both letters carefully. "We find our work is increasing and we were looking for a new clerk to join us." He looked at the letter again. "I understand you have recently left Eton. Had you thought of studying law at Oxford?"

"It is not possible for me to go to Oxford," stated Maxwell.

"So you intend to study Law in your own time? Very commendable. What have you been doing since you left Eton? We expect any young man we take on to be diligent and hard working."

"I have assisted a gentleman over some property management, and also assisted another gentleman over a family matter which required me to leave London for a few days." It was astounding how the words just came out. He must be a quick-witted natural. He said nothing about painting in his spare time, and if he was expected to be diligent and hard-working, then he was not likely to get much of that.

Mr. Wagstaff appeared to be satisfied for he said, "Now let me introduce you to my partner, Mr. Bickerstaff. He led the way to a room wherein sat his partner, also elderly. "Ah, Mr. Bickerstaff, I would like to hire this young man, Mr. Romford, as our new clerk, subject to your approval, of course."

Mr. Bickerstaff looked Maxwell over as if he were appraising an objet d'art. "Do we have a sample of his handwriting?" he enquired.

"Oh, dear me, no." Paper, pen and ink, and a sheet to copy were produced, and Maxwell copied out something about laws in his best handwriting and showed it to Mr. Wagstaff.

"Look, Mr. Bickerstaff," said Mr. Wagstaff, "no ink blots. What do you think?"

"I think he will do very well, Mr. Wagstaff. Has remuneration been discussed at all?"

"Oh, dear me, no."

Maxwell was introduced to their present clerk, Mr. Prendergast, and then sent on his way with a book of laws under his arm, and a promise of remuneration which sounded reasonable to him, and was told to be back next Monday morning at nine o'clock sharp.

He walked back to Grosvenor Square feeling pleased. At last he had something.

He spent the next few days reading the book of laws which covered a vast array of subjects from treason to straying animals. He also sat in the public gallery of the Old Bailey to listen to a few trials, which impressed his new employers when they asked him later what he had been doing since they last saw him.

He duly arrived at the premises at nine o'clock on Monday to learn that both solicitors would be in Court all day, and it was left to Mr. Prendergast to show him what to do, which consisted of writing answers to various letters already drafted out. Simple enough once he had deciphered the spidery handwriting.

Maxwell soon learned that the constant repartee between Mr. Wagstaff and Mr. Bickerstaff was their way of relieving the stress of their cases. One time during this situation he caught Mr. Prendergast looking at him, who then winked at him and smiled. Maxwell smiled in return and settled down to his work.

CHAPTER TWENTY-FIVE

At Windsor

Father and son returned to Windsor for a few days, and Barrandale was glad to be there. He always felt more at peace in the country; here, the house was home.

Wasting no time, the next day they had ridden round the entire estate with Dashell explaining more of his ideas. How much parkland could be set aside to graze sheep and cattle, how much for hay, and how much to be ploughed under for grain. There was a never ending demand for oats and hay, and any surplus after their own needs were met could easily be sold. More livestock could be raised; more crops could be planted, and so could orchards be enlarged. He sounded so enthusiastic it made the future look brighter.

"You amaze me," said Barrandale in wonder. "You are becoming quite a farmer."

"Well, sir," replied Dashell, "if that is what it takes, then that is what I shall be—a yeoman farmer. I once vowed I would do all I could not to lose the estate. For our own sakes, and Caroline's too."

"Very commendable, my son. Now let us look at the beech avenue and the pine trees."

When they rode along the beech avenue and saw what remained of the two lopped beeches, Dashell almost regretted giving the order; they looked so stark, even grotesque. He looked at his father in dismay. "What do you think, sir? Perhaps the entire trees should have come down."

Barrandale looked at them carefully. "I almost regret to say I agree with you. But some of these trees are so old some branches may need to be lopped for safety. Their condition should be discussed with the men first before coming to any decision."

"I think we have seen everything," said Dashell. "Shall we return to the stables? I am anxious to learn what Samuel says about our two hopefuls."

Barrandale laughed. "Yes, I know you are."

Lively and Daisy Chain had just come in from their gallops and were standing in the stableyard being given a good rub down.

Samuel explained his training methods to both their lordships: brisk early morning canters and good gallops in the afternoons. There were also plenty of fences and ditches on the estate for Lively to go over.

"I am sure, sir," said Samuel to Dashell, "that the ride to Yorkshire strengthened him considerably and he is now easier to handle. He is coming along very well. In fact they both are. They have been on Ascot racecourse to get them used to being on one."

"Do you think they could be raced soon?" asked Dashell.

"Yes, sir, I believe they could, especially the filly."

"Very well, Samuel. We will come and watch them tomorrow afternoon."

The next afternoon Dashell and his father came away really impressed with the two horses. Daisy Chain proved herself to be a real flyer, and Lively jumped over obstacles as though he enjoyed it.

When asked about a jockey, Samuel said that a young lad from the estate riding the filly had the makings of becoming a good one.

"If you please, Lord Barrandale," said Samuel, "there is something else I have to mention, and that is a wheeled horse-box will have to be provided. Daisy Chain could be walked to Ascot is she races there, but being walked farther away takes too much out of a horse. I believe there is an old wagon here that could be rebuilt into one."

"Very well," agreed Barrandale. "I am sure our carpenters could do this."

Seated again in the sitting room father and son discussed what they had done and seen that day.

"I hope we will be able to meet all requirements to begin racing," remarked Barrandale. "Choosing of racing colours, registration of entrants to races, and entry fees, and so on. I hope we are not taking on more than we able to handle."

"There is no alternative if we are to make our way," Dashell pointed out. "By the way, as steeplechasers carry heavier riders I thought I might try my luck in one or two races. Gentlemen do ride their own horses."

Barrandale looked at him sharply. "I would prefer you did not," he said sternly. "In fact I might forbid it."

Dashell stared at him. "I beg your pardon, sir," he said coldly, "but did I hear you correctly?"

"You did. May I remind you that these races can be extremely dangerous; riders can get badly injured, or even killed. If you die, then we all die, and so does the estate. And think of Caroline."

Dashell flushed at the strong rebuke. If he lost Caroline it would be unbearable, but if she lost him? "As usual, sir, you are quite right," he eventually admitted.

During the following days Simmonds showed them round the house explaining which rooms had been closed and where the furniture had gone. Some to other rooms and some put aside for sale.

"I have kept strict lists and inventories of all items," said Simmonds, "and an account of all payments received in return as they have been given to me. If I may say so, sirs, Johnny Faulkner has been amazingly good. He has worked very hard and has been here several times and has given me all receipts and payments down to the last penny."

Dashell smiled at that. "I knew he could be trusted," he said to his father.

As it was, the wonder of Simmonds and all the other servants had been put to rest by what Samuel had carefully told them of the association between Lord Lonsdale and this Johnny, and they now regarded the latter as some kind of hero.

"Before you go, Simmonds," continued Dashell, "I have pleasure in announcing my betrothal. The lady is Miss Caroline Waterton, younger daughter of the late Sir Arthur Waterton and the late Lady Isobel Waterton. No date has yet been arranged for the wedding, but you will be kept informed."

Simmonds' face lit up. "Congratulations, sir. I will inform the other servants. Which suite shall be prepared for her?"

Dashell glanced at his father. "The large one overlooking the garden at the back. Miss Waterton will be bringing her own maid. Some items of furniture from her old home will be brought here. And also, would you inform the head gardener I wish to see him tomorrow at two o'clock."

After the servants' evening meal, Simmonds stood up and called for the attention of everyone. They braced themselves, hoping they were not going to hear that more of them were being let go, and were delighted to learn of the betrothal of Lord Lonsdale to a Miss Caroline Waterton. Simmonds then said to the housekeeper, "Mrs. Whiteside, would you see that the large bedroom suite overlooking the back garden is prepared, and also a room for Miss Waterton's maid, who will be coming with her.

And also, Hitchcock, Lord Lonsdale wishes to see you tomorrow at two o'clock. That is all."

There was a buzz of excitement from the servants at this welcome news, and Simmonds was asked to convey their congratulations to Lord Lonsdale. Perhaps there was hope for the House of Barrandale after all.

The next afternoon Dashell met with Hitchcock, and discussed with him the layout of a new rose garden. "The lady is having the rose bushes from her old garden brought here," Dashell explained. "They were her mother's and she did not wish them to be left behind. And there may be other plants as well. Johnny will be bringing them at some time."

"Very good, sir," replied the old gardener. "I will draw up some plans."

The day before their lordships planned to return to London, they were again in the sitting room. Simmonds had gone away with the tea tray and they could talk in comfort.

"I think the last few days have been gratifying," remarked Barrandale. "I feel so much has been accomplished. I am pleased with Samuel's training of those two horses, and I believe you are too. Oh, by the way, I plan to give you Daisy Chain as a wedding present, and they both may race in your name."

"That is most generous of you, sir. Even so, we will make it a joint ownership."

Barrandale bent his head in acknowledgment. "But you will be the senior partner. And I like the fact that Caroline is having some of her furniture sent over, including the old piano," he added with a smile.

"Yes," said Dashell. "Yet she was rather diffident about it, moving her things in while we were having things moved out. She did not wish to embarrass you."

"Of course she does not. And she wanted her mother's roses as well? I like the sound of that too. She is a dear girl."

"Of course she is," replied Dashell. "That is why I am marrying her."

Barrandale just smiled. "I am very pleased at the way Maxwell is turning out, the way he has thought out everything for himself. I am sure he will do well."

"And how do you feel, sir?" asked Dashell. "I have noticed a difference in you. You seem more resolute, as though you have a new purpose."

"Yes. I believe I have. One must be philosophical, I suppose. And tomorrow, we will go to the new house."

"And I shall also look forward to hearing what Sir Ryder has learned from his visit to the Irvings in Sutherfield," said Dashell.

CHAPTER TWENTY-SIX

....

At Grosvenor Square

Lady Smythe welcomed Caroline's return most warmly. "Truly, my dear, I have missed you. But what is this, child? You look pale. I hope you did not do too much."

"Oh, no, ma'am, not at all. It was the storm on Saturday night. We hardly slept a wink. And then I played the piano all last evening, and we sang all our favourite pieces, but we did all we set out to do."

Caroline began telling Lady Smythe what other news she had, which did not amount to much, except to say the missing key had been found, and what items of hers were being taken to Windsor.

In turn, Lady Smythe told of her own news. "I had a letter from Mrs.Farling and she wrote quite a lot about your visit, and only wished it could have been longer, and was sorry she had to ask you to leave." She gave a little smile. "I am very fond of her, but oh dear, she writes just like she talks. She is a little lonely I think and I am glad her brother will be living with her. It may encourage her to go out more. But I must tell you that Sir Ryder has returned from his visit to Sussex and is anxious to see you. He will be coming here tomorrow afternoon."

The next afternoon Sir Ryder duly arrived and kissed Caroline on each cheek. "That is an uncle's privilege, m'dear," he chuckled. "I am fast learning my new duties." He sat in a comfortable chair and Lady Smythe tactfully left them to talk together, "I have so much to tell you about my visit to Sussex, and the Irvings are anxious to meet you, and thank you most sincerely for your decision about Waterton Grange."

"It was the least I could do," replied Caroline gravely.

"Now," continued Sir Ryder briskly, "this story about your mother must be made known to people, for this wrong must be put right. It has gone on far too long." He paused as though waiting for a possible objection; and Caroline in her turn thought rather irreverently it seemed as though her uncle, an admiral, was laying plans for a campaign.

She looked back at him steadily. "Please continue."

"Very well," he said with a look of approval. "Within London Society, so I am told, there are certain people who may best be described as 'professional gossipers,' although I believe they can be known by other names, but for the time being we will call them that. I understand you never tell them anything you do not wish other people to know, but on the other hand if you do wish something to be known, then you 'hire' them, so to speak." He finished those words as though it sounded distasteful, as indeed it was to a man more used to straightforward dealings.

"But what do you mean, Uncle Ryder?" protested Caroline. "I have no means to pay them."

"You are not expected to do anything, my dear girl. You leave everything to me. As I was saying, I have approached two of these people and will arrange to meet them when Dashell and Lord Barrandale return to London."

"Dashell?" asked Caroline in surprise. "Will he be there?"

"Of course he must be there; it will add weight for the two of us to corroborate what we say. These people do not know why they have been asked to come; I only informed them they would find it interesting." He finished speaking, while Caroline was not sure how she felt. She was about to say something when the admiral began talking again.

"Now let me tell you of my visit to Sutherfield, a charming village in Sussex. The Irvings are very good people and we were all delighted to renew our acquaintance with each other. Sir Richard remembered your father when he was a boy and told me many anecdotes about him. I told him to remember all he could, for you would be bound to ask him when you met him. They asked me to tell you they are looking forward to meeting you."

"That is kind of them. I shall look forward to meeting them, too," said Caroline.

"Indeed you shall. But all that can be arranged later. One thing at a time, my dear." He clapped his hands on his knees. "Let us talk of other things. How did you get on at your house on Becket Lane? Have you decided what to do with it?"

"Yes, I have decided to sell it but have no idea how to go about it. Can you help? What should I do?"

Sir Ryder pursed his lips as he tried to think. "Well, shiver me timbers," he said unconsciously lapsing into naval vernacular and scratching his head, "I'm dashed if I know much about that sort of thing myself. Ah, I'll tell you what. I will approach the estate agent who sold me my house and ask him to take on the matter for you. That's the best I can do."

"I think that is very good of you," said Caroline. She looked at him hesitantly. "Uncle Ryder," she began.

"Yes, m'dear?"

"I would like Johnny Faulkner to continue to use the old stable behind the house until it is actually sold, if that is possible. He has been using it for a while and I said it would be all right. He keeps his horse and cart there," she explained, "which he bought with the money Dashell kindly gave him."

"Ah, yes. Johnny," said the admiral, thoughtfully rubbing his chin. "I have heard so much about him. A very resourceful young fellow. I will pass on your request to the estate agent when I see him. I suppose he could be regarded as a caretaker if he still lives there." Sir Ryder had always liked the sound of this young man; and had he but known it, Johnny had passed the "bridge test" in absentia. "Are you sorry to be leaving the house?" he wondered.

"No, not at all," answered Caroline. "It would be far too large for just me and Hannah. We would probably have closed some of the rooms."

Sir Ryder did not stay much longer after tea, but before he left he told Caroline everything would be all right. Caroline, however, felt that events were happening too quickly to be comfortable, and said as much to Lady Smythe afterwards.

"Well," replied Lady Smythe, "he is certainly not one to let the grass grow under his feet, if that is the right thing to say about someone who has been on board ships most of his life." Or as Sir Ryder might have described it, "He now had a strong wind to fill his sails."

Maxwell paid a surprise visit one day, as his aunt had told him that could, and was introduced to Caroline. So this was the lady who had captivated his brother's heart, and no wonder. She was a beauty. "I am very pleased to meet you, Miss Waterton," he said gravely.

"I am very pleased to meet you too, Maxwell," she replied sweetly, "but do please call me Caroline," thinking how much like Dashell he was.

"All right, thank you—Caroline," he said with a smile.

"Now sit down, both of you," commanded their aunt, "and tell me your news, Maxwell, if you have any. I have been thinking of you."

So he proceeded to describe to them all he had been doing, ending by saying, "I am becoming quite interested in the Law." Then in turn he was told how Lady Smythe and Caroline had driven past the new house twice and thought it looked beautiful.

"But enough of that," declared Lady Smythe, "we had a most interesting time with Sir Ryder yesterday. He told us about his visit to Sutherfield, and it was amazing what he found out. Caroline, perhaps you would care to tell Maxwell some things?"

Caroline was not too sure how much he knew, but as he had accompanied Dashell to Yorkshire then he must have been told some of her story. Although they were about the same age she was not too used to young men, nor was he used to young women, but it was different when she asked about his ride with Dashell. By the time he finished telling her they felt like old friends.

"I have so many sketches," Maxwell told her. "Perhaps you would like to see them," wondering with inward delight what she would make of that sketch of Dashell.

"Yes, I would love that."

CHAPTER TWENTY-SEVEN

Father and Son Return From Windsor

Dashell and his father went straight to the new house in South Kensington as the old house in Park Lane was now empty. They looked over the whole house and declared it was very fine, albeit a lot smaller, but knew they would be comfortable there.

During the absence of their lordships' Matthew had led all the servants to South Kensington for them to get acquainted with the place, and Cook said she was very pleased with the new kitchen, to Matthew's silent relief.

Dashell, of course, lost no time in going over to Grosvenor Square.

"Dashell!" cried Caroline, when he announced himself. "How lovely to see you."

"One thing I like about you," he said as he kissed her gently, "is that you are always pleased to see me."

"Of course I am. But only one thing? Could there not be more? I must learn to tease you, too."

"Good for you!" laughed Lady Smythe. "It's what he needs."

Dashell told them what he and his father had been doing while they were at Windsor, but said nothing about the new rose garden as he wanted to surprise Caroline.

He in turn learned that Maxwell had paid a visit and had been introduced to Caroline.

"He is very like you, Dashell," said Caroline. "I thought him a pleasant young man."

"Of course he is," murmured Dashell, "if he is like me."

"And he told us about your ride to Yorkshire, and all sketches he did," continued Caroline, ignoring his interruption.

"Oh, yes," said Lady Smythe, "he also said he had obtained a place in a solicitors' office and told us all about it. And then Sir Ryder came and told us about his visit to Sussex, and what else he had been able to find out."

"Oh, yes," replied Dashell, "I shall be seeing him tomorrow evening. He left a letter for us to see on our return."

"That will be the arranged meeting, will it not?" Caroline asked.

"Yes," said Dashell, but did not enlarge upon the matter. Nor did Caroline wish to say anything more, either. A few moments later when she slipped out of the room to say something to Hannah, he immediately turned to his aunt and said, "I must speak to Caroline privately. It really is time I told her the truth about her parents and sister. So much has been happening there never seemed to be an opportunity. Perhaps I could come here for luncheon on Sunday?"

Lady Smythe barely had time to agree before Caroline came in. "I just remembered I had to remind Hannah about something," she said.

There did not seem much more for anyone to say, so Dashell ordered his horse to be saddled.

His aunt stared at him. "You came on horseback?"

"Yes, I had to," he replied, and explained about the increase of distance that now lay between their two houses.

"Oh, how tiresome it is all going to be," she sighed.

"I could not agree more," Dashell replied. He said goodbye to them, and told Caroline he would see her again on Sunday.

On his return Dashell met Maxwell coming down the stairs and they both went into a sitting room. "I have just come back from Aunt Letty," said Dashell, "and heard all about Sir Ryder's visit, and yours. So you have met Caroline. She thought you were a pleasant young man."

"That was nice of her to say so. I think she is very pretty; and I now know why you kept grinning to yourself during our ride together. I told them quite a lot about our travels as they were interested, and no, I hardly said anything about Sir Arthur."

"Thanks for that. I was hoping you would not," said Dashell. "I shall tell Caroline everything when I see her again. They told me you had found some position at a solicitors' office. How did you get on?"

Maxwell described it all, and then showed Dashell the Book of Laws he had been told to read. "Quite impressive, isn't it? "Oh, by the way, did you watch those two horses at their gallops? I thought they were really good."

"So did we," replied Dashell. "Father was quite surprised."

CHAPTER TWENTY-EIGHT

The Meeting

Friday came at last and Dashell took his seat beside the Admiral in his carriage.

"I am glad we could have luncheon together," said Sir Ryder. "I have engaged a private room in a quiet place where we will not be disturbed. The other two have been asked to come at three o'clock, and they have clear directions how to get there."

"All this is very good of you, Admiral."

"Aye, I know, and I don't mind telling you I am not exactly proud of what I am doing, but I can see no other way to vindicate Isobel, and vindicate her I will. There are newspapers of course, but I don't like that idea much, either. Too impersonal."

"I am certainly behind you in all this," said Dashell, "and my father would agree."

They did not talk much more and they soon arrived at their destination. After a light luncheon and the table had been cleared, they settled in comfortable armchairs and spoke of the matter again.

"Now," began Sir Ryder in his decisive way, "we must agree on what we are going to say, and also what we are not going to say. What I mean is that we must not contradict each other. Everything must be crystal clear, except for one thing," looking hard at Dashell.

"And that is?"

"We still do not know how Isobel had all those jewels in her possession. We may never know. We do know she sold one item to send her girls to that school, and there were still a great many left. We will just say she had them with her at the time of her abandonment. We will also assume she was given some money. No mention will be made of all the other jewels found. It will only make things more complicated and could lead to very awkward questions. Agreed?"

"Agreed."

"Good."

"But there is something I would like to mention, Sir Ryder."

"Yes?"

"We may be asked the whereabouts of Caroline and I would not wish it to made known where she is living."

"Ah, yes. Well, let's just say I have made her my ward and she is living under my protection. By the way," continued the Admiral, "do you know either of the two men coming? Jonas Kidd and Philip FitzHerbert?"

Dashell shook his head. "No, I do not know them but I have heard of them." *I don't really like doing this,* he thought. *My darling's name to be mentioned to the likes of them, and yet,* he reminded himself, *I'm doing this for Isobel, not Caroline.*

They looked up sharply at a knock on the door and a servant silently entered with two bottles of wine and some glasses, as ordered by Sir Ryder, and left as quietly as he came.

Sir Ryder settled back in his chair again. "Now we wait."

Almost on the stroke of three there was another knock on the door and the two expected callers were ushered in. Dashell knew what their types would be like but the Admiral not so much, being more used to muscular, rough-and ready sailormen. The latter stared at both of them as they came in. They wore high-heeled shoes, with large silver buckles, satin coats and breeches, powdered wigs, and each carrying a scented handkerchief, as was the fashion for men who habituated salons. Sir Ryder almost audibly gasped, and never even attempted his "bridge test". He glanced at Dashell to see what he thought.

"I am Jonas Kidd," said one of them, "and which of you gentlemen is our host?"

"I am," Sir Ryder managed to reply.

"And I am Philip FitzHerbert," said the other, "and who is this other gentleman?" he enquired, staring at Dashell.

"I am Lord Dashell Lonsdale." He too stared at them, thinking they reminded him in some way of the two moneylenders, but were preferable to them.

"We have come here with some apprehension, Sir Ryder," said Kidd, who appeared to be the spokesman. "Are we to be faced with a call of blackmail or a case of litigation? We find it passing strange that we have actually been requested to come when often we are asked to go, sometimes forcibly. We know what manner of men we are. What gossip are we to hear that you promised we would find interesting?"

Sir Ryder let them talk and respected them for what they said about themselves, as far as he could. He glanced at Dashell again, who seemed to be thinking the same thing.

"Pray sit down, if you will," said the Admiral, remembering his duties as host. "Perhaps a little wine while we talk?" He opened a bottle and poured some wine into the glasses and handed them round. "What you are about to hear is definitely not gossip, but plain truth. And a tragedy, too. A terrible wrong took place many years ago which has to be put right, even after all this time."

"Most intriguing," they murmured, "and you require our assistance in spreading the word? This is why you asked us to come?"

"Yes, it is." replied the honest Admiral.

"Is it possible we could be sued for slander by the other party?"

"I doubt it. But if any accusations arise they can be pointed directly at me. You will have nothing to fear. You have my word."

"And you, Lord Lonsdale? Are you not a son of Lord Barrandale? We have heard he is a worthy man, although not so fortunate as he once was."

Dashell's face darkened at this reference to the loss of their family fortune. "Yes, I am a son of Lord Barrandale."

"Ah. So it is possible it could concern a lady."

Dashell felt his ire rising but before he could say a word Sir Ryder cleared his throat noisily and said firmly, "Let us begin. Any agreement can come after we have spoken," which sounded sensible to both Kidd and FitzHerbert. "No doubt you have heard of Lady Catherine Bretherton?" Sir Ryder continued.

"Oh!" they both cried, flinging their hands in the air. "Who has not heard of her. A most unpleasant woman."

"Er—yes, quite. Now Lady Catherine had a younger sister, Harriet, who married the youngest grandson of the late Duke of Fennshire, while Catherine herself married a mere distant cousin of the family. Catherine never had any children of her own but Harriet had a daughter, Isobel, an only child. Isobel's parents died when she was still young so she went to live with her aunt. Knowing how ambitious and scheming she was, Catherine made good use of her connections to the Fennshires through Isobel. The Brethertons had a country house in Sussex where Isobel grew up and where she played and associated with the children of the local gentry, and probably with the village children as well.

"Even at that young age, Isobel showed signs of becoming a beauty and having strength of character. This encouraged Catherine to make use of her niece so she made sure Isobel had the best education she could provide. She was taught some

French and Italian, she had music, singing and dancing and painting lessons. She learned to play the piano, she was taught fine needlework, and all the social graces; for who knew whom she might marry?" Sir Ryder paused to take few sips of his wine.

"All this is quite interesting, Sir Ryder, and no doubt leads up to what you really have to tell us?" murmured Kidd.

"It does indeed, but be patient if you will." Sir Ryder took another sip of wine. The other two looked at Dashell, who had not said anything yet.

"By the time Isobel was nearly seventeen," began Sir Ryder again, "Catherine had made what she considered to be a very good match for her to a young member of the French aristocracy whose family had escaped the Revolution in Paris and who were still living in England. A very noble and ancient family. What a catch! What could be more brilliant. Catherine had access to the English Court through the Fennshires, and she would have access to the French Court, now that their aristocracy was beginning to return to their country.

"When Catherine returned to Sussex from London after a long absence, to prepare Isobel for her future, she was met with the news that during her said absence Isobel had married Arthur Waterton, her childhood sweetheart, son of the local village squire."

"Ah," said Kidd and FitzHerbert, "this is now becoming interesting."

"Knowing this woman's shrewish and vindictive temper, you can imagine her reaction. Shock. Disbelief. Blind anger. I could go on. This must have been the first time she had ever been thwarted in her plans. For one thing, she tried to get the Bishop to declare the marriage illegal and to dismiss the officiating priest, and he refused to do either. By the way, the marriage was not an elopement; it was a quiet ceremony in the parish church of

Sutherfield. One of the witnesses was an old friend of mine whom I met again recently and who told me much of what happened then. By the way again, Arthur Waterton's mother, Margaret, was my sister, and I knew Isobel as a young girl."

"Oh," said FitzHerbert with a faint smile, "we were wondering how you knew all this and where you fitted in."

Sir Ryder smiled faintly in return, and continued. "Vindictive or not, Catherine was forced to swallow her rage and to accept the situation. Not only that, she had the humiliating task of having to return to London to inform the young Frenchman that his intended bride had recently married someone else, just to have that incident shrugged off as of no consequence. All that education spent on that girl and wasted on a mere son of a baronet who would never be anything else. How she must have seethed! She must have been filled with implacable hatred for Isobel, but she accepted the situation with what ice-cold grace she could. She bided her time for revenge while the two innocents believed themselves forgiven. She had planned, but Providence or Destiny, call it what you will, decided otherwise."

By now Kidd and FitzHerbert were leaning forward in their chairs as they waited for Sir Ryder to continue. "Go on," they urged.

"Arthur and Isobel were as happy as the days were long. First one daughter, Maude, was born, and then a second daughter, Caroline; and still Catherine waited. Now, we are not sure how what happened next came about. Sir Arthur, as he now was, had travelled up to Yorkshire to attend to some matter concerning the late Lord Bretherton's estate. Whether he was asked to go or he offered his services, we do not know, but we know he went. He travelled by himself with his coachman. Just the two of them. Now, Lonsdale, perhaps you would describe what happened next."

"Thank you, Sir Ryder," said Dashell as two pairs of eyes turned to him. "What I am about to tell you I learned when I travelled to Yorkshire recently to try and discover the truth even after nearly twenty years, and I will tell you this now to keep the continuity. I should also say I was accompanied by one of my brothers.

"Apparently the weather in Yorkshire, when Sir Arthur got there, had been extremely unpleasant, intermittent thunderstorms, driving rain and wind for days on end. The innkeeper of the inn where they stopped for the night urged him to stay until the weather improved, but in Yorkshire that could take some time, so he left in the morning. Another thunderstorm broke out soon afterwards and the carriage turned round to go back to the inn, but there was a terrible tragedy. While passing a hillbank, the rain-soaked earth collapsed and completely buried the entire carriage. Horses, man and coachman."

Dashell stopped at the cries of horror from Kidd and FitzHerbert. "How tragic. What a terrible coincidence!"

"Indeed it was," agreed Dashell. "I learned that it was a lonely road, one stagecoach each way once a week, and not many other travellers. The accident was not discovered for two days and it shocked the locality. The road was cleared after much work by local labourers and the two bodies were taken to a barn attached to the inn. They were recognised as those of Sir Arthur Waterton and his coachman. Whatever papers that were on them were so mud—and rain-soaked, for the roof of the carriage had been broken and dislodged; they could not be read. On inspecting the inn's books, Sir Arthur had only signed himself as Waterton, bart, Sussex, and coachman. It was revealed at the inquest that Sir Arthur was twice heard to address his man as "Edwards". That was all that was known so it was impossible to trace them or to notify anyone. The bodies were given decent burial by the local parish, and as the innkeeper told me, they waited for enquiries to come about an overdue carriage. I should make it clear that my brother and I stayed at the very inn Sir Arthur had stayed at all those years ago.

"Now, I have here sketches made by my brother of the two headstones and you can see how desolate they look. Just the plain names and the dates of death."

Kidd and FitzHerbert took the sketches and scrutinized them very carefully. "As you say, Lord Lonsdale, they are bleak looking; but do please continue." Sir Ryder and Dashell looked at each other significantly: the other two were obviously keeping their interest.

"After nearly two months or so, according to the innkeeper," said Dashell, "two agents did come, making enquiries about an overdue carriage. They never said who they were acting for, but we believe it was for Catherine Bretherton. They listened to the story as told by the local authorities, they were given the dried-out papers from the two bodies, still impossible to read, and the death certificates for the two men as written out by the local coroner. Then still without a word they repaid every penny spent by the parish, and went on their way. What was considered puzzling was that nothing was ever said about new headstones, either then or later, so the originals were left in place as you can see from the sketches. It somehow gives me the impression that Sir Arthur, at least, was abandoned and forgotten.

"To return to Catherine in London, we believe that when she learned what had happened she seized upon Arthur's death as an opportunity at last to wreak her vengeance on Isobel. We surmise that somehow she got Isobel to come to London on some pretext or other and to bring the two infant children with her. Or they may have been there already, we have no way of knowing. She must have told Isobel about Arthur's death and then cruelly and deliberately abandoned her in London. We learned later that Isobel was threatened and told that if she tried to say or do anything her children would be taken away and she would never see them again. Barely given time to grieve for her husband, bewildered, terrified and alone, given some money and allowed to keep what few jewels she had, she was left alone in a poorer part of London."

Dashell finished speaking for the moment amidst horrified cries of "Shame! No, no! Of all the damnable things to do!"

"How did Isobel survive?" Kidd asked, once their disgust and indignation had subsided. "Do you know what happened? And did that woman regret what she had done and tried to make redress?"

"No, she did not," said Dashell with a short laugh. "Again I found out recently what she did do all those years ago. She approached the priest of the parish church where the wedding had taken place, the very same man incidentally, and told him a dreadful carriage accident had taken place and that the entire Waterton family had perished."

"She told him *what?* How do you know that, anyway?"

"There is inside that church a certain marble tablet on a wall which Catherine requested be made with the exact wording she wanted chiseled into it, to be set up for all to see. When I wrote to the present incumbent and asked him to make discreet enquiries about the Waterton family he enclosed with his reply a charcoal rubbing of that tablet, and he also informed me there had been a memorial service for them. I brought the rubbing for you both to see."

Wondering, Kidd and FitzHerbert took it and read it together, their faces blanching as they did so. They looked at Dashell, then at Sir Ryder, and back again to Dashell, dumbfounded. "Catherine did this? She actually dared to do it?"

"Yes," replied Dashell steadily. "She declared them all dead, knowing her actions were just to suit her own ends. She lied to the priest. She ordered that tablet cut with its chiseled lie, and put inside a church of all places. Then she asked for a memorial service to be said for all four members of the family, knowing that only one member was actually dead and the others still alive."

Both Kidd and FitzHerbert sat silent and stunned. "It is almost impossible to believe such a heinous act," the latter said at last, "but believe it we do. Now we understand why you asked us to come." Gone were their mincing ways and their foppishness. They looked as stern and resolute as men of their calibre could. "Lord Lonsdale," continued FitzHerbert, "you have more than once said you would tell us how all this knowledge came about. Perhaps now you will do so."

"Indeed I will. Then I think you will have more proof," and paused while Sir Ryder poured more wine for their guests.

"So," began Dashell, telling his story yet one more time, "one afternoon in Oxford Street several weeks ago, I noticed a young lady endeavouring to cross the busy street towards me and in her haste she tripped and fell just as she reached my side and was almost under the wheels of a cab. I assisted her to her feet and could see she was quite shaken, and by this time her maid had joined us for she herself had been delayed in crossing the street because of all the traffic. I hailed a cab for the lady and overheard the maid give the address to the driver."

"Ah," said one of them, "the beginning of a liaison."

"Shh!" remonstrated the other. "Don't interrupt. Let Lord Lonsdale speak."

"Yes," smiled Dashell, "I was greatly enamoured of the lady and called upon her the next day to enquire after her well-being. In fact, I called upon her more than once, and eventually learned she was living alone with a stepfather who took very little notice of her; and that her mother and sister had died a year or so before."

"And the lady's name?" murmured one of the men.

"I will just call her Caroline for now."

"The same name as the younger of the two infant daughters," observed the other one wisely.

"Yes," agreed Dashell. "Now, I must digress here and tell the story as told to me by the maidservant, Hannah. Apparently Isobel, left alone and almost destitute, caught the attention of a gentleman who was very touched by her situation and that she was recently widowed, and offered her marriage as protection. Such was her position that she had no choice but to accept. Also, with a change of name she could not be traced easily, should Catherine ever wish to do so; and it offered her a roof over her head. It seems odd but this man was very retiring and kept himself in the background and allowed Isobel to go her own way.

"Isobel had hired a country girl, the said Hannah as nursemaid, later to become maidservant, who became devoted to her mistress, and who told me many things about her. She said that for the first two years she was with her mistress, Isobel feared for the safety of her children and could hardly let them out of her sight, probably remembering Catherine's threats. At the same time she seemed to be waiting for a letter, which never came."

At this point Sir Ryder gave a cough, thus drawing attention to himself. "I think perhaps I can explain that. As her great-uncle, Isobel could easily have written to me, but if she did, I never received her letter. All this happened about the time I was Acting Governor in Jamaica. A ship known to be carrying letters and supplies foundered and sank during a violent storm as it neared the island. And believe you me," he added with jutting jaw, "if I had known of all this, Isobel and her children would have been under my care and protection; and that woman's treachery and perfidy would have been exposed long ago. But please continue, Lonsdale."

There were murmurs of, "How tragic. How sad," from the other two.

Once again Dashell took up the story. "Hannah went on to say that eventually her mistress made up her mind about the situation and devoted herself to her children. Now, we know Isobel was talented and well-educated for a girl in those days and we know why. This enabled her to teach her own girls everything she knew, for we believe it was her intention to fight back in the only way she knew how. Not only did she teach them but she also took in pupils to teach them what she could, and saved every penny possible with one purpose in mind. That was to send her daughters to a respectable ladies' school with the hope of finding influential husbands for them and, with their help, to declare who she really was.

"Eventually the girls were sent away for a year, but tragedy struck again. All this driving force and effort over the years had over-taxed this gallant lady's strength, and one day she and Hannah had gone out for a long walk and got drenched in a cloud-burst. They struggled back as best they could in their soaking wet dresses and Hannah put her mistress to bed. This took even more of Isobel's strength and she became seriously ill. The doctor was called but she died a day or so later, just before Maude and Caroline were due to return home. They were heartbroken to hear the news and you can imagine their distress. As Caroline herself told me, it was weeks before they could really believe it.

"If that was not enough, there was yet another tragedy. Maude missed her footing at the top of a long flight of stairs in their house and fell to the bottom, breaking her neck. Again Caroline was desolated at losing her sister. It was shortly after that incident that I met Caroline in Oxford Street, as described to you."

The other two shifted in their seats and made murmurs of sympathy, and asked, "What about the stepfather? He does not seem to figure much in the story."

"No," replied Dashell carefully. "I did meet him once and he was not a very prepossessing man. He was out of the house a great deal and, like many wives, Isobel had no real idea what he did except he had a business of some kind in the City. Two deaths so close together disturbed him greatly and he became even more distant. As it happened, his health was not at all good and he died from some kind of seizure a short while later.

"Caroline was now entirely alone, and as she had it in mind to move from that house and dispose of any unwanted items, she and Hannah began going through all the rooms.

"This was how a portrait was discovered hidden away in the attic at the top of the house. It was a portrait of Sir Arthur painted by Isobel. Also discovered amongst her personal items were several documents, including the birth or baptismal papers of Maude and Caroline. It was obvious that Isobel had never taken her second husband into her confidence for she would not have hidden those things away, so perhaps she wished to keep her true identity to herself. Nor, according to Caroline, did she ever tell her or her sister their real name. I think Isobel was going to reveal the truth in her own time, but the tragedy was that she died before she could."

"Oh, that poor, poor lady," said Kidd, "just when she had almost reached the end of her struggles."

"Yes," sighed Dashell, "I quite agree. But I will continue. I would like to mention that Caroline has told me she is the living image of her mother."

"I can verify that fact," said Sir Ryder quickly, "if I may interrupt for a moment. I met Caroline recently, and when she entered the room where I was sitting it was as though Isobel herself had walked in. It gave me quite a shock; it was so uncanny."

"Quite remarkable," murmured the others.

Once more Dashell took up his story. "It was through those certificates that I learned the two girls were born near the village of Sutherfield in Sussex. I therefore wrote to the rector of that parish with the results you already know. And also, by a truly astonishing coincidence the gravedigger's old uncle's neighbour, an ostler at some coaching inn, heard of the accident and had told him it happened in Yorkshire somewhere. My brother and I therefore travelled to Yorkshire to learn for ourselves what had happened, which we have already told you. During our absence discreet enquiries were being made about the Watertons and possible next-of-kin. On our return I wrote to Sir Ryder with the information that his niece Isobel and her children had not died as had been declared." Dashell looked at Sir Ryder. "Would you continue, sir?" and once more two keen pairs of eyes changed direction.

"I can tell you, sirs," said the Admiral, "that I had never received such a shock in all my life. I was staggered, dumbfounded in fact, and called round on Lord Lonsdale and demanded an explanation in no uncertain manner, and thus learned the whole terrible truth." He paused for a moment. "That ends our story, but not what we wish to do. We wish to do for Isobel what she was not able to do for herself, and that is to declare the truth, and for me to acknowledge that Caroline Waterton is my long-lost niece."

Kidd and FitzHerbert looked at each other. "May we speak, sirs, and ask a few questions of our own? Although your narrations have been very clear, we are still apprehensive about one matter and that is, we may be accused of slander by the Duke of Fennshire and of distorting the facts."

"If anyone is accused of slander," stated Sir Ryder, "it will be Lord Lonsdale or I, and there is much evidence to support our claim. You are merely stating what we have told you, and if anyone distorted the truth it was Catherine Bretherton. She cannot deny she had that marble tablet cut. I doubt if the Duke of Fennshire knew anything about it, and if he had he would most certainly have put a stop to it."

"Very well," said Kidd, "we accept what you say. Then he asked, "What happened to the baronetcy after Sir Arthur died?"

"It passed to a distant cousin, Sir Richard Irving," said Sir Ryder, "whom I knew years ago. When I visited him recently to tell him the truth. he was astounded, as was Lady Lucy. He told me Catherine had shut herself up in her country house in Sutherfield and was almost a recluse. She hardly ever goes out."

"Is she still alive then?" queried FitzHerbert. "No one has seen her for years."

"We believe she went abroad to avoid answering awkward questions," observed Sir Ryder drily, "and when the old Dowager Lady Anne Bretherton died shortly after Sir Arthur, apparently she found it all too much; or so she said."

"That's right," replied FitzHerbert, "I remember now. Then when she eventually returned to London she tried to re-enter Society but she had been away too long. Society had almost forgotten her and was tired of her interfering ways anyway. In the end she retired to her country house, as you said."

"Just one final question", said Kidd "what happens now about Caroline, the last of her family?"

"Once I heard her story," said Sir Ryder, "I made her my ward and she is now under my protection."

"What did her stepfather think of that?"

Dashell spoke up. "As I told you, he died recently. I understand his health was not good and he had some kind of seizure and died almost at once. Another tragedy, one might say."

"So what will become of her now she is alone?" persisted Kidd. "We may be asked this," he pointed out.

Dashell smiled at that. "Caroline and I are betrothed."

"Ah-h," they both smiled in turn, "so there was a lady after all. A mutual attraction, no doubt."

"No doubt at all," agreed Dashell.

Kidd and FitzHerbert stood up, thus indicating the end of the meeting. "Gentlemen," Kidd said, "I think I can speak for both of us. You have asked us for our assistance in this amazing matter. You have told us a terrible story and we also feel the truth should be made known, and we agree to do what you ask."

"Thank you, both of you," said Sir Ryder, "that is how I like to think of it. Now, have you any conveyance?"

"We ordered a hackney carriage to come," said Kidd, "but before we leave, we cannot help saying again that words fail us at what you both have told us. It is incredible that this amazing story was revealed following a chance meeting between you, Lord Lonsdale, and the younger daughter, Caroline. Surely it was not coincidence but was meant to be. That is how we like to see it. Good night, Sir Ryder, and to you, Lord Lonsdale." They left the room, each one carrying a well-filled leather purse which he weighed in his hand.

Sir Ryder and Dashell sat down again and almost visibly relaxed. "I think this meeting went very well," said Sir Ryder. "What we told them was certainly not what they expected to hear."

"In fact," added Dashell, "they were astounded. I was watching their faces."

"So was I," said Sir Ryder. "When they first came in I don't mind telling you I wondered who we had asked to come, but by the time they left just now they were quite different men. Care for some more wine before we leave? By the way, there has been no answer yet to my advertisement about the Webster servants. It may possibly be too late after all these years."

They were soon on their way, the carriage stopping first at the new Barrandale House. "Good night, Lonsdale. We will wait for the outcome. I think it could be interesting."

"Yes, indeed, Sir Ryder. Good night."

Sir Ryder was right about the outcome being interesting. What dismayed them, particularly Caroline, was the part of the outcome that was completely unexpected.

CHAPTER TWENTY-NINE

Dashell Speaks To Caroline

The next day after Dashell had a long talk with his father about the evening before, he asked Maxwell if he would do something for him. "I wonder if you would go to the church where Isobel and Thomas Wardlock were married, according to the documents we have, and search through the records. I want to be sure about something. I do not know how far away it is and I could order the carriage for you." He hesitated a moment and said, "On second thoughts perhaps you could take a cab as it would be less conspicuous, and I could give you your fare."

Maxwell left with the directions given him and duly arrived at the church. He paid off the cab, remembering to be inconspicuous. Once inside the church he looked around. A door opened and a clergyman came out and looked curiously at Maxwell.

"Do you require some help, young man?" he asked.

"Yes, if you please, sir. I am a solicitor's clerk and I have been sent here to look through the marriage records, beginning about twenty years ago. It is to verify a marriage actually took place here."

"Oh, I see," said the clergyman. "All those kinds of records are kept in the vestry if you would care to come back with me." Maxwell did so and waited while the appropriate volume was found and placed on a table for him. "I have some things to attend to," said the clergyman tactfully, "and will leave you for a few minutes."

Maxwell started looking at the dates and soon found what he wanted. There it was: Thomas Wardlock, bachelor, and Isobel Louise Waterton, widow, and the name of the officiating priest and signatures of two witnesses. Isobel had obviously made no mention of her title "Lady". He made a note of the date and left the register on the table and closed the door behind him.

He examined the wooden plaque at the back of the church on which were painted the names and dates of all the priests who had been in office over the years. So the present one was not the officiating priest back then. He slipped some coins into the poor box which were meant for his return fare, and walked all the way back. Dashell was not there when he arrived at the house so he sat down and read his Book of Laws and waited.

Dashell eventually returned without saying where he had been and promptly asked him how he had got on.

"I found the place all right," explained Maxwell, "and some clergyman let me into the vestry to look at the Register of Marriages. It is there. Thomas Wardlock and Isobel Louise Waterton, except she made no mention of being Lady Waterton. If you don't mind me asking, why did you want to be sure when you already knew?"

"I wanted to be sure because Wardlock was a forger and he could have forged the documents himself, thus deceiving Isobel. It was just a thought that came to me last night, and as he was known to be an actor he could easily have hired like people for a false marriage."

"Well, I looked at the plaque at the back of the church listing all the vicars they have had and the name of the one who signed the document was there."

"So it appears the marriage was a genuine one, which does relieve my mind," said Dashell, "and as Isobel was later known as Mrs. Wardlock there is no possibility of a scandal there. That is probably the only decent thing Wardlock did for her."

"There is another point too," continued Maxwell thoughtfully. "The date of marriage does prove Isobel was alive after the time she was declared dead." He fidgeted a little before adding, "How did the meeting go last night? If I may ask."

"Oh, it went very well," said Dashell, and gave Maxwell an outline.

Dashell called round at Grosvenor Square on Sunday and learned from Chadwick that Lady Smythe was spending the afternoon with a friend, and he wondered if his aunt had deliberately taken herself away. "Thank you, Chadwick. I will announce myself."

Caroline looked up in delight when he entered the salon. "Dashell! You said you would be calling. Aunt Letty is with some friend of hers."

"Yes, I know. Chadwick told me," kissing her on the cheek. "I do not wish to see my aunt, I want to see you. Alone. Where is Hannah?"

"She is in the other room. Sewing, I think, or perhaps resting." Then Dashell took her by the hand and led her to a sofa where they sat half-facing each other.

Caroline looked at Dashell carefully. "When you say you want to be alone with me and sit down with that look on your face, it means you are going to be serious about something."

"Yes, you are right," he said, cursing himself for what he had to tell her, but it had to be done before any tales got back to her. Everyone knew, and Caroline was the last to know. "Caroline, I have to tell you something which I have known for a while, and now I think this is the right time to do so." Caroline's eyes widened again and she drew in her breath sharply. What had he got to say to her? "Caroline, my darling, you have to be very brave, as I know you will be."

"Haven't I always been?"

He smiled at her and then became serious once more. He took hold of her hands again. "Caroline, I have to tell you the truth about the deaths of your father, mother and sister."

"What do you mean?" she asked. "What else is there to know?"

So slowly and carefully Dashell told her that her father had been buried in a landslide in Yorkshire; and that her mother had been smothered by her stepfather; and that her sister's foot had tripped on a string stretched purposely across the top of the stairs, placed there by her stepfather. By the time he finished she was white-faced and her hands felt cold in his grasp.

Caroline cried out at last, "But *why?* Why be so cruel? What had my gentle mother and sister ever done to him?" Dashell thought he knew why, because Wardlock was a strange man with an unreasonable hatred for those who had what he had not. "Oh, I am glad he is dead, even if you think ill of me. I do not know how Mother endured living with him, and for all the help he gave us we could have done just as well without him."

She stood up and went to look out of a window, collecting her thoughts, while Dashell sat back and waited. He was surprised and braced himself for her reaction, expecting her to weep copiously, or to have hysterics, or rail against her stepfather as a murderer. He was surprised when she simply turned and came back to sit beside him again.

"Dashell, you may think me strangely quiet at what you have just told me. I have long accepted their deaths, but the manner of them does distress me. There is now something I must tell you, believe me or not as you will. Do you remember after we had tea together at the Tea Rooms and we had returned to the house and were in the front garden looking at the rose beds? Something surprised me and I turned round just as that blackbird flew out of the tree?"

"Yes, I do remember. Blackbirds have a way of doing that."

"I turned round, not at that, but because I distinctly felt the presence of Mother and Maude; not in any way to frighten, but just an awareness of them. I think they were trying to say they were alive spiritually and I was not to burden myself grieving over-much for them. Don't you see, Dashell, Step-papa did his worst and he failed. Then the other day when I was in the front garden before I left that house, I again felt Mother's presence. It was almost as though she was asking for her roses to be moved and not to be left behind. I was so glad when you agreed they could be moved to Windsor." She paused for a moment, still looking steadily at him. "Have you ever sensed anything like this? Or does it all sound too fanciful to a man?"

"No," replied Dashell slowly, "I can't ever remember anything like that happening, not even when my own mother died. Have you ever felt your father close to you?" he ventured to ask.

"No, I have not. Perhaps because I never knew him, and it was all so long ago. Maybe Mother did. I hope so," she said with a wistful smile. "Poor Father, it must have been dreadful for him."

Dashell hesitated then said, "There is something more to tell you, if you can bear it."

"I am sure I can. Is it about the meeting last night?"

"Yes. Sir Ryder and I met with these two men we engaged to spread the truth about Isobel. The very truth she was not able to say for herself; and it must be told. We were very discreet and careful of what we said. We hardly mentioned your stepfather at all and your uncle wanted it declared publicly that you are his long-lost great niece. I also hardly need to tell you that they were amazed and astonished at what we revealed to them, so now we will wait and see what the outcome will be."

"I suppose so. You are both very kind. Is there anything else you should tell me?"

"Yes, there is something you ought to know. I asked Maxwell to go to the church where Wardlock and your mother were married, to examine the Register of Marriages. The names and date were there so that proves it was genuine, so that at least was something he did do for your mother."

Caroline did not answer. Instead she stood up and remarked, "Would you think it ill-mannered of me if I said I would like to be alone for a while?"

"Of course not."

They went to the door together and Caroline took hold of Dashell's hand and held it against her cheek. "Thank you, Dashell, for being who you are."

For answer he took her in his arms for a more fond farewell, and held her for a few moments, touched by her words. "I will see you again."

Caroline returned to sit down while Dashell went to look for Hannah in the other room. "Hannah, I have told Caroline at last how her parents and sister really died. It was a shock to her, yet she is taking it very well. Now she has asked to be alone. Would you look in on her in a little while to see she is all right?"

"I will indeed, sir."

Caroline had heard Dashell's footsteps and guessed he had gone to speak to Hannah and then heard him pass the salon door as he left. She sat silently without weeping for no tears would come. She wondered again about that strange man. Why such behaviour towards the three of them. Her mother, then her sister, and she was very nearly the third. What a blessing he was not their real father. Her father's portrait came to mind. What a contrast.

He would never have behaved like that. Anger rose against her stepfather. There were no regrets over his death. Or was that wrong of her? She wished her thoughts would stop crowding in all at the same time.

The door opened and Hannah quietly slipped in and sat down beside her young mistress. She had always known when to come in at the right time.

"Dashell has just told me," said Caroline. "You knew, didn't you?"

"Yes, dear. I knew. But Lord Lonsdale asked me not to say anything. He said he would tell you in his own time."

Caroline said nothing at first, then asked, "What happened to that cushion with the embroidered daffodils?"

Hannah had to confess. "I gave it to Johnny and told him to get rid of it somehow. I don't know if he has yet. I will ask him the next time I see him. Please don't be angry with me, Miss Caroline, I did not know what else to do."

"Of course not, Hannah. I could not possibly have kept it." Then after a brief silence she said, "Knowing what we know now, and even after all the happy memories we do have, we could never have stayed in that house, could we?"

"No, dear. Not now."

CHAPTER THIRTY

The House Inspection— And More

True to his promise Sir Ryder approached the estate agent who had sold him his own house and requested him to take on the sale of the house, 29 Becket Lane, in Fulham. Two building inspectors were duly sent to look over the house and then make their report. They arrived when Johnny was still clearing up after the storm, who promptly asked them what they were doing walking round the property.

"We are here to look over the house and grounds prior to its sale on behalf of the owner, Miss Caroline Waterton, at the request of Sir Ryder Wyecross," they explained. "Would you be the caretaker? We were told there was a young man, Johnny Faulkner, living here and who was still using the stables."

"Yes," said Johnny, "I am Johnny Faulkner."

They looked about them and could not help remarking that the storm had done considerable damage. Then they asked Johnny to show them the extent and boundaries of the grounds. Finally they wanted to go inside the house and would he have the keys to the front and side doors? Johnny took them into the kitchen and gave them the front door key, but haggled about keeping the one for the side door. How was he to get in, he wanted to know. Well, yes, he supposed he could get in through a ground floor window, which remark was regarded with suspicion, so they let him keep that key. Johnny went back outside and left the two men to their inspection.

Starting with the ground floor kitchen areas they gradually covered the whole house. They sucked their teeth, shook their heads, made notes, and tut-tutted their way from one room to another, as they found out how much the house had been neglected over time. Some window frames had become warped. One or two doors did not hang correctly. Plaster on some ceilings had cracked badly. Paintwork was peeling and chipping. The front stairs creaked loudly. The gouge marks on the hall floor were quite noticeable. The paper on some walls had faded where the sun had shone on it. The door at the bottom of the stairs to the attic rooms had been forced open, thus badly splintering the doorway because the key had been lost and the lock had to be broken, as Johnny told them later. The attic rooms were in poor shape; one room had dry rot in the floor. Quite unsafe. Some roof tiles had been displaced by the recent storm and rain had poured in, leaving a very bad stain on an inside wall. There was some evidence throughout the house of woodworm and carpenter ants.

The outside fabric of the house had come away in places; likewise the roof needed repair as other tiles were loose or broken. It was obvious the house had been neglected for years. They spoke to the young man who told them he had been in the house for nearly five years, and the old man who had died recently had hardly spent a penny on it.

The house, together with the stabling, would cost too much to repair, and it was their respectful and considered opinion it should all be pulled down. The land itself could be sold as it was quite valuable and in a good position.

There were many items that could be saved, however. Some marble fireplaces, the wooden panelling from a downstairs room with its beautiful matched carvings; some good window frames; and several solid oak doors; and as much wood as possible from the floors. This was the report handed in by the two inspectors.

The estate agent approached Sir Ryder with the report, who read it through carefully. He was surprised, and yet not surprised. The agent said he would be obliged if he could receive a letter of agreement from the owner to the pulling down of the house, as the work could not commence until then. Sir Ryder promised he would see to it.

The next day he called round at Grosvenor Square to speak with Caroline and let her read the report for herself. The condition of the house was not good and he could see no reason to keep it if it was going to cost more to repair than it was worth. Caroline was an intelligent, level-headed girl who knew her own mind, and he had become quite fond of her.

Caroline had just come in from a walk with Hannah, and was now sitting with Lady Smythe.

"Uncle Ryder," she cried. "I had no idea you would be calling."

"I have been in touch with some estate agents as I promised I would," he explained, "and here is the report from their inspectors. It is not good."

Caroline took it from him and read it through carefully, and then looked at her uncle in some surprise and concern. "As you say, it is not good. I had no idea it was in such disrepair. I suppose living there one got too used to everything and would not notice it."

"Quite right," agreed Sir Ryder. "You will see it is recommended the house be pulled down and anything that can be saved will be saved, and that the only thing of real value is the land itself. It is not for me to say but I would suggest you would agree to this. Nothing can be gained by trying to sell the house, and anyway I doubt if anyone would want it."

Caroline was disgusted and horrified at this further proof of her stepfather's indifference, and she could not understand his reasoning behind it unless he was so tight-fisted he could not bear to part with any money. Her one-time plan to sell the house and purchase a smaller one would never have succeeded, so she readily agreed to the inspectors' suggestion.

"Ah," said Sir Ryder with his brisk manner. "I thought you would. I therefore took the liberty of drafting out a reply to the estate agents for you. You do not have to copy it word for word, but it will just give you an idea of what to say."

Caroline dutifully took it and read it through. "You are very thorough," she said with a little smile. "I would just like to add that the stables must be left until last so Johnny can stay as long as possible, and that he may take whatever wood he wants from the old trees in the orchard."

"That's very good of you," said her uncle, with a look of approval. "I am not expecting you to write anything right away, you can do that later this evening. I will send my man round tomorrow afternoon and then he can take it to the agents for you."

"That is very kind of you," said Caroline.

"Well, there is no point in delaying anything."

Lady Smythe had been listening to all this and smiled when she caught Caroline's eye. Later Caroline remarked to her that she felt she should have replied "Aye, aye, sir," to everything her uncle said, which brought chuckles from both of them.

Sir Ryder did not stay much longer, leaving soon after tea. "Thank you kindly, Lady Smythe, and you, Caroline. I enjoy coming here." He went away surprised at his own remark. Well, he did enjoy coming here. Perhaps ladies did have a way of endearing themselves—depending on the ladies, of course.

Caroline showed the report to Lady Smythe who expressed her own surprise. "Uncle Ryder is quite right," said Caroline, "but you know what this means, Aunt Letty, that I have nowhere else to go and must needs trespass further upon your generosity to allow me to stay here."

Lady Smythe promptly sat by Caroline on the sofa and put her arm round her shoulder. "My dear, dear girl, of course you may stay here. I would not dream of sending you away. I know if I did, Dashell would give me a dreadful scolding."

Caroline laughed at that. "Thank you, Aunt Letty, you are very kind. Now, would you excuse me for I would like to speak to Hannah."

Hannah looked up when Caroline came to join her. "I must show you this," began Caroline. "Uncle Ryder called here this afternoon and brought this report about our old house." She pulled up a chair next to Hannah and they read it together.

"Oh, my," exclaimed Hannah in horror a minute or so later. "It really sounds awful. I had no idea it was as bad as that."

"Nor did I," admitted Caroline.

"Well, I knew about the cracks in the ceilings and the stuck windows and a few other things, but, oh dear."

"I know," agreed Caroline, "and as Uncle Ryder said, there is no point in trying to keep it. He drafted out a letter of agreement for me and we can read this together as well. I will add that the stables are to be left until last, and that Johnny can take what wood he wants from the old trees in the orchard."

"So that will be the end of the house," Hannah ventured to say.

"Yes," said Caroline slowly. "It does sound final to have it pulled down. Our old home, such as it was."

"In fact, the only things to survive will be your mother's roses," continued Hannah.

"Yes," agreed Caroline, turning to her with a smile. "Mother's roses. Her spirit did win out in the end. And Aunt Letty has kindly agreed we can stay on here. That makes us sound like two orphans," she added, with a sad little laugh.

"I suppose it does, Miss Caroline," smiled Hannah. "No place to call home."

Caroline wrote out the agreement that evening and the letter was left on a table in the hall downstairs. Chadwick was informed that Sir Ryder's manservant would be coming for it the next day.

When Johnny returned to the stables late one afternoon he was surprised to see some scaffolding had already been put up which must mean the house was going to be pulled down. The house was empty now except for the few things in the kitchen he needed for himself. Everything else had gone. He must call on Miss Caroline to give her the money from the sale of the unwanted items from the house, and to say her own furniture was now at Windsor. What a job it had been to get that piano onto the cart even with a ramp he had made. It had taken Andy and himself some considerable effort, but they did it.

The sale of 'is Nibs' stuff brought in a fair sum which Miss Caroline said he could keep, for she wanted none of it. Well, he didn't want it either, not after wot 'e did. And that went for his old clothes and bedding, which he took with the money to a mission hall in the East End somewhere. He grinned at the memory of it, the looks on the faces of the people there, too astounded to think of anything to say. It made him feel good to do it for probably 'is Nibs had never given as much as a penny or a ha'penny to charity. Nor even a farthing. Now he, Johnny, had done it for 'im, and serve 'im right too.

The next morning when the workmen arrived, the foreman approached him. "Are you Johnny Faulkner?" he asked. "We were told there was a young caretaker here."

"Yes, I am Johnny Faulkner," replied Johnny.

"Ah. Good. Now let me see," said the man, unfolding a piece of paper and turning it the right way round. "We have been told to leave the stables until last, and that you can have whatever wood you want from the old orchard. I understand the owner of the house has made a point of that. So there we are," he concluded, folding up his paper.

Johnny looked at the scaffolding with interest. "Where will you begin?" he asked. He was always ready to learn.

"Oh, always inside a house. Everything removable is taken out first. Now, if you don't mind, young man, we must get on with our work."

Johnny turned away as well, for he had his own work to do. He had left the digging up of the roses until last and he must now get on with it for he did not want workmen trampling over everything. There were seventeen bushes in all and each one had to be wrapped round in wetted sacking with as much root ball and earth as possible. He placed them in the carriage house where they would be out of the way, and no need to worry about making a mess, not when the building was going to come down eventually. When that was finished he had to dig up the spring bulbs, which was easier said than done. They were scattered about in the front and back gardens and he could not remember exactly where. Well, he did his best but knew they were all mixed up.

While Johnny had been working, the foreman had taken a look at the stables as a matter of course and was surprised to find a large horse and a covered cart there. He had imagined there would be a mere pony and trap. "Are they yours?" he had asked Johnny in wonder.

"Yes," replied Johnny proudly. "Me uncle died and left me some money so I bought them, and now I'm in business for meself."

"You are a very lucky young man," remarked the foreman. "Are you for hire then? I mean, do you do odd carting jobs?"

It was Johnny's turn to be surprised. It had been at the back of his mind what to do when work between Park Lane, South Kensington and Windsor came to an end. The journey to Windsor with the plants would be the final one of all; and he would not have the stable here much longer either.

"Yes, I would do odd carting jobs," he answered quickly. "I hafta do a delivery tomorrer and I'll be gone all day. Why, do you know of anything?"

"I may do," replied the foreman slowly, "I can let you know later."

Ever the optimist, Johnny felt better already. "Thanks." Then he told the foreman he wanted to show him something, and led him to the downstairs room in the house and showed him the carved panelling, and pointed out the little keyhole and the swivel door in one of the panels.

The man whistled in surprise. "I would never have guessed. But it would have been found when dismantled." He peered into the recess and then stretched out his arm and felt all round with his hand, but it was quite empty. Johnny had made sure of that. "Is there one on the other side of the fireplace?"

Johnny shook his head. "No, just the carved panelling. That's the only one there is." He had made sure of that too, by fingering and testing every piece of carving.

"Well," said the foreman, "I must say it is beautiful panelling. It will be well worth saving the matched pieces. A very clever place to conceal things, too," he added, looking at the recess again, while Johnny just smiled.

CHAPTER THIRTY-ONE

Johnny Continues To Be Helpful

J ohnny set out for Windsor early the next morning and for once Goldie had a light load behind her as she trotted her way along. In a way he was pleased to be going as he would be seeing his friend, Samuel Cullen, again. He did not know Samuel had allayed the suspicions the servants at Windsor had about him and his connection with Lord Lonsdale. Samuel had told them Johnny had undoubtedly saved the life of Miss Waterton, the future Lady Lonsdale, which was why Lord Lonsdale was so very grateful.

When Johnny arrived, Hitchcock was informed the lady's roses were here. Johnny explained to him he had wrapped up the roses carefully, but was sorry the spring bulbs were all mixed up as he had half-forgotten which of them had grown where.

"Never mind, lad," replied Hitchcock kindly, "they can all be sorted out in the spring when they start to bloom. I can tell a lot just by looking at them anyway. They can go in one of the greenhouses until I know where her ladyship wants them planted."

Her ladyship! thought Johnny. Of course, he means Miss Waterton. That seemed to put even more distance between them. He went to find Samuel and cheered up when he was told he could have lunch in the servants' hall when it was time. He had brought his own just in case but he could eat that later. He and Samuel always had a lot to talk about and the latter was surprised to learn the old house was being pulled down.

"Doesn't surprise me," confided Johnny. "I had a real good look at it and it is terrible in some places. 'Is Nibs hardly spent a penny on it."

"What will you do for work now that this is your last time here?" asked Samuel.

"I don't know. Something will turn up, I suppose."

After lunch, Johnny went to look for the head gardener and was told he was in one of the greenhouses. Hitchcock looked up in surprise to see him approaching. "If you please, sir," began Johnny politely, "I would like to arsk yer somefink."

Hitchcock looked more closely at him. So this was the lad who had saved Miss Waterton's life, and who had found a trainer for their lordships' racehorses. "And what did you want to ask me?"

"Well," began Johnny with a gulp, "I've bin doing odd jobs of work and some gardening and I've bin arsked to find some rose bushes. Could yer tell me where I could find some so I c'n tell the person 'oo arsked me?" Most of what he said was true and the rest he made up, but he didn't care. He wasn't going to tell anyone he wanted a rose bush as a wedding present.

"Well, I don't really know," replied Hitchcock carefully. "The only place I can think of is Kew Gardens. Perhaps your person might try there." Johnny thanked him very much but turned away thinking it did not sound too helpful.

When he returned to Becket Lane he saw more scaffolding had been put up. The workmen had begun gutting the house from the inside, eventually leaving just the shell. They explained to an ever-interested Johnny they would break up the roof and walls, keeping all the re-useable tiles and bricks and window frames, and so on. And those rooms in the attic which had not been used for years had dry rot there. Considering the condition of the house it was a miracle the floor had not come crashing down about people's ears, they remarked, with that air of cheerful gloom workmen sometimes have. What had been the front garden was now trampled down by many boots coming and going.

When returning from his work one day, a huge bonfire had been lit to burn off all old and splintered wood. It still gave off considerable heat and Johnny had to stand back as he watched it. Then he suddenly turned on his heel and went towards the stable and came back with the embroidered cushion Hannah had asked him to get rid of. He had hated having it there but had never known what to do with it. Now he had a chance to dispose of it for ever, and with sure aim he threw in onto the bonfire and watched while it burned to ashes.

CHAPTER THIRTY-TWO

The Admiral Receives A Reply To His Advertisement

Sir Ryder was in his living room warming himself in front of the fire, thinking over that talk he and Lonsdale had with those two men, and how well it had gone. He thought of the Websters, and the second advertisement placed in the newspaper asking for their whereabouts.

There was a knock on the door and Tidmarsh entered. "This letter has just been delivered, Admiral," he said.

"Leave it on the table, Tidmarsh." He was in no hurry at the moment for he often received letters.

"Aye, aye, sir."

All that changed when he opened it. The long awaited reply from the Websters at last! It was short and to the point, from John Webster himself, and in a fairly decent hand. Now they might have an answer to that final question: how did all those jewels come to be in Isobel's possession? And what else might they know?

Dear Sir Ryder,

In answer to your enquiry I am employed as a manservant and my wife as cook-housekeeper to a gentleman, and he it was who drew our attention to your advertisement as to our whereabouts. If I may be so bold to remark, my wife and I were greatly surprised to hear from your goodself after so many years. Our gentleman has kindly given us time to call upon you, and we would be pleased to come this Thursday, if it is to your convenience. In view of our gentleman's kindness we would not wish to be late in returning.

Yours respectfully,
John Webster

After hastily writing to Lord Barrandale and Dashell, Tidmarsh was sent round with the Admiral's letter and came back with the reply that they were ready and willing to come to his house as requested. He also wrote to Lady Smythe and said he would call the next day and would be obliged if she could give him the jewels Isobel had so carefully kept. He would explain why when he came. He now wrote back to John Webster taking some pains to explain why he had been anxious to trace them after all this time, and would they come this Thursday as they suggested.

Sir Ryder duly called round at Grosvenor Square. "Just to inform you again, ladies, I finally heard from John Webster. He was once footman to Sir Arthur; and Joan Cooper, as she was then, was maidservant to Isobel. Then later they both attended to the Dowager Lady Anne Bretherton until she died, so I think they may be able to tell us a great deal."

"I hope so," said Caroline. "I would love to speak to other people who knew my parents. I think it is wonderful the way they came forward."

"Caroline, my dear," said Sir Ryder, clearing his throat, "I can understand you are anxious to speak to these good people, but that is not the primary reason I asked them to come to relate all they know. Another reason is that people who have something to tell do not speak freely in front of too many persons, especially if they are strangers to them. They are more at ease with just two or three. You understand, of course?"

Caroline, feeling rebuked, agreed. "I had not thought of it like that. I am sorry."

He looked at Lady Smythe. "I trust you also understand, marm?"

"Of course, Sir Ryder," she replied.

"And those jewels. I wish to take them away with me and show them to the Websters. I am interested to see if they recognize any of them."

"I will have them ready for you."

"Good. I have asked Barrandale and Lonsdale to come on Thursday for luncheon and to stay for dinner. The Websters have been asked to come during the afternoon. Now that is all settled let us talk of other things."

CHAPTER THIRTY-THREE

The Situation Is Explained To The Websters

L ord Barrandale and Dashell duly arrived at Sir Ryder's house in Hampstead. Their carriage returned to South Kensington as their host would see them driven to their door.

"Welcome, gentlemen, welcome," cried the Admiral when Tidmarsh announced them. "Come in and sit down. A little brandy or port wine before luncheon? I feel this is a momentous occasion to hear what the Websters have to tell us. Perhaps a great deal or perhaps nothing much at all. We shall see."

Once again they rehearsed what they were going to say, and what they were not going to say. "We will tell them that Isobel and Maude have both died," said Sir Ryder, "but not how they died. If they knew that they might wonder if anything was said to the authorities."

"Which could be very awkward for us," Barrandale pointed out.

"Yes, indeed," said Sir Ryder, "but I trust you both will agree. We will tell them what we know first, and that may put them at their ease."

At about three o'clock Tidmarsh entered the room and announced, "Mr. John Webster and Mrs. Joan Webster." They came into the room looking like the servants they were, simply but respectably dressed in black.

"Come in, Webster. Come in, John, and you, Joan. It has been many a year since we last saw each other," said Sir Ryder, trying to put them at their ease.

"It has indeed, Sir Ryder," answered John gravely. The two servants were still feeling awkward because of the number of years that had passed and the fact that Captain Wyecross was now Rear Admiral Sir Ryder Wyecross, and that he had wanted to trace them after all this time. They looked nervously at Lord Barrandale and Dashell, wondering who they were and why they were there.

Sir Ryder saw this and said, "These two gentlemen are Lord Barrandale and his son Lord Lonsdale, and they feature a great deal in the story we shall relate about Isobel and her two daughters."

The Websters replied with slight bows, "Your lordships," and sat down at Sir Ryder's bidding, obviously not used to doing so in such company.

"Miss Caroline Waterton and I are betrothed," explained Dashell, and their faces showed their delight, and that remark put them more at ease.

"As we say, it has been a long time," repeated Sir Ryder, "and they were happier days then. But I am sure you are wondering why you have been asked to come to tell us what you know of the so-called disappearance of Lady Isobel Waterton." The two servants grew tense and glanced at each other, giving the others the impression that they knew quite a lot. "So now let us begin," said Sir Ryder firmly. "We will tell you our side of the story first and you will see how it all unfolds." He nodded at Dashell.

So for yet one more time Dashell began his story, being as clear and concise as he could, for there always seemed to be a lot to relate.

At the mention of the deaths of Isobel and Maude, John and Joan had given low murmurs, "Oh, no."

Dashell saw their sympathy and smiled at them, but continued, "We know from Caroline that her mother, who had been well-educated, taught Maude and her everything she knew. Now Isobel also had in her possession a quantity of jewels which were of great value"—and here again the Websters looked at each other—"and she sold one or two items to help pay for her daughters' fees, carefully keeping the receipts. So the two girls went away for a year.

"Some time after they left, the stepfather, whose name was Thomas Wardlock, suddenly wanted to know why the two girls had gone. Up to that point he had taken very little, if any, notice of them. He found some private papers belonging to Isobel, marriage and birth certificates for instance, which he would not give back unless she told him how she found enough money to send the girls away. She refused to do this, merely stating she had saved everything she could from teaching.

Dashell continued describing everything, finishing with the memorial Lady Bretherton wanted placed inside the parish church at Sutherfield. "By the way, have either of you seen that tablet?"

"No, your lordship," said John. "We left soon after the old Lady Anne Bretherton died, so is must have been put up afterwards."

"Here is the charcoal rubbing the Reverend Swanson sent to me," said Dashell, and handed it to them and watched for their reaction.

They took one look at it and cried out in distress, "But this is for all of them!" The look on their faces was one of bewilderment. "But that is impossible!"

"I shall continue," said Dashell. "I then travelled up to Yorkshire, accompanied by my brother, to where Sir Arthur had been buried. We learned that he and his coachman had died in a landslide caused by days and days of rain."

The Websters gasped in astonishment. "Do you mean the whole carriage, sir?"

"Yes," replied Dashell quietly. "The whole carriage and pair." Pale faced, they listened as Dashell continued his narrative.

"On our return to London I immediately wrote to Sir Ryder Wyecross, for during our absence enquiries had revealed that he was Isobel's relative, informing him to his enormous surprise of all I had found out about Sir Arthur Waterton and Lady Isobel and their two daughters."

"And I may tell you that I had never been so astounded in all my life," stated the Admiral. "Never."

"So we are fairly certain that Catherine Bretherton seized upon Arthur's death as a chance to abandon Isobel and her girls as punishment for marrying him without her prior knowledge, thus upsetting all her schemes."

When Dashell finished, John spoke. "I think my wife would agree with me that we appreciate being taken into the confidence of you three gentlemen. We were amazed and greatly puzzled that you, Sir Ryder, would try to trace us, although we had seen your name in the newspapers more than once. We read the papers once our gentleman has finished with them, which can sometimes take a number of days. When he pointed out to us your advertisement, we wrote a reply immediately."

"I am more than glad you did," said Sir Ryder." I was beginning to lose hope of hearing from you at all. After a lapse of so many years anything could have happened. And the three of us could not understand how all those jewels came into Isobel's possession.

He eyed them keenly. "We would like both of you to tell us all you know of the situation between Arthur and Isobel Waterton and Catherine Bretherton, for we believe you can tell us a great deal. I had been watching you as you followed Lord Lonsdale's narrative."

"Yes, Sir Ryder, there is a great deal we can tell," admitted John, "but I think my wife should speak first, for that is where our story begins."

CHAPTER THIRTY-FOUR

The Websters Tell All They Know

Joan was understandably hesitant at first as she sat beside her husband. "I think I need hardly tell you, gentlemen," she began, "what kind of person Lady Catherine Bretherton really was, if I may speak my mind. As you know, Sir Ryder, I was nursemaid to Isobel as a child in Bretherton Hall, then maidservant to her before she even married young Arthur. Lady Catherine had watched over Isobel, trying to turn her into what she wanted her to be, not what Isobel was meant to be, but Isobel was incredibly strong but not exactly self-willed, if you can understand what I mean. Catherine had great plans for her niece with her own ambitions in mind, and it was a tremendous shock to her to hear that Arthur and Isobel had married without her prior knowledge. This fact, of course, completely did away with all her own ambitious plans for herself. I know she bitterly regretted allowing them to be together so much when they were growing up.

"On the surface she was quiet, but underneath she was nothing of the sort. She behaved kindly towards them as though she had forgiven them, and even gave them a carriage and pair as a wedding present. Yet, I felt she planned some terrible revenge.

"The late Lord Bretherton had some land in the North of England, in Yorkshire, I believe, and some question arose about it—I do not know what—and Lady Catherine was going to send some agent or other to see about it, but Sir Arthur, being the gentleman he was, offered to go himself. He left in a day or so in his new carriage with Edwards driving, not knowing when he would return, as it could take several days to travel and then attend to the matter. Lady Catherine then left to go to her town house in London and Isobel remained in Waterton Grange with the children, and I stayed with her. So the days passed, rather too many for my liking, for travelling could be dangerous and accidents could happen, and even Isobel was beginning to wonder.

"About two months or more after Arthur's departure a letter came from Lady Catherine brought by a hired carriage to the effect that Arthur was in London and would Isobel come and bring the two children with her. She did not mention me but it would be natural for me to travel to London as well. Isobel was delighted to think of seeing Arthur again, although she was surprised at being asked to bring the little girls. I, on my part, was more than surprised, I was suspicious; but I did not say as much to Isobel. Once or twice in the past I had seen Lady Catherine's mask slip, her face revealing black, implacable hatred, even evil. The first time I could have been mistaken, as it happened so quickly I wondered if I actually did see it. And then I saw it a second time. However, as a hired carriage had been sent, Isobel could not refuse. So we hastily put together all the things we thought necessary and left, leaving John in charge.

"Aye, that's right," he agreed, "I felt uneasy too, but what Lady Catherine wanted, she always got."

"As you may already know," continued Joan, "Lady Catherine had two houses; the town house in London and the country house in Sussex. She therefore had quite a number of servants and I need hardly tell you they were all terrified of her, for she was known to dismiss a servant at any time or that she would take a sudden dislike to one of them, or she would sometimes rage at them for some trivial offence.

"So the carriage arrived at the London house, Isobel of course expecting to see Arthur. However, she was told that he was staying somewhere else, as what with having guests in the house she did not want them disturbed by children crying. That sounded reasonable enough, but I did not like it. If that was the case, why was Isobel asked to bring them?

"There must have been something in my look or manner for shortly afterwards she dismissed me, giving me some money for my return journey, and my young mistress was quite distressed to see me go. Lady Catherine had no right to send me away for I was a Waterton servant and no longer a Bretherton one; and I suspected she did it because she wanted me out of the way. From what you gentlemen have said I believe she learned Arthur was already dead and that she had planned everything and knew exactly what she was doing. Well, like it or not, I had to return and with plenty of misgivings, I can tell you."

Here she stopped speaking and looked at John, who now took up the story.

"I could hardly believe my eyes when Joan returned alone and at what she told me. What was going to happen to our young mistress left alone with two little children? I was beginning to have some misgivings and suspicions, myself. Well, three or four days later a letter came to me from Isobel. Then when I read it, well, Joan saw the look on my face and came over to read it with me, and we had to read it more than once.

"Her letter said that she was taken by Lady Catherine in her carriage, with the little girls and everything she had brought with her to the place where she believed Arthur to be. When they arrived there was no Arthur, and her aunt told her the terrible truth that her husband had died in a carriage accident and that she was taking this opportunity to abandon her in London and to declare her and her children dead, that they had all died in the same accident, as punishment for daring to thwart all her plans for her. She was in a terrible rage and threatened that if she tried to say anything to anybody, her children would be taken away from her and she would never see them again.

"Oh, how I remember the words she wrote," said John. "Oh, my dear John, my dear John, I must needs be dead to all who know me for my babies' sakes, but I beg your help if you will, in this respect." And then she asked me if I could somehow bring her all the certificates that were in Arthur's desk. And in particular she asked for his portrait and what jewelry of hers we could find, and her clothing and any other things belonging to the children. Then she told us where to find the money Arthur kept hidden away, as we would need it to come to her. We found the money and it was quite considerable. How to get everything to Isobel without the knowledge of Lady Catherine was the difficulty, but we could not waste time.

"We gathered everything together as well as other things we thought needful, and took the portrait out of its frame for easier carrying and put the frame itself in the attic. Now, all that was left in the stables was a pony and a small cart which I ordered the boy to get ready. We told the other servants we had to take some things to Lady Isobel and we would be away two or even three days, we were not sure.

"We knew we were taking a great risk but our mistress desperately needed our help, so we left that afternoon with me driving, and we stayed overnight in Dorking. We hired a carriage to leave early in the morning, and leaving the pony and cart behind, we travelled up to London to the address of the inn we had been given. Thankfully it was on the south side of London and we found it without too much trouble. It was called The Star Inn, but we never dreamed it would be in such a poor and run down part of London. I do not know how Lady Catherine could have been so cruel and vindictive to do what she did.

"Isobel had been waiting with what hope and patience she had and saw us arrive and ran to the top of the stairs to greet us."

Here John stopped and looked to his wife to continue.

"That's right," she said. "I hastened upstairs to her and she flung her arms round me, weeping, and thanked us again and again for coming. "Indeed, I had not expected you to come so soon," she cried. I well remember those words too.

"We dared not stay long; for one thing we had ordered the carriage to wait, and while Isobel and I talked, John saw that everything was brought into the room. We could see she was pale-faced and in shock over the past events, but she was resolute for she always had inner strength, and told us again what her aunt had done. "I must and I will be strong for the sake of my little ones" she told me.

"Then she astonished us with her plea that I stay with the babies while John took her back to call on her great aunt, the old Dowager Lady Anne Bretherton, who lived in the same house as Lady Catherine." Joan paused significantly after saying those last few words.

"It would be another great risk for us to take," said John, taking up the story again, "but she begged us." 'I know I am supposed to be dead but I must tell Great Aunt Anne that I am not, and perhaps she can help me.' "I am not sure how she thought the old lady could help but we could not refuse, especially when Isobel said her Aunt Catherine would be in London for many days and would know nothing about it. We had not been in the room more than an hour before Isobel and I left.

"Well, we made our way back to Dorking without any trouble and stayed overnight. We had made our plans that we would take the pony and cart deep into the woods near the end of the house, tie the pony to a tree, and make our way into the house and slip into the old lady's rooms. I knew how to get into the house at that end and would open a door for Isobel. So that is what we did.

"The old lady showed no great surprise to see us for Isobel often went to visit her. Isobel tried to get her to understand what she was saying but I don't think Lady Anne completely grasped everything. She was getting old and frail but she suddenly understood that Isobel was in great need of help because Lady Catherine was threatening her in some way.

"There was no love lost between Lady Anne and Lady Catherine, in fact she thoroughly detested her daughter-in-law and her arrogant ways, and here was a chance to defeat her. Hastily ordering me to fetch a large linen bag from her dressing-room, she got up, frail as she was, and began picking jewelry off her dressing-table and putting it in the linen bag I held for her. Then she opened the drawers underneath to see what more she could find to put into the bag until there was a considerable amount. 'There' she said, her voice cracking, 'Do you worst now, Catherine, if you have not done enough already.' I still remember those words. I helped her back into her chair for I could see she had become exhausted from that exertion, and I think she fell asleep. There was nothing we could do and we dared not stay any longer. Isobel kissed her and said, 'Goodbye, Great Aunt, and thank you,' but I don't think she heard.

"So we slipped away as quickly and quietly as we came and made our way back to the pony in the woods. Isobel was weeping as we walked and I had one arm round her to comfort and steady her, I felt so desperately sorry for her. I am positive no one in the house ever saw or heard us. I wondered if she should appeal to the

Duke of Fennshire, that is, the old one, not the present one, but she would not hear of it. He was quite a formidable gentleman, I believe, and Isobel was too terrified for her children.

"We drove back to Dorking, and again leaving the pony and cart, hired another carriage to London and so to the inn where Joan was anxiously awaiting us."

John paused in his talk and begged leave to pour himself a little water from the pitcher on the sideboard and to give some to Joan.

Dashell heard eagerly that Isobel had been given the jewels, and said, "We could never understand how she had so many in her possession, and there was always the nagging doubt of how she obtained them. What a relief to know the truth at last."

Sir Ryder then spoke up. "I must interrupt your most enlightening narrative, John. Did Isobel mention writing to me at all? From what Hannah told us later, she appeared anxious to receive a letter, but which never came, and I would be the only other person she could approach."

John shook his head. "No, Sir Ryder. It did cross my mind at the time, but because Isobel was so adamant about not approaching the old Duke, I did not like to say anything more to her."

"Ah," said Sir Ryder sadly, "I believe she did write to me but I never received the letter"—explaining why—"so that poor girl must have felt absolutely deserted."

"Is there much more you have to tell us?" asked Barrandale.

"Yes, your lordship," answered John, "considerably more." He put his glass aside, and continued.

"We all met up again in London and how glad we were to do so. We did not dare stay long for we never knew what Lady Catherine might do. So we all, including myself, tearfully said our goodbyes, Isobel resolving to be brave, yet fearful at the same time. We kept a little of Arthur's money for our return journey and gave the rest to Isobel. She could not thank us enough for what we had done to help her and begged us to remember her in our prayers, which indeed we have done ever since. Then we left, and Joan and I have never been so heavy-hearted.

"We returned to Dorking, then drove all the way back to Waterton Grange, thankful to be there and relieved to learn nothing untoward had happened during our absence. But oh, never had we known the house to be so quiet and empty, almost desolate. Then about a week or ten days after our return we received three letters, almost one after the other.

"The first letter, to our great surprise, was from Isobel, again thanking us for our help. Then she said a very kind clergyman told her that there was another gentleman who had heard of her predicament—without saying how he had—and was deeply touched by it"—and here the other three men all glanced significantly at each other—"and offered her marriage as protection. Such was her situation and predicament that she had no choice but to accept, for it was far too unsafe to sell any jewelry so soon; and it would afford her a roof over her head, as well as a change of name so she could not easily be traced. The gentleman found a nursemaid for her—'but I do not like her, so I shall find another of my own choosing,' she wrote. Here again the other men glanced at each other. Then she asked us to burn that letter and the first one, if we had not already done so. In respect to her wishes we did burn them. So that was the last we heard from her. And all these years we have sorely wondered what became of her.

"The second letter was from Lady Catherine, and our hearts almost stopped when we received it in case she had found out something. But it was merely to order us to close the house and dismiss the servants, and she actually sent us some money for this and for the last of our wages. That took us by surprise, for

Lady Catherine was not known to be generous in this respect. She continued to write that it was her duty and grief to inform us that all the Watertons, Sir Arthur and Lady Isobel and both infants had all perished in a tragic carriage accident." Here, John paused in his talk and held his wife's hand more firmly. "Sirs, I need hardly tell you our true thoughts on the matter, but we obeyed her orders. In fact, we did not dare disobey. We put the house in order and dismissed the other servants. One more thing, we burned the frame that had held Arthur's portrait.

"The third letter was from the old Dowager Lady Anne, in fairly firm handwriting for someone her age. Was it true, she asked, that all the Watertons had died in a terrible accident? Lady Catherine had just written and told her, and that Waterton Grange was to be closed until the next heir took over. If this was so, would I accept the position as her personal footman and Joan Cooper as her maidservant? She said she was tired of all the constant change of servants. She never knew who to expect to come and attend to her and she would much prefer to have her own.

"Well, Joan and I gave this a great deal of thought and we decided that we would attend to Lady Anne. Rightly or wrongly, we knew she was getting very frail and we therefore would not be there for long. Again, it was a risk, for sooner or later Lady Catherine was going to find out about the missing jewels, yet on the other hand we felt we should be there for the old lady's sake. So we accepted her offer; and after Waterton Grange was closed we began our duties in Bretherton Hall.

"We settled in very well. The old lady did require a great deal of attention and now with me to carry her she was able to get outside more as I would push her in a wheeled chair. She enjoyed this very much. She never mentioned the visit of Isobel and I wondered if she even remembered, although she must have known some jewelry was missing. She was still sharp-witted at times but at others was becoming quite forgetful. However, she spoke to me one day and said, 'You and Joan are serving me very well, so I will write out a letter of reference for the two of you'. And this she did. We were both very touched by her concern for us, as what with the sudden death of Arthur, we would get no such letter. Nor could we expect one from Lady Catherine.

"We had been at our new place about a month when Lady Catherine suddenly returned. We learned that she would be attending several balls, and the Prince Regent himself would be in attendance on different occasions, so she planned to look through her dresses in her wardrobe. I had taken the tray from Lady Anne's evening meal back to the kitchens and on my return to her suite, Lady Catherine happened to see me. 'What are you doing here?' she demanded. 'You were supposed to have left Waterton Grange with all the other servants. Why are you here?' I explained that I was now personal footman to Lady Anne and that Joan Cooper was her maidservant. 'I see,' she said in her icy way, and her eyes positively glittered, and I could see she was greatly displeased. Then she turned away, but it did not bode well. Then I told Joan what had happened. And now I will let her continue," once more giving her hand a gentle squeeze as though to give her confidence. She responded with a hesitant smile at him.

"Before I continue, gentlemen," said Joan, "may I say that we have both spoken freely because we had your assurance we could do so in safety, but now I must beg to ask again, as—as—" then she stopped.

Barrandale was quick to understand. "You have something of a more serious nature to disclose. Is that it?"

"Yes, Lord Barrandale," she said, grateful for his understanding. "Yes, I have."

Barrandale looked at Sir Ryder and then at Dashell. "Gentlemen?"

"You have our word," they each said. "You may speak freely."

"Thank you, sirs," replied Joan, gravely. "As John has already said, he came and told me Lady Catherine had spoken to him and asked why we were there. Our first thought was how to explain the missing jewels if she was ever to ask. We had to protect Isobel and Lady Anne, and between the two of us we decided to say that a thief must have got in somehow and stolen them. A strong agile man could have climbed up and got inside. We tried to explain to our lady, and she seemed to understand.

"We learned that Lady Catherine was returning to London that day and her coach was ordered for two o'clock. Lady Anne had finished her luncheon and John had taken the tray away, while I tidied up the suite and prepared her for her afternoon nap. I was in the dressing-room when I heard footsteps approaching and Lady Catherine walked into the suite without knocking. I dared not make myself known, but I could see everything through the crack of the half-open door.

"The look on Catherine's face was—was not very pleasant. Without any greeting at all she said, 'I understand John Webster and Joan Cooper are here as your servants. Why did you ask them to come? I told them to go when Waterton Grange was closed.' 'Yes, I know,' replied Lady Anne, 'but I wanted them here as my servants. I am tired of all the changes amongst your own. I never knew who would come to attend to me next.' I think this was something Catherine had not expected to happen, our going there. I could see she was furious, even more so when the old lady said, 'If you came here just to quarrel, then would you go away and leave me alone.'

"Lady Catherine controlled her anger and said, 'I came to ask if I may borrow a certain necklace of yours. The pearl and amethyst one. It will go so well with the gown I am wearing.' Without waiting for an answer she turned to the dressing-table and stopped short, and screamed when she saw the emptiness. She swung round. 'Where are all your jewels?' She then opened the top drawers and saw some more had gone, and screamed again. 'Where are they?' she demanded, but the old lady began to laugh at her. "Perhaps a thief came in and took them. Yes, that's right. A thief came in,' and laughed again, but it was not a natural laugh. I was fearful that what John and I had done would become known, that she would unwittingly give us away.

"Lady Catherine became even more angry and seized the old lady by her shoulders and began shaking her. Then Lady Anne cried out, 'What did you do to Isobel?' 'What do you mean?' Lady Catherine screamed again. 'Isobel is dead, I tell you, or if not, then she should be. Tell me! What do you know about it?' She shook her even harder, snapping her head backwards and forwards, and then she struck Lady Anne across her face. The old lady gasped and went limp and slid to the floor.

"All this time I had been watching through the crack of the half-open door. I did not dare move, terrified Lady Catherine would discover I was there. She was staring down at Lady Anne on the floor, her arms rigid by her side and her hands clenched; and the look on her face was absolutely evil; and I thought how terrified Isobel must have been if she had seen that same look. Then Catherine turned away and left the room.

"I simply sank to the floor, still unable to move, even to attend to my lady who was beginning to mumble and moan. I stayed where I was in case she came back, and waited to hear the coach drive off, and I cannot tell how long it was. Eventually I heard it and I got to my feet with some effort and crept to a window and watched it go, marvelling at Lady Catherine's indifference. My next thought was get help for Lady Anne, to find John as soon as possible, although I was still shocked at what I had witnessed, for I truly believe Catherine contributed to the old lady's eventual death. I went out along the corridor, still shaking, and even had to use the walls for support, when thankfully I saw John coming. He hastened towards me, alarmed at my appearance. 'Quickly, John!' I cried. 'The old lady'. He ran past me and I turned and followed and we lifted her onto the bed. At first John thought she had had some kind of seizure, as indeed she had, and could hardly believe what I told him. Lady Catherine, or not, I said, we must send for the doctor. I know she has gone for I heard the coach leave." Here Joan paused and turned to John.

"I ran down to the servants' quarters and asked for the doctor to be sent for; that we had found our lady on the floor and she was unconscious. I knew from the butler's response that nothing had been said to him by Lady Catherine; nor did he show any great surprise, for such an event was half-expected. Eventually the doctor came and took a look at her, also showing little surprise because of her age, and said the redness on one side of her face must have been when she fell onto the floor.

"We sat with her day and night, taking turns to watch, or else to sleep in an armchair. She lingered for more than two days, never regained consciousness, and died on the third day in the late afternoon. We again sent for the doctor and after a brief examination he pronounced her dead and left the certificate with us. Perhaps it was just as well he did not look too carefully or ask too many questions, for later when Lady Anne was laid out Joan told me Lady Catherine's fingers had left bruises on her shoulders and upper arms where they had gripped her.

"The next morning we sent word to Lady Catherine at her London house. We told her that the Dowager Lady Anne Bretherton had been found unconscious on the floor of her suite, and that she was put to bed and the doctor sent for, who said there was very little he could do for her because of her age. We told her we had sat with her day and night and she died in the afternoon on the third day. We received an answer from Lady Catherine telling us to make whatever arrangements were necessary, that she was too occupied with other matters to attend the funeral herself, but that she would make any payments to the Rector the next time she returned to Bretherton Hall. That was all she said. No regrets or anything.

"So we approached the Rector and he helped us make arrangements. The funeral was quiet but quite a number of country folk came, not too surprised at Lady Anne's passing, but some did wonder at the absence of Lady Catherine.

"After Lady Anne was decently buried Joan and I made arrangements to leave for we were no longer needed. We had previously told our lady that the two of us planned to wed but that we would stay with her until the time came. She was very pleased for us and said that when the time did come we were to take a certain porcelain dish that Harriet, Isobel's mother, had given to her. In fact she insisted we take it. Rightly or wrongly, for there is only our word she said that, we did take it and it has been in our possession ever since.

"Then when Joan and I were wed we made our way to London to seek a position together as footman and cook-housekeeper, but as soon as we got to London we called at The Star Inn where Isobel had been. We did not hold out much hope of learning anything but we knew we had to try. The innkeeper and servants remembered the lady with the two little girls and that she had gone away with a gentleman, but beyond that they knew nothing or where they all went. We asked if anyone else had made enquiries, for we thought Lady Catherine might have tried to get the jewels back, but to do so would be to expose her own lie. We were told no one else had asked. Regretfully and deeply saddened we turned away. There was nothing else we could do," and sighed as he repeated, "There was nothing more we could do. So that is it, gentlemen, we have spoken at length and have told you all that we knew and did."

The tension in the room eased now that the two servants had finished speaking. The three gentlemen had followed every word, Dashell sometimes sitting forward with his elbows on his knees.

"I think you had done more than enough," began Sir Ryder. "I greatly admire you both for the risks you were prepared to take for Isobel. Surely it was above and beyond the call of duty," which was exactly the sort of thing the Admiral would say.

"What you have related to us is absolutely amazing," commented Dashell. "I shall certainly tell Caroline all that you have told us. She is very anxious to hear for she knew you were both coming here this afternoon."

Joan smiled at that, and asked diffidently, "Lord Lonsdale, would it be possible for us to meet with Miss Caroline? She was a tiny baby when we last saw her and she must be quite grown up now."

"I am sure it will be possible," replied Dashell with a laugh. "She still wants to learn all she can about her parents, particularly the father she never knew."

Now Barrandale spoke up. "We are glad at last to know the truth about the jewels, even with the tragic outcome. We also feel that Lady Catherine went abroad to avoid any awkward questions about the Watertons and Lady Anne, and then returned when she felt people might have forgotten. People had not forgotten her, yet she was not welcome in Society again, so she retired to Bretherton Hall and shut herself away. You have told us so much it is only right we should tell you some things."

"Thank you, your lordship." John now became diffident. "May I ask another question, gentlemen, if you see fit to answer?"

"Yes, of course you may."

"The man whom you said married Isobel, was he a good man?"

The other two men looked quickly at Dashell, who hesitated a moment before he answered. "We believe he was at first, but he could have been better in later years. But we also know he married her for his own purposes."

"Oh," said John and Joan together. "What she must have endured," added Joan.

The general feeling was that talking had come to an end, but Sir Ryder said, "I would like to show you all the jewels we now have in our safekeeping, but before I do, could you describe them as far as you are able?"

"We will do our best, Sir Ryder," replied John, "but they were all placed into the bag so quickly. There was that pearl and amethyst necklace, and I think I recollect a plain pearl one, and oh yes, a diamond and emerald one, and many rings, brooches and earrings. Lady Anne gathered up everything all at once so it rather difficult to remember exactly."

Sir Ryder appeared satisfied. He went over to the table and opened the linen bag for John and Joan to see them.

"Oh, yes, I do remember some of them," said John after taking a careful look at them, "but perhaps Joan is more familiar with them."

Joan had also been looking carefully at the jewels. "I don't see that particular pearl and amethyst necklace," she said in wonder, "the very one Lady Catherine wanted to borrow."

"No," replied Sir Ryder. "Unwittingly, that was the very item Isobel sold. It is described on the receipt she kept and I am very glad she did keep it. But what a remarkable coincidence she chose that one to sell."

A few more minutes were spent talking and the two servants were thanked again most warmly for what they had done all those years ago, and for being instrumental in helping to close the story of the Watertons. Nor would they take any reward, stating that their reward was being able to do all this and to reveal the remaining truth.

Sir Ryder rang the bell for his manservant. "Tidmarsh, see that John and Joan have some refreshments before they leave."

They followed Tidmarsh out, delighted with the assurance from Lord Lonsdale that he would tell everything to Caroline, and that she would be anxious to see them herself within a few days.

"Well," said Sir Ryder, as he poured out some wine, "a most gratifying and incredible story. In fact, the whole story from the time you first told me, Lonsdale, until now, and also what took place beforehand has all been utterly amazing; and I have a feeling it is not over yet."

"Oh? Indeed?" queried Barrandale, surprised.

"No, because we cannot keep those jewels for they are not ours, and under no circumstances whatsoever are they going back to Catherine."

"Of course," replied Barrandale. "Certainly not."

"Are there any Brethertons left at all?" wondered Dashell. "Catherine never had any children so I suppose the next-of-kin would be the Fennshires."

"Yes. Well. Let us see what happens," said the Admiral. And there the matter stayed.

After their evening meal and they were settled comfortably again in the sitting-room, their conversation reverted once more to past events.

Barrandale shook his head sadly. "Four tragedies, Arthur, Isobel, Maude and now Anne; all untimely deaths. And there was one other particular thought that came to mind while listening to John and his wife, and that was how much had depended upon the willing help of ordinary servants. Those two had the courage to do what they did to help Isobel; they took the risk and they succeeded. Then look how much Hannah and Johnny helped Isobel, especially the former."

"It was also Caroline whom Johnny mostly helped," said Dashell quickly, "and look what he has done for you and me."

"Yes," said Barrandale. "How right you are."

CHAPTER THIRTY-FIVE

Kidd and
FitzHerbert Tell All

Jonas Kidd and Philip FitzHerbert had been faithfully carrying out their commission, and astounded listeners were asking, *What is this you are telling us? You mean that eminent men like Sir Ryder Wyecross, Lord Barrandale and Lord Lonsdale, actually asked you to do this? Why?* Because they want the truth revealed. *Truth about what?* Listen and we will tell you. It concerns Isobel, niece of Lady Catherine Bretherton. *Who? That awful woman! How does she come into it? Oh, yes, we remember Isobel. A lovely girl. Wasn't she supposed to marry some Frenchman? Catherine was always arranging other people's lives. Interfering woman. Shh! will you. Don't keep interrupting. Go on, do,* people urged the speakers, ready to hang on every word.

All unknown to Catherine, Isobel had married her childhood sweetheart, now Sir Arthur Waterton. In spite of initial anger and fury and the humiliation of having to inform the French aristocratic family, Catherine pretended she had forgiven them for doing this, but she had not. About three years later Sir Arthur died while in Yorkshire attending to a matter concerning the estate of the late Lord Bretherton, *Oh? How did he die?* The whole carriage was buried under a landslide while travelling along a lonely road, after days of unrelenting storms and rain, and it was not discovered for two days. *Oh, how dreadful, dreadful!* amidst cries of horror. *What happened then?*

When Catherine learned of the news she seized upon the opportunity to wreak her revenge upon Isobel, and declared the whole family had been travelling in the carriage at the time and all had died. In other words she declared Isobel and two children were dead, when in fact they were not. *She did what?* Then after tricking Isobel to come to London from Sussex with her two little daughters, she told Isobel that Arthur had died, and then deliberately abandoned her in a poorer part of London and threatened her that if she tried to say anything her children would be taken away and she would never see them again.

So that was her punishment? with gasps of amazement from the women and quite a number of men. *Just for thwarting Catherine's plans for her? It can't really be true, can it? Oh, it is. Well, nothing that wretched woman did would surprise anyone. But how terribly cruel. So then what happened?*

Almost destitute Isobel married again to protect herself and her children with a different name, but her new husband was not all that helpful, as it later turned out. *What husband is,* muttered some. However, she survived. Remembering her own education she took in pupils and taught them music and singing and fine needlework, and saved every penny she could. She also taught her own daughters all she knew and sent them to a school for ladies, hoping for fine husbands, and eventually to declare the truth with their help. *Oh, how brave she must have been,* said some. *But that could have taken years,* said others. Yes, it did, but she also had the help of two devoted servants. *Oh, so what happened next?*

Tragically, Isobel died just before her two girls returned home from this school. *Oh, poor Isobel, after all her struggles.* Then after that, Maude, the elder daughter, missed her footing and fell headlong downstairs and broke her neck. *Not more tragedy, surely.*

So that just left the younger daughter, Caroline. *What about the step-father, couldn't he have helped?* No, because he had died too. *Humph. Just as well. So that left Caroline all alone?* No, not quite. Sir Ryder Wyecross is her great uncle and he has made himself her guardian. *Could not he have helped at the time?* It is possible Isobel wrote to him, but it is not known for sure, for any letter would have gone down in a supply ship during a violent storm in the Caribbean. All this happened about the time Sir Ryder was in Jamaica. *So Isobel was completely alone and friendless?* Yes, she was, and don't forget those very real threats of Catherine to take her children away. *Poor, poor Isobel,* murmured some as silence fell.

There was something else Catherine did after she abandoned Isobel. *There was? What more could she do? What was it, anyway?* She had a marble memorial tablet cut for the whole Waterton family and put on a wall in the parish church in Sutherfield for all to see. It was worded exactly as Catherine wanted. And then she ordered a memorial service for the four of them, when in fact only one family member was actually dead.

There was a stunned silence as the meaning of those words sank in, followed by cries and gasps of disbelief. *She—did— WHAT? How could she! How dared she! And what hypocrisy! Surely she has damned herself.* Then shortly afterwards the Dowager Lady Anne Bretherton died. *Not surprising, considering her age.* And Catherine said it was all too much for her and she went abroad, probably to avoid any awkward questions. *Guilty conscience, no doubt,* said some. *And good riddance too,* sniffed others. *Never could abide the woman.* Then when she returned to England she tried to continue her ways, but she had been away too long and people would have nothing to do with her. *Haven't seen her for years. Where is she anyway?* She buried herself in her country house in Sussex. *Let's hope she stays there.*

So this whole story, this whole truth, gradually came to light because one afternoon in Oxford Street Lord Lonsdale came to the aid of a young lady who had tripped and fallen down. Her name is Caroline, and she turned out to be the younger daughter of Isobel, and it all unfolded from the chance meeting. *What a delightful coincidence! So what happened to Caroline?* She is now betrothed to Lord Lonsdale. *Well, of course she must be. What a silly question. And how romantic!*

So, said Kidd and FitzHerbert, we have done what we were commissioned to do. Sir Ryder has done for Isobel what she was not able to do for herself—to declare the truth of what occurred all those years ago. *Ah,* remarked some wisely, *how true it is, that saying, 'Be sure your sins will find you out'.* Er, yes, quite, agreed others, a little less assuredly.

Such was the scenario which was repeated again and again in salons and drawing-rooms across London. Quietly at first, until it gained momentum and came out into the open as the full treachery and horror that it was it took hold, and rocked Society for some time to come.

CHAPTER THIRTY-SIX

Caroline Is
Told Everything

Dashell lost no time in relating to Caroline and his aunt almost word for word all that the Websters had told them.

"Like Sir Ryder said, it was amazing we did hear from the Websters after all these years and that they were able to tell us so much we needed to know, and a great deal more we knew nothing about. We know now how Isobel had those jewels; that she was given them by her great aunt. The story of a thief breaking in and frightening the old lady to death was just put out by Catherine to hide the truth. And that, my dear ones, must go no farther than these walls, for it would be unpleasant for us if the truth did get out."

"But how brave John and Joan were," remarked Caroline. "I truly must speak to them myself and thank them for what they did for my Mother. And yet," she continued, trying to search her memory, "I do not remember Mother ever mentioning their names to either Maude or me. In fact, she hardly ever spoke about herself at all. And how strange that the necklace Catherine wanted to borrow turned out to be the very one Mother sold."

"Has Sir Ryder still got the jewels?" asked Aunt Letty.

"Oh, yes," replied Dashell, "they are in his safe keeping. As he said, under no circumstances are they going back to Catherine. I think he has in mind to return them to the Fennshires."

"I must ask them to come here," said Caroline, "for I am so anxious to meet them."

Dashell laughed. "I think they are as anxious to meet you. And I did warn them to expect a lot of questions."

Later Caroline told Hannah everything she had learned, who listened with awed, wide-eyed interest. "Oh, my, I think they were very brave taking such risks. What if they had been found out?"

"I dread to think," replied Caroline, "but as they said, Catherine could hardly have exposed her own lie."

A few days later they were all seated in the small salon. John and Joan were eager to meet the one who had been a tiny baby when they last saw her. They expressed amazement at the likeness of Caroline to her mother.

When Chadwick announced, "Mr. and Mrs. Webster," Caroline had stood up and came forward to welcome them and bade them sit down. "This is my maidservant, Hannah," she explained to them. "She too, was a wonderful help to my Mother." On such a common ground the three servants took to each other immediately, as Hannah had commenced where Joan had been forced to leave off.

"Lord Lonsdale has told me almost word for word all that you related to the three gentlemen the other day, and I must thank you both sincerely for all the risks you took. Lady Smythe, Lord Lonsdale's aunt, knew of Lady Bretherton, and said she was a most formidable woman."

Chadwick came in with the tea tray, giving the servants considerable private pleasure at being treated as guests.

"If you please, Miss Waterton," began John hesitantly, suddenly feeling his age, now that a one-time baby had grown into a beautiful lady.

"Please call me Miss Caroline. There is no need for formality."

"Thank you—Miss Caroline. Joan and I have had in our possession this porcelain dish ever since we left Bretherton Hall. Lady Anne said that if anything happened to her we could take it. It was given to her by your grandmother, Lady Harriet, as a present. We have no knowledge of the occasion."

"Oh, it's beautiful," said Caroline, as she carefully took it from him and examined it. "You say my grandmother gave it to Lady Anne, who would have been my great, great aunt. So probably my Mother would have seen it."

"Oh, yes, many a time," said Joan quickly. "She loved that kind of thing. But John and I feel you should have it. It is almost as though it has come home."

Caroline smiled gently. "That is a lovely thought. I shall take great care of it."

The afternoon passed all too quickly, not nearly enough time to say all that had to be said, and all that Caroline wanted to hear. "We have barely told half of it," said John.

"Then we must meet again," said Caroline, "for there is much we can tell you, too."

John and Joan did come to meet with Caroline again to tell her more about her parents. The three servants would meet by themselves sometimes, and it was the beginning of a lasting friendship between Hannah and Joan for they had much in common.

CHAPTER THIRTY-SEVEN

Enter The Duke

I t was inevitable that a certain story should reach the ears of the Duke of Fennshire himself. At first he heard it with disbelief, then disgust, and then a deepening anger when assured it was so, but his anger was not directed at those circulating the story. Why was Rear Admiral Sir Ryder Wyecross one of the instigators anyway? That was because his sister Margaret, was Sir Arthur Waterton's mother.

Fennshire knew the Admiral was beyond reproach; he would never jeopardize his own character. Likewise Lord Barrandale was a man of integrity, so why would he cast doubt upon himself? And his son, Lord Lonsdale? Like father, like son. For all that he would call upon Sir Ryder and hear the story from the source itself.

Within a day or so Tidmarsh announced to Sir Ryder "the Duke of Fennshire."

"Will you take a seat, General? A glass of wine or sherry, perhaps?"

"No thank you. I prefer to stand. You do not seem surprised at my coming, Admiral."

"No, General, I have been half-expecting you."

Fennshire frowned slightly at what he took to be a familiarity, but it was too trivial to make an issue of it. Besides, he was here for a specific reason. "I have come because a certain incredible story has reached me, but I wish to hear it from you, even though I feel it to be true. Neither you nor Lord Barrandale nor Lord Lonsdale would spread anything if it was not so. From all that I know personally of Catherine Bretherton I can quite believe she is capable of anything. But I would like to hear it all again from you."

"Very well, for there is much to tell you."

"In that case, I will sit down and accept your offer of a glass of sherry." Like the Admiral, the General was a man of action, accustomed to issuing orders and to being in control of any given situation, but he also had the grace to listen. He settled into a chair as the Admiral placed his glass on a small table beside him.

So once again Sir Ryder carefully outlined the story while the Duke keenly and patiently, listened. "...and now," Sir Ryder concluded, "we have just recently learned of further evidence of Catherine's cruelty after her abandonment of Isobel and her children."

"You have? And how did that come about?"

"I advertised in *The Times* for the whereabouts of John Webster, one-time manservant at Waterton Grange, and for Joan Webster, formerly known as Cooper, one-time maidservant at Bretherton Hall and then later at Waterton Grange after Arthur and Isobel married. I had almost given up hope of hearing from them for what we wished to learn had happened years ago, when to my surprise and delight they did answer. They were asked to come here and, in the presence of Lord Barrandale, Lord Lonsdale and myself, told us a most amazing and incredible story, which I will now relate to you."

Once more Fennshire listened, yet interspersed the words with dark mutterings, such as "that damnable woman," and "if she had been a man she should have been horse-whipped."

"Now," continued Sir Ryder, "there was something else the Websters told us which threw a great deal of light upon a certain puzzling situation. But I should first tell you that this was one subject that was not mentioned to either Kidd or FitzHerbert for we did not wish it to become public knowledge, and that was that Isobel had in her possession a quantity of jewels. A considerable quantity of jewels," he repeated, "which to her credit she very carefully kept hidden away, except for one item which she sold when her girls went to that school, and for which she kept the receipt."

He ceased talking and looked intently at Fennshire, who looked back at him for a moment or two. Fennshire then said, "Are you referring to all the jewels Catherine told me had been stolen? She said some thief had climbed in through the upper window into Anne's suite, which had literally frightened her to death. She was still quite distraught about it."

"Hmm. Distraught, was she? Well, let me say she did not tell you the truth."

Fennshire's face darkened angrily. "What do you mean?" he said sharply.

"We learned the truth from the Websters, from Joan in particular, who witnessed a scene between Catherine and Anne."

The duke sat up straight in his chair, his eyes fixed on Sir Ryder. "Go on."

So Sir Ryder carefully repeated and in detail all that John and Joan had told them some days ago.

"That means there never was a thief," said Fennshire slowly. "Anne actually gave the jewels to Isobel."

"Yes," answered Sir Ryder. "Catherine just made up that story to cover up their disappearance, and the fact of Anne's death. And we are fairly certain that was why she went abroad, to avoid answering awkward questions."

"What a damnable, detestable woman. Never could stand her, myself. So she lied to me and to all and sundry. And she virtually killed Anne. And then got the servants to make arrangements for her funeral, which she did not attend." Disgusted, Fennshire got to his feet. "Where are the jewels now?" he asked sternly.

Sir Ryder, who had been watching him, answered, "I have them here," and produced the bag from a drawer in his desk, then went over to a table, followed by Fennshire, and emptied it out. "Do you recognize any of them?"

Fennshire looked them over, his mind still filled with Catherine's duplicity. "Can't say I do. Jewels were never much in my line."

"Nevertheless," said Sir Ryder, "they must be returned to you as there is no one else who can have them," replacing everything into the linen bag and handing it to the Duke. "They most certainly cannot go back to Catherine. Are there any more Brethertons?"

"No, Catherine is the last. And as far as I am concerned the sooner she goes the better." He turned to leave, and then said with a smile, "At least there is one happy outcome from all these hateful incidents, and that is the wedding between young Lonsdale and Caroline Waterton, and I wish them both well."

"Ah, yes," smiled Sir Ryder. "A delightful couple. I have great respect for Lonsdale, and Caroline is a lovely young woman."

"Just like her mother, you say? I remember seeing Isobel just after her parents died when she had gone to live with Catherine. She must have been about nine years old at the time. A very pretty child. But I will not take up any more of your time, Admiral, and I am more than grateful for everything you have disclosed to me, and also for your discretion."

CHAPTER THIRTY-EIGHT

The Duke Calls At Bretherton Hall

A few days later splendid coach drawn by four superb black horses swept through the village of Sutherfield, causing villagers to stare open-mouthed at it, and pulled up outside the parish church. A tall, set-faced man of military bearing stepped out of the coach, entered the church, and looked to the wall on the left. He ran his eyes along until he saw what he wanted and moved over for a closer look. He stood staring at it for several minutes, and then turned and went outside. He then walked round the churchyard until he found the grave of Lady Anne Bretherton, and stood regarding it thoughtfully for a while. With a sigh and a shake of his head he returned to his coach.

The coach travelled a few miles along country lanes, still causing those who saw it to stand and gape, until it swept up a much neglected avenue to pull up at the front entrance of a house that had known better days. The tall man once more stepped out and stared about him with ill-concealed amazement and disbelief, while his aide rang the bell. The man had to ring two or three times before there was an answer. Eventually an elderly manservant opened the door which creaked on its rusty hinges.

"Yes?" he asked a little tremulously, as if surprised that someone should knock on the door. Then he blinked and straightened up as best he could. "Your Grace," he stammered. "I beg your pardon, we were not expecting you. No one calls these days." He limped to one side as Fennshire and his aide entered the hall, the former's observant eyes taking in every detail.

"I have come to see Lady Catherine," he said. "Where may I find her? I shall announce myself."

"Lady Catherine keeps downstairs all the time now, Your Grace," said the old servant. "You will find her in the drawing-room overlooking the garden."

Fennshire strode away, signing to his aide to remain in the hall. He knew well enough where to go and entered the room wondering why it was so dark, or had the old servant made a mistake? The room smelled as though it needed a good airing. Nothing much had changed; it was always as he remembered it, except for what appeared to be a pile of coverings or some other fabric on one of the sofas. With an exclamation of disgust he went over to a window and flung back the curtains, letting in some much needed light.

At the same time the pile on the sofa moved and a cracked voice spoke hoarsely. "What are you doing? The light! The light! It hurts my eyes! Pull them back!"

At the first sound of the voice Fennshire gave a violent start and spun round with an audible gasp, and stared in horror at the creature speaking to him. A skull-like head had risen up and a pair of bony hands clutched the edges of the coverings.

"Who are you?" it asked. "You are not Blundell. He would never have opened them. Who are you?"

Fennshire gasped again. "Catherine! Great heavens, can that be you?"

The sunken eyes opened wide, blinking in the unaccustomed light. "Henry! Why are you here? You have not been here for years." A bony arm was raised to shield the eyes. "Are you going to close the curtains?"

With a shrug he closed the curtains but opened others behind Catherine instead. He was not about to stand and talk in semi-darkness. "I won't waste time," he began in his forthright manner, "I don't particularly relish being here even though I came here for a reason." The figure on the sofa did not move, making itself even more of a caricature. "There is a certain story going the rounds of salons in London which has now reached my ears, and which I believe and know to be true."

"I am surprised at you, Henry, listening to gossip," replied Catherine, now gaining a little more strength, "I would have thought better of you."

"Ah, but this story is very different. It is the story of how, many years ago, a certain young man died and somebody seized upon that incident to declare that his family, consisting of his wife and two little girls, had died with him, when they had not. In fact, they were cruelly abandoned in a poorer part of London and left to fend for themselves. Do you recognize yourself in this, Catherine? Well, do you?" he demanded.

"Why should I care about what happened years ago?" she replied, "Isobel died, and those two wretched children."

"Oh, but they did not. They survived. They lived to tell the tale. That is why I know what I am talking about." Fennshire was not going to say that Isobel and Maude really had died, comparatively recently. Let Catherine think all three were still alive.

She made a strange noise as she drew in her breath sharply. She stared at Fennshire with an even more ghastly look on her face, while her fingers plucked at the coverings. "How can they be alive?" she asked, her voice sounding cracked and strained. "I made sure they would die."

"Well, they did not," repeated Fennshire bluntly, "so that marble tablet on the wall in Sutherfield parish church which you had carved to your exact wording, is nothing but a damnable and despicable lie. I don't know how you dared to do it. But the truth always comes to light in the end."

"Isobel deserved it!" Catherine could contain herself no longer. "Stupid, stupid, little fool, marrying that equally foolish boy. I had much better plans for her."

"You used Isobel to further your own scheming ambitions, you mean. Just another one of your pawns. You never really cared for her, your sister's only child." Fennshire saw his words had hit their mark. "If you still lived in London you would never dare show your face outside."

"I have no desire to live in London. I shall end my days in this place. My home."

"In this place," scoffed Fennshire. "When was the last time you went outside to the gardens or even looked through the windows and saw all the tangled flowerbeds and overgrown trees? And the lawns would need a scythe to mow the grass down. It would take an army of gardeners to put it all right." Fennshire showed her no mercy. "There are cobwebs and dead spiders everywhere. Even walking here from the front door a mouse scuttled out of my way. Bretherton would turn in his grave if he could see it."

"There are not enough servants. They will not stay; and the ones I have are too old."

"You never could keep servants with your vixenish temper."

"I have no money to afford many servants. Not since that thief broke in and stole all those jewels."

"Thief be damned. You lied to me about that. There never was a thief. You made that up to hide the fact that you shook Anne to death."

Catherine seemed to shrink into herself. "How do you know that?" she whispered hoarsely. "How could you possibly know that? Of course they were stolen. How else did they disappear?"

Fennshire had no scruples about telling her the truth; let Catherine think Isobel had told him. "After you abandoned Isobel she came back to seek help from her great aunt, and Anne gave the jewels to her. She kept them in safekeeping all those years, except she sold the very one you wanted to borrow from Anne. The remainder are now in my care. And you are not going to get hold of them." He left it at that. Let Catherine think that was how Isobel had survived—selling off the jewels as necessary.

There was silence in the room as Catherine tried to comprehend how Isobel could possibly have come back and then left again. Her lips moved as though she was trying to say something, staring at Fennshire as if he were her Nemesis. Eventually she managed to form a few words in a whisper "I—want—those—jewels."

"All you want are the jewels? Is that all you can say?" Fennshire felt his anger rising. "You killed Anne and you thought you had killed Isobel and the children. Have you no thought for them?" He stared down at the wretched creature and felt disgust and loathing. "I often wondered what Bretherton saw in you. Probably nothing at all. You probably schemed your way into your own marriage. I can see now how you sent him to an early grave." Still no word or sound from Catherine. "When you die," he continued, "there will be no service for you. There will be no memorial tablet on the wall for you. You will just be buried. Nor will I come to your funeral." With that he turned on his heel and left the room.

That seemed to rouse her at last for she called after him, "Henry! Henry! Come back!" He heard her cries but ignored them, and as he strode away he inadvertently glanced at the hole in the wainscoting where the mouse had disappeared.

When he reached the hall he saw the old servant struggling up from a chair. Sitting down was something a servant should never have done, but Fennshire said nothing. Anyone who had been in Catherine's employ for several years deserved a little sympathy. He spent several minutes speaking to Blundell who answered to the best of his ability, and finally issued some orders to him. "Did you hear all that, Fabian?" he asked, turning to his aide.

"Yes, your Grace."

Blundell closed the door behind them after watching the coach drive off, and went away with his back a little straighter and a gleam of hope in his eye. Yet a little fearfully, he entered the room where Lady Catherine was and closed the curtains Fennshire had left open.

Two days after the duke had left Bretherton Hall in disgust, the old servant sent word to him that Lady Catherine had died. She had refused all food and drink and when her old maidservant had prepared her for bed and bade her goodnight that second evening, she remained sitting up, her hands clutching the coverings to her and just staring straight ahead. She was in exactly the same position when the servants entered her room the next morning, staring in front of her with unblinking eyes, which terrified them. The local doctor was promptly sent for who pronounced her deceased, and the Reverend Swanson was also notified, who began making funeral arrangements, as requested.

As predicted, the only ones to attend were Swanson, his church warden, and the grave diggers. A few curious passers-by stopped to watch, standing well back.

Blundell carried out the Duke's orders and hired house servants and gardeners from the village to clean Bretherton Hall from top to bottom and put some semblance of order into the grounds outside. It took days to go through the whole house as some rooms had not been touched for years, in particular Lady

Catherine's old suite. Under orders from her it had been closed off and left. There were piles of old letters and other papers in her bureau to go through, and Blundell helped Fabian as much as he could.

CHAPTER THIRTY-NINE

The Unwelcome Outcome

The more people heard that amazing, incredible story, the more it caught their imagination. In drawing-rooms and salons and elsewhere, it all the talk. What is Caroline like? Is she really that beautiful? Well, her mother was, so it is said. Where is she living? Nobody knows. She is betrothed to Lord Lonsdale. Of course, he was the one who found her. Oh, how romantic! But his family is now practically penniless, so what can he offer her? She is penniless too, by all accounts, so are there not many other men who can offer her more? Sir Ryder Wyecross may be her great uncle, her mother's mother was his sister, Margaret, but she is also distantly related to the Duke of Fennshire, for did not her paternal grandmother, Harriet, marry Philip, the youngest grandson of the old Duke of Fennshire, father of Henry, the present one? Therefore Philip would be paternal grandfather to Caroline. Hmm. A very interesting connection.

So the search began for Caroline, for not a word had been said where she might be. She could not possibly be with Sir Ryder, for there was no lady there to act as chaperone. Nor would she be with the Barrandales, for the same reason. She could be in some unknown place in the country somewhere. True. But is it not possible she could be with Lady Smythe, sister to Lord Barrandale, aunt to Lord Lonsdale? There have been rumours of a young woman living there, and what better chaperone than Lady Smythe?

It was not long before trinkets and tokens began to arrive at Smythe House, all addressed to Miss Caroline Waterton. "Why am I being sent these things by people I do not even know?" she asked "and how do people know where to send them? Dashell told me nothing was said where I was living."

Lady Smythe sighed. "I think that people have now heard your mother's story and wish to compensate by offering to take care of you."

"Take care of me?" echoed Caroline. "You mean they are offering me marriage? Even when an announcement about our betrothal has been put in the newspaper?"

To her embarrassment and mortification the situation did not stop there. It increased slowly and gained momentum. More trinkets and tokens arrived, which were immediately returned. Miniature paintings of those requesting her hand in marriage, with promises of undying love. "How absolutely impossible, when they have not even seen me," cried Caroline furiously. More wealthy applicants offered riches beyond her desire or need. Silks, satins, furs, jewelry, carriages, fine country houses. Travel to anywhere she wished. "I have no need or desire for any of these things! How dare people do this. Surely they know I am betrothed to Dashell."

Lady Smythe had known some of the names and recognised many faces in the miniatures, and had more than once made exclamations of horror. "He is much older now! That must have been painted years ago! And this one, an absolute rake. Oh, my goodness, I thought this one was already dead!"

Caroline went through a range of emotions: feeling mortified, insulted, embarrassed, and shaken by the whole situation which was so completely unexpected. She also had a strong notion that not all offers were honourable, although many women would have jumped at these chances, but she had no desire to be a "kept" woman. Did they think she could be bought by a trinket or two, knowing full well she was already betrothed and wearing that man's ring? Or did they infer he could not provide for her? She did not know whether to be angry or disgusted or laugh at them for their stupidity. At least she had some satisfaction in pointing out in her replies that all their attention was quite unwelcome. And how was she to explain all this to Dashell anyway. It was an insult to him, and to kind Lord Barrandale.

There was something else that distressed Caroline, and Hannah too, for of course she had told all this to her faithful maid, and that was any walking in Hyde Park was no longer possible because they were getting too well known and she had no desire to attract any more attention. There was nowhere else they could go. Kew Gardens were too far away and Oxford Street too crowded. Barrandale Park was quite out of the question, the house on Becket Lane no longer existed, and she almost wished she could go back to Farling House, but that was also impossible. No access to fresh air and a daily walk, plus everything else, was enough to give anyone headaches.

It was not possible to keep it from Dashell, nor did Caroline try to. He was aghast to learn what had been happening. "It must be the result of Kidd and FitzHerbert doing what we asked them to do, to spread your mother's story. There is no blame attached to them, of course. It has obviously caught people's attention."

"I don't like it," Caroline stated flatly. "I think it is horrible. How can people be so insensitive to our forthcoming marriage? Those who choose to ignore it are not honourable, in my opinion."

Dashell, however, felt differently. He had read some of the letters Caroline had shown him and knew at once he could not possibly offer the same because of the loss of the family fortune, and his heart sank. Those letters were also insulting for they inferred the Barrandales were not able to provide for Caroline, and in some degree they could be right. He must be honest about that. Like his aunt, he had recognised some of the names and knew them to be very wealthy men. But what kind of men? One or two of them were old enough to be Caroline's grandfather and it disgusted him that they would even think of writing.

"Caroline," he began hoarsely, "you have been offered things I could never possibly give you. They are far beyond my reach, and all I have to offer you is an old ring and a one-horse carriage. I love you dearly, far more than I can say, but I would never stand in your way if you wished to accept any offer." What it cost him to say that! To be giving away all his hopes and dreams of their life together. And supposing she did accept an offer? He could not say anything more. He turned away to stand with his back to her, not wanting to see her face or what she was thinking.

Caroline listened to his words in silence. She sensed his hurtfulness and dejection, although he tried not to show it, and felt her love for him. She moved quietly over to him and placed her hands flat against his back and rested her cheek in the space between, and gently said, "Yes, it is true; I have been promised many things, which I have no use for and do not even want, but you are the only person who has promised me a rose garden."

Dashell caught his breath at her words as he realized what she meant. He turned round slowly, wondering, as she smiled at him, then held her close to him and she felt his tears on her cheek. "Bless you, bless you, my dearest, darling Caroline. I will never forget what you have just said," and kissed her again and again. When he finally let her go he said, "It is time we made plans for our wedding. Come and sit down."

"Aunt Letty should be in soon," remarked Caroline, as she sat next to him. "She had a luncheon engagement with some friends. She is a little late."

"Probably still talking," Dashell smiled, now feeling much happier.

Caroline smiled too, for woman-like, she had already given thought to their wedding, but of course it had to be discussed with all involved. Usually everything was done by the bride's family, but the only family Caroline had was Sir Ryder and apart from giving her away he could not be expected to do anything else.

The two of them sat on the sofa, Dashell with one arm round Caroline's shoulders and his free hand holding one of hers. Caroline was not quite sure if this was proper, but if not—well, never mind. And Aunt Letty returned all too soon.

"For heavens sake, Dashell! Are you here again? You might as well take up residence here and be done with it, but don't you dare do so!"

"Before long, my darling aunt, I shall cease to come at all for I will have spirited Caroline away. We have just been discussing our wedding plans."

Chapter Forty

An Unwelcome Caller

There was one person who never took the trouble to send anything to Caroline but who made his way straight to Sir Ryder Wyecross.

"Lord Carley, Admiral," Tidmarsh announced one afternoon, as Lord Carley strutted arrogantly into the room, which did not go well with his host. Sir Ryder stared at him in disgust. He saw Tidmarsh still standing by the door waiting for a sign, and gave him a slight nod. Tidmarsh noiselessly closed the door behind him but remained in the hall on the alert.

"I do not believe I know you, sir," began Sir Ryder.

"Lord Carley to you, sir," retorted the other, causing his host to regard him with even more distaste. "I am the younger son of the Duke of Fennshire."

"I have had the honour of meeting the Duke and I have a high regard for him," said Sir Ryder, trying to be polite, but at the same time shuddering at the figure in front of him.

"You are very kind," replied Carley with a slight bow as manners dictated. He was forty years old, but tried to look younger. A pock-marked face, reddened by excessive drinking and indulgence, with a permanent ill-natured expression giving the impression of a thoroughly dissipated person. He sat down without being asked to do so, which no polite person would have done. Sir Ryder remained standing with his hands behind his back, waiting for the other to speak.

"It has come to my knowledge," began Carley, after looking round the room as though expecting something better, "that there is a newly-found female relative of ours, albeit a distant one, one whose discovery is comparatively recent. Such is her situation that I believe we Fennshires should take her into our care. After all, we are better able to provide for her than anyone else. With us, she will have everything she needs or wants."

"What are you suggesting?" asked Sir Ryder. Strange, Fennshire had never mentioned this when they were together the other day.

"What I have just said," replied the other somewhat testily. "The family she appears to be associated with now is in no position to afford her anything. How can they when they are practically penniless?"

"They are not completely destitute," said Sir Ryder coldly. "They have ways and means of recovering their losses."

"So I have heard," sneered Carley. "And they think they can do so against the best racehorses people have, when all they have is an old stallion, three carriage mares and two unknowns. They will be laughed off every racecourse in the land." The thought of that caused him to laugh derisively.

The Admiral held his peace. He knew nothing about horses. The sea and ships had always been his life. "You have not yet told me exactly why you came here."

Carley gave a smile which made him look hideous. "I would like to meet the fair Miss Waterton, the lovely Caroline. We are distant cousins, you know."

"Yes, you are," agreed Sir Ryder, "but are your intentions honourable?"

Carley gasped out loud but did not succeed in hiding that look in his eye. "Sir! This is outrageous!" he spluttered. "I came to ask for Miss Waterton's hand in marriage."

"You what!" roared the Admiral. "With your reputation! Over my dead body! Do you think I would hand over that lovely girl to you? If you do mean marriage, which I doubt. You know perfectly well she is to marry Lord Lonsdale and she is fully aware of his circumstances. He has kept nothing from her. Do you think she would prefer you to him?" For a moment he compared the athletic upright Dashell with the figure before him—what a comparison! "Do you think she would break off her engagement for you? No man of honour would even suggest this. And any breath of knowledge that she had been seen in your company would sully her reputation at once."

Carley's face had been getting more and more suffused. He was enraged. "Sir!" his voice quavering, "You are insulting! You are insufferable!"

"You have been nothing but insulting ever since you came here."

Carley's eyes narrowed. "Be careful, sir," he warned, his voice menacing, his true nature showing at last, "I am not known as Devil Carley for nothing."

"All the more reason you are not going to see Caroline. Nor will you approach her in any way whatsoever. And if you dare take that coach of yours into Grosvenor Square I'll—I'll have you keelhauled. I'll—I'll have you strung up on a yard-arm." Sir Ryder paused for breath. "By George, if you had been on one of my ships it would not have taken the other officers long to throw you overboard to teach you a lesson." He was indeed speaking from experience for he had known this to happen. He regarded the other with a jaundiced eye before saying, "Good day to you, sir," and rang the bell for Tidmarsh, who responded with alacrity. "You will leave my house before my man puts his knee in your breeches."

By now Lord Carley was white, not with anger, but with fear, for like all bullies he was a coward. Tidmarsh held the front door open for him, and he stumbled outside and into his coach.

"What did you think of him?" Sir Ryder asked Tidmarsh when he came back.

"A very nasty piece of work, if I may say so, Admiral," he grinned. Master and man had often sailed together and understood each other well. "And I know he would have been thrown overboard."

Sir Ryder grunted in agreement. "I am going to write a letter which I will have you deliver. I will call for you when I am ready."

"Aye, aye, sir."

It gave Dashell quite a surprise when he read Sir Ryder's letter requesting him to call at his earliest convenience, and why. "I had a call from Lord Carley who asked for Caroline's hand in marriage, and I flatly refused to agree and ultimately showed him the door. Knowing his reputation I would not trust him one inch."

Nor would I, muttered Dashell to himself. And to think of that man putting his hands on…He promptly blocked the thought. Why, why was it, that when all seemed to go well for the two of them something always happened to spoil it?

"I came when I could," he eventually said to Sir Ryder, when he was sitting in the front room with his host, and learned more about the unwelcome caller and his offer.

"I ordered him out of the house," concluded Sir Ryder.

Dashell scowled at what he was told and then said, "If I had him in a boxing ring he would not last one round with me."

"And I would be there to cheer you on," and they both laughed.

Dashell frowned again. "You don't think he would cause trouble do you? You cannot trust him."

"He would not dare," stated Sir Ryder. "I shall never mention this to Fennshire."

"No. Nor will I speak of this to Caroline. It would only alarm and disgust her, and she has had enough as it is."

Sir Ryder stared at him. "What do you mean?"

So Dashell told him of all the gifts sent to Caroline which were promptly and firmly declined and returned. That this attention must be the result of all Kidd and FitzHerbert had been telling people. "We never thought this would be the result, did we? At least not to this extent. People must have surmised where she lived."

"So that's why Carley came to me," remarked Sir Ryder. "Did Caroline receive anything from him?"

"Not to my knowledge. I am sure my aunt would have seen anything. By the way, I will disregard his insults about my family; nor I will mention them to my father. But perhaps we may talk of something else."

"By all means."

"Caroline and I have been discussing our wedding plans."

"Ah, yes, that reminds me," said Sir Ryder. "I may have spent most of my life on board ships but I have learned a thing or two. I understand it is the bride's family that pays for the wedding, and as I am Caroline's only family member I can guess what that means. I must speak to Caroline about it."

"That is very good of you, sir."

"Not at all, not at all," replied Sir Ryder, with an affable wave of his hand.

After Dashell had gone, Sir Ryder was left scratching his head and muttering, "Dashed if I know what to give 'em for a wedding present." Perhaps Lady Smythe could suggest something. Women were much better at that kind of thing.

The next day, Sir Ryder called at Grosvenor Square for he had another reason for doing so, and had enjoyed a cup of tea with both ladies in the pleasant salon.

"Now, Caroline," he began. "Dashell came to see me yesterday and told me you both are making your wedding plans; but he also told me something else that displeased me very much. I understand you have been receiving some unwanted attention for several days." He held up his hand when Caroline tried to speak. "Dashell was quite right to inform me and I am glad he did. You are my ward and I am your guardian and I will not have you distressed in this way."

Lady Smythe spoke up. "I fear the blame should be with me, Sir Ryder. I knew the names and the people, and suggested everything should be returned."

"Which I would have done anyway," declared Caroline stoutly.

"If there are any more offers of any kind, Caroline," said Sir Ryder sternly, "you will give them to me, and I will give the senders answers they will not forget." Those last words caused the two women to exchange looks, but there were no smiles this time. "Now, Caroline, we will talk of other things, such as your wedding plans. I will be only too happy to give you away as I am your nearest, and indeed only, male relative. And you may have all you desire, and no expense spared."

"Oh, Uncle Ryder, that is so kind of you, but we do not want an elaborate wedding."

"Oh, really," he said, sounding surprised. "I was expecting to do a fair amount of quibbling," with a wink at Lady Smythe.

"Now you are teasing me."

"Perhaps just a little," he chuckled in reply.

Lord Carley never did approach Caroline in any way whatsoever, or took his coach into Grosvenor Square, although he still rankled at the words spoken to him by the Admiral, and his own undignified hasty exit from his house.

On rather short notice he was invited to join a deer stalking party in the remote Highlands of Scotland. The party was a small one, and the shooters were divided into two groups, and Carley was repeatedly told not to wander about. Of course, the inevitable happened and he was mistaken for a stag in the failing light and was brought down, thus bringing about his own demise.

CHAPTER FORTY-ONE

Preparations—and More

All wedding plans had finally been arranged. "At last this day has come and I think we deserve to go away somewhere," remarked Dashell. "Where would you like to go? Although I think I can guess where you will suggest"

Caroline smiled. "You are probably right, and the Irvings did say they would like to meet us, and we have invited them to our wedding. Do you think we could go to Sussex, if it is not too expensive? I would dearly love to see where my parents grew up and played together, and perhaps talk to some older village folk who still remember them."

Dashell laughed. "I was expecting you to say something like that and I am sure we can manage it."

The wedding was to take place at Fulham Parish Church. Caroline knew many people there, many of whom would not be able to travel to Windsor.

During the next Sunday morning service when the banns of marriage were announced they caused a ripple of surprise through the whole congregation, who had to wait until they got outside to talk about it.

Our Caroline? whom nobody has seen for some time, and is now known by her real name of Waterton, is now to be married? Where has she been living now that the old house is being pulled down? She is now residing at a house in Grosvenor

Square. But that is where the gentry live. How does she come to be there? Wait a moment, she was seen weeks and weeks ago with a gentleman in the Tea Rooms and she addressed him as Lord Lonsdale. And how, pray, did our quiet Miss Waterton come to meet such a gentleman? He must have wealthy connections. Well, well. Invited or not, we will certainly go and watch the ceremony.

Sir Ryder decided upon a full dinner service for twelve with all the accompanying dishes; together with a matching tea service for the same number. Lady Smythe gave Caroline a silver-backed brush and comb set for her dressing-table, and she gave the same to Dashell but of a more masculine nature. Maxwell finished another of his paintings and had it framed.

Caroline had carefully kept the money Johnny had obtained from the sales of various items and paid a call to a jeweller where she bought a gold and diamond pin for Dashell for his cravat. She also bought a silver watch and chain which she left at the jeweller's to have some engraving done.

Lord Barrandale had already given the filly Daisy Chain to Dashell; and he bought something for Caroline which no one else could do without embarrassing the family. He ordered for her a new one-horse carriage. It was to be painted dark brown with red leather upholstery and the wheels and shafts were to be picked out in yellow.

When it was ready Johnny was hired to take it to Windsor, and was warned by Reuben to be very careful with it. He was also handed two letters from Lord Barrandale to be given to Simmonds. Johnny duly delivered the carriage and the letters safely, and was left to walk Goldie all the way back to London, well paid for his efforts.

Hannah begged leave to go on some mysterious shopping errand of her own, and came back with a beautiful pair of white kid-leather gloves. Something that would be useful and not just admired and put into a drawer and forgotten. Johnny had not yet made up his mind, but there was time yet.

A group of Dashell's friends banded together and bought a twelve-year-old mare, in foal to Falcon. "She's good," they told him. "She won three races as a two-year-old and the Oaks as a three-year-old, and she has produced some damn good foals. She has the idiotic name of Daybreak. Apparently she was born at the first glimmer of dawn, so she got saddled with it, so to speak."

Dashell returned the compliment and asked Martin Ellersby to be his best man and called at Martin's rooms to discuss details with him. He was therefore not at South Kensington when Fabian, the Duke of Fennshire's aide, called at Barrandale House.

"His Grace sent me to speak to you," explained Fabian to Lord Barrandale, "and I have a great deal to tell you."

Barrandale related everything to Dashell on his return. "First of all, I requested Fabian to convey our condolences to His Grace on the death of his son, Lord Carley."

"I suppose we must be polite," said Dashell a trifle sourly, thinking of all that Sir Ryder had told him of Carley's visit and his request for Caroline's hand in marriage, "but undoubtedly he will be no great loss."

"Er, yes, but as you say, one must be polite," replied Barrandale, surprised at the tone of Dashell's remark. "But wait, there is more to tell you. I have hardly begun. Fabian informed me that the Duke had visited Sutherfield Parish Church, and we can guess why, and then called on Catherine Bretherton and spoke with her for some time. A few days later, Blundell, the old butler there, sent word that Lady Bretherton had died. Fabian went to the house to make arrangements for the funeral as Blundell would need help.

"Fennshire gave orders for the house to be cleaned from top to bottom, inside and out, and the grounds be brought to some semblance of order. The place had been neglected for years and was in a deplorable condition. When going through Catherine's bureau, Fabian found these hidden at the back of a drawer." Barrandale handed two pieces of yellowed paper to Dashell with a significant smile. Dashell took them and gave a cry of astonishment. "Yes," continued Barrandale, "the death certificates of Sir Arthur Waterton and his coachman, Edwards. Fabian said he had been specifically told to look for them."

"So she had these hidden away all this time," said Dashell, "and the agents who went looking for that overdue carriage all those years ago were sent by Catherine, and they were given these papers, and they then gave them to her."

"And Catherine did not give Arthur's to Isobel," Barrandale pointed out, "nor could she give the one for Edwards to his family either, without giving herself away."

"What a damnable woman," remarked Dashell. Then after a pause he said, "I will not tell Caroline just yet, it will only bring back memories and she is so happy just now."

"There is something else that may make Caroline even more happy," continued Barrandale with a smile. "You know Isobel spent a great deal of her childhood at Bretherton Hall; Fennshire has given permission for Caroline to go to the Hall and take anything she wishes in memory of her mother. I took the liberty of informing Fabian you would be going to that part of Sussex after your wedding. He asked that once you have called there, or decide not to go at all, would you let him know, as the house will then be put up for sale. Apparently neither Fennshire nor his other son, Lord Runcorn, wants it."

"That is wonderfully kind and generous of him. And Caroline has already said to me she would like to go."

"Wait. There is more to tell you."

"More?" echoed Dashell.

Barrandale smiled. "Fennshire is giving us a mare from his own stables," pausing at the look of surprise on Dashell's face. "Her name is Sorelle. She is ten years old, never raced, and has an as yet unnamed foal at foot, by Trojan."

Dashell shook his head in wonder. "It is all so incredulous. I never expected all this. And from Fennshire himself. I, or we, must thank him for this. Is there anything more? Although I doubt there can be."

"Oh, yes there is," said Barrandale with a laugh. "Fennshire has expressed a desire to meet Miss Waterton."

"Really? Well, I am sure it can be arranged. But all this is an honour."

"Yes, it is," remarked Barrandale thoughtfully, "and I like to think there is something deeper here," looking at Dashell intently.

"And that is?" queried Dashell, beginning to catch his meaning.

"To begin with, Fennshire and Wyecross are old acquaintances, they have known of each other for a long time. Fennshire had heard the story circulating the salons and called on Wyecross and learned more. Everything, in fact. He went to Sussex, first to Sutherfield and then on to Bretherton Hall, where he challenged Catherine and satisfied himself that what he had heard was true, because Isobel's story greatly intrigued him.

"Like the rest of London Society, he not only knows her story, he also knows ours, and it could be his way of acknowledging how much we, or rather you, have done. He is a man of the world, and when it becomes known that he requested to meet Caroline no one would dare turn their backs on us. Also, the gift of that mare would ensure our acceptance on any racecourse in the country."

"I see what you mean," Dashell said slowly in agreement, "and if you are right then he is a most remarkable and generous man."

"And that reminds me," continued Barrandale briskly, "I must write at once to Simmonds so he can inform James and Samuel to make ready for the arrival of the two mares. They could come at any time. And I will also inform Reuben here."

"Let's hope events are changing for us," said Dashell, even if he did sound trite.

News of the impending wedding between Lord Lonsdale and Miss Waterton was received with joy by all at Barrandale Park. Simmonds had received his orders from Lord Barrandale, and in turn issued his orders that all guest rooms be prepared, even temporarily opening up some that had been closed although it was not known for sure how many would be required. The suite for the new Lady Lonsdale had already been prepared and the furniture brought from Becket Lane was in place. The housekeeping was always well run but even so Simmonds thoroughly checked everything.

Hitchcock also made sure nothing was out of place. Work on the new rose garden had progressed as planned although it was a long way from being completed.

In the stables all stalls and loose boxes and the yard itself were swept out and kept clean as far possible. The arrival of Daybreak and Sorelle were eagerly awaited, and their loose boxes were prepared with plenty of deep litter.

At the Wheatsheaf, ale flowed freely as the locals, tenants and neighbours alike celebrated the coming wedding. All agreed how good both their lordships were. Look how Lord Barrandale forgave us our rent that terrible year a while back. And look how Lord Lonsdale has made great changes to the estate for good, for he is determined to keep it in the family. Every evening as people spilled outside at closing time they would take instinctive glances at the night sky trying to judge what tomorrow's weather might be, for they were going to do their part by working their land as much as possible.

CHAPTER FORTY-TWO

To Return to Johnny
and Becket Lane

The time was fast approaching for Johnny to leave Becket Lane. He had been to see Hannah a few times and had told her he had disposed of that cushion. He had had several odd hauling jobs, and had obtained a regular job of delivering furniture for a workshop, but that was only once a week, as items were finished.

The old stable now looked stark and desolate by itself. It felt quite eerie. Johnny was glad tomorrow would be his last day when he would load his cart and leave for ever. But tonight he would celebrate by going to the Bishop's Head Inn and have a good meal. He would even buy some of his favourite meat pies.

A cab pulled up outside what was once number 29 Becket Lane and two women stepped down and looked about them in dismay and unbelief. Where was the house they were supposed to be looking at? Even the cabman was nonplussed. "The sign distinctly said Becket Lane," he said "and there's the number, 29, on the gatepost there," nodding at it. "It must be right."

"Well, where is it then?" snapped the younger of the two women, "where's the bloody house?" She strode up what was left of the front path which now led nowhere, then back again. "What the hell is he playing at? He said he had written a new will, and this is what he promised me? There's nothing. I haven't seen him for weeks and weeks, anyway. Where the hell is he? I'll chew his ear off when I do see him. Mark my words." She swung round on her older companion. "Can't you say anything, Nan?"

"I would if I could get a word in edgeways."

"Pah!" snarled the other. She stood there, still fuming. "If he's changed his mind and left me for someone else, I 'll kill him. I really will," her tone indicating she really would.

Nan had been taking a more careful look around her. "Perhaps it caught fire and burned down," she suggested, without much conviction.

"Nah," said the other, after considering the possibility.

Then they saw someone coming along the road towards them. "Here," said Nan, "let me ask this person if he knows anything. And you shut your mouth and keep quiet. Excuse me," she began politely, as the person drew level with them, "but someone we know used to live here. Do you know what happened to this house?"

The man stopped and blinked in surprise, looking at the large patch of ground indicated to him. "Well, er—miss, I don't know that much. I heard an old man used to live here, but he died."

Died!" cried the two women in unison, and looked at each other blankly.

"Yes, that's right. He was found by a servant lying dead on the floor some weeks ago. That's all I know."

"What did I tell you," screeched the younger woman. "He tricked me, he did. He made me think I was coming into some property, and now look at it. What the hell am I expected to do with what's left?" She swung round. "What happened to the house?"

"Well," began the unfortunate man cautiously, taking a step backward, not liking the woman's temper, "I heard it was in such a terrible state it had to be pulled down."

"What!" she stormed. "And we came all this way for nothing! And he was going to leave me a tumble-down old house!" Choking with rage she gave vent to it by kicking a wheel of the cab, accompanied by some very unladylike language.

"Here!" cried the cabman indignantly. "What the hell do you think you're doing?" If the so-called lady could use some strong language, then so could he. "Just you damn well stop that!"

She shouted something at him and went on kicking, accompanied by more angry protests from the cabman, until Nan intervened.

"Davilla! Will you stop before I clout you one. If you don't shut up and stop your horrible language I'll get in the cab and go off without you."

Davilla did stop but only because her toes were hurting. She stood there panting. "Serve him right he's dead. I never liked him all that much anyway."

"Well," said Nan, "it's no use crying over spilt milk. I never liked him that much either. He used to give me the creeps." She jerked her head at the cab. "Come on, Davilla, get in." Swallowing her wrath, Davilla, did so after giving one more look round at what she thought she had, but lost. Nan spoke to the cabman, "Would you take us back to where you picked us up?"

"I'll be more than glad to," he muttered, not caring if he was heard.

During all this time the man had been standing to one side listening open-mouthed, while at the same time the two women had completely ignored him. He stood watching the cab until it was out of sight and then gave one loud, joyful whoop. What a coincidence for this to happen on his last night! What a wonderful ending! It could not have been better. But for the precious pies in his hands Johnny would have done handsprings or cartwheels or something, but all he could do was bound from one side of the carriageway to the other, whooping his way back to the stable.

He had recognised the name Davilla immediately. So that was Davilla Spendham, was it? Old Nibs' fancy piece. Two of a kind if you asked me. Well suited to each other. Now she had been done one in the eye, too. And if she knew he had burned that will, whew!

But what a wonderful story to tell Hannah! Just wait until she heard it. What a laugh! The mere thought sent him chortling again. Then he stopped dead. Oh, no, he almost forgot. He could never tell her. She would be horrified to learn he had burned that second will. She might let it slip one day to Miss Caroline what he had done, and then it might reach Lord Lonsdale. That would never do. Just think of the trouble that might cause. With a sigh he set down his pies on a ledge in his sleeping area and went and told Goldie all about it instead.

The next day he loaded up his cart with his few belongings, which included garden tools he was told he could keep, the pots and pans Hannah had given him, and an old brazier he had found somewhere for whatever cooking he wanted to do, and the sawn up wood from the trees in the orchard. He bundled up what hay and straw he could, and took the bin with Goldie's oats. He was not too fussy about cleaning out the stable, not when it was going to be pulled down. He gathered up the reins and left.

He had been hired to clean out an old cottage where an elderly couple had lived for years, but had not done much about it, and the family now did want something done about it. In clearing the garden, Johnny found five downed arches with climbing roses still attached. What a find! Here was his wedding present for Miss

Caroline! He cut them free and wrapped sacking round them. Any further pruning could be done by the gardeners at Windsor.

When he finally returned to his rented stable he found a message from Hannah about taking the Barrandale servants and herself to Windsor in his cart, and he was to speak to Matthew about it. The arrangements were that later he was to fetch Hannah from Grosvenor Square and all the servants from Barrandale House and go straight to Barrandale Park in Windsor, as everyone would be required to work there.

Although the wedding was still several days away James was going to make sure everything would be in readiness. Her ladyship's new coach would be kept in the carriage house until required, everything else inspected more than once, so that not a horsehair or blade of straw or hay was out of place. James knew from experience that visiting coachmen would cast critical eyes around to see how well other establishments were run.

Likewise similar activities were being carried out inside the house. Rooms that had been closed were opened up for any visitor staying overnight, the housekeeper checking everything. The cook was going through her recipe books for special delicacies to be served on the day. All in all, the servants were busy but they were excited, too.

CHAPTER FORTY-THREE

The Wedding At Fulham Church

The wedding was here at last, with the weather promising fair and all last minute preparations had taken place. A large crowd of well-wishers and onlookers had gathered outside waiting to see "our dear Caroline."

The carriages began to arrive. Lord Barrandale and Dashell had travelled together. Other carriages came, one with Lady Smythe and Maxwell. Several guests were on horseback, and local boys were only too willing to hold the horses until owners came out again. Two quiet people arrived by cab, looking like the respectable servants they were, who slipped inside the church and preferred to sit at the back. And the vicar welcomed them all as they came.

Everyone eagerly awaited the carriage containing the bride-to-be; surely it should be coming any minute. Their patience was soon rewarded as another carriage pulled up. A man stepped out, resplendent in his Naval uniform of a Rear-Admiral, who turned to help out Caroline, the bride. Oh, how lovely she looked. And what a pretty dress! With his cocked hat under one arm, and Caroline on the other, Sir Ryder proudly led her inside the church.

Caroline had many thoughts as she walked slowly along. Yes, indeed, she had known from the first time she and Dashell met that it was meant to be, although at the time she had to disclaim it. It was not until the name of her real father had been discovered that she let her love for Dashell blossom, especially when he said he could give her a home and gardens to walk in and call her own; but all else he could offer her was an old ring and a one-horse carriage and a new rose garden. All that was far more precious to her than anything else she had been offered. And it was a marriage with love as the mortar between the two of them; it was not a cold loveless marriage of convenience which she had dreaded.

With the double entry doors to the church wide open, Dashell had heard the activity outside. He, too, had been thinking of all that had occurred since he first met Caroline. How it was that one mystery after another had appeared. When one was cleared another one appeared, until he wondered how it would all end, but the day he thought might never come, had come. And now his Caroline was here.

The rector was now standing with his back to the altar, smiling as she approached. As she drew level Dashell turned to look at his bride. Their eyes met. How lovely she looked! How splendid he looked! She saw a tiny silver holder in Dashell's lapel containing the most perfect pink rosebud anyone would wish to see. The sun was shining brightly through the stained glass windows and people may have been mistaken, but did he wink at her? And did she wink back? Surely not, perhaps she was just blinking back a tear.

The rector began the service. "Dearly beloved…" and so on to the exchange of vows.

"I, Dashell Roland…"

"I, Caroline Diana…"

…and through the service until Martin Ellersby, Dashell's best man, produced the ring. Dashell slipped it onto Caroline's finger and the vicar pronounced them man and wife, and said, "You may now kiss the bride." *A silly thing to say really,* thought some, *as if any prospective bridegroom had not been practicing enough already.* Dashell had long waited for this moment when he could truly call Caroline his own and he kissed her gently, with sighs and murmurs of approval from the congregation. They turned and walked proudly towards the doors, holding hands, smiling at their guests until they were outside.

Unbeknown to all who were inside the church, those who were outside had been talking, positive the bridegroom was the same man who had been seen with Miss Caroline in the Tea Rooms several weeks ago. And she had addressed him as "Lord Lonsdale." So if that was correct then Caroline would be Lady Lonsdale. Whatever next. And how did quiet Caroline come to know him, anyway? But oh, what a topic of conversation for everyone for days to come!

Then the cry went up from those closest to the doors. "Here they come!" And everyone craned their necks forward to see them.

Dashell and Caroline left soon afterwards, travelling in Barrandale's carriage, for he would travel with Sir Ryder. Dashell's friends surrounded him to congratulate him before he did leave and addressed him as Lonsdale. Well, there was the proof, thought those who overheard.

So one by one carriages and riders invited to Windsor left, and gradually the area outside the church was cleared of well-wishers, though some still lingered to talk.

CHAPTER FORTY-FOUR

At Barrandale Park

About twenty men were waiting at the head of the poplar avenue for the bridal carriage a good hour before it was reckoned to come. When Reuben saw the crowd he knew what was going to happen and stopped the carriage for the men to unbuckle the harnesses to take the horses out. Surprised why they had stopped Dashell enquired and was told, "Don't you worry, sir, we are going to pull the carriage ourselves."

"What are they doing?" whispered Caroline, and Dashell explained.

Some ropes were quickly attached, and with a nod to Reuben who had remained on the box to apply the brakes where necessary, the carriage started forward; while the horses were led to the stables. Those not pulling the carriage ran alongside, so they could tell any grandchildren in later years that they were proud to be there that day to escort Lord and Lady Lonsdale to the house.

Simmonds and Mrs. Whiteside and all the other servants, as well as Hannah, were waiting to greet them. Dashell said to Caroline, "This house will be your home for the rest of your life," and carried her over the threshold amidst cheers from everyone.

"Thank you, everyone," laughed Dashell, "thank you one and all."

"And thank you all too, you have given me a wonderful welcome," said Caroline, amidst more cheers.

By now carriages and riders were arriving and Dashell and Caroline stayed in the entrance hall to greet their guests.

A buffet meal had been set out on long tables and chairs had been provided along the walls for those wishing to use them. Once everyone had arrived and had assembled in the great hall, the call went out from Sir Ryder for a toast to the bride and bridegroom. "May they have many happy years together."

"To the bride and bridegroom!" they all replied, and raised their glasses.

"And now," stated Lord Barrandale, "let me say the house, gardens and grounds are open to all who wish to look around. Please enjoy yourselves."

Many of the guests knew each other, but still Lord Barrandale, Lady Smythe and Sir Ryder moved among them, making sure no one was sitting or standing alone, or else encouraged dancing among the guests.

At some time or other Dashell indicated to Dr.Meldicott and the Reverend Sudbury that he wished to speak to them privately and led them to a small private room. "I am sure you are wondering why I wish to speak to you, and regret introducing a matter of a sombre nature but I may not have another occasion to speak to you. I believe you both know Caroline's mother and sister died far too soon. It has been in my mind to arrange the removal of their remains to the Waterton vault in Sutherfield in Sussex. There is also the removal of Sir Arthur's remains from Skorrcliff in Yorkshire, but that is another matter. After their tragic separation I would like to feel Arthur and Isobel may be together at last, and Maude will not be left behind. I trust I have your concern and sympathy over the situation?"

Both listeners glanced at each other. "That is a most considerate and generous gesture," said Dr. Meldicott.

"I am sure it can be arranged," added the Reverend Sudbury, "but it will take time."

"I will approach the authorities and begin the arrangements," said Dashell, "and I would appreciate your attendance in due course, if you both agree. I will only mention this to Caroline when an opportune moment arises. Now, shall we return to the others?"

A number of guests were outside on the terrace or moving slowly through the gardens. Some had wandered through to the old rose garden and into the new one being designed but there was not much to see there just now. Dashell explained to Caroline he would take her through it when they had the place to themselves.

Dashell's friends had surrounded him asking him questions. *Dashell, you lucky devil. She's a beauty. How on earth did you find her?* It's a long story. *Has she any sisters?* She had one, but she died. *Oh. Any cousins perhaps?* Yes, some, I think, but they are distant cousins, and they are older anyway. *There could be second cousins by now and never mind being distant.* Well, Sir Richard Irving and Lady Lucy are here and they are the parents of the cousins, perhaps you could ask for introductions. *Don't be such a devil, Dashell, how can we do that when we haven't even seen them?* What about the girls already here, Caroline's friends? She could arrange introductions. *Mm, yes, there are quite a few pretty ones here, come to think of it.* Well, now, there's your chance.

Caroline, on her part, managed to whisper to Hannah, "Would you tell Johnny I wish to see him before he returns to London, but do not tell him why."

"Of course not," Hannah whispered in return, knowing what was afoot.

Lord Barrandale and Sir Ryder had been having a quiet conversation and his lordship learned something that surprised him; Lady Smythe and her old friend, Mrs.Farling, were sitting together. Mr.Talbot was having a discussion with a group of men. Some of the other ladies, Isobel's old friends and now Caroline's, were quite content to sit and watch what was going on and catch their breath, as someone described it.

Sir Richard and Lady Lucy were with Dashell and Caroline, discussing their coming visit to their house in Sutherfield. "When you come there may be some items you would like to have, Caroline. After all, they might have been yours anyway."

"That is most kind of you, Lucy," said Caroline. "As a matter of fact the Duke of Fennshire has given us permission to go to Bretherton Hall for the same reason. That was where Mother spent her childhood."

"Oh yes," laughed Richard, "what a dreadful state that house was in when Catherine died. We heard it took days for all the clutter to be taken out. Some chairs and other things were so riddled with old mouse nests or moths that they had to be burned. But that is enough of that. You may stay with us as long as you like."

"That is very good of you, Richard," said Dashell, "but we do not wish to inconvenience you. Is there a local inn where we could stay?"

"There is," stated Richard, "but you are not going to."

CHAPTER FORTY-FIVE

The Next Few Days

B y late morning all the guests, except Sir Ryder, had left; and several young ladies were only too delighted to have carriages escorted by young men on horseback.

When they had waved goodbye to the last carriage, Dashell took Caroline by the hand and led her to the new rose garden he had planned for her. "This is my wedding present to you, except it is a long way from being completed." They went slowly round as he pointed out the various walks and beds already staked out. "I can show you the plans which Hitchcock still has, and anything can be changed, of course, if you wish.

Caroline shook her head gently. "It is going to be beautiful. I shall come to love it."

Dashell began to laugh. "I must tell you this: Johnny gave five rose root balls to Hitchcock as his wedding present to you. Hitchcock is fairly sure that from the age of them and the spade marks, he must have dug them up from somewhere. Johnny said they were climbing roses."

"Knowing Johnny, I can quite believe this of him."

In time when the roses had grown and covered trellis arches, visitors to the garden would remark about them. "What beautiful roses," they would say, "what a lovely scent." Caroline would say "Yes. They were a wedding present." "Really? What a charming idea." Then bury their faces in the blooms again. "Mmm. Delightful."

They returned to the house through the old rose garden. "This was Mother's," said Dashell as they walked about. "She loved it very much. Now, we should return indoors so you can speak to Johnny."

Johnny had been ushered into a small room but he did not know why, and was somewhat reassured to find Hannah already there. "Wot's 'appening? I'm glad to see yer 'ere 'cos I wuz beginning to fink I'd somefink awful. Why are we 'ere anyway?"

"I'm not supposed to say anything," she answered mysteriously.

Just then footsteps were heard and Dashell and Caroline entered the room.

About fifteen minutes later Hannah and Johnny left the room, the latter tightly holding a packet he had been given. He surreptitiously put a finger on one cheek where he could still feel the light imprint of Caroline's kiss on it. But it was the gift he had been given that had made him catch his breath. It was beautiful. It was a silver watch and chain, and engraved on the inside of the flap at the back were the words, *With my love and gratitude, Caroline.* He could only stammer his thanks, for he had not expected this.

"But for you Johnny," Caroline had said, "there would not have been today, for which both my husband and I must thank you."

"Indeed we must," Dashell had added, "and you have also done a great deal for my father and me, which we will not forget. And now I believe my wife has something else to say to you."

"Yes, Johnny. We will be leaving for Sussex the day after tomorrow and will be staying at Waterton Grange near the village of Sutherfield in Sussex. We need a carter to take away some items from there, and from Bretherton Hall, and I would like you to do this even though it is a long way to go."

Johnny jumped at the chance. "Of course I will, Miss Caroline—er, I mean yer ladyship." thinking he would have to work round his Thursday deliveries somehow.

When they had left the room Johnny turned to Hannah. "So this was the surprise you were not to tell me," he grinned. Of course he would wear the watch and chain with pride but he would have to conceal it somehow. He had seen enough poverty on the streets of London to know the watch could be stolen, and that must never, never happen;

Hannah did think of something when he asked her. "Leave your waistcoat with me and I will sew an inside pocket for you, and you can pick it up when you return from Sussex. You can still wear your other coat."

"I knoo you'd fink of somefink, 'annah-me-girl. You're a marvel."

"Oh, go on with you," she laughed.

As Dashell and Caroline also left the room he said to her, "Your carriage, my lady fair, has been ordered for two o'clock."

"My carriage," echoed Caroline with a laugh. "How lovely those words sound. Never in my life have I owned such a thing. How kind your father is. The way he described it, it sounds wonderful."

After luncheon the Barrandale House servants were getting ready to leave. Their boxes had already been placed in Johnny's cart and he was on his driving seat, and was heard to remark it was the first time he had sat down since he arrived on Friday, which caused much merriment. "That goes for us as well!" said many others. The cook had given them pies, cold meats, bread and cheese so they would have something for their supper when they got back. Johnny had some as well. Goldie was tossing her head up and down; she had been in a stall for three days with nothing to do and was ready to be on her way.

CHAPTER FORTY-SIX

The Carriage Ride—And More

"Your very own carriage, Caroline, my dear," said Lord Barrandale proudly. "My wedding present to you. Leonard, your coachman, will look after you when you go visiting round the countryside."

"Indeed I will, Lady Lonsdale," answered Leonard gravely.

"And this is your very own horse," said Dashell. "Her name is Flame. Now, we are ready to go for a drive," and handed Caroline into the carriage. He sat beside her and knocked twice on the roof of the carriage. "That's what you do when you want the carriage to move."

Barrandale and Sir Ryder waved them off. "Enjoy yourselves."

"Well, there they go," remarked the latter as they stood watching it roll away. "I may be a sentimental old fool, but I will warrant this marriage will last, although I have no experience of such matters."

Barrandale smiled. "If they are as happy as Alicia and I were, then it will."

Quite oblivious of those sentiments Dashell and Caroline had settled themselves down comfortably. "What a lovely shade of red," remarked Caroline as she ran her hands over the upholstery.

"I love the smell of new leather," said Dashell, "it always reminds me of saddles." By the way, you knock twice on the roof of the carriage when you want it to stop. Always knock twice to make sure the coachman heard you."

"Oh. Thank you for telling me. Is there anything else you wish me to know?"

"Oh, yes, plenty." He put his arm round her and pulled her close to him, while Caroline laid her head on his shoulder. "I can assure you that this behaviour is now perfectly proper."

"Absolutely, I quite agree," murmured Caroline. "Where are we going?"

"Oh, just to show you the local countryside. Windsor, of course. We could stop to look round the castle if you wish."

"I think I would rather just sit here with you."

"Thank you for the compliment. I think that deserves a kiss. Or two."

After a moment or two, Caroline reminded Dashell they were supposed to be looking at the countryside, but he merely replied that he knew it well enough already. "But don't I get to look at it?"

"If you insist," he said with a mock sigh, "but at least I have got you all to myself, now that the milling throngs have gone."

"I rather enjoyed seeing everybody, sharing our happiness" said Caroline. "So many people helped us discover the whole story about my family it would have been unkind to leave them out. I am so glad we planned the wedding the way we did; for as you said, what were a few days when we have the rest of our lives together." She turned her head to look at Dashell. "You are very like your father, you know. Very kind and considerate."

"That was quite a speech you made. And your regard for me is overwhelming. Very seemly in a new little wife."

"There you go," laughed Caroline, "teasing me again. I suppose I shall have to get used to it."

"You probably shall," agreed Dashell. "What are you laughing at?"

"I was remembering the time you followed Aunt Letty's carriage because you wanted me to say three words to you."

"You little rogue."

"Oh, no. Those were not the words at all."

"You are impossible."

"Those do not sound quite right either, although they are certainly familiar."

"Would 'I love you' be right?"

"How did you guess?" smiled Caroline.

"My memory must be better than yours."

She turned to him. "I love you. Now it is your turn to say it."

"I love you, Caroline. I always have," as he kissed her mouth, her face, her throat; and the passing countryside was forgotten for a while.

"Dashell, may I talk to you about something?"

"Of course you may, except you have done nothing but talk ever since we set off."

"No. I mean seriously."

"That will be a change. What is it about?"

"Well, when you asked me to marry you, I asked Aunt Letty what a Lady of the House was supposed to do. Mother had always taught Maude and me to be diligent in a genteel way, as she described it; and I am not one to sit around and just be 'grand' and actually do nothing."

"Oh, I see what you mean. You will be expected to see the house is well run and that the servants are in order; and that reminds me, I must have Mrs. Whiteside show you round the house. And you need to be the gracious hostess at any functions we attend or hold ourselves. My mother was very good at keeping her eye on everything, but as she died some years ago, I suppose Mrs. Whiteside has been managing the household as best she can.

Then there are the estate grounds and gardens which Hitchcock can show you.

"Such as?" Caroline was quite fascinated.

"Well, let me see. The Italian Garden, the White Garden, the Bluebell Woods. All the various walks through them, and along the river. The orchards, the fish pond, all the greenhouses, the kitchen gardens, the home farm and dairy. Everything down to the last hen house. The stables too, if you wish."

"Did your mother really know all about such things?" asked Caroline in wonder.

"She did indeed."

"Aunt Letty also mentioned Lady Alicia had afternoon tea once a week with Mrs. Whiteside to discuss household business, as she described it. Oh, Hannah asked me what her duties are now, and I want her to remain as my maidservant."

"I think Aunt Letty left out one thing the Lady of the House is supposed to do, unless she expected me to mention it."

"Oh, what is that?"

"She is expected to produce heirs."

Caroline felt her face turn scarlet. "Dashell!"

"Had you not thought of children?"

"Well, of course, but…"

"There aren't going to be any 'buts' my girl. Not if I can help it."

Caroline asked, "What shall we do tomorrow?"

"I know you are trying to change the subject but would you like to go for a ride? I will come with you. We could go round the estate."

"It is so long since I have been on a horse I am sure I shall be nervous."

"You must not be, or the horse will sense it from you and that will make it nervous. Besides, it is almost impossible to fall out of a side-saddle."

"That kind of comfort just makes it worse," protested Caroline, "but I will try."

"I knew you would," smiled Dashell. "Flame has been very well trained."

"What do I do about a riding-habit?" asked Caroline.

"There is a whole wardrobe of spare clothing in the house. I am sure Mrs. Whiteside will be able to find you something."

The carriage had gone along the poplar-lined avenue and was now approaching the house. "Do I knock on the roof to stop it?" said Caroline.

"Not this time because it will stop anyway." When it did Dashell jumped out and then turned to help Caroline out. "Thank you, Leonard, you have done very well with Flame. I know Lady Lonsdale enjoyed the ride."

"Thank you, your lordship."

"Leonard, would you inform James to have Sparkle and Flame saddled and brought round at ten o'clock tomorrow."

They turned to go into the house and Caroline said she would go upstairs before tea at four o'clock, while Dashell went to join his father and Sir Ryder in the library.

"I must freshen my face and hands and tidy up my hair," she remarked to Hannah, glancing at the little clock on the mantelpiece, a wedding present from a friend. Just gone twenty-five past three.

"Oh, by the way, Miss Caroline, Mrs. Whiteside brought two riding-habits for you to try on. They are hanging up in the dressing room. I am sure one of them will fit you."

"I shall be riding out tomorrow morning, so I will try them on after tea. I spoke to Dashell about your duties here and I said I want you to remain as my maidservant."

"I am only too happy to be here with you, Miss Caroline. I will certainly do anything required of me while I bide my time waiting."

"Waiting?" repeated Caroline, mystified. "What do you mean? Waiting for what?"

"Why, till I be nursemaid." Never had Hannah sounded so down to earth.

Once again Caroline felt her face turn scarlet. "Hannah!" She had barely recovered from Dashell's teasing, when the little clock mercilessly chimed quarter to four and she was compelled to go downstairs to join the gentlemen for tea.

Earlier, after they had watched the new carriage roll away, Barrandale and Sir Ryder spent a quiet time together. To begin with, they indulged in something even earls and admirals might enjoy, and that was an afternoon nap. The latter did not actually sleep but remained in a deep doze, still able to dwell on his thoughts.

Mainly it was to think to himself how much had happened since receiving Dashell's fateful letter some weeks ago, in fact on the same day of the luncheon with his old shipmates. What a surprising coincidence. He had not been at his best that day for at the back of his mind was the nagging thought that he was facing a rather bleak and lonely old age, reinforced by the knowledge that he believed he had no relatives. Even since that luncheon he had learned of two more shipmates who had "slipped anchor." He had likened himself to an unseaworthy ship being tied up in dock that nobody wanted or knew what to do with; or being beached like some old hulk and left to rot, buffeted by wind and tide.

It had all changed after he heard the incredible story about the Waterton family. Caroline, whom he understood had died with the others, was the one link to him because he was her great uncle; and now with her marriage to Dashell he had been drawn into friendship with the Barrandales.

That, too, was interesting in its own way. Almost all his life had been spent on board ship, therefore any friends were naval men, not having the time or opportunity to mix with landmen. Since his first angry meeting with them, he now regarded Barrandale as a very fine fellow indeed, and also the two sons he had met. Pity about the other one, the cause of the family's financial embarrassment. Also, through the Barrandales, he had renewed his friendship with the Irvings. No wonder he felt so much better about himself.

A slight sound caused him to open his eyes and glance at Barrandale, who was beginning to awaken and stir. "Did I disturb you, Admiral?"

"Not at all, not at all," he replied affably. "I have not really been asleep."

Barrandale stood up. "Would you care to join me on the terrace?"

"Of course." They started walking slowly up and down, deep in conversation.

"Admiral," began Barrandale thoughtfully, "Dashell mentioned to me that he had a particular subject he wished to discuss with the two us. Have you any idea what it is?"

"None at all. But as he asked if I could stay another day it must be of some importance if it requires privacy. He said he wanted to wait until everyone had gone."

"Hmm. I wonder what it can be." Barrandale paused before adding, "Well, I trust his judgement so we will have to wait and see." Again he paused, then said, "I do sincerely thank you for your part in the wedding arrangements, or rather the—er—finances. I do not find such discussions easy for they embarrass me."

"Then say no more, my dear fellow, I was only too happy to do so. I am Caroline's only relative so she had no one else to ask; and besides, I believe the bride's family does pay for the wedding. In truth, I felt I was doing it for both Caroline and Isobel. By the way, I made enquiries at the Admiralty and at Greenwich Docks about which ships set sail for Jamaica when I was there. The supply ship that went down in that storm did contain a number of letters, both official and personal. I am quite convinced in my own mind that Isobel did write to me, and it still grieves me greatly that her letter never arrived. How different the outcome would have been if it had." He came to a standstill with a sigh, and then said, "I shall leave tomorrow as planned."

"Will you stay for luncheon? There will still be time for you to travel to London."

"Thank you Barrandale, that will do very well."

"I have enjoyed your company, Admiral. Perhaps I may sound a little selfish," continued Barrandale, "but I am so pleased there is a new Lady of the House. When Alicia was alive we used to hold a small private dinner party once a month or so with just a few guests at a time. Alicia was there for any other lady invited but after she died it was not so easy. To continue would have meant gentlemen guests only and such a party can lack a certain lustre, if you know what I mean, and I rather lost heart. My sister would sometimes act as hostess at official functions but she began to find it too much. Perhaps I may invite you from time to time? You will be a most welcome guest."

"I shall be delighted to accept at any time, Barrandale. You are most kind."

"By the way, have you seen Dashell's wedding present to Caroline? A new rose garden? There is not much to see at present but the planned layout indicates it will be splendid."

"I have heard about it," said the Admiral. "That was a lovely idea of Caroline's to bring over her mother's bushes from the old house."

"Yes, it was. And our young hero, Johnny Faulkner, gave Caroline five climbing roses as his wedding present," said Barrandale. "It will take a few years for everything to get established but the end results will be beautiful."

They returned to the house shortly before the carriage returned.

"I trust you both enjoyed your ride?" enquired Barrandale politely, when Dashell entered the room.

"We did, sir, very much," replied Dashell, without adding that precious little of the countryside had actually been seen.

"You look blooming, my dear," said Barrandale when Caroline came into the room, which did not help her composure at all; nor did the warm welcoming smile from Dashell. It was almost too much and she sat down rather unsteadily. Fortunately Simmonds brought in the tea tray just then which put a momentary stop to any conversation until he had left the room.

Dashell came to her rescue. "Caroline, dearest, we must discuss our visit to the Irvings in Sussex. I think we should be ready to leave on Friday."

"And you may have the use of my carriage," said Barrandale firmly. "It is larger and it will serve your better. Reuben will look after you both, as I know Stephen will look after me. So that is all settled."

"So will you be staying at Waterton Grange?" asked Sir Ryder.

"Yes, we will, for a few days," said Dashell. "Sir Richard insisted."

"We shall also call at Bretherton Hall where my mother lived as a child," said Caroline. "The Duke of Fennshire kindly gave us permission to look over it."

So the conversation continued along these lines until Caroline excused herself, saying she wished to try on the riding-habits Mrs. Whiteside had found for her.

"Now that we are alone," began Dashell, "I would like to mention the subject I wish to discuss with you both. I had already mentioned it to Dr.Meldicott and the Reverend Sudbury before they left the other day, but I have said nothing to Caroline yet. That will come later."

The other two men turned to him immediately, their interest quickened. "We are both greatly intrigued," murmured Barrandale. "Pray continue."

"It is that as the final chapter of the Waterton story has virtually closed, I have seriously considered the possibility of having the remains of Isobel and Maude exhumed and taken to the family vault at Sutherfield church. Then likewise Arthur's remains will be removed from Skorrcliff and taken to Sussex. The whole episode has affected me greatly and it would give me peace of mind to know they were all together at last. May I have your comments and observations? If either of you think this is foolish on my part, you may say so."

Neither of the other two spoke at first because this was not what they expected to hear, and it took them by surprise. Then Barrandale said, "I had no idea this was what you had in mind. Could such a thing be possible?"

"How could it be arranged?" queried Sir Ryder. "Such a request would have to go through the proper channels and I imagine that could take time."

"As it happened, Meldicott and Sudbury saw my point and offered to make enquiries on my behalf."

"I cannot help stating the obvious," remarked Barrandale, "but will this not be very expensive?"

Dashell knew that would be mentioned and said, "I believe I have enough money of my own to cover any expenses."

"Wait a moment," said Sir Ryder sharply, "may I be allowed to assist in this matter? The Watertons are my family too. As I mentioned to Barrandale earlier today, what I have done has been as much for Isobel as for Caroline. Like you, the whole story took hold of me, and this last gesture surely will bring closure at last. Do not make me insist, but I will if I have to," with a look that indicated he was not used to defeat.

Dashell met his eye with a smile. "In that case, I shall accept your offer."

"So that is settled," said Sir Ryder, slapping his hands on his knees. "So what do we do now?"

"We wait to hear from Meldicott and Sudbury," said Dashell. "I really have no knowledge of such matters. While I am at Sutherfield I will speak to the Reverend Swanson, to make known our intentions to him. Then I will write to the authorities in York and to the parish priest at Skorrcliff."

Barrandale remarked, "This is going to involve a great deal of arranging, but I applaud your sentiments."

"Thank you, sir, and I am prepared to do it."

All this led to more discussion about attendance at the exhumations and re-burials and it was agreed it was not necessary to travel up to Yorkshire, but they would attend at Fulham churchyard, and Dashell and Sir Ryder attend at Sutherfield.

Hannah had already laid out a riding-habit for Caroline to try it on. "What do you think, Hannah?" she asked, surveying herself in the mirror. "What does it look like from the back?" Hannah did not know much about such garments but thought "it would do." Caroline took off the habit and put on her own clothes again. "Hannah, would you go downstairs and tell Mrs. Whiteside I would like to see her."

"You wish to see me, Lady Lonsdale?" said Mrs. Whiteside a few minutes later, standing with her hands respectfully clasped together.

"Yes, Mrs. Whiteside. First of all, thank you for bringing me these riding-habits. This one here fits quite well. Now, I understand Lady Alicia used to have afternoon tea with you once a week to discuss household affairs. I would like to continue with this arrangement on my return from Sussex. Also on my return I would like you to show me over the whole house."

"Very good, ma'am."

"While I am away, perhaps you could find some work for Hannah to do. She is very clever and can do almost anything," turning to her with a smile.

"I believe there is some work, ma'am. There used to be a sewing woman who left on her own accord quite a while ago and we did not replace her. I know there is a great deal of household linen to be looked over for repairs and alterations, as well as clothing."

"Thank you, Mrs. Whiteside, that is all. Would you take this other dress with you?

The housekeeper went away with a good impression of the new Lady Lonsdale. She was just what the house needed. She liked Hannah, too. In fact, everyone liked Hannah.

Caroline went to join the gentlemen downstairs. As she closed the door behind her she did not notice Dashell's look of warning to the others, and went to sit by him.

"I was just saying that I shall be leaving tomorrow," said Sir Ryder.

"Oh, Uncle Ryder, we shall miss you. But you did speak of it earlier, I believe."

"And I shall miss you all too," he replied gallantly. "You have all been very kind to an old man like me."

That evening Barrandale and Sir Ryder found plenty to talk about, and Dashell and Caroline went away by themselves for a while.

CHAPTER FORTY-SEVEN

Sir Ryder Returns To London—And More

The next morning Sparkle and Flame were led round to the front of the house to the stone mounting block. Usually riders mounted in the stableyard, but Dashell knew Caroline was inexperienced and did not wish her to be embarrassed in front of servants.

At ten o'clock Caroline appeared looking absolutely charming, and stepped onto the block and settled herself in the saddle and gathered up the reins, while Dashell adjusted the stirrup leathers for her.

"You look a born horsewoman," he told her.

"Thank you," she said, knowing he was trying to make her feel relaxed.

They rode all over the estate and the quiet countryside. Caroline had almost forgotten how exhilarating cantering could be. Dashell, who was partly ahead, turned round in the saddle, and called out, "Enjoying yourself? How do you like your horse?"

"She's beautiful. She goes very well."

Before long they were back at the stables, Caroline looking flushed and happy. "That was a lovely ride, Dashell. You showed me so much."

"There is still more to see which I can show you after Sir Ryder has left," said Dashell.

"More surprises?" asked Caroline. "I should love to go riding again tomorrow."

"We are supposed to be leaving tomorrow," Dashell reminder her. "But we could ride before breakfast, if you get up early enough."

"All right. Will you be up in time?"

"I think you are teasing me now," said Dashell.

"Of course I am."

Luncheon was pleasant but sad knowing another goodbye had to be said. "Not really goodbye, Sir Ryder," protested the others. "You are a member of our family now."

He was deeply touched at that and could only say, "Thank you, thank you."

Soon Sir Ryder's carriage was at the door. He shook hands warmly with Barrandale and Dashell, and kissed Caroline on each cheek. "Mind you keep her happy," he admonished Dashell, "or I will want to know about it."

"Have no fear, Sir Ryder. I certainly will."

"Well, there he goes,' remarked Barrandale. "I have greatly enjoyed his company." They went back inside and returned to the sitting-room. "What time will you two be leaving tomorrow?"

"I will order the carriage for eleven o'clock as her ladyship wishes to ride out at eight o'clock, if you please. So that means I must be up early too."

"He is a terrible tease," said Caroline to Barrandale, in a mock confidential whisper.

"Then you must tease him too," he whispered back.

"Now, sir," continued Dashell. "I am going to show Caroline over the grounds and gardens. We will join you later."

"You have mentioned some things to me already," said Caroline, tucking her hand under his arm "I am looking forward to seeing them all."

So together they went through the various gardens, the orchards, the farm, right down to the hen houses; and Caroline just had to ask which hen house was the last one.

"I don't know," replied Dashell with a smile, "I don't think Mother ever told us." That set them chuckling again. "Let's go down to the stables now."

Reuben was pleased to show Lady Lonsdale round and she learned all the horses' names.

They walked back through the bluebell woods, bare now, but the ground would be well covered in the spring; as other ground would be covered with spring flowers.

"So, my lady, I think you have seen everything."

Caroline was amazed at how extensive it all was. "It's all so beautiful."

"Now I will show you the tree out of which I fell when I was a boy. I was about thirteen at the time. I remember my parents were very displeased as I could have lost an eye. Strange to look at the tree now, it looks so much smaller."

They walked along slowly until they came to the bench along the river pathway. "It's all so beautiful," murmured Caroline again, as they sat down. "I love it all already. What is that wooden building over there?"

"That's the boat house where the rowing boats are kept. My brothers and I used to have such great times together. I will take you out rowing one day; you will love it."

They slowly returned to the house. "You must love it all too," said Caroline.

"I do; very much. We were all born here and grew up here. It is part of me. I can't explain it. It's like belonging to the land itself. I can well understand how shocked and devastated Father was at the realization he might lose it all."

Caroline glanced at Dashell, knowing how and why that nearly happened, and saw the set jaw and angry frown, and slipped her hand back through his arm.

Dashell began talking again. "Some time ago I made a solemn promise to myself that I would do everything in my power to save the house and estate, even if it meant ploughing or scything and stooking hay with the men. I will not lose it."

Caroline looked up at him again, admiring his resolution. "Is there any way I may help? I have many a time seen people working in hayfields. I am sure I could do the same."

Dashell stared at her and saw how earnest she was. "Bless you no, but on second thoughts," he added with a wicked smile, "perhaps you could."

"I could become a dairymaid and learn to make butter and cream. Except we were never taught these things at the Academy."

Barrandale, looking out of a window, wondered what they were laughing about.

CHAPTER FORTY-EIGHT

The Visit to Sutherfield

Caroline was down before Dashell the next morning. "You hardly give me time to open my eyes," he protested, pretending to be still sleepy, yet the look he gave his wife was one of pride and admiration. "Come, we will go straight to the stables this time."

The horses were ready and waiting and Caroline stepped confidently to the mounting block and into the saddle, while Dashell quickly mounted Sparkle. As they moved off he reminded Caroline they could not be out too long this time.

"Enough for us to enjoy ourselves," she replied.

Dashell smiled, remembering the time many weeks ago when he had pictured the two of them riding through the estate. All too soon they had to return.

Once again a carriage waited at the front door with trunks and boxes strapped on.

Caroline had made a special request to Dashell to pass a certain place as they went through London. He had frowned a little at first and then agreed.

Barrandale came to see them leave, and sighed as he turned to go back indoors again. Just as he had become used to having people around him once more, he was now left by himself again.

Dashell and Caroline sat back in their seats and made themselves comfortable. "Now I have got you all to myself again," he said, as Caroline rested her head on his shoulder. The special request she had made to Dashell was on his mind. "Do you think it is a wise thing to do?" he asked gently.

"Please, Dashell, I want to do it. Otherwise I will always wonder, and I may never have another opportunity."

"All right then. Reuben knows where to stop."

Eventually the carriage stopped outside an old inn which probably looked much better twenty years ago, situated in a mean-looking street in a poorer part of London. Dashell looked up at the sign to make sure it was the correct one. It was the same inn Isobel had been taken to all those years ago, tricked into believing she was going to meet her husband Arthur there.

"What an awful place," murmured Caroline. "My poor darling Mother. To be left there by herself with Maude and me when we were still so tiny. What cruel deception. And then John and Joan came to help us. I will always, always bless them for that. Then Thomas Wardlock found Mother and married her for his own purposes. It is strange that because of him we survived, and yet because of him, two of us died."

"I think we should go," Dashell chided gently. "You must not dwell on it. Your mother and sister are at peace now from what you told me."

When they arrived at Waterton Grange and Sir Richard and Lady Lucy came to the door to greet them. "Welcome! Welcome! Come inside. The servants will see to everything."

Caroline looked about the entrance hall with great interest. So this was where her parents had once lived, where Maude and she had been born. She and Dashell followed Richard and Lucy upstairs. "We use the rooms Arthur and Isobel once had," explained their host, "and your room is just along here. Now, we will leave you until you join us for tea. We can show you round the house and gardens later, if you are not too tired after your journey."

After a leisurely tea, Dashell and Caroline described their journey, and Richard and Lucy were intrigued to learn they had stopped at the inn where Isobel had been abandoned years ago. "John and Joan Webster told us the name and where it was," as Caroline described it. "I wanted to go and look, and now I can be at peace."

Later that evening, Richard showed them where Arthur's portrait had hung. "I always remember it being there, and when we moved here we found it had simply disappeared. We looked all over the house for it, attic as well, and we could never understand how or where it went. All the old servants had gone so there was no one to ask. But now we do know what happened to it."

"I can tell you it is safe at Barrandale Park," said Caroline.

The four of them strolled round the gardens one time, and Richard remarked they were very much as Isobel must have seen them. "We have done very little to change anything, except for planting a few trees here and there."

Caroline asked if she might walk around by herself and be alone with her thoughts. When she joined them, she asked if she might take a few rose bushes with her when they eventually returned. "I would love to have them replanted in the new rose garden." The Irvings thought that a charming idea and readily agreed.

She also expressed a desire to walk along paths and lanes where her parents had once walked and sit under the same trees. Dashell accompanied her to the church for he wished to make himself known to the Reverend Swanson.

When Dashell left Caroline, he looked around the churchyard to find the grave of Lady Anne Bretherton, Isobel's great aunt by marriage; who helped Isobel so much and was shaken to death because she had done so. He stood looking at it for several minutes recalling the words spoken by the Websters. He moved slowly towards another part of the churchyard where someone else's grave lay. Did he really want to see it? After all, they had travelled all this way to see other things so he might as well.

The grave looked so plain and cold, just a flat slab of stone like the one for Arthur. Nothing was known about Arthur, yet the villagers of Skorrcliff had done what they could. A great deal was known about Catherine but nothing was said about her, just her name and dates of birth and death. How right the Duke had been.

He turned away and entered the church and walked along the aisle on the left looking for that infamous tablet. Yes, there it was, still declaring its hideous lie to all and sundry. He and Sir Ryder had already discussed a new one had to be made.

The Reverend Swanson had been in the vestry making sure everything was in order for a parish council meeting that evening, and as he shut the door behind him he caught sight of a gentleman looking at a certain memorial tablet on the left hand wall of the church. Someone whom he did not recognize. It was the second time an unknown gentleman had entered the church to look at the same thing. One of the village women who helped clean the church had seen a tall, upright man come in a while ago who stood looking at it. The gentleman had gone away in a coach drawn by four black horses, which the whole village was still talking about. Now there was this second person looking at it. Very intriguing. He would go over and introduce himself and perhaps he might learn something

Dashell turned at the sound of approaching footsteps. "Good afternoon," he said. "Am I right in thinking you are the Reverend Swanson?"

"I am indeed, sir. And you are?"

"I am Lord Lonsdale. You will recall I wrote to you some weeks ago asking for certain information concerning the Waterton family, and you sent me a charcoal rubbing of this tablet, and I was greatly shocked at what I read."

"I do indeed remember, your lordship, but I beg your pardon, I had hoped it would be helpful to you."

"It was. Very helpful." Swanson looked surprised at Dashell's answer. "You see, these words are a complete and utter lie because Lady Waterton and her two infant daughters did not die in that accident, as declared by Lady Bretherton. In fact they were never in the carriage with Sir Arthur."

"What do you mean?" cried Swanson. "I know there was a memorial service for them. I have seen it listed and dated in an old register."

"Oh, yes," agreed Dashell, who was beginning to feel he had been too blunt, "there certainly was. But the only person who actually died was Sir Arthur."

The Rector was stunned. It took him some moments to comprehend what he had been told, and he had an uncomfortable feeling something was terribly wrong. He looked sternly at Dashell. "That is a very serious statement you have just made, Lord Lonsdale. I trust you know what you are saying and that you have proof?"

"I certainly have."

"Then come with me to the vestry where we may talk."

"If you please, I would prefer we go outside. My wife, Caroline, is the sole survivor of the Waterton family and she is looking at places her parents knew in this area. We agreed to meet in the churchyard."

Swanson glanced involuntarily at the incriminating tablet. "You claimed just now that Lady Waterton and her daughters did not die when Lady Bretherton said they did, and now you state this Caroline to be the sole survivor. I do not understand."

"It is a long story," said Dashell, and turned to lead the way outside, followed by a now rather grim and determined Swanson. They sat down on a bench which happened to be so placed that Caroline was sure to see them when she came to meet Dashell.

So once again Dashell told the story, trying to be clear and precise and not too long. Swanson was obviously an educated man and was able to follow and assimilate the narrative, his face registering his thoughts at the same time. He never took his eyes off Dashell as he listened to every word.

"This is truly an amazing revelation of the truth," he ventured to say at last. "All this was in the days of my predecessor, but I am sure he acted in good faith. I had heard that Lady Bretherton tried to get him dismissed and have the marriage declared illegal, but the bishop at the time refused to do so. So that was her terrible revenge on those two unfortunate young people; to seize upon that opportunity to declare them all dead. I do not know how she dared to do what she did. I must confess words fail me."

"Had you ever met Lady Bretherton?' asked Dashell.

"No, your lordship, but one does get to hear things," replied Swanson carefully, with a faint smile. "After her death some of my parishioners were hired to help remove and burn various items from the house, and I understand nothing had been touched for years and everything was in an appalling condition." He paused to contemplate the situation and then asked, "What will be done about that tablet on the wall? It cannot stay there."

"No, of course not. It could be moved now if you agree, and a new one will be put up in due time. I have already consulted with Sir Ryder Wyecross about this. Now, there is something else I must mention to you."

"And that is?"

"Arrangements are being made for the remains of Lady Isobel and Maude to be exhumed and brought here for re-burial; and likewise Sir Arthur's will be brought down from Yorkshire. All this will take time of course but I trust you will understand. Oh yes, there is something else. The coachman who died with his master will not be left behind. He is known by the name of Edwards and nothing else is known about him, but he was possibly a local man and may still have family here."

Swanson, who had been wondering how many more incredulous things were going to be said to him, slowly shook his head. "I am unable to say. I will of course mention this to my parishioners and perhaps some of the older ones may remember." He had already thought of the meeting to be held that evening when he would have to tell the members that an old tablet on the church wall would have to be removed, and that in time there would be four re-burials. He could just see the looks on their honest faces when he explained why all this had to be done. He was equally appalled at having to tell his bishop about the false service, as tell him he must, and could not imagine what his Right Reverend lordship would say. The parish of Sutherfield would never be the same again.

He became aware Lord Lonsdale was regarding him quizzically. "I beg your pardon, I was just thinking of the effect all this will have on the parish. People will hardly believe it. And yes, of course, I agree to your request and I must inform my bishop of that. I completely understand your sentiments."

Dashell had caught sight of Caroline not too far away coming slowly along the path leading to the lych-gate of the churchyard. "There is one more thing I would like to mention, for the third time," he said with a deprecating smile.

"And what is that, your lordship?" Swanson smiled back at him.

"My wife is approaching and I would like you to meet her. Would any of your older parishioners remember Isobel as a child, and even Arthur? I understand they played together as children, and I am sure Caroline would dearly love to hear anything they could remember."

"I will certainly mention that also," promised Swanson. "I sincerely hope so, although it would be recalling events that happened nearly forty years ago."

Caroline had savoured each moment as she walked, trying to imagine her parents on the same paths, and that she and Maude could have been with them as children growing up. She paused under some old gnarled trees, supposing them to have been the same ones. It was a beautiful warm day, bees buzzing, the smell of wild flowers and growing crops, and cows standing in the shade on the far side of a field.

As she returned and crossed the churchyard she caught sight of Dashell talking to another man, and from his clerical garb she guessed him to the resident priest. The two men got to their feet as she approached them.

Dashell put his hand out to her. "Caroline, dearest, I would like you to meet the Reverend Swanson, who is the rector here. We have been having a most enlightening conversation."

"I am pleased to meet you, sir," she said to him.

"Your ladyship," he replied gravely, trying not to stare at this sole survivor.

"Revered Swanson thinks some of his older parishioners may remember your parents when they still lived here."

Caroline's eyes lit up in delight. "Oh, I should so love to speak to them."

They talked some minutes more until Swanson said, "I must now beg leave to excuse myself, Lord Lonsdale, Lady Lonsdale," and with a bow went his way.

"Did you enjoy your walk?" asked Dashell.

I did, until I had to shoo some cows out of my way. They sounded cross when they moo-ed at me."

"C-cows!" said Dashell, trying not to laugh. "Oh, my brave little d-dairymaid! You told me you thought to become one. Did you not stop to get acquainted with them?"

"Certainly not," she retorted, beginning to laugh too. "Perhaps it was just a passing fancy anyway."

"You disappoint me. Maybe you should try something smaller, like sheep. Or perhaps keep hens and collect eggs. That should be even safer."

"Dashell, you really are impossible!"

He smiled and shook his head. "We ought to return to the house, but before we do I must speak to you about something. We can sit down on this bench together."

"Oh, Dashell, no. When you get all serious like this and hold my hands I know you have something dreadful to say to me."

"Once when I held your hands it was to ask you to marry me. Was that so dreadful?"

"Now you are teasing me again. No, of course not," she added hastily, yet sensing Dashell was concerned about something.

So Dashell explained that he, his father and Sir Ryder were in agreement that the remains of her mother and sister were to be brought here for re-burial, and the remains her father, and also the coachman who died with him, would be brought down from that lonely village in Yorkshire. They felt that Arthur and Isobel should be together again after being so cruelly treated. And of course, Maude would join them.

Caroline closed her eyes and tried to picture the situation. There was no necessity now to return to Fulham, because the old house on Becket Lane had gone for ever. Bury them at Windsor? No, they had never known Windsor. Let them be together again in a setting they both knew; where they had grown up as children; where they had been married; and where they would have ended their days anyway. Sentimental? Probably. But Dashell was right.

She opened her eyes and looked at her husband. Holding one hand of his in her own she raised it to her lips and kissed it. "You are a wonderfully kind and thoughtful man. Now we must pray it can be done."

Dashell touched her cheek gently, reflecting that it would likely take a great deal of prayer. "We must return before the others wonder where we are."

Two days later Dashell and Caroline visited Bretherton Hall. They had not expected such a large house and there were still some servants putting things into order. Blundell had been informed Lord and Lady Lonsdale would be coming. They could go over the house and grounds as they wished and could take away anything they wanted. They were shown which rooms were Lady Anne's, and which had been Isobel's as a child.

Caroline was beginning to be disappointed in Bretherton Hall. It was not a happy house like Waterton Grange. Isobel's bedroom and schoolroom were completely empty, devoid of everything, cleared out long ago on Catherine's orders, leaving a dusty silence that conveyed nothing. It was the same in Lady Anne's rooms. Nothing in them at all.

Dashell pointed out the dressing-room where Joan Webster had hidden when Catherine had quarrelled with Lady Anne. He half-closed the door and could well understand how she had witnessed the scene through the crack. They turned away and returned downstairs, leaving the oppressive silence behind them.

They looked at family paintings which meant nothing to them. Other paintings did not appeal to them. An easy chair caught Caroline's eye, and she sat in it to see how comfortable it was, and decided to have it.

The gardens outside were not much better. They would have been lovely in their heyday but were now just sad, with many bare patches where overgrown bushes had been pulled up. There were some beds of roses that needed pruning. Hitchcock would to see to them when they were moved to Windsor.

Back indoors Blundell took them to a small room where a tea table was laid out. "I must apologize for the simplicity of it all, but there is only myself and a kitchen maid left, and we will be leaving soon. His Grace has kindly offered us places in the pensioners' cottages on his estate, for we have no where else to go." The door opened and the elderly maid carried in a tray.

When the two servants left, Caroline could not help remarking how such a stern man as the Duke could have a touch of kindness about him.

"Rather like turning two old workhorses out to grass."

"Dashell!"

Before they left the house they showed Blundell the items of furniture they wished to have moved, as well as some old rose bushes from the garden. He was a little nonplussed about that, but was told the carter who was coming would dig them up.

That evening over dinner, Dashell and Caroline described their visit to Bretherton Hall; what a large place it was and with a forlorn sense of neglect.

"Oh yes," said Richard, "stories have been circulating in the village about conditions there. Servants moving chairs and sofas only to have mice scuttle out of them. Cobwebs and dead spiders all over the place. Chimneys not swept. Rooms not aired for months, possibly years. Curtains bleached by the sun and the linings just rotted."

The next morning Sir Richard learned that the young carter had come and had loaded his cart, and that the gardener had taken him to the rose beds.

"May we go outside?" said Caroline. "We must make sure Johnny takes the right ones."

Johnny had made quite a start with his digging, watched by the Irving's gardener who did not like having his garden "messed up," but who did allow him to borrow a wheelbarrow.

"Hello, Johnny," said Caroline. "You found your way here all right?"

"Oh, yes, Miss Caroline," he answered with a grin "How many should I dig up?"

"You may have all the ones in this bed," said Richard. "There are nine of them."

As the Reverend Swanson feared, the startling news he had disclosed to the parish council meeting shocked and astounded them beyond measure. It rocked the whole village off its feet when the news began to spread about. The church congregation swelled in number the following Sunday, mostly by those hoping to hear more and those who rarely went. Heads turned and necks craned as worshippers tried to get a look at the infamous memorial on the wall.

Swanson appealed to the older people to try and remember all they could about Isobel when she was a child at Bretherton Hall, or as a young bride at Waterton Grange. Later when Dashell and Caroline visited these people, some did their best to relate what they remembered, but Caroline could not help feeling she was just an object of interest to them. The inn was another well-attended place in the village. The more imaginative, or inebriated patrons, when turned loose at closing time, swore blind they had seen the ghost of Lady Catherine walking about the churchyard wringing her hands. Other villagers were too terrified to go anywhere near the place except in broad daylight.

Apart from all that, the Irving's two guests enjoyed themselves. They walked most days or sometimes took a carriage ride to local places of interest. They played cards in the evenings, or Caroline played the piano for them which they loved, and always encouraged her to play more. Once when the four of them walked out together past the cow field, no cows were to be seen. Dashell muttered something which sounded like, "It must be milking time."

All too soon the day of departure came. "So much water has passed under the bridge," Richard reminded them. We must keep in touch for it may be a long time before we meet again." And so with handshakes and kisses Dashell and Caroline departed.

"Well, what do you think?" Dashell asked Caroline as they travelled away.

She thought a little at first. "Richard and Lucy are such dear people, and I am very fond of them. But I am a little disappointed that other things did not turn out as I expected. But I am glad we came and did what we did and now I, at least, can put it all in the past. And you?"

"I like them both very much too, and Richard is a good man at heart. And I wanted to introduce myself to the Reverend Swanson. I am sure what I told him has the whole village buzzing like a wasps' nest by now."

They made their way straight to South Kensington and remained there a few days.

In a similar way Johnny was disappointed. He wished he had been able to speak more to Miss Caroline, or her ladyship as he should have said. The old days had certainly gone. He reached Barrandale House and made his first delivery and then travelled on to Windsor with everything else. He told Hitchcock he had two lots of rootballs carefully labelled that were to be kept in separate flowerbeds because they came from different places, according to her ladyship's instructions.

He met Hannah, and was delighted with the inside pocket she had sewn into his waistcoat for his silver watch and chain. Later, he would have the actual sixpence Lord Lonsdale had tossed to him all those weeks ago attached to the chain. He had guarded it carefully, for that was something else he would never part with.

He and Hannah had a long talk together. She asked him about his future, now that he had finished all the hauling for the Barrandales. He said he had that carting job for the furniture firm which was now one day every week, but agreed it was not nearly enough. He supposed he could become a cab driver, except that Goldie was far too large to be a cab horse. Besides, he always remembered the drivers at Paxton's Yard coming in with coughs and sneezes and sore throats, but going out again the next day, not daring to lose any earnings as horses still had to be fed. Anyway, there was still that money to come from Uncle Joe, and there were his own savings, so he would see.

Hannah and Johnny said goodbye sadly, knowing it could be a while before they saw each other again. Hannah would always be with Lady Lonsdale and Johnny would now be working on his own.

CHAPTER FORTY-NINE

The Return to South Kensington

"Welcome, Lord Lonsdale, Lady Lonsdale," said Matthew, "Welcome to the new house. I trust you both enjoyed your travelling."

"Thank you, Matthew, we did," said Dashell. "It does feel good to be here. Has anything happened during our absence? Or any note from Lord Barrandale?"

"No, sir, not at all. It has been very quiet."

Dashell nodded briefly. "So all must be well at Windsor." Then turning to Caroline, he said, "Now, my lady fair, let me show you to your rooms," and led her upstairs till they came to the door to her suite. "Now close your eyes," he said. She obediently did so as he guided her inside. "Now you may open them. Do you like them?" he asked, boyishly eager for her response. "I chose them for you but you may change to others if you wish."

"Oh," she replied, looking about her. "These rooms are beautiful, so airy and light. And I love the view of the gardens from the windows."

"Now I will show you my rooms," which were just as pleasant but more masculine.

That evening after they had dined they were quite content to sit together and enjoy each other's company, Caroline with her head on Dashell's shoulder. "Happy?" he asked.

"Wonderfully," she replied, glancing up at him, whereupon he promptly kissed her, not wanting to miss an opportunity.

"Happy?" he asked again.

"Well, I'm not so sure."

"What you mean, my darling, is that you want me to kiss you again, and I'll be only too willing to oblige." After several minutes of contented silence, Dashell said, "I think we should visit Aunt Letty before we leave for Windsor. She would be rather hurt if we did not. And I also want to call on Sir Ryder because he will want to know how everything turned out at Sutherfield. I promised I would. And Caroline, I would prefer to be on my own when I do call."

The afternoon of the next day they had an unexpected caller, which took them both by surprise when Matthew announced, "Inspector Cockburn, sir."

Dashell and Caroline looked at each other in astonishment. For what reason would he come? Dashell stood up, while Caroline remained seated. "Show him in, Matthew."

Inspector Cockburn entered the room his usual brisk self. "Thank you, Lord Lonsdale, Lady Lonsdale," with a bow in Caroline's direction. "I will only take a few minutes of your time."

"If you wish to speak to my husband," began Caroline, rising from her chair.

"Oh, no, Lady Lonsdale, it is you I wish to see, if you would be so good," causing her to sit down again, with another look of surprise at Dashell, "but first may I congratulate you both on your recent wedding. I saw the announcement in the newspaper."

"Thank you, Inspector," they replied together, still wondering why he had come.

"Now, I am here with regard to the late Thomas Wardlock, with particular reference to all the money and valuables he had accumulated. We have been able to return a great deal of this to various people, thanks to his own record keeping, but a certain amount is still unclaimed. We have done our very best to trace everyone but it has been difficult. Some have moved away or have even died, their families or next of kin unknown. This brings me to the point of what to do with the unclaimed money, because in accordance with the terms of Wardlock's will it all comes to you, Lady Lonsdale. The amount unclaimed is quite considerable, almost five hundred pounds."

At the first mention of Thomas Wardlock's name, both Dashell and Caroline had stiffened, the latter in particular. She had thought she had put all this behind her and in truth she had almost forgotten him. Now everything came flooding back. Why did this have to happen? Not that she blamed Inspector Cockburn. He was only doing his duty and therefore he had to come; and now he was looking at her, obviously waiting for an answer.

"Truly, Inspector," said Caroline, "I am at a complete loss what to say. I never thought such a subject would be mentioned. And it is a great deal of money." She thought how her stepfather had deceived and robbed people by cheating them, and decided she wanted no part of his ill-gotten gains; not if some unfortunates had died in poverty and want. Yet on the other hand, could not all this money help the impoverished Barrandale estate?

She looked at Dashell. "It is your decision, Caroline. I will abide by it."

Caroline made up her mind. "Thank you, Inspector Cockburn, for what you have told me. But recollecting how the money was obtained to the distress of so many people, I do not wish to accept it, and would prefer it be given to charity. I do not know how. Perhaps you could advise me."

Dashell was very touched by her reply. So was the Inspector. "That is most generous of you, Lady Lonsdale. Indeed, there are many mission halls and orphanages in London which will be more than grateful to receive any amount. You may trust me to see the distribution is carried out."

Caroline inclined her head. "Thank you, Inspector."

"Thank you both for your time. I will see myself out," said the Inspector, with a bow to each of them.

Inspector Cockburn kept his word and saw that the money was given to various charities in London, to the surprise of those in charge of them. How may we thank our benefactor? they wanted to know Alas he is deceased, and wished to remain anonymous, was the tactful reply. They would have been horrified to know where it really came from.

That evening Dashell and Caroline were still discussing the Inspector's visit. "I hope I made the right decision," said Caroline. "I was completely taken by surprise but what else could I do? I did not want the money although I could have taken it and offered it to you for the estate."

"Oh, no," protested Dashell at once. "Like you I am disgusted at the way it was obtained. Let us hope it can now help those in need. We know we can trust Inspector Cockburn. Besides, neither my father nor I would wish our estate or houses be tainted in any way."

Dashell called upon Sir Ryder and told him about their visit to the Irvings in Sussex. "I introduced myself to the Reverend Swanson and he could hardly believe what I told him. Poor fellow! He said his parish might never be the same again."

"I can certainly believe that," snorted the Admiral. "That woman has left a legacy of trouble."

"Yes," agreed Dashell. "When Caroline and I visited Bretherton Hall, Anne and Isobel's rooms had been completely emptied. Very obvious when other rooms were still furnished. I know she was disappointed. But to get back to Swanson, he will see about arrangements for the re-burials, and Richard will let us know in time how everything went. And also this Edward Edwards, Arthur's coachman, does not appear to have any family remaining in Sutherfield. A widower, his only son moved away many years ago and on one else in the village remembers anyone else. Swanson will see that a new memorial tablet will be cut according to the wording you and I agreed upon."

"Very good, very good," said Sir Ryder. "Do you see any need for us to travel to Yorkshire? It is rather a long way."

Dashell shook his head. "No, I don't think so. At least not to Yorkshire, but we will certainly be at Fulham; and perhaps also at Sutherfield as Richard might like us to be there with him."

Dashell and Caroline paid a call on Aunt Letty, Dashell deciding he should accompany Caroline after all. She was delighted to see them again and to hear about their stay in Sussex.

"Richard and Lucy wished us to convey their greetings to you," said Dashell.

"That was most kind of them," replied Aunt Letty, graciously inclining her head, but sniffed in disgust to learn there was very little to see at Bretherton Hall as Anne and Isobel's rooms had been completely emptied. "That showed that woman had a guilty conscience," she stated grimly.

"Yes, I was rather disappointed," agreed Caroline with a sigh, "but I did so enjoy all else. Imagining my parents playing and growing up as children, or walking in the countryside, or living at Waterton Grange. Now I feel all that can be put behind me and closed, like the ending of a chapter in a book."

"What an apt way to describe it," remarked Aunt Letty.

They stayed a little while longer until they could see Aunt Letty was getting tired. Dashell and Caroline glanced at each other. "Perhaps we should be going now, Aunt Letty, but we wanted to see you again before we returned to Windsor. It could be a while before we see each other again."

"Oh, don't say that," she protested, "because I know I shall miss you both."

"We will write," promised Dashell, "or at least Caroline will."

"Humph. You are talking like a husband already."

"Of course I shall write," exclaimed Caroline, "and that's a promise."

Aunt Letty watched them go downstairs, yet did not hear Dashell say to Chadwick, "Keep on eye on Lady Smythe for me, will you?"

Later that evening Dashell remarked, "I think we could return to Windsor tomorrow, now that we have done our duty calls, as one might say."

"I don't think Aunt Letty would like to be referred to as a "duty call," Caroline remarked, with a chuckle, "nor, I am sure, would Uncle Ryder."

CHAPTER FIFTY

New Beginnings

The next morning Dashell asked Caroline, "Will you be glad to go to Windsor?"

"Oh yes, I will," she said at once. "I shall always think of Barrandale Park as my home, especially as everything seems to be there."

"I know exactly what you mean. I expect Father will be glad to see us, too. And no doubt," he added, "you will renew your acquaintance with your beloved Flame."

"Of course, I shall," said Caroline. "That goes without saying."

"Welcome back, Lord Lonsdale, Lady Lonsdale," said Simmonds, when they arrived.

"Thank you, Simmonds. We are both pleased to be home. How is Lord Barrandale? Nothing untoward has occurred, I trust."

"His lordship is very well," replied Simmonds. Then turning to Caroline, said, "There have been a number of letters come for you, Lady Lonsdale. Hannah has them in safe keeping for you."

Barrandale was pleased to see the two of them again. He had been a little lonely after so much hustle and bustle and had been somewhat hard-pressed to fill in his time, and now he welcomed them warmly. "Welcome, Dashell, and you, Caroline, my dear. You look as charming as ever. And I am all agog to hear your news.

But first things first: I am sure you wish to refresh yourselves after your journey. I will wait until you both come down again."

Caroline went upstairs to her rooms to receive another welcome from Hannah.

"It's lovely to be back here again, Hannah. To be home." She took off her coat and matching bonnet as she spoke and laid them on the bed. She went to a window over-looking much of the garden and wondered how Hitchcock had been getting on with the roses from the two old gardens, for surely Johnny would have brought them by now. To her, they were the best keepsakes of all. She turned round as she remembered the letters that had come during her absence.

"Here they are, Miss Caroline," said Hannah. "I put them on the bureau for you. There are quite a number."

"Seventeen!" exclaimed Caroline in surprise, after she counted them; thank-you letters, and invitations from local people to visit them, as she found out when she read them later.

She joined the gentlemen for tea, taking part in the conversation about their times in Sussex, and then returned upstairs, leaving father and son to talk together, for she knew Dashell had much else to discuss with him. Besides, she had a great deal to tell Hannah.

When the evening of talking was over, Barrandale went up to his own bedroom musing over the words the other two had used, that there were going to be some "new beginnings." It was a most apt way of describing it, for over the next few months several new starts were going to be made.

Caroline went out riding every morning accompanied by Dashell, and on a few occasions by Barrandale. Dashell declared her to be quite indefatigable.

"What am I to do?" he complained to his father once, tongue in cheek. "At first she was too nervous to get on a horse and now she won't get off. I shall be exhausted if she keeps up this pace," which remark caused Barrandale considerable amusement. Caroline's next love was Dashell's wedding present to her: the new rose garden. It was gradually taking shape as all plans were being followed. Three special beds had been laid out. One contained the roses from Bretherton Hall, the second those from Waterton Grange, and the third the ones from Becket Lane.

Mrs. Whiteside showed Caroline over the whole house, which took almost the whole day. Caroline commenced the Friday afternoon teas with her to discuss household needs and affairs, during which time she also learned a great number of interesting and amusing snippets about past and present Barrandales.

One great factor was that Rosedale Manor had been sold, to the relief to Barrandale and Dashell alike, for it meant the loan from the bank could now be paid off. Yet on the other hand they were regretful and saddened to see it sold, leaving only memories behind. Dashell, on his part, held the private hope that in the future it might be possible to buy it back, but only time would tell. Although the estate was now debt free it would have to be worked hard to remain solvent.

In time, London authorities gave permission for two certain coffins to be exhumed in the Fulham parish churchyard. The party attending at four o'clock one cold morning consisted of the Reverend Sudbury, Sir Ryder Wyecross, Dashell, and two officials. They watched in silence as the gravediggers worked away and then placed the coffins in the waiting hearse. Papers were signed, money paid, and hands shaken before everyone left.

Earlier, when arrangements had been made, Dashell mentioned it to Caroline. "It will mean being there at four o'clock in the morning. You may wish to attend, but I would prefer you did not."

Caroline had immediately stated that she did not wish to attend. It was no place for her, even if it did concern her two dear ones. Neither did Lord Barrandale attend.

When the rector of the Skorrcliff parish church learned of the requested arrangements, of necessity he had to inform his parish council and it caused quite a stir. Prunty, the innkeeper, who happened to be on the council, was as astounded as were all the others. At last, after all these years, someone had come forward to claim relationship. Now, perhaps, the mystery might be solved.

So those two gentlemen brothers had not come by accident. Nor had he been fooled by their seemingly disarming interest, not when he had gone looking the next morning and had found their footprints by the two graves, which showed they must have been standing there for some time. And yes, he was glad he had given them such a detailed account of the accident.

He had never said a word to anyone then, but perhaps he should now. He cleared his throat, thus catching everyone's attention, and began to speak.

As previously agreed, Sir Ryder and Dashell did not go to Yorkshire, but sent trusted agents. They were paid half of what they asked and would be paid the rest when they proved all had been done to everyone's satisfaction.

As promised, Sir Richard Irving witnessed the two re-burials, and wrote to Sir Ryder and Dashell on each occasion, describing the events.

Caroline made use of an alcove along one of the corridors at Barrandale Park. On one side hung the double portrait of herself and Maude, and on the opposite side was the painting with Windsor Castle in the distance, and on the middle side was the portrait of her father. Underneath that portrait was the small table brought from Waterton Grange with the pretty porcelain dish placed upon it, which had been owned by her maternal grandmother. The cross-stitch picture that had been in the front parlour of the old house on Becket Lane, was too large to fit into the alcove, so it was hung on the opposite wall of the corridor, still facing the alcove.

The small armchair from Bretherton Hall which she had liked so much was now in her suite. Caroline had told Hannah the story of mice scuttling out of various chairs and sofas, and this one had been thoroughly looked over for any indication of them.

There were new beginnings with the horses too. A new one was bought locally so Leonard could accompany Caroline when she rode out if Dashell was not able to be with her. Also purchased was a new pony to replace Dandy, whose work now was to help keep down the grass in the orchards.

The mare, Daybreak, duly had her foal, which later would be named Phoenix, after the mythical bird "which rose from the ashes." He would signify new hope for the stables.

Samuel requested permission to speak to Lord Barrandale and Lord Lonsdale to discuss Lively. He explained respectfully that he could train a flat racer but he found it difficult with a horse that wanted to jump. In the end Lively was leased to a trusted farmer neighbour who rode him in the hunting season, as this was the best way to keep a steeplechaser in training. Samuel also respectfully asked if a more worthy name could be found for the horse, as it seemed a name did have an effect on something. So Lively was re-named Lionheart, as befitting his courage and ability.

Daisy Chain had been entered in two races and won both of them, with her jockey wearing the Barrandale colours of dark red and pink. Both Barrandale and Dashell had attended the first time she ran, but on the second occasion, at Newmarket, only Dashell was there. There was a crowd of owners round him congratulating him on his horse's second win; certainly a filly to be watched next season, they said.

A certain gentleman approached Dashell and requested permission to call upon him when he returned to London. Dashell agreed and took the card handed to him and glanced at the name: Viscount Ogilvy. It meant nothing to him.

Dashell remained in London for several days for he had some business to attend to, besides dining out with a few racing owners. By that time he had almost forgotten the incident at Newmarket until Matthew announced one afternoon, "A gentleman by the name of Viscount Ogilvy wishes to see you, sir."

Dashell could not think why the man wanted to see him, but hoped he would be brief. "Show him in, Matthew."

"Thank you for agreeing to see me, Lord Lonsdale," said Viscount Ogilvy, "for I believe my request took you by surprise when I approached you at Newmarket, but I will only take up a little of your time." Dashell stiffened at the Viscount's next words. "I am here at the request of your brother, Walden, for I made a promise to him just before he left for India."

Dashell's face darkened as he stared at Ogilvy. "You saw my brother? And you made him a promise? For what reason?"

"I called upon him at Hyde Park Barracks as the result of a letter he wrote to me. He requested me to approach you if our paths should ever cross; and on no account was I to approach Lord Barrandale."

"And what is all this about?" asked Dashell, still frowning, angry at all the thoughts brought back to mind. Damn Walden. Why did he have to do this?

So Ogilvy carefully outlined the whole story. The cruel duplicity and treachery of Lassiter. How young men were singled out, flattered, cheated and duped and brought to ruin, to the very edge of despair, and some even to suicide. Then the two money lenders moved in and offered ways to repay debts; and how they knew when to do this showed those three rogues were in league with each other.

Walden had been one of those singled out, for it was known his father was a wealthy man. He does not expect forgiveness, explained Ogilvy, but does ask for understanding.

Ogilvy went on to say that Lassiter was found floating face down in the Thames, stunned first by a blow to the back of the head and then left to drown; and that Lee and Macy had fled to the Continent with their ill-gotten gains before the authorities caught up with them. It was still not known who had killed Lassiter.

Still frowning, Dashell spoke. "Thank you for your explanation, Ogilvy. Have you heard again from my brother?"

"No, not at all. I did not expect to."

Dashell nodded briefly. "Well, I do appreciate your coming."

"And thank you for your time and patience, Lord Lonsdale," said Ogilvy, "I now consider myself released from my promise. I will see myself out." He gave a slight bow, left the room and closed the front door behind him.

Dashell remained standing for some time, thinking. Did he really care about Walden? The damage had been done and could not be undone. But what was Walden trying to say? That he had been very foolish, that he had been taken in by this charismatic man, like so many others. Yes, Lord Barrandale was once a wealthy man; so if Walden had not been singled out, then it could have been Maxwell, or even himself.

Then again, he wondered, should he tell his father about Ogilvy's visit, although Walden had the grace not to want him approached. What good would it do anyway? It would only open up newly-healed wounds. If the occasion and opportunity ever arose he might consider it, but for the time being, let sleeping dogs lie. He was still in a sombre mood when he retired that night.

Dashell did not feel much better the next morning when he returned to Windsor. Too much anger still remained, especially when he remembered how much their father had changed. Yes, he could understand more now, and even wondered what Walden was doing now.

His carriage was nearing Barrandale Park, and thoughts of Caroline came closer to him, which were never far away, anyway. Any time now she would be in his arms and give him a welcome home. He smiled in anticipation.

Caroline did indeed give him a welcome. Never had she looked as beautiful as she did now. Dashell regarded her almost in awe.

That evening Dashell, his father and Caroline were in the library, the two men talking about Daisy Chain and her two wins, and the various invitations given to Dashell to dine with racing owners. "I explained that you and I were joint owners, sir, so I am sure you will be included too," said Dashell.

Caroline did not join in the conversation but had listened with great interest, nurturing her own increasing love of horses. Anyway, she had something else to think about.

Barrandale tactfully said he would retire early, and bade them goodnight.

It was still a little early for the other two to retire, so Caroline suggested that as it was a lovely calm evening they might go for a moonlight walk. Dashell, a little surprised, agreed, remarking she must be a romantic.

"Of course I am. And I have missed you." They walked slowly along, savouring the smell of the flowers, and stopped to listen to a nightingale singing.

"More romance," began Dashell, smiling as she turned towards him, then she told him they were expecting their first child. He caught his breath. He gave a great whoop of joy, silencing the nightingale, seized her by the waist, lifted her up and whirled her round, and just as suddenly put her down with a gasp of horror. "Caroline! What have I done! I should never have done that. Please forgive me, I just got carried away. It's all so wonderful. You don't think it harmed the baby, do you?"

"Oh, Dashell, I am sure it didn't," she said, seeing how contrite he looked. "It is far too soon anyway. Nor am I likely to break like a china ornament."

He gave a sigh of relief but still held Caroline very carefully in his arms. "You are a very clever girl, you know."

"You come into it as well," was the muffled reply. "We will have to tell your father," she added, when she could.

"Not now. He will be so excited he won't sleep a wink all night. And I don't think I will either. I will have to ask him what he did when he knew he was going to be a father for the first time. Of course, that would have been me, wouldn't it?"

Caroline was laughing before he finished speaking. "Dashell, do be serious."

"Yes, I suppose so. Now we will have to think of names."

"Dashell," began Caroline slowly, "if it is a little girl, or if we ever have a little girl, I would like to call her Isobel Maude."

"No need to ask why, but just suppose it is a little boy?"

"Oh, in that case I will leave his names to you."

So that was the agreement. Caroline had already chosen names for a girl, and Dashell would choose names for a boy.

When told the next morning, Lord Barrandale was overjoyed, declaring it was the best news he could have heard, and congratulated them both heartily. Now the House of Barrandale could raise its head again and look to the future.

Simmonds was given permission to inform all the servants, which he did at the first opportunity, to their great delight.

It so happened there was one area where Dashell and Caroline had a strong disagreement, and it was over her wish to go riding every morning. Dashell, annoyed, reminded her she was carrying their hopes for the future; and that if he was prepared to give up hunting and racing, then she could give up riding; and Caroline, not wishing to cause any real dissension, agreed to abide by what the doctor said. The doctor said it would be all right for the time being, as long as she was careful; and that meant just riding about the countryside.

One other person who was delighted with the news was Hannah. When she and Mrs. Whiteside had looked through the household linens, they came across some infants' clothing, now musty and yellowed with age. Hannah had regarded them in dismay, thinking they should not be used again. Mrs. Whiteside was inclined to agree, although she admitted she knew very little of such matters. But Hannah did. She said she would unpick them and use them as patterns for the new.

Caroline was astonished when Hannah showed them to her; she could not imagine how someone the size of Dashell has once fitted into them. "That reminds me, Hannah, we must bring out those little things Mother kept and look through them again."

Hannah was eventually driven in the trap to Windsor to purchase lengths of suitable fabric. Later, she was as happy as a lark as she stitched away. Caroline, of course, did a considerable amount of sewing as well.

Dashell was still marshalling his thoughts from that call by Viscount Ogilvy. What if Walden had not been so much in debt and everything had gone on as usual? The estate would have been just the same; no servants let go. Maxwell would have gone to Oxford and studied architecture, although he was developing a real interest in the Law. And Caroline? Well, he would have married her anyway. Yet they would still have had to make the acquaintance of Sir Ryder Wyecross just to find out her parentage.

They might have sold Daisy Chain and Lionheart without realizing their real potential. And what a loss that would have been. Now with Daybreak and Sorelle and their foals; and Amber and Russet in foal to Raven, they could build up a really fine stable. Flame never did produce a foal so she remained her ladyship's horse.

They had gathered in the library one evening and Dashell sat watching Caroline and his father. Again that thought came into mind; that chance meeting between himself and Caroline. If he or she had been a few minutes earlier or later, they would never have met each other. It was a thought that would haunt them both for the rest of their lives.

Caroline had finally finished stitching the slippers Mrs. Farling had given to her, but unfortunately they proved too small for Dashell. However they fitted his father perfectly.

"Thank you, my dear," he said, "I shall wear them with pride, and they are very comfortable," proving the point by looking down admiringly at them and turning his feet this way and that.

"I will make a pair for you, Dashell, now that I know your size," promised Caroline.

Surprisingly however, Dashell associated such slippers with older men like his father. "Thank you, but I feel you are trying to turn me into a contented husband. I don't feel old enough yet."

Both Barrandale and Caroline stared at him in surprise. "But you are content, aren't you?" demanded his father. "What has age got to do with it?"

Dashell could find no answer to that as the others looked at the blank look on his face. "Yes, I suppose I am," he admitted, and joined in with the laughter.

In due course a little girl was born, mother and daughter doing well, and great was the grandfather's pride when Isobel Maude was laid in his arms.

Lightning Source UK Ltd.
Milton Keynes UK
UKHW010225250123
415851UK00002BA/13

9 781956 074529